The

DIVINE LEDGER

The Eve of Humanity - Book One

Nov 2018

Kevin Weisbeck

Kevin Weisbeck

The Divine Ledger
An Owlstone Book

All Rights Reserved

Neither this book nor any portion therof may be reproduced or used in any manner without the express written permission of the author, except for the use of brief quotations in a book review.

Published as a Print-on-Demand book
through CreateSpace, an Amazon Company,
for the author Kevin Weisbeck.

Printed in the United States of America
This is a work of fiction. Names, characters, and incidents either are the product of the author's imagination or are used fictitiously. Any resemblance to actual persons, living or dead, or events is entirely coincidental.

Artwork by Dan Huckle, Okotoks, AB Canada
Danhuckle.com
Editing by Marius Oelschig and Sherry Kasper

Copyright © 2018   Kevin Weisbeck
ISBN 978-0-9917566-0-5
First printing, April 2018

The Divine Ledger

Dedication

I dedicate this book to everyone that has been on this journey with me. Your kind words and support have meant the world to me.

I also dedicate this book to Doris and Franklin. These two cats have been with me on this journey from day one. Sure, they didn't contribute very much, and on more than one occasion they interrupted me with a poorly-timed hairball exorcism, but they've always meant well.

And when I was too tired to carry on, they would walk across the keyboard. I doubt very much that a million cats, given a million years, could type anything other than:

ppppllollllkjjjhhhhhtttttttttdzasssswwwwwwwqqqqqqqqq

A special thank you to Tony Lawton for an important cover edit and to John Barrie for his proofreading advice

Kevin Weisbeck

Prologue

Havana, Cuba

The old woman reached for the leather-bound book with her scrawny fingers. She hesitated, hands inches away from touching it. This wasn't right. But, if this man was being truthful, she'd finally get the one thing that had eluded her an entire lifetime. Although this wasn't how she'd expected it to happen, destiny, much like desperation, sometimes had to be nudged down its own path. God would need to be side-stepped.

Her eyes drifted up to the tall, dark man. He returned a hopeful smile and nodded for her to continue. Three sparrows fluttered onto a nearby windowsill. They peered in as the man put a hand on the old woman's shoulder. He had promised her a lot and the price was her trust.

She turned back to the book, placed a hand on it and closed her eyes. The leather was soft. She felt its energy flow freely through her fingertips. When she reopened her eyes, a name had trailed its way across the cover. It was her name, embossed upon the tattered leather surface as if magic had placed it there and, in a way, it had.

The ghost of a smile drifted across her face, flattening a few wrinkles and causing a dozen others. "You weren't lying."

"I was not." He moved closer. "Now open it. You deserve this."

She took a moment and glanced around the room. Her life hadn't been that bad. She had a lovely one-bedroom apartment full of antiques that looked as good as the day they were made. Her curtains, somewhat dated, were cream-coloured with age and speckled with tiny faded yellow buttercups. She loved buttercups. They had been her mother's favourite.

"Can I…" She reached for the corner of the book, desperate to open it and read the first entry.

"Go ahead. It's yours now, Mrs. Encinoe."

Although he had no intention of giving her the book, he also knew that no one would come looking for it in an old woman's apartment. The man sat down in the chair beside her.

Another bird flew onto the sill, jostling the other three for a better view. The man looked over towards them but remained calm. "We need to hurry."

Outside, thousands of sparrows began to swarm.

Chapter One

Puerto Vallarta, Mexico

A warm breeze gentled its way off the Pacific Ocean making Victor, the man with the soft English accent, wish he'd spent more time in places like this. The absence of rain was such a welcome change from the Seattle drizzle that he had grown accustomed to over the last year. A worn canvas duffel bag, its contents currently the most important part of his life, sat on the floor resting against his foot. It was imperative to have that bag close. He leaned back and let the sun warm his skin as he took a sip of tea. It immediately altered his mood. God, how he hated drinking this shit.

"Anyone for tennis?" The stranger's voice cut through the calm.

Victor watched as the young man wove his way through the tables looking for an opponent. The man was wearing a sweater like a child might wear a cape. Victor held the cup close to his lips as he imagined the sleeves of that sweater tightening until the man's face turned red. He'd watch the fear slowly drain from the man's eyes as they bulged in their sockets. Then he smiled and took another sip as he tried to shake the thought away. Thank God for those Anger Management classes.

Tennis courts and spoiled tourists were the collateral damage of five-star resorts. Victor closed his eyes, willing this sweater-caped idiot to leave.

"More tea, Mr. Vicar?" Pedro stood with a glazed stare as he patiently held the teapot at the ready. His were the eyes of a gentle culture born to siestas and serving others. Victor could appreciate that.

"That's Victor. Victor with a 't'." There was a pause while he watched Pedro comprehend the error, much like a small child might. Then he softened his English accent and repeated the name. "Vic-tor."

Pedro nodded his head, eager to please. His eyes became spirited, reminding Victor of a puppy he'd once owned. The thing could fetch newspapers, slippers and even bottles of beer. It would have learned to talk and even pronounced his name correctly, if he'd asked it to. That kind of loyalty was refreshing. "Si, Vicor. I give more tea, Mr. Vicor?"

This was obviously a society of optional schooling. Victor conceded and forced a smile. "No thank you, Pedro. I have a lot to do today and I've travelled quite a distance."

"Things to do?" Pedro's eyes widened. "This is Pedro's job."

Victor thought about that for a second before setting his teacup down. Maybe this guy could open a few doors that might otherwise be closed. "Do you know of a place: La Playa de Los Muertos?"

Pedro's pleasant demeanour sobered. "This is not a place for the Gringo. It is not safe. The Gods forbid anyone but close family to go there."

"I understand, but I cannot fulfil my purpose without a visit to the place." A well-mannered smile remained fixed upon Victor's face. "If you want to help me, you need to take me there."

Pedro almost dropped the teapot as he placed it on the table. "Mr. Vicor. The translation for this place is 'Beach of the Dead'. There is a cemetery. The spirits are no longer controlled by their bodies or by our God. They want to pass over to the other side.

The Divine Ledger

Memories from tragic deaths hold them back. They are angry spirits. They seek revenge. They become ghosts and animals and can hurt you. I do not know your purpose, but this is not the place for it."

Pedro's words landed like snowflakes on a young lad's tongue. Victor lapped them up and welcomed their ominous weight with an eagerness that he'd never felt before. This beachside cemetery, ripe with angry spirits, was just the place. "Take me there."

"You don't understand, Mr Vic—"

"Can you take me today?" It was time for the language that Pedro's people understood only too well. "I have money, and I'd be happy to pay you for your time."

Pedro took a second before nodding.

"Great." Victor got to his feet. "Shall we get started?"

Pedro followed Victor as they made their way to his room. He remained a respectful step behind him and stopped at the door.

Victor opened the door and invited him in.

"Do you have a car, Mr Vicar?"

"No." Victor hadn't wanted his name in the system.

"Maybe we cannot go then."

Victor pulled four hundred pesos out of his wallet. "Which Compestalla bus do we need to take?"

"The five-forty-seven." Pedro took a deep breath and exhaled slowly. "The place you want is an hour up the coast in a small surf-town called Sayulita."

"Thank you. Now that wasn't so hard, was it?" He gave Pedro a pat on the back. "Trust me, we'll be fine."

Pedro shrugged. He knew *he'd* be fine. It wasn't the land they needed to fear, nor was it the difficulty in finding the beach. It was the locals. They didn't need, or favour, the gringos toying with their culture. They might tolerate him if one of their own was being paid.

Pedro picked up the grey duffel bag, slung it over his shoulder and took a spot by the door to wait. "Mr. Vicor will let me carry his bag, no?"

A bleached skull, aged like an old sepia photograph, slipped past the zipper that had pulled partially apart. It landed on the floor with a deadened thud. In that moment, every other sound on the planet fell silent to the skull that slowly rolled across the hardwood floor. While Pedro stood frozen, Victor calmly picked it up, blew the accumulated dust off its brow and placed it back in the bag.

"I'll carry my bag." Victor snatched the bag from the man and headed for the door. "I don't mean to be short, Pedro, but this is my bag."

Pedro nodded and kept his eyes to the floor as he obediently followed, now two steps behind the man who dressed well, spoke oddly, and had a bag of skulls.

A black bag, handcrafted from some of Italy's finest leather, was gently kicked under the bed before they left. Among its contents were some of the rarest surgical instruments that money could buy. Victor had acquired quite a collection, mostly gifts from surgeons who had owed him favours. If anything ever happened to these items he'd be angry, but he'd survive. The frayed duffel bag however, was as priceless as the air in his lungs.

As they headed downstairs, past the shops outside the lobby, Victor found a hole-in-the-wall cigar shop. He headed over to it where he argued with an ornery old lady over the price of a couple of hand-rolled Cubans. She held firm on the price until the howl of an old bus's brakes announced that it was time to go. She quickly took his offer of forty pesos. Better forty than nothing at all. He grabbed the cigars and boarded the bus. He'd have given her fifty if necessary.

They travelled through the jungle as they made their way along the narrow coastal road. It took longer than the intended hour. That was how things worked in Mexico. At one point the bus stopped for fuel. The driver pulled the money from the box of fares and handed it to a small child who, in turn, raced it to the lady drinking beer in the shade. It was his mother. She took the money and the boy returned to top up the tank.

Further down the road, cattle and ranch-hands blocked the road. Victor noticed that the men's faces were painted as black as night. He wiped at the filthy window to no avail. "What's that all about, Pedro?"

The Divine Ledger

"They are the Heguerros. They believe that the colour black protects them from the evil spirits." He pulled a tattered rag from his pocket and wiped the sweat from his brow. "We're very close Mr. Vicor. Are you sure you—"

"I'll be fine." A smile returned and this time it was a sincere one. He gave Pedro a reassuring pat on the shoulder. "But thanks for asking. You're a good man."

Pedro returned a bewildered stare. The English accent had vanished.

There was no more talking as they got off the bus and walked amongst the people of the small village. With only seven streets in total, it only took five minutes to get to the other side. A handful of restaurants were littered with tourists who swilled beer and gazed out over the ocean. Nobody noticed the two men as they passed by.

The Pacific Ocean gently rolled up the beach towards them. Children played in the water and the gringo women tanned their flabby bodies on hotel towels. One woman, well in her nineties, offered them the use of the washroom for a mere five pesos. It seemed that everything had a price in Mexico. It was a hard culture, one that the tourists seldom noticed.

The beach, populated by white skin and screaming children, was anything but terrifying. "Are you sure this is La Playa de Los Muertos, Pedro?"

"No, Mr. Vicar." He pointed past the beach to where a resort was nestled amongst the jagged rocks at the point. "It's past the Villa Amour Resort. I will take you as far as the jungle. I will even wait for you, but I cannot go into the jungle."

"That's quite alright. I'll be able to take it from there."

This time Victor followed a respectful step behind Pedro and made a point of openly paying him when they arrived. They parted company over a cold beer and a handshake. Victor passed through the opening in the fence. Soon, his gait laboured from the weight of the duffel bag as he manoeuvred his way across the exposed roots and rocks. The colourful orange and yellow buildings disappeared behind the trees as an overgrown road turned into a jungle floor.

Kevin Weisbeck

Most gringos, and the resort was full of them, had been told that the beach was named after the cemetery that one had to pass through to get to it. They were also told that man-eating pumas often frequented the area. The information was appreciated, even though it was all a lie, but honesty wasn't good for business. Murderous cats were easier to accept than the truth.

Pumas or no pumas, Victor soon found himself standing at the edge of the graveyard. The headstones were scattered across the hillside like windblown flowers. He gently placed his duffel bag beside the headstone of one Hector Fuentes, took a deep breath of the mossy wet air and let a grin spread across his face. He'd experienced many things in his days, but nothing as spiritual as this. His heart pounded in his chest as he slipped off his shoes, lit a cigar and cracked one of the two ice-cold beers that he'd brought from the resort's outdoor lounge.

His bare feet stirred the dust, and hopefully the spirits, as he walked amongst the eclectic maze of headstones. Poorly-kept figures of the Virgin Mary were decorated in bright, bold colours. They were anything but haunting.

Victor unzipped the duffel bag, exposing twelve skulls. From a side pocket inside the bag he pulled out a case, slipped a knife from it, and sliced his palm. It was instinctive to want to tend to the wound, but today he'd let the earth taste his blood. Drops of blood spattered and landed amongst the headstones, the graves, and the statues as he chanted the words that he'd etched into his brain.

"Bones of the dead, you cease to be, I lift your soul, I set you free. Bones of the dead, you cease to be, I lift your soul, I set you free. Bones of the dead…"

Chapter Two

Washington DC, USA

Greg Miller didn't feel dead in his dream, but a bone-chilling cold bit at his toes as the coffin's lid closed down on him. The darkness was absolute and then suddenly, he was free, floating out of the box and up from the soil like a balloon. He could see the white granite of the tombstone that marked his grave. It read 'Gregory Michael Miller, Born September 24, 1962 – Died ...

That date was hidden as hundreds of sparrows blanketed the ground, covering the far-right corner. Below his name and the dates, three cheesy words read *Rest in Peace*. Those three words, ones that he had always hated, never ceased to confuse him. Peace should be a cold beer on the back deck, not being stuffed in a box lined with fake silk, salmon- coloured to boot. His blank stare was interrupted with a bang. It was a door being slammed shut, putting him back in the coffin.

Lumps of fabric dug into his back as he tried to move around. Obviously, the dead weren't supposed to care about comfort. And as for those three words, who would have picked them, his parents? He didn't remember his real mother or father. The memories of them had faded like a morning haze burnt off by the first hours of sunshine. Maybe his adopted parents chose them. They hadn't done much else.

Greg worked his hands from his side and up to his chest. Then he placed his open palms on the underside of the lid and shoved up as hard as he could. The casket resisted at first and then popped open to an assault of daylight, allowing the dream to end.

"Shit." When Greg woke up he was on his back. His arms were outstretched, pushing the blankets away from his face. "What the f—"

He let the blankets fall to his side, rolled out of bed, and stumbled to the bathroom. There, last night's scotch streamed into the toilet as if it wouldn't end. There had to be at least twenty-six ounces, he thought to himself as a hint of a smile nudged at the corner of his mouth.

Slumped against the wall of the shower as he did his business, Greg let the other dream surface. It was a dream that had visited him almost every night for the last twenty years. The first dreams had introduced a small boy to him, a boy he felt a connection with.

In the most recent dreams, the boy had grown to a mature twenty-two years old. A thin nest of stubble formed on his chin. Regardless of his age, the boy would take his hand and lead him down the street. It was always the same street. The only difference was that the small child had aged as Greg had aged. Twenty years had passed since that first dream and the small boy was now a man.

Greg's wife, Anne-Marie, when she was still considered his wife, used to tease him about those dreams. It wasn't long before he regretted mentioning them to her. Her mumbled and somewhat derogatory comments often warned him about bringing home strays. Then she'd head off to see Danny, her tennis instructor, while her still-in-the-bag tennis racket sat in the hall closet. It was a detail she often overlooked. Perhaps she didn't care to hide it any more. Greg never called her out on it. This was Washington DC and he knew he played as big a role in the failure of their marriage.

At the time, he had given their relationship a year to play itself out. It only took three months. A lease for an apartment, closer to downtown, was signed later that week. A truck would arrive to move his stuff. He took one last look around. Strangely, he knew he'd miss this place. Dysfunctional as it was, it was home.

The dreams of the boy had become a bigger part of him than he wanted to admit. In them he walked with the child down a narrow, crowded street that was littered with debris. There was an unknown urgency as they glided through the crowds of locals. Were they looking for something? It was possible, but he had no idea as to what, or who.

The crowds parted. People watched him and the odd one couldn't refrain from touching his shoulder as he passed. No matter what happened, the young boy continued to tug on his hand.

In an attempt to shake off the dreams, Greg dressed and headed downstairs. Breakfast was the usual coffee and toast. He ate it while standing over the sink. Grabbing his briefcase, he popped the last bite into his mouth. His job, as much a ball and chain as his wife was, kept him on the run. And like his wife, it challenged him and kept him from having a life of his own.

With his coffee cup now empty and in the dishwasher, he made his way to the garage. The door opened, allowing the morning to wash away the darkness. Greg tossed a small suitcase on the passenger seat, slipped behind the wheel of the Mercedes, and turned the key. The car rolled back into the street and he waited while the garage door closed. It didn't always stay closed. The odd time it would touch down and then start back up again. The garage would remain open all day. Why did he still care? It wasn't his house anymore. Old habits died hard.

While the door closed, the boy from his dreams drifted back into his thoughts. Did the child have a name? The kid was Hispanic with well-tanned skin and chestnut eyes. A full head of long curly dark hair graced his head. It was much like Greg's before the greys had grabbed a foothold at his temples.

In the dream, the boy often mentioned a Papa. Was Greg that Papa? The feeling was as natural as the crowds they passed. Although poverty-stricken, they seemed content. Most looked at him as they passed by, this stranger from the States with one of their own.

Kevin Weisbeck

The boy always stopped at the same spot. There was a street sign attached to the corner of the building. The sign read 'Calle.' and Greg knew he'd been there before. There'd be a doorway, stairs, and a dark abyss with exposed power lines and cracked cement walls. It always looked the same. He knew this place.

A car horn snatched Greg from the trance. "Move it along, Miller!"

The words were sarcastically playful as Ted Wilson passed him in his Jaguar. Ted meant no ill will by his arrogance. The man was born an asshole and took pride in the role. Greg gave him a polite wave, knowing that next Monday he'd be wondering where that Miller guy went. And by midweek, Miller would be forgotten, and the next victim would be chosen. It was the way these guys worked.

"Back at ya, you miserable ass."

Ted's middle finger waved as he sped off. "Good one, Miller."

For the last time, Greg took a moment to say goodbye to his neighbourhood before driving away. Mrs. Johnson's wisteria, draped with a full bloom of white flowers, looked as fruitful as ever. She was the only one that ever looked out for him. It usually came in the form of a timely wave, a small brown bag of peanut butter cookies or a sympathetic smile when Anne was in one of her moods. Now in the rear-view mirror, his life, the white picket fence and the tall Dutch elms slowly dwindled until they were gone.

On the freeway, his thoughts swarmed like angry bees. None of the dreams had ever made sense to him, that is, until yesterday afternoon. Greg had always thought it peculiar that the dreams evolved. As he aged, so did the young child. All the people in the dreams aged. Now as a young man, the boy still grasped Greg's hand and led him down the street. The dreams had occurred so often that the people in them were like family, friends and neighbours.

But the dreams were nothing more than the subconscious rantings of a man who'd managed to mess up his life, right? And they'd been no more than dreams until yesterday, when he was with Anne's family watching her Aunt Diane's vacation video. She'd recently returned from Cuba.

The Divine Ledger

Greg had nothing against her family. It wasn't their fault Anne was giving him the boot after twenty years of marriage. They were good people, they had taken him in and loved him like a son from the beginning. Sure, he was nothing more than a son-in-law, but her mother made him cabbage rolls the German way, with bacon and hamburger. Her father had taken him marlin fishing. He knew he'd miss them more than he'd miss Anne.

Most of the visit had been spent staring across the room at his soon-to-be ex-wife. Was it wrong to still be in love with her? Could there be a part of Anne-Marie that wanted him to stay? She loved him in the beginning. His trance was rudely broken by a scene from the video.

He could feel the blood drain from his face when the video got to Obispo Street. Thoughts of his wife and the love they once shared were quickly replaced with a panic he'd never felt before. There, in Havana, was a busy little shopping street. There was lots to see and more to spend money on. More important than that, it was the street from his dreams.

It had everything, from the debris that hadn't moved in decades to the potholes that got larger as the years rolled by. There was a doorway, their doorway. This had to be the boy's home. His Aunt had called it Obispo Street.

Greg said nothing as he tried to catch his breath. He continued to watch in silent amazement as the peanuts disappeared from the candy dish, one by one. The place was real. Later that night he went online and found out that Obispo Street was actually called Obispo Calle. The Obispo part had been missing. Why the hell had this come to him now, after all these years?

That night Greg booked a flight to Cuba, via Mexico. Even though he had seen his grave, he knew he was anything but dead. So what was up with the crazy coffin dream? If the boy was real, could his death also be real? Was the clock ticking?

Sleep never came on the flight to Mexico, but it did on the connecting flight to Cuba. As he slept, another dream came to him. In this dream a cemetery sprawled for acres. The boy, now a man, took his hand and instead of leading him to that broken-down apartment, he dragged him through the rows of tombstones. The cemetery sprawled in every direction and as far as the eye could see. In the distance thousands of sparrows were gathering.

Chapter Three

Vancouver, Canada

Violet took a gulp of the mud in her favourite coffee mug. It was the usual blend of the cheapest coffee she could afford, mixed with the impatience of not letting all the water run through the machine. The mug was a white one, with a large yellow smiley face. A bullet hole and accompanying trickle of blood sat between the eyes. It was a get-well gift from the boys at the precinct, the first time she had been shot. She took another mouthful and let the coffee work away at clearing the lingering haze of last night's shooting.

She took a seat at the table of her travel trailer. It was the kind that folded down into a bed when needed. Unable to find a deluxe model in her price range, there was no queen-sized bed or even an actual mattress. Her clothes closet was under the four inches of foam. It was added padding for her bed and sleeping on your pants and shirts kept them pressed. The two hundred and forty square feet of living space was all she needed, all she could handle.

Kitchen cupboards doubled as storage space, less the shelf needed for two coffee mugs, a plate, a glass and some mixed cutlery. Since toast was all she'd ever cooked, all she could cook, the stove had become the home of her belts, ball caps and shoes. Actual meals consisted of the stale Danish and doughnuts found at the precinct's break room, unless the traffic cops beat her to them. Damn, how she hated those flat feet.

Popping the last two Advils from the bottle that sat beside her service revolver, she threw them to the back of her mouth and washed them down with another swallow of coffee. Sure, there were days when being a traffic cop might have been a safer choice than homicide, but how much fun would that have been? Nobody ever got shot at while writing parking tickets, except for Danny Parker. In his defence, how could 'Meter Maid Dan' have known the car he was leaning against was a waiting getaway car? Maybe the fact that the driver was wearing panty hose over his head?

She rubbed at the bandage on her forehead. Who was she kidding? Getting shot, more a bloody graze than anything else, allowed her to draw her revolver and fire back. Car tires squealing, guns blasting, and the heart racing—it was everything the brochure had promised. It never disappointed.

Passing out in last night's jeans and blouse simplified her morning routine. She grabbed her gun, slipped on a mixed pair of pink and black flip-flops and opened the door to her trailer. The mid-morning sun greeted her as she ran her fingers through her blonde mane. She scratched at her scalp and squinted as she tried to locate her car. It wasn't in the driveway.

She brushed her hand over the front of her jeans and found a lump of keys. That could only mean one thing. "Damn you, Anthony."

Violet stepped back inside and panned the trailer for her phone. Detective Walsh was the name she pulled up from the contact list. He always worked days and she trusted him. It only rang twice.

"Walsh here."

"Neil, I need a ride. What's your ETA?"

"I'm halfway up Hastings. Where's your..." He stopped. "I don't want to know, do I?"

"You do not. See ya in five."

The Divine Ledger

The black and white pulled into the driveway in three. The lights and siren allowed him to cut through the traffic. "Morning Stormm. I'm guessing Barn's Impound?"

"The guy's relentless, Neil."

"Here's a thought. Pay him what you owe him."

"What?" Her eyes rolled. "I can't believe you. If we all thought like that, there'd be no need for guys like him. He'd end up unemployed. Then he'd have to turn to a life of crime and drugs to make ends meet. We'd probably end up shooting him in some crackhouse. Call this my way of look'n out for the little guy."

"Sure, we'll go with that."

"Hey, I do what I can." Violet pointed to the back alley as they got closer. "I don't have his money, Neil."

"Why am I surprised?" He shook his head as he cranked the wheel. The car slowly growled to a stop on the loose gravel. "I'm gonna drop you here, Stormm. Give me a minute to put some distance between us. I have a pension to think about."

"You'll never live long enough to worry about it with that wussy attitude."

Violet got out and watched as he drove off. He didn't share her spirit or her blood, but he was family - they all were. That's why she carefully counted to sixty before slipping into the impound yard through a cut in the chain-link fence. She'd put it there two weeks ago.

A black 'sixty-eight Dart GT sat in a stall patiently waiting for her. The car was a stallion and commanded respect. It didn't deserve to be caged like a Topaz or a Pinto. In true Mopar fashion, the car had the infamous thick stripe across the trunk. The stripe was a violet one and gave the car more than just personality. It gave the car attitude.

Crouching down, Violet worked her way along the driver's side of the car and unlocked the door. She crawled behind the wheel, slipped the key into the ignition, and gave it a turn. The car came alive with a throaty rumble that sent a flock of magpies fleeing for a nearby power line. "I missed you this morning, Babe."

Tires howled as the car left the stall. The back end swung around and Violet faced the exit as she hammered the brakes. Then the engine revved in short bursts as she inched forward. She hand-cranked the driver's window down. "Open the gate, Anthony."

"I can't do that, Detective Violent Stormm." The voice came from a rotund man who stepped out of the small booth at the entrance. Holding a large hoagie in both hands, he started toward her.

"It's Violet, without the 'n', you ass. Now open up." The engine snorted again, and she grabbed another three feet of pavement. "Open up."

"That's not how it works." He tossed his sandwich down on the dusty hood of a nearby Cadillac before taking his place in front of the gate. "Was that Neil dropping you off?"

"Nah. It was Jake." She hated Jake. The only time she ever saw that ass-clown was in the break room. On more than one occasion she'd caught him eating the only cream-filled Long John. The shit-eating grin, stretched across his face, was a sure give-away that he knew she loved those things. "Yeah, it was Jake Turner."

"Where's my money, Stormm?"

"I need my car, Anthony."

"That's great. I need a wife with tits like watermelons." He laughed as if the comment was worth a chuckle. It wasn't. "Maybe you'd have my money if you didn't hand so much of it over to that deadbeat ex of yours."

She took a deep breath and started counting. She got to six before stopping. "You know better than to go there."

"Whatever. Am I wrong?"

She thought of her service revolver tucked in her pants behind her back. Putting a thirty-eight slug in this guy's leg wouldn't get the gate open, but it would feel good. As tempting as that was, she knew idiot-face wasn't the enemy. "I'll get you your money by the end of the week."

On her command, the four hundred and fifty horses were released. It launched the car forward, drawing two black lines in the asphalt.

Anthony stepped back to the shack and pressed the button. The gate started its slow, chugging journey across the entrance. Violet slammed on the brakes, this time stopping a few feet from the

The Divine Ledger

half-open gate. It was a bit anticlimactic as she sat there waiting. Anthony moved back in front of the car. He leaned forward and placed his chubby hands on the mirrored finish of the hood.

Cringing at the thought of the greasy smudges on the paint, Violet's eyes narrowed to angry slits. "Don't."

"You know I always get my money." His stare held hers through the windshield as he made his way to the driver's side door. "Look, I know your situation with your ex is kinda difficult, but I can't afford to carry you any longer. He needs to find his own money, and you need to pay me. I'll give you one week, but nothing more."

"Or you'll do what, steal my car again?"

"First of all, it's not stealing. You owe me the money. And no, I don't want the car." His eyes locked on hers like a father's might when he'd reached the end of his rope. "I'll be forced to take the damn trailer. That's what you owe the money on."

"End of the week!" With that she tromped the pedal and left the lot sideways.

But the man was right, she owed him money and her salary wasn't enough to help Bradley and pay the bills, especially if she kept getting shot. She couldn't expect it to.

During her two-year stint as a homicide detective she had been shot twice, not counting the grazes. In the first instance, she had taken a bullet to the abdomen. She left blood all over the Gilford Mall as she continued to chase the perp. There was no letting this one get away. The slime had taken his daughter with him on a bank job. He'd also left her behind to save himself when the shooting started.

By the time she had caught him, her store-bought vanity tan had paled to a peachy white. Because she couldn't trust herself to stay conscious, she cracked the man on the head with her revolver. Then she emptied the bullets out of the chamber of her gun and handcuffed it to her wrist. When the backups found her, she was unconscious in a puddle of her own blood. That was exactly what the brochure had promised. She was off for eight weeks. Only a portion of her wages was covered. That part had been in the fine print.

The second time she was shot was during a drive-by while she was staking out a drug house. A black SUV had showed up at two in the morning and a guy in the back seat sprayed her car with bullets. She never even got her guns drawn. Violet took two slugs, one in the shoulder and one in the leg. She was lucky to be alive. It also meant six weeks on short-term disability pay.

Even with full pay, it was hard to cover the bills and cut a cheque for Bradley. Too bad Anthony didn't understand. Instead he kept impounding the only thing that she and Bradley still shared, the black 'sixty-eight Dart with the violet stripe across the trunk.

Chapter Four

Sayulita, Mexico

Hector Fuentes had died in 1976 from a fall off a rooftop. He was a once-famous cliff diver from Acapulco. He used to dive from the towering cliffs of La Quebrada. Now, the only sign of his existence was a weathered four-by-eight slab of hand-mixed concrete that sat on the ground like a curbstone. Two large cracks had the one corner dipping slightly. They allowed for several weeds to reach out from whatever was below. Although aged and crumbling, it made a fine spot for Victor to sit.

He crouched and parked himself against the name on the partially toppled headstone. Then he made himself as comfortable as he could. His duffel bag was pulled to his side and he unzipped it, letting the sadness and betrayal waft from the opening. That wasn't what concerned him as he took a drag on his cigar. He was worried that this might not work.

Victor took a few moments to settle his mood before carefully reaching inside the bag and retrieving one of the skulls. It was that of a Harvard man named Alexander P. Newton. The 'P' stood for Percy. Despite being highly educated, the man's world was dreary and pathetic. He aspired to more and might have had it, had a trek from Atlanta to Vancouver not changed all that. The man thought he was going to a seminar. His life would be the first of twelve taken.

With cigar in hand, Victor held the skull up to the sun and admired the beauty of the man's cranium. Thick smoke slithered through the open eye sockets as if Alex himself was the one smoking. The smooth surface of the occipital bone felt good against Victor's fingertips, enchanting him. Alexander had been returned to his rightful place on the planet. The man had lived, and he had died. Wherever he was, touched by the angry spirits of this cemetery or lost in a void where life used to exist, he was an abomination that had to be stopped.

With some formality, he set the skull down by the headstone and removed another from the bag. Simply by size and feel, he could tell who they were. Each skull was as unique as the person it belonged to.

"Hello Elizabeth, it's been a while."

Elizabeth Dearns was a young woman who loved 'The Beach Boys'. At the age of sixteen, she knew all she needed to know about them. She also knew all she needed to know about her parents. Unlike the songs of fun and sun, her Mom and Dad were out to get her. They chose her friends, made far too many rules and couldn't understand her need for the occasional sip from their liquor cabinet. She just wanted to live life and they were holding her back. So, with the coaxing from her boyfriend, Jeremy Stalwart, she quietly slipped away, trading the comforts of home for the adventures of a lifetime.

They found that life in the big city. But then Jeremy died, a drug deal gone horribly wrong, and she was alone. It wasn't what she expected. Sure, she had the option to call home, but she wasn't ready to do that just yet. Too bad the streets hadn't killed her before he had to.

Victor got to his feet and carefully paced off eight steps and set her skull down amongst a pile of rocks with no headstone. The anonymity of the grave seemed fitting. He finished the first beer and tossed the bottle into the jungle, wishing he'd brought a case.

The Divine Ledger

Jane Lizzy Travis, a lonely schoolteacher from Virginia, had been walking home from a New Year's Eve party when she got the call to go to Vancouver. There was a gala honouring her achievements, or so she was led to believe. Her skull was scarred from a fracture that ran the length of the occipital plate. Victor hadn't caused it. Messy killings were not his style. The scar was caused when she was twelve. A ski accident during a school outing had caused it and almost led to her death.

Victor had picked her up at the airport and she'd been a chatty one. Her blur of words was simple. Peter was an ass, her mother didn't help matters, her brother should just butt the hell out and she'd never date again. He enjoyed her rant. After she had exhausted her rage, Victor saw to it that she'd never have a bad date again. He set her skull down on a gravestone facing an ocean hidden by the palm trees. "Now you can enjoy your freedom, sweet Jane."

One by one he extracted the twelve skulls from the bag. He took a moment to reflect on each one before setting them down in their carefully chosen spots.

There was a decorated surgeon from Boston who only needed four more jumps to say he'd parachuted one hundred times. Another skull belonged to a woman who owned seven cats. Her brothel in Atlantic City gave her quite a list of connections, each one trusting her discretion with their lives. Every skull held a story. Victor had learned them all before ending them in mid-chapter.

The only one he regretted was a young woman named Gerty from Kettle Falls, Washington. She was a girl that could barrel-race with the best of them. The woman had filled her life with magical energy and hard work. Had she been allowed to live, she would have been a champion. Her life was far brighter than the others, but he had still taken it. If he had to do it over he might have left her alone, let her live out her life and die at eighty-four, as she was fated to do. Then again, why take that chance?

No, he was right to have killed her. He gently kissed the skull before setting it down amongst some roses he'd taken from an adjacent grave.

Victor closed his eyes and took a final puff of his cigar. The humidity from the jungle reminded him of Cambodia—four mercenaries, a one-legged hooker and two blind mules hauling forty kilos of heroin. Now that was one crazy weekend.

He downed a good portion of his second beer and took a long look at the last mouthful through the neck of the bottle. What he'd done years ago was supposed to have ended all of this. He had really hoped it was over, but knew the other shoe would fall someday. He drank the last of the beer and tossed the bottle into the jungle.

Several days ago, an unexpected package had arrived at his hotel room. He hadn't opened it right away, didn't have to. Instead, he cracked open a bottle of tequila and didn't stop drinking until the worm was gone.

How many would he have to kill this time?

Chapter Five

The streets of downtown Vancouver were abnormally quiet as Violet made a detour on her way to the precinct. Often the urban crowds flocked to restaurant patios and parks when the days were this nice, but they were mysteriously absent. There weren't any artery-clogging accidents or street corners packed with anxious pedestrians running five minutes late. It was more like a casual Sunday.

Violet rolled down the windows and cranked the music as she enjoyed her morning cruise along Marine Drive. She was almost at Bradley's place when her phone went off. She slowly pulled the phone out of her jeans pocket, its vibrating the only pleasure she'd felt in weeks. The thought was shrugged off with a chuckle. "Stormm here."

"Where are you?"

"Damn." It was the Sarge. He must have noticed she was absent at the morning briefing.

"Excuse me, Detective Stormm?"

"I mean morning, Sarge. Sorry, Sir." She felt an instant need to lie, call it an intuition. "I was just about to call…uh."

"Save it." Sergeant Crowley had never pretended to understand her. A good part of his job was babysitting and sorting through the strengths and weaknesses of the newer detectives. Misfits like Violet were trouble, but there was always something in them worth moulding. Stormm had many talents, albeit masked in the many layers of irresponsibility. "I don't have the patience today."

"It's not like that Sarge. I just…"

"I need you to go to the airport. There'll be a ticket waiting for you."

"I'm guessing there's been a murder?"

"Not exactly."

"Is this a forced retirement?" She knew she could do a lot worse than sand-blown beaches, but this wasn't the norm. She could also do a lot worse than a forced retirement at the age of twenty-seven. If only it were this easy. "Like, am I coming back, Sir?"

"I need you to check out a crime scene. You'll have no jurisdiction, no authority, and no say in how they conduct the investigation. You're just a shadow."

"Seriously? Then why don't you send one of the flunkeys?"

"I am." There was a brief pause. "That shooting last night caused a lot of media noise. The mayor was asking for a suspension. This was what I talked him down to."

"This ticket, you're sure it's a return flight?"

He stifled a laugh, not wanting to encourage her. He was three years from retirement. He'd mentored all kinds of crazy and Violet was no exception. Her tactics could steer an ocean liner into an iceberg on a Panama Cruise, but she got results. This was a cold case that she had shown interest in back when she was a wet-behind-the-ears cadet. If anybody could crack it, she could. She was tenacious

"Why me, for the record?"

"For some reason people like you and they trust you. It's like the whole world opens up to you."

"I don't understand."

"Believe me, I don't either, but I need you to go to Mexico and sweet-talk the authorities down in Sayulita. I'll make sure the case files are at the airport when you get there. You wrapped up a case last night. Other than the big shootout at the supermarket, it was a good job. You might want to formally apologise to the store owner for trashing his produce section."

"The perp was a big guy. I never told him to fall against that stack of watermelons."

"And the grapefruits, the cantaloupes and the apples. You could have clipped him a lot quicker than you did."

But she had enjoyed the chase. "Fair enough. So why the Vancouver Homicide Department, Sarge?"

"We got a courtesy call from a detective in Puerto Vallarta. It has a major similarity to a case you showed interest in a while back. I figured you might be interested. The situation is a bit odd, but I trust you."

"Uh, for real?" She thought he was going to choke on the words.

"That, and Jerry talked me into it."

Jerry Fhitzer was a cop and a good friend. These days Jerry was happy to sit behind a desk. He'd been the lead officer on one of the grizzliest crimes that Vancouver had ever seen. The case had rattled him for weeks. It had started with two headless women found on the beach in Kitsilano. In the weeks that followed, headless body after headless body had surfaced in a variety of locations. There had been no connections, no leads, and it had all stopped as suddenly as it had started.

"What am I walking into?"

"They've found a collection of skulls, Stormm."

She felt a rush of blood in her face. "Is it safe to assume, twelve?"

"They didn't say, but when I heard about it I thought of you. Are you going to be okay with this?"

"I guess."

"When you get there, you'll meet a Captain Sosa. Just remember to be polite. This isn't our jurisdiction and we need everything this man can give us." He waited.

She answered knowing that, over the phone, he couldn't see that her fingers were crossed. "I can do that."

"We've told the Detective that you have ties to one of the dead. He seemed sympathetic. Use that to talk him into handing the skulls over to us."

"What have they figured out so far?"

"Not much. You'll be landing there this afternoon. Captain Sosa will pick you up at the airport and take you straight to the site. You're not afraid of spirits, are you?"

"You mean like tequila? I've always been a little scared of the bite-back, but I can handle it."

"I meant ghosts."

"I can't believe you're asking that, Sarge. There's no such thing as Hocus Pocus, voodoo, or any of that ghoulish crap."

"That's good, but these people are all freaked out about the crime scene, so tread lightly. I want those skulls. They're Mexican jurisdiction until we can do the forensics and DNA testing. You match them to our case and they're ours."

"Is that all?"

"I got another call from Bradley."

"My Bradley?"

"He had questions about some secondary disability pay. Any idea what he was talking about, Stormm?" Although he already knew why, he had to do his due diligence.

"Nothing, Sarge. I'm pulling into his driveway as we speak. He's been a little confused since the shooting. I'll talk to him." She ended the call.

From the driveway she could see him sitting in his wheelchair at the front door, and he was angry.

"Ah, shit."

Chapter Six

Bradley was helpless as the coffee cup took a slow-motion tumble onto his lap. He couldn't feel the steaming hot brew, but it would burn his skin all the same if he didn't clean it up right away. For that reason, he grabbed a tea towel, mopped at his unresponsive legs while he wheeled his way to the front door. Like some paranormal warning, he always spilt his coffee when she dropped by unannounced. Today was no different.

From the ramp at the front of his house, he saw his girl rumbling her four hundred horses up the street and into the driveway. Violet was driving the car like she'd stolen it, and that warmed his heart. Somebody should, now that he couldn't.

"Damn it, Violet." His chest tightened as the car rolled to a stop. "Are those fingerprints?"

Violet remembered Anthony's greasy paws and quickly got out, pulled at the bottom of her t-shirt, and proceeded to rub the hood clean. "Asshole-face had her last night."

"Hey, if you need a few dollars, let me know. She doesn't belong there. I can help."

"I'm good."

He watched her rub the hood back to a shine. Then he noticed the white square of gauze at her hairline. "What happened to you?" He tapped his forehead when she looked up.

She reached up and pulled the bandage off, revealing a row of eight stitches. "It's nothing."

He leaned forward to get a better look. "Were you shot again?"

She tossed the bandage behind one of the dead Cedars. "Barely. Now can we change the subject?" She knew what was coming next. It was the you-have-to-be-careful lecture. God how she hated that one.

"Shit, Violet. What is that, three, four, and this one's a head shot. You've gotta start being more careful—"

"Enough! I said I'm not talking about it, so pick another topic."

"Okay, did you find out anything about that secondary disability?"

"You were injured in the line of duty." She shrugged. "I think the first disability is for normal crap, falling down stairs, back strains, and paper cuts. Yours was worse, a line-of-duty thing."

"Don't get me wrong. I'll take the money from them. I just don't want them changing their minds a couple years down the road and wanting it back."

"Oh, no problem there." She quickly tossed another lie onto the pile. "I talked to the precinct lawyer and they can't ask for it back."

"Good." He started up the ramp. "What's the visit for?"

"Guess who's going to Mexico."

"That's great. If anybody needs a vacation, you do." He found it easy to be happy for her. "Right on. Don't forget the sunscreen. I don't need ya coming back looking like any dang minority."

"Shit, Bradley. Be nice, eh." She gave him a playful smack in the arm as she looked around for the eavesdropping neighbours. "No, I'm off on business."

"What the hell are you doing there?" Then he remembered who he was talking to. Violet was also Victoria, the Canadian diplomat, Veronica, the reporter and the never-to-be-forgotten Vivian, the investor who had embezzled millions. That was never proven. And who knew how many other identities she had created. When he first found the stack of little blue passports, he wondered if she was even a cop, but only a cop would throw themselves at danger the way she did. "Is this police business, or…"

She put his mind at ease. "Police stuff. Some kids found a bunch of skulls."

"Damn, Violet. How many?"

"Not sure, but I have a good idea."

He rolled past the coffee maker to the fridge and grabbed a beer. "Want one? We can talk out back."

"Let me." She popped the caps off with his lighter and handed one back to him. Then she started to load the dishwasher with the plates from the sink.

He spun around, catching her leg with the chair.

"Ouch."

"What are you doing? You don't live here. My house, my shit. I'm quite capable of loading my own damn dishwasher."

Violet bent down and rubbed her shin. "Too bad you're not capable of steering that thing."

"Stop acting like I'm fucking useless."

"Nobody called you useless." Violet grabbed her beer and headed for the back patio. "For the record, I think you're more of a prick than anything."

Bradley smiled, slammed the dishwasher door shut, and put his beer in the cup holder. He could have cut her some slack, but she needed this. Maybe to a degree, he did too. They weren't a couple anymore. She no longer lived with him and the sooner they got that figured out, the better.

He had spent a month making the place more him, less her, and it wasn't an easy task. Everything she had done to the place over the last two years had worked. Her constant nagging had the bathroom looking great, the bedroom cosy, and the living room welcoming.

Everything, from the paint on the walls to the many plants, to the colour co-ordinated toaster, was her idea. He had hired painters to come in last week and change everything. And when they were done, it sucked. Twice he sat in the middle of the living room with his phone in hand. He wanted to get the painters back but didn't.

"What took you so long." Violet had only been waiting a minute, but he had started it. She'd finish it. "You get lost in your own mess?"

"Like you…" He stopped and took a long cleansing breath. "Never mind. You're off to Mexico. You know I can help at this end if you want it."

"Always." She leaned back in her chair. Neither of them wanted to fight, but it came so naturally. "You still got all your gear?"

"Are you kidding me? The spare room has been transformed. I have all my computers hooked up. I even got a hold of a used carbon-dater. I bought a used titrator, HPLC machine and some new-tech facial recognition software. Hell, I'll be the guy James Bond goes to when he needs help."

"I see you've kept yourself busy."

His head slumped. "What else am I going to do? When do you leave?"

"I should be at the airport in an hour. I just wanted to see if I could call you, you know, if I need some of this fancy-shmancy help."

"I've always got your back. You know that."

She got up and gave him a hug. "It means a lot to me."

He watched as she got up and walked back into the house. It was nice of her to stop by. "Hey, slob-girl. You forgot your empty bottle. You think this is some kinda barn or something?"

Her hair shook from side to side as her middle finger playfully waved back at him. She made her way through the house without looking back. The good-byes were still the hardest part.

Chapter Seven

Varadero, Cuba

Greg stepped through the airport doors and the Cuban humidity hit him like an ocean wave. It exuded red clay and stuck to the inside of his lungs like peanut butter. The distant sweet aroma of the smouldering Cohibas rode the winds throughout the island. It was Fidel Castro's trademark cigar. Back in the day, when Greg used to smoke, the Cohiba was a coveted and highly illegal treasure. These hand-rolled masterpieces were cherished with every slow, long drag that he sucked into his eagerly awaiting lungs. But, after a doctor's long-winded lecture, smoking reluctantly gave way to jogging. Now, years later, the taste of those damn cigars had returned and they smelled amazing.

Salsa music, as distant as the beach party it emanated from, filled the warm night air. Stars dotted the darkened sky, looking more like illuminated snowflakes suspended in time. Palm trees swayed in the tropical breeze as if dancing. They thirsted for a good storm. Instead, they got discarded candy wrappers, cigar butts and crushed beer cans. This wasn't the image the travel brochures had portrayed, but at least he was finally here.

With his carry-on in tow, he slung his jacket over his shoulder and looked across the parking lot at no less than a dozen buses. They were a lot newer than he'd anticipated. This was a good thing, as one of them would be his ride into Havana. He'd imagined a cart, pulled by a donkey. He imagined sitting in the back with the hay and the family dog.

Greg stopped to take it all in and, as if his brain was a car's GPS system, recalculating, recalculating. He took a deep breath, but it didn't calm the second thoughts of being there. The dreams that he'd been having since he was nineteen were coming to life.

"*Buenos dias. Copacabana?*" A short, well-dressed local man held up a sign that read the name of the airline he'd just flown in on. A straw fedora, the typical hat you'd expect to see, sat crooked on his head. It matched his off-centre smile as he repeated the hotel's name. "Copacabana?"

"*Si.*" Greg glanced at his watch. It was four in the morning. It had been close to midnight when he'd left. Buenos noches was no longer pertinent. How the time flew. "Buenos dias." He'd given himself a Spanish lesson on the plane. Now was his chance to use it. "*Como esta?*"

"*Bien, gracias.*" The man affected a welcoming smile, worn like a birthmark. "*Habla espanjol?*"

Greg stood there looking at the man. He doubted that 'habla' meant food or drink. Screw the lessons. It was late, or early, depending. "My Spanish is very poor. My apologies."

"Not to worry. I can talk English some." The man's smile grew even larger as he dragged Greg's carry-on to one of the smaller buses. There were eight people already seated in it. They weren't from his flight.

"We wait for you."

An instant flush of guilt washed over him. How long had they waited? Were they mad? It wasn't his fault…the plane…what could he say? "I'm sorry, I didn't…"

"Oh no. They no wait long. It all good. This is vacation time." He slid Greg's bag into the luggage compartment. Reading the nametag, he turned back to him. "Small suitcase, Mr. Miller. You no staying long in Cuba?"

The Divine Ledger

Greg shook his head. "It's Greg, and I really don't know."

The man was puzzled, his smile never wavering. Most tourists came for a set time, ready to pack in as much fun and sun as possible. But for this gringo there was no plan and no way of knowing what to expect. He didn't know that Greg came with the hopes of finding answers to questions he didn't know to ask yet. Again, he found himself recalculating, recalculating.

One of the seats at the very back of the bus seemed to be calling him. The bus reminded him of his high school days, minus the chaos of being a crater-faced teenager. As he passed by everyone, he got smiles and head nods. Two women, he quickly put them in their late thirties, acted interested…in him. Did he look good for a man his age? They must have thought so.

Regardless, no one was upset about the wait. They were all looking forward to the two-hour bus ride into Havana. There they could check in, unpack, and start enjoying their holiday. Greg would be tossing his suitcase on the bed, grabbing a coffee and taking the first cab downtown.

Palm trees passed at speeds that almost scared him. Maybe it was the potholes that tossed him around in his seat, or maybe it was the fog, thick from a warm ocean. Either way, a frayed seatbelt was available and he wasn't embarrassed to use it.

Greg closed his eyes, not because of the driver's death-wish, but to contemplate whether there was another reason for being there. Could it be that this was an escape from his wife, Anne? She had held his heart captive for eighteen years and still might. He knew no other way. Only distractions or death could exorcise the woman from his heart and only if he was smart enough to allow it. Was he?

The last few years had been painful. They held the memories he could let slip away into the abyss. The years prior to that, after they met, when their love was stronger than the world, were the years he held close. There was skinny-dipping in the moonlit Demster's Pond, late nights with popcorn and scary movies and the ever-enjoyable drives through the countryside. Those memories had burrowed their way deeper into his heart than a rabbit in its hole when winter came.

After savouring those thoughts for a while, Greg reopened his eyes. The lights were off and everyone was snoring. He had tried to contemplate what to expect, but anything was possible. More than likely, he'd find nothing more than an interesting vacation, which wasn't a bad thing. He was years overdue to get away. As a hobby-writer he might even dig up enough inspiration to write that novel. He'd never make enough to quit his job, but maybe he could scratch some alimony-free pocket money.

Still nagging at him was that dream of his tombstone, the one that had woken him in a cold sweat. It brought a crazy energy to this place. The tombstone, the boy, and that street were real. Was his death going to be real too?

Outside the window of the bus, a dead tree stood in the distance with several crows perched in it. The hazy reflection of the moon on the ocean and the drifting fog framed the birds like a scene from an Alfred Hitchcock movie. He had read somewhere that a group of seven or more crows was called a murder. As they got closer to the tree, he couldn't help but wonder what they would call the hundreds of sparrows that accompanied them. Each one of the birds had locked their gaze on him, heads turning in unison as the bus passed. And under the tree stood a tall man, half-hidden in the shadows. He wore an oversized leather coat and a large-brimmed black hat that hid his face.

They knew he was coming.

Chapter Eight

Puerto Vallarta, Mexico

Violet awoke as the plane touched down on the Mexican tarmac. She gathered the victim's folders and stuffed them into her shoulder bag. Seat 27C was ridiculously comfortable compared to the bed back in her trailer. She had slipped into a deep sleep shortly after takeoff.

As she got ready to leave the plane, she noticed a young boy of about nine looking back at her from his seat a few rows forward. Was he smitten with a schoolboy crush? She politely shot him a wink. His eyes flared and he abruptly dropped behind the back of his seat.

She turned to the middle-aged computer nerd on her left. "How cute was that?"

He cleared his throat as he gathered his comic books. "You nodded off a while back. You know you snore?"

"Pardon?" She didn't understand.

"You were out cold." He pointed to her face. "I took the liberty of putting a few red sticky dots on you. That kid probably thought you had some freaky measles thing going on."

Violet ran her fingers over her skin, picking them off as she found them. "Why would you do that? How old are you?"

"It was a boring flight. If you think about it, it's kinda funny."

She opened her bag, revealing her service revolver. "Capping your ass would be funny too, but you don't see me—"

With that, the stampede off the plane started, the nerd leading the way. "Gun! She's got a gun!"

In seconds, all one hundred and forty-seven passengers were leaving their bags behind and screaming. Captain Sosa wouldn't need the cardboard sign that his secretary had made for him. It had read 'Storm', missing the second 'm' purely by accident.

Violet slumped when she saw him. "I am really sorry about that, Sir. It was poor judgement on my part. I assure you it won't happen again."

He looked at her, pulled off one of the dots that she'd missed and shook his head. "The man who started the stampede, he is a teacher at my daughter's school. She will be happy when I tell her of this story."

"Really?"

"The man failed her on a final exam because she forgot to put her name on her test paper. He knew it was hers but felt the need to make an example for the others."

"You're a Captain. You could arrest him for bad hair. I'd have …"

He cut her off. "We don't work that way here."

"Of course not. Sorry."

The man led her to his pickup and slipped behind the wheel while Violet grabbed the passenger side. Sitting in the box were four young soldiers, each holding an M60 machine gun. And there she was, worried about a handgun in her bag.

Heading up the north coast, it took only forty-five minutes to arrive at the crime scene. Violet listened to the stories of the Heguerros and of La Playa de Muertos. She smiled politely as she remembered her orders to respect their childish concerns. Ghosts ranked right up there with Ninja Turtles and she had no time to sensationalise a crime scene. The man who had murdered twelve people years ago in Vancouver, had left the skulls at a cemetery in Mexico and she wanted to know why. Messed up ideals were rolling around in that twisted mind of his and it was her job to either find out why or, at the very least, to extinguish them.

The four young soldiers hopped out of the truck when they pulled into the parking lot of the Villa Amour. Violet was given a quick tour of the cemetery and she immediately started to nose around. The skulls were scattered amongst the tombstones. Violet saw no apparent pattern. There were no pentacles or ancient symbols that she could see. That didn't mean Bradley wouldn't be able to see something. She pulled out her phone and opened the camera app.

She gave the skulls a quick count. "Twelve?"

"Si. Is that the number you were looking for?" The Captain asked.

"I'm pretty sure we have the matching bodies back home."

She started taking pictures of everything and scratching notes. Missing things that seemed trivial had happened on more than one occasion and Bradley never hesitated to scold her for it. He was all about the trivial and the stupid. Later tonight, he'd get to scour the photos and notes for the clues that everyone else missed. He'd get the pictures as soon as she got to the hotel. Surely there'd be WIFI?

Violet turned to Captain Sosa. "My Sarge mentioned that you might allow these skulls into Canada?"

"I'm going to say yes, but it won't be right away. We have an intelligence department that wants them first." He paused. "I was told of your friend. I'm sorry."

"Thank you." She masked a sad face. She had lied to her own Sergeant about knowing one of the victims in order to get access to the case. Even Bradley hadn't figured out she was lying. He had also helped her by forwarding confidential information.

Blonde hair wisped over her eyes as the breeze blew across her face. She calmly removed a "scrunchie" from her wrist and pulled her hair back. "I guess I should have asked if it was okay to take pictures."

"Be my guest." The Captain replied.

She continued to snap images and occasionally stopped to refer to a file. These skulls were the ones from Vancouver. Two of the skulls had bridgework done to the upper front teeth. There was the skull of Jane Travis with her deformed occipital bone scarred from a skiing mishap, and that of Vern Dickenson, the one Violet claimed to have known. Gertrude Helmsworth's was also there. She was the last one killed and a minor celebrity on the rodeo circuit.

Seeing the pictures of each victim put a lump in her throat. It was a tough image to push away. Back in Vancouver, the funerals had all been closed-casket and in twelve graves there were bodies without heads. Violet held Gertrude's skull with an extended arm. Would they dig her up to make her whole again? "You deserve to be complete."

Back at the truck the four soldiers were interrogating two local boys. Violet overheard the conversation. The men were threatening to shoot the boys if they didn't talk. At the very least they would be hauled into Puerto Vallarta for questioning. The boys still refused. This was a different generation and kids knew they had rights, even in Mexico.

Violet walked past them to the bar at the patio lounge. She returned with a cold beer in her right hand and the rest of the six-pack in her left. Her blouse was dangerously unbuttoned to show the boys an eyeful of cleavage. "Hey, you guys thirsty?"

Their fifteen-year-old eyes lit up like lighthouse beacons as they followed her to a nearby picnic table. Whether it was the cleavage or the beer, it didn't matter. She was about to question them on her terms.

"Do you guys live around here?"

A boy opened two beers and handed one to his friend. "We're not talking. Just drinking."

"No, that's fine. I couldn't give a shit about this murder investigation. My boss, back in Canada, hates me and sent me here." She let her eyes toy with the talker. "So, what do you do for fun around here?"

"We party." They laughed. "And we don't talk to cops."

"I got that, and I can't blame you. Bad shit happens when you talk to cops. Trust me, I now." She took a long swallow of beer.

It was cold and a welcome contrast to the heat. "You got a girlfriend?"

The boy sucked half the beer back, almost choking on it. "I have many girlfriends."

Violet smiled. "These are lucky girls, eh?"

He squirmed at her openness. It required another mouthful of beer. "Lady, are you hitting on me?"

"Me, no. I'm not pretty enough for a guy like you. Besides, I'm an asshole cop, remember?"

He downed the last of his beer and motioned for his friend to do the same. The boy did, so she followed suit and started to open a second round.

"You're not an asshole cop. You're okay." He took the beer from her and drank. His eyes were starting to squint. "You're too cute for a cop."

"And you're quite a gentleman." She tapped her beer against his. "A toast to pretty girls."

"To pretty girls," he repeated.

Violet took her beer to half-full. "So…"

"Tony. It's Tony."

"Tony, just between you and me, did you see what happened here?"

"Hell ya." He shook his head. "But you wouldn't believe me if I told you."

"Try me, handsome." She leaned forward, letting her shirt pull apart a bit.

There was no hesitation as his vow of silence shattered. Soon he couldn't shut up. By the time the beers were done, she had to stop him. He was rambling.

The man that had brought the skulls was white, six feet tall and older. He was a well-dressed man and had skin like hers, pale. Violet had thought her tan was pretty good. Down here it was nothing more than a tease. They added that the man had cut himself, chanted a verse over and over and strategically placed the skulls before leaving. They had watched him pace off the steps and set each skull to face the ocean. They'd been pulled out of a duffel bag. The bag had been tossed into the jungle, along with another skull.

"Wait, there's another skull?" She was back in detective mode, but they were too drunk to care. "We only found twelve."

"He placed twelve. He studied twelve. The last one was thrown into the jungle like a football. It was dark with shadows, but we saw it." His beer was empty and the distant look in his eyes told her they'd had enough. "Can we have a skull?"

"Asshole cops. They won't even let me have one. You should have grabbed one when you had the chance." She puckered her lips as she put a finger to them. "Keep this to yourselves, okay?"

"No problem. We don't talk to cops, remember?"

"You're a good man, Tony."

With that she downed her beer, pulled out a pad and pencil and set it down. "Let's see if you can remember what this guy looked like."

The two took turns correcting each other while she scribbled, shaded, and erased. They eventually agreed on a face just as Tony's friend ran to the fence and produced a pile of vomit. Tony laughed, which gave Violet her cue to leave.

Captain Sosa met her at the truck. Hopefully she could redeem herself for the airport incident. "Did they know anything?"

She handed the picture to the Captain. "The perp has a face."

Chapter Nine

The cab driver dropped Greg off in downtown Havana, next to a building riddled with hundreds of bullet holes. He started counting them, but lost interest at fifty. He'd picked up a map in the lobby of his hotel. It was a simple tourist map. Obispo Street was south a few blocks and with any luck there'd be a coffee shop along the way.

The crowds, mostly tourists from Eastern Europe and Russia, moved in all directions, yet the smiles were scarce. It seemed there was an unwritten law about enjoying oneself amongst such poverty. The locals didn't mind the tourists and went about their business, welcoming the invasion of money. A few of them played on heartstrings, begging for pesos. Greg wasted no time weaving through the pan-handlers, side-stepping crumbled remnants of balconies that had crashed from the buildings years before.

His eyes, now stinging from the lack of sleep, searched for any resemblance of his dream. Streets were becoming familiar, the buildings becoming those from his dream-walk with the boy. Greg let them lead him to the doorway. It was real. He needed to touch it, put his hand on the doorjamb.

As with most of the buildings, the doors were seldom closed. A dark opening invited him in and he obliged. No longer baking in the hot morning sun, the shade of the apartment was cool. He felt for a light switch and instead rubbed his hand against an exposed piece of rebar. In his dreams, wires hung from the tall ceiling and fallen plaster from the various cracks littered the stairway. His dreams were surprisingly accurate.

He knew that entering the home of his make-believe world was wrong. It didn't stop him. As he took each step, he listened for voices, followed by foot steps, or the slamming of a front door. The only noises were the ones that came from the street. On the second floor of the apartment a gentle breeze tossed a tattered kitchen curtain gently against a fridge. A picture, drawn by a small child, was taped to the side of the fridge. Greg had to take a closer look. Had the boy from his dreams drawn these pictures? He must have. In the bottom corner of one of the drawings was a poorly scribbled name. The boy that had been taking his hand and bringing him here had a name. It was Ricky. Greg took a minute to let it absorb. The boy had looked like a Ricky.

A voice bellowed up the stairs. "Is somebody up there?"

Greg froze. As a government agent from United States, he knew he was trespassing and Communist Cuba was the worst place to be doing that. It wasn't an America-friendly place. He could only imagine what they'd do to him if he was caught. Then the heavy feet started to shuffle up the steps. They were quick and not the steps of a fat man, but of a heavy man.

A gruff voice belonged to them. "Who's up there?"

Why the hell was he in there? What if these guys took him out back and put a bullet in him? He watched the stairs, expecting a head to emerge. Then the breeze brushed the curtain across his arm. It was his signal to go. Greg awkwardly climbed out the kitchen window and started his shimmy down the water pipe. It creaked and shed its filth as he worked his way down it. The last seven feet was a jump because the voice was now at the window.

"Stop right there. I want to talk to you."

The Divine Ledger

Greg wished it were that easy. Instead his feet hit the ground and he found himself running down the lane. Instead of looking back, he quickly melted into the crowd.

The drumming of his heart continued until he knew he wasn't being followed. At that point a drink was in order - a stiff drink. The map was quickly unfolded, studied, and folded back up. The Foridito was a bar and it was close. It ended up being right around the corner.

The place was busy, with wall-to-wall tourists. Greg glanced at his watch. It was ten in the morning. Early drinking must be a vacation thing, Greg thought, or there were a lot of sleep-deprived people running around chasing dreams. He grabbed a table at the far end of the room. That way he could keep an eye on anyone that entered.

He kept the other eye on the waitress as she shuffled her way from table to table. She was an attractive woman, dressed in a man's formal black suit, minus the jacket. The material was threadbare from years of slinging drinks. As she swept by his table she asked. "What will it be?"

Greg took a second to study the woman. She was beautiful in a simple kind of way. Long chestnut hair was pulled back in a loosely wrapped bun. Her smile was fatigued, but her eyes sparkled like those of a schoolgirl. And all that in a body that was forty something going on thirty. There was something special about her that he couldn't place, something familiar.

She grew impatient as she continued to look down at her pad. "Do you want a daiquiri, Sir?"

"A daiquiri?"

"Yes. This is the famous Hemingway bar. Everyone comes here to have one of his famous…" Her eyes finally looked up and met his. She quickly looked away.

"Do you have scotch?"

The eyes, the voice—It was him. "Scotch, of course. I'll be right back."

"Hey, are you okay?"

Half-hiding her face she turned and left. Greg shrugged it off and waited for her to return with his drink. When she didn't, he worked his way through the crowd to the bar. As he arrived, a couple slid their empty glasses forward and pocketed their coasters as souvenirs before leaving. He grabbed one of their stools.

"Hey, bartender!" He had always wanted to say that in a bar like this. It was straight out of an old western, with the kind of bar-counter you wanted to slide a pint of beer down. The beer would glide to a graceful stop in front of the hombre that had ordered it. Nothing would spill. The image was a good one, except that this aged and rugged bar was littered with frilly yellow daiquiris. It was a pitiful sight.

"Whatcha want, Buddy?"

"I lost my waitress. Girl about forty, dark hair, five-foot seven-ish and good looking. She took my order a while ago and I haven't seen her since."

"I don't think so, Buddy."

"What do you mean?"

"Look around. We only got waiters."

"But I saw her. She..." Greg looked around. The man was right, but he had seen her. She had taken his order.

When he looked back to the bartender the man was setting a scotch down on a coaster. Then he left to whip up another batch of daiquiris. Greg panned the room for the woman but saw nothing but tourists and the man at the blender who had just lied to him. Where had she gone? He turned back to his drink and took a swig.

How had the man known he wanted a scotch?

Chapter Ten

The scotch went down like recycled turpentine. That meant a second was out of the question. Instead, Greg left the bar and started walking the streets looking for the woman. She had seen something in his eyes, as he too had seen something in hers. There was a familiarity that made him curious. And then there was her sudden disappearance.

Time passed, and he couldn't find her. Had there been more time, he might have stayed downtown longer, but he needed to get back to the hotel for a couple hours of sleep. It was a victory that he had arrived and that he had found the place. With an exact address he could start asking questions. Who lived in this place? Who was Ricky, and did the boy have a father? What happened back at that Floridito bar?

He'd left word with his secretary that he might need a little legwork done at her end. He mentioned the dreams and she was not only intrigued but looked forward to his call. They'd start with the address. Marisa had also become single recently. She was cute, and they had always engaged in innocent if unprofessional flirting. For Greg it was harmless. Both had been stuck in unsatisfactory, desolate marriages. When he told her about going, she'd joked about going with him. He had toyed with the idea but knew it would have been a mistake.

Greg fumbled with the buttons on his phone as he tried to send her a text. His phone had no bars. He'd have to call her from the hotel phone.

Back at the bullet-ridden building, Greg tried to find a cab. When he first arrived there the street had been littered with 56 Belairs and 57 Chevys. Each one had a Lada four-cylinder engine. They were the only replacements for the eight-cylinder engines that had given up years ago. American parts were impossible to come by. The cars were all for hire, but at the moment there were none in sight.

There was, however, a bus rolling up to the curb. Greg moved to the back of the line and boarded. "Does this bus go to Copacabana?"

"Si, Copacabana. Ten Peso."

"Si." He dropped the coins in the shoebox that was taped to the dashboard. It was half full of coins and paper pesos. Back home the thing would have been ripped off the dashboard, tucked under somebody's arm and quickly turned into drugs or a gun. He looked around. Everyone sat quietly, eyes front. So, this was Communism.

As the bus departed he took a seat on the upper deck. He wasn't sure if the direction was right, or how long it would take. It didn't matter. He closed his eyes. He thought about the tombstone. If it were really his, how could he stop it from happening? If popular opinion was correct, death couldn't be stopped. But what if it wasn't his time? What if it was all some mistake? He opened his eyes to see a young woman taking a seat. Her body was sculpted to perfection. Her curves stretched at the fabric of her dress and left little to the imagination. Greg smiled. There were worse places to die.

The bus lumbered through the streets. He swayed from side to side in his seat, occasionally looking ahead in hopes of seeing his hotel. Instead he saw buildings ready to topple, fifty-year-old cars and, of course, the long hair and bare shoulders of the young woman three seats away.

Suddenly the cemetery came into view as they rounded a corner. Like the apartment, it was a perfect copy of his dream. He reached for the wire to stop the bus. There wasn't one. What did they do here, jump?

A chubby white lady tapped him on the arm. "You have to go down to the front. Then he'll stop."

"Thanks."

The lady was right. Greg raced off the bus and was across the street before his sanity could catch up. The wrought iron and whitewashed pillars kept him from entering. There had to be a gate. He walked down the sidewalk and, as it turned out, there were several. The cemetery sprawled for several city blocks.

Greg became energised with a second wind. The need for sleep was pushed aside as he methodically tried to view as many headstones as he could. Soon the heat was draining him. It came from the sun, came up from the ground and was intensified by the headstones.

Not a blade of grass could be found anywhere. Concrete, marble and crushed rock covered the earth as if this was another planet. He'd read several hundred names and his head swam. Greg looked around. He hadn't even put a dent in the cemetery, and what was that odd sensation? Was he being watched? Several times he'd stopped and looked for the eyes.

"Can I help you, Sir?"

Greg was startled to see one of the locals. "Do you know this cemetery well?"

"I do."

"How many graves do they have here?"

"Just over eight hundred thousand." He smiled politely. "With room for one million."

Greg's knees wobbled. "Are you kidding me?"

"No. Are you looking for anyone in particular?"

"You might say."

"I know who. Is it Santiago Alvarez, Hubert de Blanck, Jose Gomez or Maximo Gomez? I am a caretaker here. I know all the famous ones."

"No. None of those." Greg scratched at his chin. "I'm looking for a Greg Miller."

"Greg Miller?" His face contorted as he thought. "Is this man a musician, a politician, maybe a baseball player?"

"No, but I think it should be a recent grave." The grave had been a dream. He was also still alive. There was no certainty that it would even be here yet. "Actually..."

Over the man's shoulder, Greg finally saw the eyes that had been watching him earlier. They were beautiful deep brown eyes, almost black, and they belonged to the woman that had ducked out at the Floridito. "Hey, Señorita. Hey."

This time the woman didn't run. Seeing him had obviously left her with a few questions of her own.

Greg quickly walked up to her. "What's your name? And why'd you leave earlier?"

She held out a handkerchief. "It's Juanita."

"Thanks, Juanita." He took it and wiped away the sweat from his forehead. "Do I know you?"

"That's not a fair question."

Chapter Eleven
Havana, Cuba

With the morning sky as blue as the ocean, Victor left his room for the lobby where he found a comfortable place to sit. He slipped his thumb under the flap of the envelope and tore it open. This time there were sixteen names in total. Most would have already been lured to Cuba, with a few still on their way. As Victor scrolled through the addresses, he noticed that only one victim would be coming from the States. That was odd.

"Coffee or tea, sir?" It was the hostess. He was standing close enough to the entrance of the hotel restaurant to catch her eye.

"Coffee, black. Do you have twenty pesos I could buy? I'll give you twenty convertible pesos."

"Si, Seňor, but our pesos aren't the ones you're supposed to use."

"I know. I want them for souvenirs."

In Havana they had two different currencies. Cubans used a local peso while the tourists used convertible pesos. Ten local pesos equated to one convertible peso, yet in a store each peso had the same value. This woman was about to turn her twenty pesos into two hundred. Victor took out the twenty and handed it to her.

"Gracias." She reached into her pocket and handed him twenty local pesos. Then she offered him the nicest spot in the restaurant, by a window. It was a reserved spot, but she'd make an exception for this man. "The buffet is out and you are welcome to enjoy it."

Enjoy? Boiled hotdogs and raisin bread didn't thrill him, especially when one of the raisins just took flight. Victor had given them a second look, hoping they weren't dead. He'd wait to find real food. "Thanks, but I'm okay."

As she left, he pocketed the money and returned his attention to the list. Victor had received the envelope back in Mexico from a child who was no older than ten. The boy refused to hand it over until he had received a few pesos for food. In Victor's experience, the envelopes had been smaller and were handed over one victim at a time. They were delivered by people dressed to appear as inconspicuous as possible. There was the fat guy at the hot dog stand in Burnaby, the skinny girl in spandex at the gym, and his favourite, an old lady at a church bazaar—selling great cookies, by the way. Regardless, Victor would receive the envelope, open it and get to work studying the instructions. The orders were never questioned. This was his role, abomination decapitation.

But things were different this time, more desperate. Now Victor was dealing with a different organisation, more of a lone wolf. But this man was just one of the crazies caught up in the shit that shouldn't be. Victor's part in this wasn't much different.

Along with the list of names, there were the usual information sheets on each person, because this wasn't about the killing. This was about maintaining order. This was about making things right.

And today, the right thing meant taking the life of one Beverly Shipstone, from Manchester England. She worked for the British Government. Her job wasn't anything as glorious as a MI-5 agent. It was more an accounting position. But this gave her access to laundered money and, whether she knew it or not, she was helping the enemy.

The Divine Ledger

"Your coffee."

He quickly covered the names with the envelope. "Thank you."

Victor finished the coffee and returned to his room. Stuffed in one of the compartments of his medical bag was a bowling ball tote, folded flat. He tucked it in his waistband behind his back and covered it with his jacket. Then he took a cab that dropped him off near his destination. The morning sun was kind, so he'd walk the last two blocks.

He entered the Hotel Panorama looking for a currency exchange. Most hotels had one in the lobby. While he waited in line, he took one last look at her photo. Beverly was a handsome woman. It was a shame to kill her, but she'd had forty years, years she didn't deserve.

When he reached the front of the line, he converted more dollars to pesos. The exchange was twelve pesos per American dollar. Perhaps he could go for a nice dinner tonight. He'd checked out a few of the locally owned places and they looked good. Wouldn't it be nice to find someone to take there? Eating alone was always such a bore.

The lobby of the Panorama was a vast open space and Victor took a seat by the fireplace. From there he could see the elevators. Beverly would have to walk past him if she wanted the complimentary hotel breakfast, and they all did. With any luck it would be better than the flies on rye back at his hotel.

A single set of eyes watched him as he sat there. They were the same eyes that watched him walk through the front doors of the hotel. Victor placed the man, a soldier, in his mid-twenties. He was young, but had the intuitive nature of a scout. He didn't know what drew his eyes to the man sitting by the fireplace and it didn't matter. Of all these people, he was the one to watch. Victor made eye contact, hoping it might ease the young lad's concern and when it didn't, he looked away. There had been no crime committed, yet.

Thinking of Beverly's bio, he'd have known some of the people she worked with. Once friends and co-workers, they had all become enemies, but she didn't need to know that. During his walk to the hotel he'd concocted a story to tell her, that he was on a working vacation, taking a break from the office. Surely that would work. It would have to, because she'd just stepped off the elevator.

Victor quickly got to his feet. That way their paths could cross. "Pardon me, Miss. As tourists, are we supposed to be using Cuban Pesos or Convertible?"

Her spirit was carefree. She stopped. "Why, Convertible, Sir."

"Bloody hell. I think I just got shagged." He pulled the twenty, that he'd bought from the waitress, out of his pocket. "Are these…"

"They're Cuban." She told him. "Worth a tenth of what you probably paid."

"Damn. You sound like you're from Manchester?"

"I work in Manchester. I was born in Bromley, and you?" she asked politely.

"Chislehurst." He laughed. "We're practically neighbours."

"We sure are." She turned to walk away, then stopped. "I hope this doesn't sound too forward, but would you be interested in sitting with me at breakfast? There's an old farmhouse in Chislehurst. I loved that place as a child. I'd love to pick your brain about it. I'm sure you'd know the one. Everyone thought it was haunted."

"Nothing would make me happier. Sadly, I must decline. I'm on Her Majesty's clock. Could I be so bold as to invite you to dinner tonight? It would be my treat. There's a locally-run place down the street. They make a great home-made pizza."

Her smile squinted her eyes and scrunched her nose. She was a handsome woman indeed. "That sounds nice. Meet me back here at say, six?"

"Six sounds perfect." Because eating alone was such a bore.

Chapter Twelve

It was Chanel#5 that sliced through the midmorning heat as Greg let the woman's beauty wash over him. A tattered sundress hung on her hips, giving her curves a certain sensuality that cemented his interest. The hem, cut just above her knees, drew his eyes to her well-developed calves. They were the calves of a woman who spent a lot of time on her feet, like a waitress. And then there was her hair. It flowed down her back and over her shoulders like melted chocolate.

Greg swallowed hard. "You know me, don't you?"

"Yes."

"Have we met?" His eyes probed hers. There was something so familiar, yet so foreign about her. She was like that distant friend you couldn't place, or that someone from your old school days you couldn't remember, except she was cute and he'd have remembered this one. Maybe he'd met in a past life, or in a … "My dreams. That's where I've seen you."

She looked down at the ground.

"I'm right, aren't I? I swear I've seen you in my dreams." Then he realised how corny that sounded. "No, I mean I've seen you in my…I mean it's innocent…I'm not a pervert."

Greg stopped himself, leaving his words as jumbled as a nest of tangled fishing line. Her eyes met his. They were as soft and dark as her hair and they were curious. She also wanted answers.

"I've had these dreams for a couple of decades. I'm sure it's you in the crowd as the boy and I walk down the street. You've always stood out and I feel a distinct closeness to you as we pass. I know it's stupid and I can't even begin to explain it, but seeing you today makes the dreams a little more real. Are they real?" He waited for her to smile, to frown, or to show some emotion. She didn't. "Talk to me. How do I know you?"

"You shouldn't have come here."

"But I did."

"Yes, you did." She smiled. "We need to get out of here."

"What do you mean? Cuba, or this place? You don't like cemeteries?"

Her expression didn't change. "Look over my right shoulder."

Greg looked. He saw a man in a long leather trench coat. He wore a large black hat that cast shadows on his face. He looked like the man he'd seen beside the tree by the ocean. "Friend of yours?"

"I don't know. Every time I come here I see him."

"You come here often?"

"I do."

"You have family here?"

"Not that I know of."

Greg forced a crooked smile. "You just like hanging out with dead people and strange men in rather large coats?"

She returned an equally crooked smile. "I have dreams too. Tell me, why are you here?"

Greg's smile disappeared as he looked up to the sky. Thousands of birds were flying toward them. "You said something about leaving. Maybe I'll take you up on that."

She looked up to see the cloud of sparrows. They came from trees, telephone wires and fence-tops. In seconds hundreds had turned to thousands, all merging into a black comet of feathers and beaks. It swayed left then right, dipping and diving in perfect harmony.

The Divine Ledger

They gathered around the man with the hat and swirled like a cyclone. It lasted less than a minute before the birds dispersed in what looked like an explosion. Both Greg and Juanita gasped. The man was gone.

Greg and Juanita decided to do the same, although not in as dramatic a fashion. Instead of feathers and fury, he walked her to a bus that carried them to the stop in front of the Copacabana. Greg exited first, in order to take Juanita's hand. He helped her down and led her into the lobby. They headed straight for the bar.

Greg had his wallet out. "Can I buy you a drink?"

She looked over to the bar and saw a few empty tables. "A Cristol please and leave it in the can. I'll grab us a seat."

Greg returned with the beer and took a seat beside her, facing the ridiculously small stage. "Bartender said there's a band starting in about two minutes. Let's hope they're good."

Juanita rolled her eyes. "How long have you been in Cuba?"

"A day."

"You might like the band then."

Two minutes into the music, Greg quickly understood. They were loud, amateurish and sought crowd participation. A sunburned couple couldn't wait to accommodate them, shaking their booties as if they knew how. It was the Cuban experience.

When the first song mercifully ended, Juanita grabbed her beer in one hand and Greg's hand in the other. "Quick before they see us."

The two hands remained interlocked as they made their way to the pool. Dozens of lounge chairs were lined up for tomorrow's crowd. They sat back on two of the chairs, keeping their hands together.

Greg broke the silence after a few minutes of confusion. She was still holding his hand, not that he wanted to let go. Her hand felt nice in his. This was a moment, something he hadn't felt in some time. There was warmth, tenderness and a need for being wanted. The last time he'd felt this way was a month before his wedding. The fact that it had ended before the vows should have been a red flag. But most flags aren't seen until it's too late. Others are ignored.

"What is this?" he asked.

Juanita shrugged. "What do you want it to be?"

"Like I should know. The only thing I'm sure of, you're a very attractive girl."

"Double thank-you."

"Double?"

"I'm attractive and young enough to be considered a girl? You're a very kind man."

"But it's true." Although she was close to forty, there were no wrinkles and barely a hint that she'd blown past thirty. "You look good."

"You do too." She placed her hand on his cheek and slid her fingers into his hair. "Such gorgeous locks."

She pulled him in for a kiss. There was no resistance. He had longed for a moment like this for years. Anne hadn't been much of a kisser, especially anything with passion. Oddly, she used to be.

The kiss, as mystical as it was, ended when a stray cat hopped up on Juanita's lap. She reached down and gave its head a scratch. "Hey handsome. What are you up to?"

The cat purred at her touch and looked at Greg. Its lone blue eye was warm and trusting. The other eye was a mass of ulcerated skin.

Juanita didn't see a collar. "He's probably hungry."

The cat meowed in agreement, so Greg got up and headed for the dining room. He returned and unfolded a napkin to reveal a boiled hot dog. "They have these things out all the time. In the morning they're called breakfast sausages, at lunch they're hot dogs and in the evening, *hors d'oeuvres*."

She pinched her nose. "They look pretty bad."

"Don't say that. He needs to think this is a delicacy."

The cat devoured the pieces as he broke them up. There were a couple more minutes of purring and petting before the cat abruptly stopped, jumped down and ran off to where a couple of cats were waiting at the far end of the pool. The three cats then ambled away.

Juanita watched the cats leave and looked back at Greg. "Where were we?"

"You were going to tell me about your dream. Then you decided to switch gears and distract me with a kiss."

"Oh, you caught that?"

"I didn't mind."

She turned to him and gently placed her hand back on his face. Her eyes locked back on his. "I didn't either."

The dizzying fog descended once more as her lips met his. They were sweet and it was abundantly clear that her story would have to wait.

Kevin Weisbeck

Chapter Thirteen

A battered blue Compestella bus pulled up to the curb an hour after Violet took a seat at the bus stop. The lady at the front desk of her hotel had given her a time, but she wasn't even close. Violet squinted to read the greasepaint scribble of stops written on the passenger side of the windshield. It was an ever-changing hodgepodge of destinations. Earlier, Violet had been taken to the crime scene in Sayulita by Captain Sosa and four armed soldiers. Sayulita was the eighth destination on the windshield.

Dressed in a bikini top, cut-offs and flip-flops, she climbed the two steps onto the bus. Violet in no way resembled a cop and that was the way she wanted it. She slipped the driver fifty pesos and took the first empty seat, three rows down on the driver's side.

Her long, lean legs curled up into her chest as she sat. A large fabric bag and a beach towel were placed on the seat beside her. An instant calm washed over her as she sat amongst the locals. They were simple people living simple lives. Then her phone rang. She had to rummage through her bag to find it. "Hello?"

"Violet?" Bradley had gone over the texts she'd sent from the crime scene. She had done well. "The pictures, did you see it?"

The Divine Ledger

"Well duh. I took the pictures." But she hadn't seen anything.

He waited her out.

"Okay, Brainiac, what are you talking about?"

"The skulls. There was a pattern."

Her feet made their way down to the floor as she sat up. "Seriously?"

"They were set out in groups. Do you know numerology?"

"No." She wanted to add that she had a life but refrained. The fact that he didn't have one was the reason she was getting answers.

"Numbers can be translated into letters. These ones spell out a name, Mary. Does that mean anything?"

"No. Not one of the victims was a Mary."

"I'd get on that. There has to be a link."

Violet tried to think as a chicken ran across her feet and under her seat. It had escaped from the boy chasing it. "Uh, maybe Mary is an anagram for army or a code name for something else. Run the family names and jobs?"

"For what?"

"Shit Brad. You're the smart one. You tell me. Maybe one of them was living with an alias. Maybe all of them had a mother named Mary."

"I can check that, but you're the one who's there."

The vein in her temple started to bulge as the counting started. It was something she'd learned to do at the precinct. She breezed past ten. It didn't help. "I need to go."

There was silence. Bradley knew what she was doing.

"Bradley, are you there?"

"I never meant to piss you off." He gave a nervous laugh. "Just something I do."

"It's not you. I'm just in a pissy mood. You see, there's another skull. Nobody knows about it. It was tossed into the jungle. I have to go in after dark, so now I'm on a bus heading back into Sayulita. And to top it all off, there's a chicken pecking at my heel. Oh, and did I tell you, the jungle is allegedly haunted."

"Pissy mood understood." It was the peace offering she desperately needed. "You said another skull?"

"I did. I'll send it to you as soon as I can acquire it."

"If you make it out, that is."

"What do you mean?"

"Violet, it's the jungle. You've got poisonous snakes, big cats, scorpions, wild boars and God only knows what else."

Violet held the phone away from her ear for a second before cutting him off. "That's enough, Bradley. I get that it's a jungle."

"I haven't even covered all the parasites or insects that could kill you."

"I said that's enough!"

"I just want you going in there with a plan. Make sure you're wearing long pants, boots, and a shirt with sleeves. And don't forget your gun." He took a minute, as if she might be taking notes. "Put your hair up too. Can you do that?

"I'm already on all of that." She said that while looking in her bag. There was no gun or change of clothes. There wasn't even sunscreen. She had a wallet with a driver's license that said she was Victoria Sawyer, a Member of the Canadian Legislative Assembly. People like that didn't carry guns or wear pants and boots in this heat. She was on vacation. "What kind of bugs are we talking?"

"Tarantulas, Violin spiders, the Puss caterpillar, Deer ticks and the Assassin bug. When that thing bites you, it looks like a mosquito bite. Thing is, the bite can kill you."

"Are you shitting me?"

"No, and here's the best part. You don't die right away. You might not even get sick right away. I heard of this guy who got bit and thought it was nothing. Thirty years later he got sick and no one could figure it out. He puffed up and died the same day. The disease can sit dormant in you for decades and then all of a sudden, boom, you're dead."

Violet pulled her feet back off the floor and tucked her knees back into her chest. Hungry animals, Mexican ghosts and time-released bugs; was it all worth it? "Thanks, Bradley. I got this covered."

The Divine Ledger

"Did you know they have a variety of honey bees that can..."

"What part of I got this fucking covered, do you not understand?"

The words popped out a little louder than she had intended. Suddenly, everyone on the bus, including the driver, was looking at the crazed Canadian Member of the Legislative Assembly.

She tried to wave it off. "Sorry, one of those silly telemarketing people. They don't know when to stop the selling pitch."

Slowly, most of the eyes returned to their own business. Some people had stops coming up, others simply didn't care. "Fuck, Brad. I'm trying to remain undercover here."

"I didn't tell you to freak out on me."

She held the phone closer and whispered into it. "I'll get the skull to you tomorrow at the latest."

"It's a human skull, Violet. How are you going to do that?"

She pressed the end button and tossed the phone into her purse. Outside the sun was setting and soon the jungle would be dark.

"One problem at a time, Brad."

Chapter Fourteen

Victor straightened his tie and checked his cufflinks as he paced the floor one last time. Then he downed his drink, stared at the empty glass and checked his watch. It was time to go. Setting the empty glass down, he grabbed his leather bag and started for the door. He stopped. Did he really want to bring it? Abomination decapitation, he reminded himself and left the hotel room. As the door clicked behind him, he immediately felt at his breast pocket. Yes, he had his door card.

The elevator ride was a quick one. It dropped him off in the lobby where, hopefully, his date would be waiting. She was standing by the fireplace. Her hair was up off her shoulders, exposing the graceful curves of her collarbone and neck. The dress she'd chosen was a stunning black knee-length number. Actually, he thought to himself, she was the one who was stunning. The dress, on its own, was nothing special.

"My apologies. Am I late?" he asked.

She smiled at seeing him. "I think I'm early."

"Would you like to get a drink first?"

"That would be nice. Do we have time?"

The Divine Ledger

"Yes. Our little pizza place is just down the street. The place is always busy, so I made a reservation. We have half an hour."

She held her arm out for him to take. The bar was by the pool just off the lobby. Arm in arm, they walked into the bar like a married couple of twenty years. "I think I'll have a gin and tonic."

He ordered her drink and a dirty martini for himself, two olives. "So why Cuba, Miss…?"

"Shipstone. It's Beverly Shipstone." She took a sip. "I won a contest. I forgot I'd even entered it. Second prize was a trip to Cuba, all expenses paid. I mean I've never thought about Cuba, but who can beat that price."

"And how have you liked it so far?"

"I just arrived last night so I haven't seen much, but…" She giggled and twirled her hair. "I like what I've seen so far."

Victor caught himself blushing. "Such flattery from such beauty. I'm truly blessed."

"What brings you to Cuba, Mr…"

"Just call me Victor, with a 't'. The locals seem to have difficulties with that."

"I know. I never knew Shipstone could be pronounced so many ways. It isn't that hard, is it?"

"I'm sure they mean well."

"What's in the bag?"

I have a few papers, important stuff. I know it sounds terrible, but I don't trust the staff. Does that make me a bad person?"

"Oh my, no. I read a few reports before leaving home. I left most of my valuables back in England." She patted his hand. It was soft, warm and compassionate. He wouldn't have expected anything less. "You have to be careful these days."

The sight of her hand on his made him uncomfortable, but he didn't pull away. Instead he took her hand and gave it a squeeze. "We should probably finish these and get going."

She let him help her to her feet. They strolled through the lobby and out into Cuba's late afternoon. It was a nice stroll to the restaurant, which allowed for some sight-seeing. She liked how the locals had fixed up their yards. As in England, most took pride in their homes, planting gardens and adding personal touches like handcrafted lawn ornaments. Granted, most were tacky, but they gave the houses that homespun feel.

"This is the place." He let go of her hand and ushered her through the gate.

The home was modest. Tables were scattered around the back yard, the dining courtyard. Large Mahogany trees and patio umbrellas provided ample shade. There were paper lanterns strung along branches, probably brought back from a family trip to Mexico.

"It's quaint." Beverly took a deep breath. "The food smells wonderful."

A darling young girl, maybe fourteen, grabbed a couple of menus and politely escorted them to a table. Victor held Beverly's chair while the girl set the menus in front of them. The girl left them with a warm smile. Moments later another pretty girl appeared with two glasses and a pitcher of cold water. She was obviously an older sister.

"You would order, now?"

Beverly reached for the menu. "I haven't really looked at…"

Victor stopped her. "That's okay, Beverly. Do you like ham?"

"Mmm, I do."

"And pineapple?"

"Sounds delicious."

He turned to the waitress. "Is the pineapple fresh?"

"Si, from my Uncle's granja de la piña."

"Your Uncle has a farm? Then we must try it."

The girl's cheeks dimpled as the corners of her mouth curled upward. "He grows the best piña in the world. You will love it."

"I believe you." Victor admitted. "Do you recommend a wine?"

"I don't know if wines are that good here. They are much better in sangria."

Victor looked to Beverly and she returned a why-not shoulder shrug.

"A pitcher of sangria sounds wonderful."

Her eyes widened. "Si, gracias. I will tell my mother. It won't be long."

The Divine Ledger

Beverly watched her leave. "Such a cute thing. I'm guessing this is also her home?"

"Yes, and her Momma's a good cook."

Beverly took a deep breath. "I wish my back yard smelled this nice." There was a slight pause. "So, Victor. What do you do for a living?"

"Let's not talk about me, I'm boring on my best day. I'd like to hear about you."

"What do you want to know?"

What more was there to know? She was kind, gracious and adventurous. Under different circumstances, he could have easily fallen for her. A part of him just wanted to hear her voice. "Tell me everything. What you do, places you've been, your childhood."

The last one was meant to make this easier.

The girl returned with the sangria and Beverly waited while it was poured. Then she took a sip. "This is good. I haven't really travelled much, unless you count work. It takes me to Russia on occasion. I've always wanted to go to Paris. Have you been?"

"No," he replied. "I've heard it's magical. So much history and let's not forget all the artwork. I'd love to get there some day."

This made her play with the tassel that was tied to the stem of her wineglass. He was a catch and they had similar interests. She could see them travelling to Paris, walking along the Seine. Her mind drifted to the what-ifs while they talked. A little too much sangria was consumed as she nibbled on what was one of the best pizzas she'd ever tasted.

Hours later they were heading back to the hotel. Would she see him again? Did he like her? He seemed interested and so attentive. Her heart fluttered as her mind floated amongst the possibilities. This was, without a doubt, one of the best dates she'd been on in a long time. She'd have to phone her friend, Nancy, tonight. This guy might be the one, or was all this too premature?

Victor walked alongside her, letting her have those thoughts. Beverly, lost in a night of bliss and wrapped up in her own haze of hope, hadn't seen his mood change.

She also didn't notice that he had led her down a back lane. They were alone now. Through all her talking and daydreaming she'd also missed the fact that he'd reached into his pants pocket and removed a cloth from a sealed plastic bag.

He stopped, turned to her and leaned in for a kiss. At that point she became very aware of him. He hadn't intended on doing this and he'd later regret it, but he had to kiss her, just once. She was an amazing woman. She just didn't belong.

When his lips left hers, he could see the longing, the devotion and the compassion in her eyes. It didn't last long. Hope was replaced by confusion as he put the sweetened rag to her nose.

"Good-bye, Beverly. I hope you enjoyed yourself tonight."

Chapter Fifteen

Violet stepped off the bus in Sayulita as the sun was just starting to set. The toe of her flip-flop caught a piece of loose trim on the bottom step and she toppled facedown in the dirt. The other passengers passed by and stepped over her cautiously, as if she might lash out at them.

'Damn it." She picked herself up and used her towel to brush away the dust. Back in Canada, someone might have helped her to her feet, but not here. No one wanted anything to do with her. That ship had sailed when she flipped out at Bradley.

Violet slowly wove her way through the streets to the other end of town. She almost jogged the beach trail to the Villa Amour and headed for the terrace lounge. Thanks to Bradley's damn bug stories, she'd need at least one beer before heading into the land of fangs and killer insects.

An ice-cold Corona was delivered and she drank it in one of the lounge chairs that overlooked the Ocean. The waves curled up on the shore. How nice would it be to forget the skull, grab a board, and ride a few waves? Would she find time to do that while she was in Mexico? The waves looked like they could get crazy if the weather turned. That would be fun.

But, she had work to do. Maybe she'd stay for a couple days after the killer was caught. She set the empty down on an end table and thought of the beetle that could kill thirty years later. Bradley had to be shitting her—he could be such a dick at times. The empty was removed seconds after it left her hand.

A young waiter gave the table a quick wipe with his cloth. "Would you care for another?"

There was no hesitation. "A Pacifico this time, port per four."

"*Si.*" He hid his grin as he left.

She thought about the beer. Seriously, was she really that afraid? Fear wasn't her modus operandi. She'd been shot, beaten up and dumped by men far too stupid to realise their mistakes. None of that had killed her. Hell, she'd had her right arm tattooed by a guy named Bruce *The Tooth Fairy* Pennyworth. He was six hundred and forty-two pounds of unbridled back hair. He had a tattoo of the tooth fairy on the side of his shaved head.

She thought of her friends back home and wished they could see how far she'd come. Top of her class, she was disciplined and loved by everyone she encountered. Well, maybe not everyone. Instead of being loved, tolerated might have been a better description, but it worked.

Damn, she hated bugs.

Regardless, the last five years had taught her that there was—how did they say—more than one way to skin a cat. Back home there was only one way, not that anyone would have skinned anything. It was barbaric. But this was a world where rules could be re-written and she was just the girl to do that. She got to her feet as the waiter arrived.

The second beer was as cold as the first, perfect in fact. Violet paid for it, left a generous tip and set it down on the table. It would be there, not *if* she got back, but *when*, she hoped.

In the cemetery the shadows were deepening by the minute. The sun was on the horizon and those once-large shards of sunlight slicing through the trees had become thin slivers. It wasn't flashlight-dark yet, but it was easy to stumble on roots, rocks and over-sized gophers. She looked around for signs that the police had been there earlier. There were none.

At one headstone a surfboard had been either blown, or knocked over. Despite the dusk, she could still read the dates and did the math. The boy had been sixteen when he'd died in the ocean, doing what he loved. She wasn't sure of this, but it seemed pretty damn obvious. It was one of her solid detective hunches. She picked the board up and leaned it back where it belonged.

Stepping over graves, she made her way to the edge of the cemetery. Scattered trees and the tall grass that crept through the picket fence, blurred the border between safe and dangerous.

Inside the fence, bodies were laid to rest, but they weren't resting. They were angry. There were cement statues, marble markers and a great number of bones below the surface. That was the safe side. Outside the fence there were snakes, spiders and killer beetles. There was also a skull and some unknown presence lurking in the shadows. She could feel it.

Her right leg pressed against the fence as she leaned over. She surveyed the mountainside, hoping to see the white orb. It would have been nice to find it, grab it and go. When had anything ever been that simple?

The tall grass swayed, but not to any particular rhythm. She was about to step over the fence but stopped. Was it the breeze or snakes? It made her wish she'd brought boots and long pants, but she hadn't. She stepped over the fence.

With her very first step she disturbed a snake. "Ouch."

The serpent struck her in the leg just below the knee, recoiled, but never got the chance to bite a second time. Violet bolted. About fifteen feet deeper into the jungle she tripped and fell. Again, like getting off the bus, it was a face plant. She was about to get up and run when she looked up to see a single eye staring at her. It was yellowish-green and unafraid. She looked for a second eye on the big cat, but it was covered in a permanently scarred wink.

It had locked its single eye on her, causing her to freeze. Damn you Bradley! "Nice kitty."

The puma crept towards her, its head keeping level with hers. Its lone eye remained focused. Had the cat been starving, it would have attacked her, a quick throat kill. It wasn't hungry.

"What do you want?"

The puma's long whiskers rubbed along her face and shoulder as it moved towards her feet. It sniffed at the ground. Violet followed it closely with her eyes. The head lowered, nudged at something in the grass. Then it looked back at her.

"What have you got there?" She slowly rolled over and sat up. The move made her vulnerable, yet she didn't feel as threatened as when she first saw the big cat. At her feet was the object that had tripped her, the skull. "Is that for me, big fella?"

She cautiously reached for the skull, keeping her eyes trained on the cat. Was she pushing her luck? The puma looked away. High up on the hillside two other pumas had gathered and were watching intently.

The skull was heavier than she thought, heavier than the others. She got to her knees, remaining as submissive as she could. The cat leaned forward. Violet raised a hand to touch him.

The cat snapped at her. Violet fought back the impulse of releasing the recently-consumed beer into her cut-offs. If cats could smile, it was. There could only be one alpha. The puma nudged the skull with its nose again. A small feathery head appeared in one of the eye sockets, causing Violet to drop it. "Shit."

The rest of the bird, a sparrow, slipped through the hole and fluttered past the cat's nose and landed on his back. The puma didn't flinch. Instead it turned and slowly started up the hill.

Violet waited while they sauntered off. Then she picked up the skull by the eye sockets like a bowling ball and bolted for the fence. There was no looking back.

The beer was still on the table where she'd left it. The sweat had evaporated from the outside of the bottle, but it was still cold. She collapsed into the chair and put the bottle to her lips. The beer went down with several long swallows. Then she looked over her shoulder toward town. It was time to catch a bus.

The Divine Ledger

Her pace was hurried as she made her way past the trinket stores, the fish taco stands and the man cooking a chicken in a truck's discarded wheel-rim. She slowed to give him a second look.

People stared at her as she passed them. The man grilling the chicken went as far as to gawk. What the hell were they looking at? Did she have spinach in her teeth, maybe a booger hanging off her nose? Then it struck her. Her knee was bleeding from the snakebite and she was holding a skull—so much for keeping a low profile.

She stopped at the spot where she'd arrived. It wasn't an official bus stop, just a field with a downed palm tree that the elderly used as a bench as they waited for the bus. There was no one there. Violet took a seat and placed the skull on the ground. A man on a donkey made his way toward her. It might have been a mule, or perhaps a jack-ass.

"*Disculpe, señorita?*"

"*Si.*" Violet answered, not sure of what he'd said.

He shook his hand from side to side. "*No hay autobuses.*"

Her Spanish wasn't the best, but it sounded like he'd just said there were no more busses. "Shit."

"*Siguiente autobus es por la mañana.*" Then he gave his best attempt at English. "Morning."

"Morning? Damn it." She got to her feet. "*Si, gracias.*"

Violet watched as the man nudged the donkey's flanks and slowly lumbered off. It had to be a stupid ass.

Her phone rang, and she yanked it out of her bag. "What?"

"And hello to you too."

"Bradley? What have you got?"

"There's another body. They just found it in Cuba." He paused. "No head."

"What? He's killing again? That's just what I need."

"Not to mention the inconvenience for the victim."

"Seriously? You want to go there after the evening I just had? How the hell did you find this out?"

"I've got a program that constantly scans police airways for keywords. When I found out you were going to Mexico I added the words beheaded, decapitated and headless. I never expected a hit, let alone one this soon."

71

"Think it's related?"

"How could it not be?"

"Find out all you can. I'll send you the skull in the morning."

"You've got it."

"And a hell of a story to go with it."

"Beers when you get back if you can send it tonight."

"Make it rum and it'll put it on a plane tomorrow."

"I'm running names of butchers, doctors, veterinarians or anybody with the skills to properly lop off a head. There can't be that many people travelling from Puerto Vallarta to Havana with those skills. I'm sure he would have flown."

"Do you really think he'd use his real name?"

"No, but he'd likely use his real face. I've tapped into the airport's video surveillance in Puerto Vallarta and Havana. I get to use my new facial recognition software."

"Okay, okay. I guess being a nerd is kinda cool at times."

"Hell, it has to be."

Violet hung up and started back toward town. She noticed that every hotel had a *no* in front of their vacancy signs.

"I sure hope the liquor store is still open."

Chapter Sixteen

Greg awoke with a smile that stretched all the way to the Florida Keys. He couldn't remember the last time a woman had drawn such passion and body-draining enthusiasm out of him. He rolled over and let his eyes embrace her. Juanita was still sleeping so he didn't wake her. Instead he stared and wondered. What was she thinking? She was a stranger and, technically, he was still married. He wasn't even over Anne yet, or maybe he was. Maybe this was just what he needed to move forward.

Juanita's eyes opened as if she could read his thoughts. "Hey."

"Good morning."

She pulled the covers up to her mouth. "Morning."

Her returned gaze was looking for options. Suddenly, Greg wanted options. He wanted to run, except this was his room. "How about I go and get us some coffee?"

Juanita nodded.

He slipped out from underneath the covers and headed for the bathroom. She stared at the door as it closed behind him. Greg had felt good inside her. There was the passion and that animalistic lust that accompanied a first-time romp. The man had done everything right, better than right. So why did she feel like she'd just slept with her brother?

In the bathroom Greg quickly dressed in a t-shirt and a pair of shorts. He looked into the mirror and shook his head. What had he just done? Although a part of him wanted to send a naked selfie of the two of them to Anne, seeing that fear in Juanita's eyes killed all the OMG sensations he was feeling. He almost wanted to take it back. That way they could go back to that flirty friendship that they had shared down by the pool?

But damn it, she was cute. She was a breath of fresh air and, although he'd be lying if he didn't admit to a bit of guilt, he deserved this. Anne didn't want him and Juanita was beautiful, exotic, intoxicating.

Stuffing a toothbrush in his mouth, he left the bathroom, stole a quick glance at her, and left. Damn it, what the hell was wrong with this?

With Greg gone, Juanita got out of bed and grabbed her clothes from the chair. Now to make everything look as good as it had last night. She settled on close enough.

The patio door beside the bed was still open from last night so she passed through it to the balcony. She took a seat in one of the rattan chairs, crossed her legs beneath her and closed her eyes. Then she took a deep breath and smiled as the surf broke on the shore. The man was awfully cute.

Greg returned a couple minutes later with the coffee. "I'm hoping you take it black."

"That's perfect." She took a sip and gave him a wink. "About last night."

"Weird, right?"

It hurt that any night that good could be considered weird, but he was right. "Don't get me wrong, you were fantastic. But, is it me or did the whole thing feel strange? I mean it was going great, until we were done."

"I think it was me. I haven't really...you know, since my wife."

The Divine Ledger

"I think you can call her an ex-wife now," she corrected him. "You have to get that closure thing out of the way. Maybe that's what this was. If that's the case, I'm glad I could be the one to help. You're a great guy."

He stifled a laugh. "I need to stop you. I didn't sleep with you last night to get over anybody. I did it because you're ridiculously attractive, intelligent, and your body emits this sexuality thing that…"

"I'll stop you there with a thank you." She raised her cup to clink with his. "I also find you moderately irresistible."

"Moderately works." He raised his cup and took a sip. "But we won't be doing this again, will we?"

"No. It's just too weird afterward." She set her cup down. "Tell me, what happened between you and your ex?"

"It's a long story."

"Well, I need to get home." She got up and took his hand. "You can tell me on the way."

The story started off as a rant about a tennis instructor as they left the room and it ended with gardeners as they made their way through the lobby.

"Seriously, Greg? It's not tennis instructors and gardeners that destroy marriages. They're the result of a marriage that's already dead. You need to ask yourself, how'd it die?"

Greg said nothing as he made his way to a '55 Chevy convertible that stood outside. He opened the door for Juanita and they both dropped into the back seat. Juanita rattled off an address for the driver and they were off.

"It's a long drive, so tell me what really happened?"

"I'm not sure. I always blamed the tennis guy, but maybe you're right. We met in high school. We were best friends. Everybody knew we'd get together some day, so it was no surprise when it happened. Soon, after the wedding bells, there was talk of a child."

"You had kids?"

"No. Oddly we only talked about it."

"Interesting."

"Why is that?"

"To me it would be a red flag if you wanted children, yet never actually had them. Did you try? Was there a problem?"

"The only problem was time." He was trying his damnedest to remember. "We just never got around to it. Before long we were drifting. It didn't seem like such a good idea to have kids. There were too many 'what ifs', if you know what I mean?"

"Let me guess. From there the drifting continued. You had work, she had tennis."

"Pretty much. What's the verdict, Doc?"

"A pair of good friends dated because that was what everybody else wanted. You were pleasing them, not yourselves. It was doomed from the word go. You two were meant to be friends, not lovers. Once sex enters a relationship, it changes all the dynamics. If your best friend cheats on their spouse, you still love them, right?"

"Of course."

"But if they cheat on you, it's a little harder to love them. Same goes with stopping dreams or stealing the years from someone's life."

"You lost me."

"She was with you when she should have been with someone else. She should have been having someone else's children, watching those children go to school, watching them graduate, fall in love. You took that from her, and she took it from you."

"What?"

"You lost those good years by forcing something that was never meant to be, and so did she. Call it a passive-aggressive thing. You put up with tennis lessons and she put up with your long hours at work." She let it sink in a little deeper. "Don't hate her. Maybe someday you can have this chat with her. I'll bet she understands and you both can move on to being friends again."

"No shit. That's interesting."

"Hey, at least now you know."

"I just never saw it that way."

"Who does? Work and resentment make pretty solid walls."

Greg's eyes widened as the cab pulled up to the curb in front of Juanita's home.

The Divine Ledger

"Are you okay? You look a little lost."

"Quite the opposite. I've been here before," he answered as he stared at the apartment in his dreams. "You know the boy, don't you?"

Chapter Seventeen

Victor dropped a large suitcase at the foot of the bed in his new room. The envelope full of names was dropped on the coffee table. Beverly's hotel was far nicer than his and the restaurant was much more elegant. The bread was fresher and the drinks weren't watered down.

He grabbed a beer from the courtesy bar, sat at the couch and pulled the list from the folder. The next name, bio and image of a man were soon stamped into his brain. They didn't have to be dealt with in any particular order, but Victor preferred the more orderly OCD approach. Order was a hard habit to break.

From this room he could see the ocean. There was something about the waves crashing on the shore, crashing on the rocks and concrete breaks. It was a power that couldn't be harnessed. It rounded rocks and toppled walls. This was raw nature and it had a purpose, because it belonged.

There'd be time to unpack later. Victor needed to go down to the lobby. There was a drink with his name on it. There were also a handful of detectives to check on. They should have found Beverly's body by now and would be looking for the rest of it. More importantly, they'd want answers. Why would someone do this?

The Divine Ledger

Why would anybody kill such a beautiful woman? But they didn't know her like Victor knew her.

In the elevator a couple was also going down to the lobby. Victor joined them. She was a heavier floral-print kind of gal in her late fifties. She likely sewed, baked, and adored all of her grandchildren the same. Victor could see her running the show at the church bake-sale and forever praying for somebody's soul.

Her husband was also in his fifties and worn weary from working at a dead-end job. It had slowly flushed his life down the sewer pipes with all the other shit in this world. Years of overtime and the need to please the boss had taken a toll. In time he stopped doing the overtime, and he argued his boss's every stupid decision. If only he'd gone to school and made something of his life. At least he had reruns of the Rockford Files and sports. Nobody could take hockey away from him. Reading these two was like reading the comic section of the newspaper.

Victor started the conversation. "Nice weather, don't you think?"

The woman was fiddling with the handkerchief. She looked up at Victor as soon as he spoke. "Did you hear about that poor woman, such a tragedy."

The man added, "I heard her head had been removed." Then he slid his thumb across his throat in a cutting motion. "Can you imagine?"

Victor nodded as he watched the man's gesture. "I heard the same."

The man shrugged. "You have to expect it in places like this. I mean, these types aren't far off being animals, don't you think?"

"Bob, please," his wife reprimanded. "Show some respect."

"Ah, Edith. Every time we come here, something like this happens. I don't know what we'd talk about if it didn't." He turned to Victor. "You come here often?"

Victor looked him in the eye and smiled. "I'm a first timer."

The stare unsettled the man. "I'm sorry. Do I know you."

Realising what he had done, Victor broke his gaze. "No. It's just, you look like a Habs fan."

"Amazing." He elbowed his wife like he'd just met a bona fide magician. "He's a Canadian, Edith."

"I've been a Montreal Canadians fan since the game was invented."

"Me too. Hey, there's a game on tonight. They're playing in Calgary." He leaned toward Victor as if he held the secret to world peace. "There's a pub close to our hotel. It's only a couple of blocks away from this one and a fellow Canadian runs it. The guy always plays the games on TV. You should join me."

"You don't stay. At this hotel?"

"No. We're in the hotel beside the one with the pub. The wife just wanted to come here and get the story on that dead girl."

"Bob, it's not like that."

"Whatever." He held out his hand. "In case you didn't catch it, name's Bob, Bob Henley."

Victor took his hand and gave it a firm shake, but he already knew the man's name. It was the next one from the list, Robert Morris Henley.

Damn if they weren't coming to him now.

Chapter Eighteen

Violet stuffed the skull amongst a pile of garbage that was stacked against the trash bin outside the Puerto Vallarta Walmart. She'd come up with a plan last night while she tried sleeping on the beach. It was windy and pebble-sized sand crabs scooted across her body every time she started to nod off. That left her a lot of time to think. Who'd have thought there'd be no vacancies in a town like this?

She stepped inside the store and suddenly felt at ease. It was wonderful how every Walmart, in every country, looked the same. The tactic was a smart one. You could be anywhere on the planet and still find deodorant, beach towels and cat litter.

After throwing a bottle of the good tequila into her basket, she headed for the crafts lane. In that aisle she grabbed glue, beads, black grease paint and anything that would dangle, dingle, or barf up glitter.

Back in the parking lot she retrieved the skull and walked back to the bus stop. Now it was a waiting game for the next Compestella. She almost looked at her watch but remembered it had disappeared at some point last night. One of the damn crabs probably took it. Her phone worked and let her know that it was still morning.

When the bus arrived, she immediately grabbed a seat beside a young girl of about ten. As a preteen, she had the two requirements that Violet needed. First, she looked like she was ready for some fun. Secondly, her parents were nowhere in sight. "Do you speak English?"

"*Si.*"

Violet pulled out the skull. "Good."

The girl's eyes widened. "Why do you have a skull?"

"Oh, don't worry." Violet tossed it up and caught it like a basketball. "It's not real." She opened the bag and showed the girl all the craft stuff.

"Are we..."

Violet took the tequila out of the bag and set it aside. "Are you good at crafts?"

"I'm the best at my school."

"That's what I want to hear." She handed the girl the glue and started to open the bags. "Let's make me a souvenir."

"Really? We can decorate this?"

"Hell yeah! I have a friend back home. I want to send this to him, but first we have to make it so scary that he cries when he opens it."

"We learned all about Cinco de Mayo in social studies. I made a mask once that scared my Dad. I wore it for a week."

Violet quietly opened the tequila bottle and took a swig. It eased the gnawing pains in her back from sleeping on a beach. "What do we do first."

"You're drinking." She laughed. "It that your breakfast?"

"Rough night."

"Here." The girl gave Violet a couple cookies from her lunch box and then took the glue and started attaching beads around the eye sockets. "You're a funny person. My Auntie drinks for breakfast sometimes."

"Mexico has that effect on people." Her phone rang, and she pulled it out. "Hola. Coma easter?"

The Divine Ledger

"What?" It was Bradley. "Hey, I just got the police report for that murder in Havana."

"So?"

"It confirmed there was no head."

Violet looked at the little girl, gluing and sticking with childlike precision. "I'll be sending you the thirteenth you-know-what in about an hour. I'll text you the flight."

"Can you describe it, mandible width, distance between eye sockets?"

"Not really."

"How come? I need this shit."

"I'd rather not say. You'll get it when you get it."

"Look. You came to me, remember? If you want my help you'll just have to get over yourself and…."

"Damn it, Bradley." She turned her head to the window and whispered. "I've got a little girl sticking beads to it."

"What? I don't think I heard that right. Sounds like you said you had a little girl sticking beads to it."

"I did."

"Shit, Violet. Aren't you gonna make a good mom someday. I can see it now. Here you go honey, hold mom's gun while I slap the cuffs on this guy. After I book him, you can fingerprint him. Then we'll go for ice cream."

Violet took a long swig before she continued. "And you're perfect?"

"Are you drinking?"

"No." She knew he didn't buy it. "Look, I need to get this thing analysed. This one doesn't belong. Are you going to do this or not?"

"You know I will. Just don't put too much crap on that thing. Everything you add makes it harder."

Violet looked over. The girl had already attached dozens of beads, most of the danglers, and she was starting to colour it with grease paint. There was little bone showing. "Looking good, Sweetie."

The girl grinned and continued.

"It'll be fine, Brad. You should be able to pick it up tonight."

"Just remember, not too much shit, Violet."

"Right."

"And try not to get that poor girl drunk."

"Fuck you." She hung up and took another swig.

"You said a bad word," the girl giggled.

"I'm sorry. He was a bad man."

"Really?"

"No, but boys can be so damn difficult, don't you think?"

"Boys are icky." She held up the skull. "How does it look?"

It was just the right amount of tacky. "Perfect, and for your troubles…" Violet handed the girl fifty pesos, good for a big bag of candy and a few sodas.

"Wow, thank you." She snapped it up before Violet could change her mind. She'd likely give it to her mother for groceries. The girl reached over and touched Violet's arm. "What's that?"

"That's my tattoo." A score of music coiled and climbed up and around Violet's arm. Four little beetles replaced some of the notes between the lines. Most would overlook them at first glance, but the girl noticed them right away. Where Violet was never a big fan of ink in places where it could be easily seen, this one was artistic and quite exquisite. "It's just a song."

"What song?"

"Yesterday, by the…"

The girl cut her off. "They're Beatles. Which one is Ringo?"

Violet didn't want to disappoint the girl, so she pointed to the last one. In truth, the four beetles on her arm represented each of her ex-boyfriends. Bradley was the fourth. As in the song, she had said, or done, something wrong and now longed for yesterday.

Four hours later the skull was on a plane halfway to Vancouver and Violet was on a plane touching down just outside Havana, Cuba. She thought of the Sarge, but decided to report back to him in a day or two. He'd want answers and, quite possibly, he'd want her to come home. This was still considered a cold case. Vancouver didn't have the funding to have one of their officers globetrotting. There'd be heat from the Mayor's office. For that reason, she'd have to lay low until she could link the murders.

The Divine Ledger

"*Hola, Seňorita.* Welcome to Havana." A plump little man saw her and waved her over to a bus full of people.

Violet walked over. "How far is it to downtown?"

"I good driver," he replied. "I take you to your hotel."

"Not what I meant, but fair enough." She worked her way to the back seat and tossed her bag on the seat beside her. The back seat turned out to be a mistake, amplifying the potholes. Good driver my ass, she thought to herself each time her butt lifted off the worn cushion. It was like he was aiming for the damn things.

She stared out the window. Trees, the ocean and a blur of ramshackle houses passed at dizzying speed. Soon it all looked the same. One thing did stand out however. It was a section of fence, down at the edge of the ocean. Hundreds of sparrows lined the top of every board. Then, suddenly, they took flight, gathered into a mass and darted for the bus. Each one dove at her window and turned away just before impact. There were so many of the damn things. Violet held her bag up between the window and her face.

If there was one thing she hated more than anything else, it was birds. She felt for the tequila bottle, but it had been left back at the Mexican airport.

So, what was the drink of choice in Cuba?

Chapter Nineteen

The cab stopped in front of Juanita's apartment, the one from Greg's dreams. It was also the one he'd been chased from, by a man who just wanted to talk. Was he the husband? Why would she bring him here if she were married? Why would she have spent the night with him?

"Do you live here alone?"

She walked through the doorway and started for the stairs. "I have a roommate of sorts."

Greg felt his gut cartwheel. "Is it…the boy?"

She turned back to him. "Yes, Ricky."

"You know him?"

"Yes."

"These dreams I talked about yesterday, he's always in them. In the first dreams he was just a kid. I've been having these dreams for some time now. Is he about twenty now?"

None of these questions seemed odd to her. "In three months he'll be twenty-two."

"Do you have a picture of him?"

"I do, but I need to change for work. I'll find it for you." She started undressing as she left through a door to the right. "Have a seat."

Greg waited until she left before he walked over to a bookcase. There was Hemingway's *The Old Man and the Sea* and *A Farewell to Arms* as well as other classics brought in from Mexico. He flipped through one. It was a Spanish version of *Zorro*.

There was also a shelf of science books. Greg pulled one out. It was a microbiology text. Beside it was a study of the human genome. Beside that book was a complete roadmap of the brain, maps included. These were intense books and each one was full of hand-scribbled notes.

He put them back and headed into the kitchen. She met him there and handed him several photos. "Here he is at different ages."

Greg took a moment to study each photo. It was unbelievable. This was not only the young boy, but he was the same child and teenager. He lowered them slowly. It was like he'd been a part of this boy's life. "Where is he?"

"Probably the University. He's a pretty smart kid."

"A science whiz?"

"A regular bookworm."

Greg paused, looking for the right words. "Has he ever mentioned any dreams?"

"You mean, has he ever mentioned you? He's a pretty close-lipped kid. I know he's dreamt of you though. We both have. In my dreams, some stranger walks through town with him. I've always wondered who that stranger was and why he's here now. I still want to figure that out."

"Take a number." Greg wanted to ask if he was her family, perhaps a son. If he was twenty-two, she might be offended at ageing her close to forty. It wasn't a stretch, but he decided on a different approach. "Is Ricky a brother?"

She gave him a playful slap on the back. "Very smooth, and thanks, but that's a no. He was just a kid that had no home. I had also seen him in my dreams and ran across him in a park one day. He was alone, so I confronted him. We just stared at each other. We knew each other. He came over and liked hanging around. It became home. I look out for him when he's around, but there are times when I don't see him for days. He's like the cats around here. Sometimes I feed him and put a roof over his head and other times he finds his own way."

"He's not family then?"

"No more mine than yours." She removed a couple of apples from the fridge and dropped them into her purse. "I have to run. You can stay if you want."

"I think I'm going to head back to the cemetery. That headstone is still bothering me."

"That's fine. If you decide to stay, mind the guys in the Lada. I'm not sure who they are, but they're always parked out front. They've been harmless so far."

"I'll walk you out."

As they reached the bottom of the stairs, Juanita grabbed him and pulled him away from the doorway. Her kiss was tender, definitely not the kiss of a sister. "Last night was a little weird, but I really enjoyed it. Thanks, Greg."

The weirdness had started to fade, or maybe it was getting lost in his wanting her again. "Maybe we'll have time ..."

She gave him another quick peck and turned to leave. "Not a chance."

Chapter Twenty

After the awkward goodbye with Juanita, Greg jumped on a bus and rode it back to the cemetery. Was it determination or sheer stupidity that had him wanting to waste so much time there? There was a headstone, his headstone, and he needed to find it.

Greg watched the birds fly over the cemetery in a dark cloud as he stepped off the bus. They flew from the power lines to the tall metal gates and trees, landing briefly before flying back. Greg looked around and noticed he wasn't the only one watching. The sight had even raised a few eyebrows amongst the locals.

The cloud of sparrows reformed and swirled as he entered the cemetery. They were flying in circles as if chasing one another. It was a playful display and the mass reminded him of a dog that might chase its tail when it thought no one was looking. The circle tightened and the speed grew. An odd humming started to fill the air as the whirling mass slowly made its way to the ground. Dust lifted, adding to the obscurity. Greg winced at what happened next.

Sparrows started crashing into headstones, falling limply to the ground. In an instant they suddenly broke apart, racing back to the power lines, headstones, trees and fence tops. What remained, after they'd finished their aerial acrobatics, was the man with a wide-rimmed black hat. This time Greg got a better look at him. He was dressed from head to toe in black, which included black leather boots and gloves. His face was the only part of him that was exposed.

Greg squinted to get a better look at the man's face, but it was hidden in the shadows of the hat. Where the hell had he come from? Had he emerged from hell? There was only one way to find out. "Hey."

As Greg started toward him, the chattering from the birds began again. The closer he got, the louder the birds became. Was it a warning? To Greg, they were just birds and he just wanted to talk.

"Hey." He shouted out again. "Who are you?"

The man didn't answer, didn't respond.

"Look, you obviously know something. I just want to ask a few questions."

Greg managed to get within one hundred feet of the stranger when the noise became deafening. With a swipe of the man's hand, the birds took flight and blanketed the ground between him and Greg. The man and his feathered insanity slowed Greg, but that wouldn't stop him. He thought of the boy and started to sweep the birds out of his way with his foot.

"Do you know the boy? Who is he?"

Twenty years of dreams had come to life on Obispo Street. He didn't know how, but he knew this man had something to do with it. It was more than just a hunch. The crazy seemed to fit with everything that had happened so far. Greg's stomach knotted as the odd bird crunched under his feet.

He was fifty feet from the man and the shadow under his hat was starting to reveal features, features that looked a lot like defects or bad scarring.

"Who are you?" Greg was more curious than ever.

The man raised a hand to the sky and was quickly engulfed in the swirl of sparrows once more. Even those crushed under Greg's feet took flight and joined them. Again, they stirred the dust as they came within inches of the ground. It lasted ten seconds,

The Divine Ledger

maybe twelve, and then it was over. The birds dispersed, finding cover in the trees and headstones that dotted the cemetery.

"No, no! Stop!" Greg watched as the cemetery returned to normal. "I just wanted to ask a couple questions."

It had only taken seconds, but the man was gone.

The dust floated in the stale air of the morning heat. All Greg had wanted was an answer. All he had ever wanted in life was the answers. Why was his wife cheating, why had his parents abandoned him and now, why were these damn dreams coming to life?

The dust eventually thinned, and when it did, he noticed a woman. Was this another trick? Her white cotton knee-length dress clung to her curves like poured milk. Blonde, loosely curled locks fell over her shoulders and down her back. Who was she, such a contrast to the man in black?

Greg blinked quickly, trying to clear the last of the dust from his eyes. When he looked again, she was gone. The dust had allowed her to escape. Doubt came immediately. Had she been standing there? But he *had* seen her. She was real. Then, by some trick of the mind, her presence became doubtful. Greg knew it was more than a trick. She'd been standing feet from where the man with the large-brimmed black hat had once stood. They had both disappeared in an instant.

He blinked again. It didn't bring her back.

Kevin Weisbeck

Chapter Twenty-one

Violet tossed her suitcase onto the chair beside the bed and took a second to admire the walls tiled in every colour imaginable. Like Mexico, everything in Cuba was either cement or tile. After the moment had passed, she walked over to the well- stocked bar-fridge and grabbed a cold beer. And why not, the precinct was paying. From the patio she could see the courtyard and pool. Beyond that, the sun was slowly dipping into the salty ocean. It was evening and still ninety-eight degrees.

She had chosen the Copacabana and, although it wasn't the one in Rio, the one that Barry Manilow had sung about, that didn't matter. It had vacancies. Besides, she wasn't a showgirl named Lola. She was a cop and a headless body had been found a few blocks away. That meant that her guy was in Cuba. He was close.

Violet was about to swallow a second mouthful of beer when her phone rang. She couldn't look. It had to be the Sarge. She waited for the fifth ring, hoping he'd give up. He couldn't scold her voicemail box. On the seventh ring, when her voicemail failed to grab the call, she picked up.

"Stormm here."

"Are you in a better mood?"

She looked at the screen. "Damn you, Brad. I thought you were the Sarge."

"Why? Are you avoiding him?"

There was a pause.

"Seriously, Stormm. You haven't told him you went to Cuba?"

"I'm waiting until I have something. Help me out. Got any leads."

"There is one. Of all the travellers flying from Mexico to Cuba, there seems to be one passenger that fits the bill better than the rest. His name is Victor Wainsworth. He's late forties with dark, greying hair. Records have him at a tad over six feet tall and about two hundred and ten pounds. I can't seem to find much else on the guy."

"Slipping, eh?" she teased. "Why him? Is he a doctor?"

"Not sure, but he had medical gear when he went through Customs. I'm trying to find out why. He was in Mexico for just two days. I'm sending you a picture of him as we speak."

Her phone chimed. She recognised the face that appeared on her screen. "Shit Brad, this is the guy I drew in my artist's sketch. He's our guy in Sayulita."

"Well, now he has a name." He paused and chose his words carefully. "Hey. I'm here at the airport."

She didn't bite. "Uh, good for you?"

"Your voodoo skull trinket just arrived." He had to broach the subject properly. "Nice work on loading the thing with all this crap."

"Come on, Bradley. The kid was having fun."

"I'm so delighted to hear that. I mean it's all about fun, eh? You know it's going to take me all night to clean this damn thing."

"Just pick them off with a screwdriver."

"What? DNA is a fine science. There's algorithms, genetic codes and..."

"Blah, blah, blah. Just tell me this, does it belong with the others?"

"From the inside of the skull I can see that the maceration process looks like it used the same enzymes, likely some cheap laundry soap. I'm guessing it was a hot water process…"

"Again, Brad, blah, blah, blah." This nerdy side was a lot more attractive when he simply spit out answers. "Is it the same?"

"It was prepared the same as the others. Good on you to keep all the teeth. I'll do the dental checks. I'm sure I can find a match."

"Hey, Brad?"

"Yes."

"I do appreciate all this. I owe you."

"I'll run a few impressions into a data bank and get you a name. You just catch this guy and don't get shot."

"I can do that. And thanks. I mean, you're always there. It's like we're still…"

"I gotta go. I'll get back to you when I find something."

"I just wanted to say…"

"I know what you want to say. I just don't want to hear it. It's over, Violet. The sooner you figure it out the better."

A click ended the conversation, along with any feelings she'd started to let back in.

"Asshole." She stuffed the phone in her pocket and walked to the front of the hotel for a taxi. There was one waiting, so she hopped in the back. "Can you take me downtown?"

"Where downtown, Miss?"

"Take me to the Policiana stationiola."

"You mean *Estación de policia?*"

She paused, giving him a chance to check her eyes in the rear-view mirror.

The message wasn't that hard to figure out for a man married twenty-seven years. "Ah, Policiana stationiola it is."

Violet leaned back wishing she'd grabbed a sandwich from the supper buffet. Maybe, if she hurried, there'd still be one when she got back. "Can we make it quick?"

Chapter Twenty-two

Victor had seen his share of sports bars in his days, but none like this one. He had drunk Stolichnaya Elit Vodka in a bar in Novosibirsk, Russia, he'd slugged back old-school moonshine in the *The Burley Hen* back in the Sawgrass Hills of Louisville Kentucky and he'd found a pub called *The Kitchen* in a town called Dildo, Newfoundland. That place looked like a big kitchen, complete with fake stoves, fridges, and checkered curtains. For some reason the people of Newfoundland had a passion for drinking a rot-gut called Screech and it had to be done in their kitchens. They did this while playing the ugly stick, a handmade musical instrument that only sounded good after far too many drinks.

All these places had one thing in common and that was multiple televisions. Some even had televisions and tables outside to handle the overflow, nature nuts and the tree-huggers that couldn't handle the smokers.

The pub that Bob had referred to consisted of a cheap neon sign, a fair-sized living room, two couches set up in the corner, a green beer fridge from the 60's and an old twenty-seven-inch Hitachi that was as thick as it was wide. At least it had colour.

Victor cautiously walked through the living room and poked his head into the kitchen. "Is this the Mapleleaf Pub?"

Bob and his friend turned and answered in stereo, "Hola."

They stood beside each other in their over-sized hockey jerseys like a pair of big kids. Bob wore the red and blue of the Montreal Canadians while his friend wore the blue and white of the Toronto Maple Leafs. Both were stout men and standing there, they reminded Victor of a novelty pair of NHL salt and pepper shakers.

"Uh, hello." Victor added his chuckle as he walked over. "Your friend is the proprietor?"

The man dumped a bag of ripple chips into a bowl and set it on the counter. "Hell, I've been called a lot of things, most of them by my wife, but that's never been one of them. Just call me Alvin." He held out his hand.

Victor took it and gave it a manly shake. "It's Victor."

"Good to meet ya, Vic."

Bob popped the top off a cold Bucanero and held it out. "Now that we've got that out of the way, have a beer."

"Thank you." Victor reached for his wallet. "How much?"

Bob proudly shrugged him off. "You're a Habs fan, so the night's on me."

"That's awfully kind of y—"

Bob cut him off. "Not now. Game's starting."

They entered the living room as the puck was dropped. The game unfolded and midway through the second period, four more people joined them. They were split, with three Montreal fans, three Calgary fans, and one that waffled. Suffice to say the war was on. After Calgary scored a third period fifth goal, the banter began to fade. The game was as good as over.

A bench-clearing brawl broke out with three minutes left to play. That was good enough for Victor. "I'm done. Thank you, Alvin and thanks for the brews, Bob. I'll be doing breakfast tomorrow around nine. Do you and your wife want to join me? I'm buying." They both smiled at the fact that it was a complementary meal.

"We'd love to Vic. I'm just gonna stay and watch the last bit. You never know, eh?"

The Divine Ledger

"Five to three is a good enough spread for me. Have a good night, Bob."

Victor left, knowing that a true fan shouldn't leave until the fat lady sang, but it was late. He circled the block five times before he saw Bob walking with a bit of a stagger down the sidewalk. "Bob." He picked up his pace to catch him. "Bob, wait up."

"Hey, Vic. You should have stayed. We fuck'n pulled it off. Pulled the goalie with two minutes left and got two goals to tie it with a handful of seconds on the clock. Knocked in the winner in OT. Six to five for the good guys."

"You're kidding."

"Nope. It was amazing. Hey, I thought you were heading back to the hotel."

"I'm trying, but I got a little crossed up at the supermarket. I didn't remember a supermarket when I came over."

"That thing threw me the first time too. You probably came up the alley when you left the hotel. Roads and alleys all look the same around here."

"Really, because I was looking, I swear."

"I'll show you. It's this way my man."

Victor obediently followed. Bob continued the hockey talk with a childlike enthusiasm. The Habs' come-from-behind win over the Calgary Flames was a miracle. They'd surely make the playoffs and, who knows, make an honest run for the Stanley Cup.

Victor let Bob go for a while before changing the subject. "So, Cuba."

Bob stopped walking. "What ya say, Vic?"

"As a kid, did you ever think you'd go to Cuba?"

"Thinking about it, I don't remember much about my childhood, probably a good thing. I was probably quite the brat. My parents left when I was very young. I don't remember them. Hell, I don't even remember the beginning of my marriage, you know, the good parts when the love was fun and fresh."

This was what Victor needed to hear. "Really?"

"Memory has always been a little sketchy though. Lots of fog for some things and other things are crystal clear. I think I got one too many knocks to the head as a kid. Do you ever get that, Vic?"

He wanted to say yes, that it was normal, but that would have been a lie. Victor did a quick shoulder check. They were alone, so he reached into his pocket for the bag. It was time.

Bob suddenly wrapped his arms around him. Victor's instinct was to knock him on his ass, a quick roundhouse. He didn't. Bob was giving him a hug. "Thanks, Vic. Wanna hear a secret?"

Victor held the bag down. "Sure, Bob."

"My wife has no use for hockey, or friends for that matter. If it were up to her we'd never leave the house. Me, I just want to get out. I don't give a damn about the hockey. I just love hanging out in the pubs. The energy is fantastic. Hell, if the team loses, that's okay. At least I'm not trapped in that damn house."

"Why don't you tell her you need your space."

"I tried that once. She read it as I didn't love her, thought I was cheating on her." He took a step back and held his arms out. "Who the hell would want this?"

Victor laughed. He didn't mean to, but Bob had made a good point.

"That woman is making me crazy," he continued. "She loves cats. We have four of them. Those damn things have become her life. Shit, she'd have tea parties and hold sewing bees with them if I let her. I can't even have friends over when she's like that. And the house smells like cat. Do you know what a cat-house smells like, Vic?"

Again, Victor tried not to laugh, but couldn't help himself. The deliveries were like he'd rehearsed this stuff. The guy should have been doing stand-up.

"Not that kind of cat-house." He shook his head and chuckled along. "Nah, place smells like a freak'n litter box. I need to get away. Ya gotta help me, Vic."

Victor opened the bag and exposed the damp rag.

"What cha got there, Vic?"

"Help, Bob." He held it up. "Do you want a smell?"

Bob leaned forward and took a sniff. "Ewe, that's kinda sweet. How's it gonna help me?"

The Divine Ledger

Victor hadn't expected that. He counted on a struggle. Was this man really that trusting, or just a fool? "I think you need a bigger sniff."

The cloth found Bob's face and after a few seconds, his knees buckled. Victor held him for a few seconds before lowering his body to the ground. The look on Bob's face was one of hopeful confusion right to the very end. How could this help him deal with his half-crazed wife, or those damn cats? Was he about to get high? Hell, he'd try anything if it worked.

Victor pulled a leather tote out of a trash bag that was stuffed in the bushes. He calmly opened it and took out the scalpel.

"Peace be with you, Bob."

Kevin Weisbeck

Chapter Twenty-three

The cab pulled up to what looked like a small castle. Violet looked up at the three stories of stone blocks as she slowly opened the cab's door. There was an eerie warmth with the early evening shadows cast by stone window ledges and archways. They didn't have police stations like this back home. It was a tad intimidating, but she could handle it. In the last thirty hours she had flown to Mexico, checked out a haunted cemetery, met a puma with one eye, slept on the beach with thieving crabs and hopped on a flight to Cuba. How bad could this be?

"Is this the…"

"This is the Policiana Stationiola." He let her pick her jaw up from the ground. "Twenty pesos."

"Twenty? You charge me that and you'll end up in there."

"Ten pesos."

Violet pulled out her badge. "This isn't Mexico, buddy. Five."

"Look lady. I have to make a living."

"What living. This is a Communist Country. All you have to do is show up. Besides, I'm paying with convertible pesos. They're worth more. I'm giving you like, fifty bucks."

The Divine Ledger

"Eight?"

Violet pulled out a handful of coins. "Here's six."

The man took the coins. "Welcome to Cuba, cheapskate lady."

The wheels of the taxi chirped, and the man raced out of sight.

An officer walked over from the gates of the stone building. "Is there a problem here?"

Violet still had her badge out and flashed it for him. "I heard there was a murder…a headless victim."

"I'm sorry. Where did you say you were from?"

"I didn't." She started to pass by him.

He politely put an arm out to stop her. "How did you find out about this murder?"

"This isn't the first victim. We had twelve in Canada."

He pulled his arm back and stepped aside. "I think you should come with me then."

Inside, the men behind all the old wooden desks were busy. It wasn't often a body was found without a head. The officer escorted her to one of the desks and offered her a coffee. She took it. She'd taken just three sips when an elderly man took a seat across from her.

"I am Captain Cerava, Miss…"

"Stormm, with two m's."

"Miss Stormm. You seem to have an advantage over me?"

"Long story short, I have a cold case and you have a body, well most of one. Do you have a name yet?"

"I am honoured that the Canadian Government would send us their help, but we have this under control. How did you hear about…?"

"I have no doubt your men are amply trained." She continued to posture. "I have information for you and I just hope my generosity is contagious."

"I'm listening."

"Several years ago, Vancouver had a number of similar crimes. There were twelve bodies found in this manner. We never caught the guy. We found the bodies over ten days and then, suddenly, the killing stopped. The guy's not a serial killer and he's not doing it for the attention. He's all business."

"That's very interesting. You said several years ago. Why does one headless body, all this time later, grab your attention?"

"Because I just flew in from Mexico where the skulls to those twelve bodies were dumped in a cemetery. I don't think it's a coincidence. This time it's Havana instead of Vancouver."

"How many does he want?"

"I don't know. We're still trying to find the link between the victims. Do you have a name?"

"We're not sure. Her finger prints don't match anything in our databanks."

"I'm pretty sure she's a tourist. As a Canadian, I have a lot more data banks to search through. I can probably get you a name if you give me a print."

His eyes studied hers. Was she on the level? What else did she know?

She pulled a handful of files out of her bag. "Because I'm a nice girl and a very trusting Canadian, I'll let you go through these. It's important we work together on this."

He browsed through a couple of the folders while she sipped on her coffee.

"Most people find our coffee too strong." He said.

"Hell no. This shit is real."

He cocked a brow and set the folders down. Then he slid one of his across the desk. Violet quickly took a snapshot of the fingerprints and sent it to Bradley in a text. The pictures were graphic for a murder. Considering the woman was beheaded, there wasn't a lot of blood. The killer was tidy.

"Have there been any hotel guests reported missing? I'm sure a hotel might have a room full of clues."

"We've been checking the hotels in the area. Most hotels wouldn't know until check-out time. Even then, it's only an issue if the hotel is full and the room is needed."

Her phone chimed. It was Bradley. "He wants to know if you have a fax number."

Violet typed as he called out the numbers. It only took a minute before the fax machine fired up and started to spit the pages out. Her phone chimed again, and she gave it a quick glance before rolling her eyes.

The Captain collected the sheets. Beverly Shipstone's profile picture was shot in front of a government office in England. The camera had caught her with a coy smile. She was only thirty-nine. The pages contained her life and hopefully clues as to why she had been murdered.

"Good work Detective Stormm. I'll find out where she was staying and start canvassing the hotels and restaurants in the area."

"Keep me posted on what you find. We'll accomplish more working together."

"I agree."

He took her number and walked her out. A few of the men were curious, wondering where this young blonde Señorita had come from. Was their Captain living a double life? Being cops, they would all come up with their own conclusions.

Violet noticed the cab parked under a lit street lamp, just outside the precinct. The driver stood beside the car in a dim evening glow. It was as if he'd been waiting for her. "You need a ride, nice lady."

Violet looked around and, not seeing any one else, she walked over. "What?"

"I watched the other cab driver treat you poorly. He is a bad man. We are not all like him."

"Have you been waiting here for me this whole time?"

"*Si.*"

"Like that's not messed up." Regardless, she opened the back door and climbed in. "Do you know of a hotel called the Copacabana?"

"*Si.*"

"And how much will you charge to take me there?"

He thought for a second. She was easy to read. "Five?"

"Good answer."

Kevin Weisbeck

She let the cab leave the curb before looking back down at her phone. The last text had been from Bradley. It had been an address.

Chapter Twenty-four

Morning welcomed Violet with a sunrise that was worth a second look. She grabbed a complimentary morning coffee in the lobby as she headed for the cabs. Her friend from last night was there, the taxi version of a stalker. That was okay because she needed a ride to the Tri-Neptune Hotel. This was where a certain Victor Wainsworth was staying, hopefully still sleeping. The hotel wasn't that far away.

She entered the lobby, pulled out her phone and started for the elevators. Should she make that call? Nah, she'd call the Sarge after she capped this creep. The coffee from her hotel was weak, terrible in fact, so she set it down on a tray of dirty dishes in a room-cleaning service cart. Had they even used beans or just ran water through a dish rag? As she set the coffee down, the odour hit her, a familiar sweetness unlike any candy. It was metallic or synthetic-sweet and it came from the laundry bag of dirty towels. She ran down the remainder of the corridor.

She pulled an overextended credit card from her wallet and slid it between the door and the jamb of room 319, Victor Wainsworth's room. With any luck the maid hadn't stopped by yet.

A better scenario would have him fast asleep. It was still pretty early.

She wiggled and twisted the card, hoping that it would unlock the room. It didn't. The new card-key doors had taken the nostalgia out of breaking and entering. A quick curse accompanied her acceptance of defeat. She slipped the card back into her wallet. Then she begrudgingly pulled out the black card. It was a card that Bradley had made for her months ago. This wasn't how the true detectives did it in the old movies, how real detectives did it years ago. Where had the romance gone? She slid the card into the slot, the door clicked and opened. At least it was efficient.

Proficiency had always been important to Bradley. He was all about keeping it simple, keeping her safe and hey, who didn't like cool technology? Why battle with a credit card when you could simply use a master key card? It worked on ninety-seven percent of all locks. He had programmed the card for her and they had argued for an hour before she finally took the damn thing. Still, whenever she had to break in to a room, she'd pull out a credit card first. Her credit cards weren't much good for anything else.

Once inside, she slipped on a pair of thin cotton gloves. He was gone and an over-eager maid had already been through the room. On the bed, two towels were twisted into a pair of swans kissing. That meant this guy had left a tip, maybe a nice one.

She immediately went to the bar-fridge. What better place to store a head. It sure beat the nightstand. There was no sign of Beverly. Three bottles of water and two beers sat on the top shelf, crowded to the left. She grabbed one of the beers and opened it. It was early, but she needed something to wash away the taste of that terrible coffee.

Over at the table a pencil and note pad sat by a remote control that probably didn't work. They never do, always needing batteries. Hell, people shouldn't be watching TV on vacation anyway. She took the pencil and lightly coloured the pad. If anything had been written on a previous page, an imprint would have been left. Something did indeed appear.

Violet studied it before realising that it was upside down. Who writes on a pad with the open side up? She read it and quickly deduced that Victor hadn't used the pad. It was a shopping list for vodka, cranberry juice, Cointreau and tampons. The first three were the ingredients for a Cosmopolitan, a common feminine drink. If this Victor guy drank those, he'd probably need the tampons.

Every aspect of the room was tidy. She checked the patio doors and found them locked. Violet knew she shouldn't be touching anything, with or without gloves. She could be smudging vital fingerprints. She also knew how guys like this worked. He was thorough and admirably professional. There wouldn't be any prints.

She stepped out onto the patio with her beer. There was a chair in the corner and it beckoned her. Had Victor sat here? She took a seat and immediately felt his presence. The lingering energy wasn't dark or sinister though. Taking a sip, she let his energy wash over her. Like a bloodhound catching a scent, Violet would take the energy and use it to find a way into the guy's head. It was what she did better than anyone else.

A baneful energy was what she'd expected. This guy was a killer, a serial killer and the nut-job types always killed with an agenda. They often blamed it on having a neglected childhood. Calling cards were usually left and some even went as far as to leave actual playing cards. They wanted people to know they weren't finished and that there'd be more until they got caught. Many of these killers knew they were damaged goods and being caught would bring a suitable end to the one thing they couldn't control. Too cowardly to stop themselves, someone else would have to do it. Other killers were just terrorists, getting off on the sensationalised headlines. They wanted people to fear them. Fear was respect, something they dearly wanted. Victor was none of the above.

From Victor's energy, she envisaged a man who was methodical and disciplined. He took his time and paid close attention to detail. This guy didn't make mistakes.

"Shit." Or would he. He thought he was dealing with Cuban authorities. Had he been sloppy?

Violet set her beer down and hurried to the bathroom. Pulling a flashlight out of her purse, she closed the door behind her and turned it on. It wasn't a normal flashlight. This one was ultraviolet. Bloodstains glowed in the white bathtub. He had cleaned the skull in the tub and, without bleach, he couldn't clean the tub properly. And then there was that faint aroma of sweetness again. This time she recognized it as chloroform. This confirmed criminal, murderous consistencies, confirmed the murderer. Victor Wainworth was her man.

So, there *was* a little bit of crazy to this guy, mixed with methodical. Although he seemed to have a set number in Vancouver, twelve, he was back to collecting skulls. What did he want with these things? Were they some kind of spiritual trade items? And why drop the others off in Mexico? Was it going to be twelve again? Did twelve even mean anything? Bradley had used numerology to find the name Mary. Coincidence? Would these skulls also be displayed somewhere, giving them Mary's last name?

Violet clicked the flashlight off and left the bathroom. Sitting back in the chair, she finished her beer. She knew the hardest part of catching crazy was thinking crazy. Some might say she was perfect for the job, but her crazy wasn't the same.

After several hours, she finished a second beer. The empties went with her. No sense in leaving her DNA behind. Outside, her cabbie friend was waiting. It was like he'd adopted her.

"I no leave, pretty woman?"

Violet crawled in the back. "Save the ass-kissing. I hated that movie."

He scrunched his face. "What's this, ass-kissing?"

With her hand she motioned it was nothing. "Where does a girl go to get a good lunch around here?"

"My cousin has a great place. I take you there."

"No cousins. I want food I can recognise."

His expression wilted, but she didn't care. These guys all worked together. His cousin probably served dog, cooked to the consistency of shoe leather.

"You Canadian?"

"Yes, but I'll eat whatever, as long as it's good."

"A Canadian owns this place downtown. I hear the food is great. Long line ups though. Maybe not now. Hard to say."

"What are we waiting for?"

The Divine Ledger

"Because I thought you…" It took him a second to realise that it was a rhetorical question. Tourists were so complex. He pulled away from the curb. "Five pesos?"

She nodded and watched as the buildings passed. Cuba was a unique place. She might even come back on a vacation some day. There was history, warm weather and no rain. The cab wheeled down several busy streets before stopping across from the Capitol building.

"We here, pretty woman."

"Thanks." She handed him his five pesos. It should have been more. "I'm done for the day. Go make a million off someone else, but think of me when you wake up. I'll need a ride."

His grin widened. "See you tomorrow, pretty wo… I mean lady."

"It's Violet." She gave him a good-on-you wink for figuring it out.

"Violent." He repeated.

"That's better, except drop the 'n'."

"Si, Violent."

"Whatever." She left the cab to see a line-up that stretched out the door.

At the top of the stairs a shouting match was in full swing. Catching every third word, Violet quickly read it as an opportunity and started through the crowd. "Excuse me. Excuse me. Get out of my way, already. Shit. Excuse me. Move it."

She made her way to the front of the line to see the host arguing with a man.

"Sorry. Please understand, we are too busy to serve singles. You take up a whole table." He pointed to the sign that read *No Single Seating*.

"But I'm hungry and I've been in this line-up for damn near an hour. You should put that sign at the bottom of the stairs."

Violet lunged toward the man taking his arm in hers. She landed a kiss on his cheek. "Darling. There you are. I thought I lost you."

He turned to her. "Who the hell…"

Her arm constricted around his, cutting his words short. "Did you get us a table, my love?" She shot him a raised eyebrow and waited for him to clue in.

The man turned back to the waiter with a shit-eating grin. "Well?"

The waiter sighed. "Right this way, sir."

She put her lips up to his ear. "Name's Violet."

He turned back to her as they walked. "I'm Greg."

"You know they're probably gonna spit in our food."

Greg looked over to the kitchen. "What?"

Chapter Twenty-five

Violet's eyes widened as the waiter walked her and Greg to the table. This place was amazing. Large timbers towered to the ceiling. The beams were magnificent. She doubted they were load-bearing, likely more for show, but they gave the place a real Canadian Rockies feel. If it wasn't for the unrelenting heat outside, this could have been Canmore or Banff. She looked over to Greg. Like a true gentleman, he had already sat down and had the menu open. She pulled her chair out and took a seat.

Greg looked up. "They've got a stuffed schnitzel."

"Will your wife be joining us?"

"Oh, I'm not married anymore." He stopped and looked up. Was this girl hitting on him?

"Isn't that a shocker," she chuffed.

Greg decided against the flirting. "Sorry. I should have got your chair. It's just that I haven't eaten anything decent since I got here."

"Okay, you got me on that one. The hotel where I'm staying serves boiled hotdogs as breakfast sausages."

He looked up from the menu again. "Mine too."

"Copacabana?"

He laughed. "Small world."

Violet let that comment hang in the air as she opened her menu. That was it for polite conversation until the waiter came. It wasn't hard to see through his nice guy act.

The waiter flipped his note pad open. "What'll you have."

Greg didn't hesitate, like ordering it quickly would get it to him quicker. "The schnitzel with a baked potato."

"And the lady?"

"See, Honey. The waiter thinks I'm a lady."

Greg looked up again, first at the waiter and then back at her. "Huh?"

She batted her eyelashes. "I'll bet the waiter even thinks I'm cute."

They both looked at the waiter and waited.

He swallowed hard. "Sorry, Miss. What did you say you wanted?"

"A husband that doesn't snore like a buzz-saw, or clip his nails at the supper-table, or maybe one that remembers my birthday. That would be nice, but I don't see it on the menu."

Both Greg and the waiter squirmed. Violet loved it. There was a sadistic pleasure to it. That had to be Victor's energy purging itself from her. Should she push them further?

Nah, she was hungry. "I'll take the lobster with fries and hold the spit. He was the one making the scene earlier, not me."

The waiter wrote down lobster and fries and started to back away slowly. He didn't turn his back to them until he was at a safe distance. Greg wanted to say no spit for his either but didn't. Surely, they wouldn't.

"And can we get a pitcher of sangria?" She turned to Greg. "You're paying, right?"

"I uh, you…"

"Thanks." She nodded to the waiter, who was halfway back to the kitchen. "We'll do the sangria."

Greg held his hands palms out. "What the hell was that all about?"

"Relax, I was just having fun." She leaned toward him. "Tell me you don't clip your nails at the table or forget birthdays."

"Whatever. Everyone has issues."

"I know. What brings you to Cuba?"

"Awe, I'm not even sure where to start. It's all a little crazy."

"Right on. I've been hitting crazy on all eight cylinders lately."

The waiter returned with two glasses and the pitcher of Sangria. Violet let him fill her glass and took a long swallow. "You go first. We can compare."

"I don't think it's a competition," Greg replied.

"Why? You scared you're gonna lose?"

"Not at all." He put his drink down and began. "I have dreams. There's this kid in them. I've watched this kid go from toddler to adult over twenty years of dreams. Crazy, huh?"

Violet nodded and let him go on. The story was a good one and she could tell he needed to get it all out. The food came while he explained about the tombstone and she refilled the glasses. By the time he was done telling her about the man and the birds, the dessert menus were being placed in front of them.

"Is that crazy enough for you?"

"Oh ya."

He gave a smirk as if he'd won. "What do you have?"

"I'll let you have this one. I've only got thirteen skulls and a serial killer."

"You're kidding, right?"

Her badge was on the table before he could finish the sentence. She opened her purse to show him the gun, a habit she really should try to curb. "I wish."

"Who is this guy? Do you have any leads?"

"I know who, I'm just one step behind on the where. The guy's meticulous and I can't afford to wait for him to screw up. I mean, who knows how many he'll kill." She closed her purse. "You having dessert?"

"No. I'm stuffed. You?"

"No."

Her phone rang. She saw the number and got to her feet looking around. "I need to take this. I'll be right back."

After the call she returned to a table to see it being cleared by two young boys. Over at the entrance, Greg was waving at her. His wallet was out.

She walked over. "Hey, I said I'd get this one. You didn't need to…"

"Relax. I didn't. I have an expense account. My boss paid."

"All right then. Same time, same place, tomorrow?"

"You have a killer to catch. Was that…"

"More dead people. They want me to go over the crime scene and do an ID."

"Sounds like fun."

"Sadly, we need bodies to find the common variable. It's hard without clues." Violet scrunched her face in an apologetic smile. It was a morbid reality. "What are you up to?"

"I have a kid to find." Juanita had offered to let him know if she heard from him. Often the kid spooked and disappeared for days. All you could do was let his friends know you were looking and wait until someone saw him.

Back down on the street, the blazing sun was waiting. Violet pulled her sunglasses out and threw them on. The lenses were tinted a deep purple. "Maybe we'll see each other around the hotel. I'll buy."

"Have you tried their food?" Greg shook his head. "I'll pass."

"Maybe a beer then." Violet headed across the street to the waiting squad car. She looked back to see that Greg hadn't moved, so she gave him a friendly wave as she got in.

The man had nice eyes.

Chapter Twenty-six

Greg wasn't sure what to expect when he stepped off the bus in front of the University. Juanita still hadn't seen Ricky and wasn't sure when she would, but there was a good chance he'd be here. Greg hadn't flown to Cuba, setting an important job aside for bird aerobatics and a one-time fling. He needed to find the boy.

The University turned out to be an aged set of buildings fronted by large towering pillars at the top of one hundred well-travelled stone steps. At the top of the steps, the statue Alma Mater stood as if it could feel the pride of its students. Several students ate late lunches and gabbed about the lectures they'd just attended, or maybe it was the beach party they'd be going to later that night. Greg didn't bother to eavesdrop.

The doors to the Aula Magna, one of the largest auditoriums in Havana, were thrust open and Greg watched as the students poured from it into the courtyard. Was Ricky one of them? He walked over and waited. Hundreds of kids exited the building and most of them looked like Ricky. They all had full heads of hair and dark brown eyes. Three of them had Greg doing a double take, but none of them were his boy.

There were surprising numbers of Asians learning Spanish and a few Cubans learning Chinese. Greg saw Russian students and a few that were too tall to be anything but Danish. There was no Ricky.

He stopped one of the students and struggled with his words. *"Donde es la oficina?"*

The young man pointed across the courtyard. "The office is just over there, Sir."

"You speak English. That's great." Greg pulled out one of the pictures he got from Juanita. "Do you know this kid?"

After a few seconds of staring, the student shook his head. "I may have seen him around, but I've never talked to him."

"Recently?"

The student shrugged.

"Thanks." Greg slipped the picture into his pocket and headed for the office.

There were two secretaries behind the counter. Greg picked the one that didn't look like she'd just eaten a basket of baby kittens. *"Escusa, habla usted Inglés?"*

"Sir, we are a leading University, teaching both Spanish and English. It would be ridiculous to assume I don't speak English."

Greg looked over at the other woman. There was a good chance he had chosen wrong. He pulled the picture out and dropped it on the counter. "Do you know this student?"

"I know all my students. I take pride in my job and make a point of knowing each and every one of my children. I think it's vital that we show our youth that we not only care, but that we think their dreams and aspirations are important. They don't come here to play games and waste time."

Greg looked to the other lady again. "Was that a yes or a no?"

"That one doesn't go to school here."

"Are you sure?"

The lady started up again and Greg walked away before she could wind up her rant. He was not a student, was all he needed, but how could that be? Juanita had told him the boy was a science whiz and that he attended this University. Had she lied to him? Had the boy lied to her?

Greg walked through the courtyard again scanning for a face. The day was cresting mid-afternoon and students were starting to leave. He couldn't afford to miss him. His eyes darted left and right, but didn't see him, nor did he see the young woman with her arms full, until he bumped into her. Books and loose pages fell to the ground.

"I'm so sorry." Greg leaned down and started to gather up the papers. "I didn't see you."

The girl quickly knelt down and helped. "I get it, I'm short."

Greg looked up to see her smiling.

"I was thinking about my homework assignment. I wasn't paying attention."

Greg handed the papers to her, picked up the books and stood up. "I'm Greg and again, I'm sorry."

She stood up, barely five feet tall, and took the books from him. "I'm Simonne."

"You obviously go to school here." He held the picture up for her. "Have you seen this kid. I think he's a student."

"I don't know if he's a student, but I've seen him around."

"Recently?"

"Why are you asking? Is he in trouble?"

"Oh, no. He's not in any trouble. I know him, and I just came by to see him."

"But you don't even know if he's a student? Doesn't sound like you know him all that well." She smiled, easing the threatening accusation. "I'm just saying."

"Fair enough. I've actually never met him."

"You said you know him."

"I do know him, sort of." He stopped himself. How could he tell her without coming across as a madman? "It's hard to explain."

"Have a nice day, Mister."

"But…" He let her go. "Damn it."

Greg continued to loiter until the security guard started to walk over. It was time to leave. He made his way down the steps and to the bus stop at the front of the grounds. Should he stop by

Juanita's place? She had some explaining to do. Who was he kidding, she'd be working. Besides, she said she couldn't see him until tomorrow. Wasn't that always the way, with women calling the shots?

Greg didn't notice the two men at first. They had got out of their car and were heading his way. "Hey Mister! We would like to talk to you."

He recognised the car and froze. These were the guys usually found in front of Juanita's apartment. Why did they want to talk to him? This couldn't be good. He bolted left and stopped. Two other men had that escape route covered. "Shit."

Could he make it across the street? Where would he run if he couldn't? At that point, it didn't matter. He took two steps onto the street and the howl of tires was instant.

A BMW slid to a stop in front of him. The passenger door had popped open and a familiar girl sat behind the wheel. It was Simonne. "Get in."

Greg did as he was told.

"I thought you were friends with these guys," she said as she tromped the gas pedal.

"These are the guys parked outside of Juanita's apartment, aren't they?"

Over her shoulder she could see the men scrambling for their cars. "They are. I don't like them."

"Me neither."

"I mean it. Be careful of them." She made a left turn and then a right, just to be sure she'd lost them before they could catch up. "I wish Ricky felt the same."

"You do know him, don't you?"

"I do," she admitted.

"How do you know him?"

She checked the rear-view mirror one last time before pulling down a side street and stopping. Greg would be safe here. Three cabs were lined up back on the main street, waiting for fares. "Come to the University noon tomorrow and I'll introduce you to him. Come by cab and make sure you're not being followed."

"I will." Greg got out and watched her drive away. Two cabs were parked at the curb. He was about to jump in the first cab when he saw her. It was the blonde from the cemetery.

She quickly turned and started down the sidewalk. Her steps were quick as she made her way through the crowd. Greg found himself sprinting to keep up. Startled pedestrians jumped out of his way.

"Wait." He was closing in on her. "Who are you?"

The woman dodged right and slipped down a back alley. Greg was three, maybe four, steps behind her.

When he rounded the corner, she was gone.

Kevin Weisbeck

Chapter Twenty-seven

The morning heat had every window and every patio door wide open at the Copacabana. The searing heat had hung on long after the day had ended. In Violet's room the early temperatures were hanging at a very thick eighty-six degrees. Sleeping in just panties on top of the covers hadn't helped. A cold morning shower did.

She headed down for breakfast and Greg saw her before she saw him. "Over here."

Violet grabbed a coffee, a juice, and a plate full of dried out Danishes before heading to his table. "Morning."

Greg eyed the plate. "And here I saw you as a fruit and fibre kinda gal. One second on the lips, an inch on the—"

"Really Greg. That's how you want to start this conversation. You forget I have a gun?"

"It's just that you're so lean, I mean healthy, I mean fit. I just assumed…"

"Ass, u, me, Greg." She dunked the Danish in the coffee and took a bite. "More you though."

"Are you always this cheery in the morning?"

The Divine Ledger

"I couldn't sleep. Who controls the thermostat in this damn country?" Her phone chimed, and she stole a glance at it while she took a second bite.

"Do what I did. Ask for a fan at the front desk and grab a bucket of ice. Put the ice in front of the fan. Doesn't last all night, but it helps."

It sounded like a good idea. "I'll try it tonight. Where'd you learn that?"

"I live in DC. Humidity's horrible up there as well."

"DC? How'd you get into Cuba? Last time I checked, these folks didn't much care for your kind."

"It's a mutual dislike, so keep the DC thing between you and me. I flew a connector through Monterrey."

Violet downed her juice and started on the second Danish. "Good food, eh."

"You remember the sausages?"

"Oh, that reminds me. I really should grab one for my friend. There's this cat…"

Greg cut her off. "One eye?"

"I guess he's pretty popular in these parts." She gave Greg a harder look. He was a charming man, in a childish kind of way. "What are you up to today, more tombstone steeplechase?"

"You laugh, but there's some crazy magic going on there."

"Magic? There's a word you don't hear from adults very often."

"Whatever. Yesterday these birds made a man appear and later, a woman. Then they were gone, poof. How would you explain it?"

"Magic would be getting the kitchen to make some bacon appear. People disappearing is just a cool parlour trick."

"It's wasn't a trick and I'm well aware it wasn't magic. Still, two people appeared and disappeared. How?"

"People vanishing? I'd say someone's messing with you."

"Maybe. Well, I should go. I have to get to the University." There was no point in working her up any further. Greg set his coffee cup back in its saucer and pushed it to the middle of the table. He looked outside. "Good, there's one cab left."

"Best of luck with the University." She started dipping the last Danish. "And good luck with that cab."

He got up. "Have a good morning, and don't forget to do the fan thing. It really works."

She watched him leave, finished her Danish and sipped at the coffee for ten more minutes. Then she slowly made her way outside.

Once again she walked into Greg arguing with one of the locals. "The man won't take me. Can you believe that?"

"You trying to go downtown?"

"Trying."

"Good morning, Miss Violent."

She opened the back door and clambered into the cab. "And a good morning to you too."

Greg stood stunned. "What are you doing?"

She slid over, leaving the door open. "Get in."

He took the spot beside her.

Her eyes met the cabbie's in the rear-view mirror. "Fifteen pesos to go downtown?"

"Fifteen?" He coughed. The blonde gringo had never paid more than five. His eyes frantically tried to find her game.

"Okay, make it twenty, but not a peso more." She added, "The man is paying. Is that okay?"

Was that a smile in her eyes? This was one strange lady. "I can do it for that."

Greg sat back. "Excellent. Let's go."

Violet gave the cabbie a wink and leaned back. "I need to go to the Policiana Stationiola again, but can you take us the scenic route, past this cemetery? I've heard so much about the place. I think I need to see it for myself."

"I knew you were a believer." Greg gave her knee a pat. "Then I'll need Obispo Street."

The cab left the turnaround at the hotel and sped off up Calle 60. He dodged and honked his way through the streets missing every pothole. Thankfully he also missed the pedestrians, not nearly as important. Within minutes the iron gates of the cemetery came into view on the right.

Violet hung out the window. "Are you seriously trying to find your headstone in there. It's huge."

"One hundred and forty acres."

"How long do you plan on living, because this might take a while. Have you narrowed it down to any particular section?"

"No. The damn birds were covering part of my tombstone in the dreams."

"Those birds?"

The cloud wove through the trees and started to form the circle. It spun faster and faster. The chattering started and soon people were stopping on the sidewalk to watch. Even the cabbie slowed to get a better look. And again, as quickly as it had started, it dispersed, leaving the man with the hat.

Greg had mentioned the man to Violet and she had been a sceptic. "See?"

But she couldn't take her eyes off the birds as they found perches. "This is crazy."

The cab started to speed up as the birds went back to their business.

"Who do you think he is?"

"Who?"

"The guy with the black hat. The one that showed up with the birds."

"There was a guy?" She strained to see through the filthy back window of the cab. "I must have missed him."

Greg shrugged. "How could you miss him? He was right there."

"Sorry. I was watching the birds."

Greg started the silent treatment and sustained it until the cab stopped in front of Juanita's place. He got out and paid the driver

Violet shrugged and stayed in the back seat. "I said I was sorry."

"And you're a detective?" Greg shook his head and started for the stairs. The cab pulled away from the curb and headed for the policiana stationiola.

Inside the apartment, Juanita had just laid out a few home-baked cookies.

"The place smells wonderful." Greg walked over to her and gave her a hug. It seemed like the right thing to do.

Juanita returned his hug with a kiss on the lips. It was a confusing sign. Was it meant to be a friendly or more a take-me-now move? Greg added a couple seconds to the hug and hoped for a clearer sign. The cookies, being all dolled up and this hug had Greg thinking that she might want to revisit mattress land. He was okay with that, but he wasn't sure about the relationship that might ensue. He was an American. It would never work.

"I baked you cookies."

That was all the proof he needed. She wanted him. "Look I really like you but…'

"But what?"

"You know, the cookies, the hug…"

"What the hell are you talking about? Do you think I made these cookies so that I could sleep with you again?"

"Uh, kinda obvious…"

"I want a damn favour, not sex."

He took a step back. "Don't I look stupid?"

She gave him a forgiving wink. "Ah, you don't look that much stupider than you did when you got here."

He took a relieved breath. "Thanks? I think I owe you a favour."

"I know this woman. She's one of the best, I swear. I've gone to her for advice on occasion. It's what she does. I know it sounds cheesy, but she knows her stuff. I'd like us to go see her, about your dreams."

"What are you talking about? What is she?"

"I'm just saying. We've both had dreams. You've been dreaming about Ricky for a long time. If anyone can figure this out, she can."

"Is she a fortune teller?" It came out like an insult. It might even have been meant as one. He immediately realised how it must have sounded to Violet. She probably thought the disappearing man was a flaky mirage. Now it was his turn, except he had crazy old ladies and crystal balls.

"She knows what she's doing."

"Sure she does. Hey, about Ricky. Have you heard from him yet?"

"No." She reached down and flipped over a sheet of paper. It was a picture Ricky had done when he was five. In it he was holding a man's hand and the man looked a little like Greg. "If there's something to this, this woman can help us. You have to trust me on this."

Trust had become a bit of a complication. What did she know and was she holding out on him? He had already decided to keep his visit with Simonne to himself. Greg reached down and touched the drawing with his fingertips. He couldn't deny that this was his dream. "I'll give you five minutes with her, then I've gotta go find Ricky."

"You won't regret it."

"Wanna bet me a handful of those cookies."

Chapter Twenty-eight

Turbulence hit the plane hard, dropping it fifty feet. For a large jetliner, fifty feet was nothing. For Jon, flying a much smaller plane, it was like flying off the edge of a cliff. He looked down at the instruments and made the necessary adjustments. At least Cuba was in sight.

He fumbled his phone back up to his ear. "Gina, have you seen my passport?"

"I packed if for you. It's in the front of your carry-on. Are you still in the air? You shouldn't be calling me. Just fly the plane."

"I'm good. I was worried that I'd forgotten it. You know they'd never allow a Columbian into the country without a passport, or a kilo of coke." He chuckled nervously and tried to let the thin strip of land on the horizon relax him.

Gina hated him flying over water, not that a crash on land was any better. At least on land they'd find his body for the funeral. "You need to call the kids when you get settled."

"I will."

"So why is your Company dealing with Cuba?"

"The Americans are getting closer to ending the sanctions. It won't be long before an American flag flies on Cuban soil again.

We have to get a jump on this. I could save a fortune routing my shipments through Cuba."

"This guy deals with fibre optic?"

"This guy deals with everything. He makes me nervous though."

"Why didn't you tell me that earlier?"

"I didn't want you worrying. I'm sure he's fine. It's just a gut instinct thing. Shit!"

"What Jon?"

There was a long pause.

"Jon?"

"It's a flock of damn birds. They're chasing me."

The dark flock had come out of nowhere. They had trailed behind the plane for a couple minutes, but soon caught up with it. They flew into the side windows and he could hear them tapping against the roof. "What the fuck…"

"Jon?"

He shoved the stick forward taking the plane into a dive. The birds followed. He jerked the stick to the left. Before the birds could catch him, he pulled back and jerked the stick to the right. Again, the plane went into a dive, so he revved the engine to full throttle. The swarm darted right, left, and remained in pursuit.

"Jon. What's going on?"

He kept the throttle at maximum speed as he lost elevation but reached land. The birds were slowly being left behind, but he'd have to slow down for his approach at the airport. They'd catch him again for sure.

"Jon?"

"Sorry dear. Damn birds caught me. I had to out-fly the little bastards."

"Where are you now?"

"I'm coming up to the airport. I've got to get going, Darling. I still need to talk to the tower and get clearance."

"I'm glad to hear you're at the airport. Don't forget to call us once you get settled."

"I will, Darling. Bye."

He dropped the phone on the seat beside him and got on the radio. "WJ221 to Josè Marti Airport. Looking for clearance to land. Over."

The Radio crackled back. "It might be a minute WJ221. Over."

"I have a bit of a situation. There's a flock of birds chasing me. Do you see them? Over."

There was silence for a few seconds. What if they said no and he had to wait? What could these birds do to him? Could they take down a plane? All they'd have to do is find their way into the engine's intake. It would make him nothing more than a newspaper headline. Surely these birds weren't that smart.

"WJ221, you have clearance. Over."

"Thank you. Over."

He pulled back on the throttle as he lined himself up. Again, the birds started tapping on the windows and the roof. He looked at the passenger window. As the birds hit the glass, they lost co-ordination and tumbled back, taking out others in the process. Damn, there were so many of them.

Again, Jon had to pull back on the throttle to slow the plane for the landing. The birds easily overtook him. Some flew in front of him, blocking his view and being chopped up by the props. Their blood turned the plane's windshield red. There was no escaping them. He dropped down quicker than he had wanted, but it was the only way he could clear the birds from his windshield. When the birds followed, he started rocking the stick.

Suddenly the engine sputtered and quit. The plane dodged, and Jon pulled back on the stick to correct it. All he could do was watch the altimeter. Thirty feet…twenty feet…ten feet and touchdown. The tires hit hard as he bounced in his seat.

At least the plane was on the ground and rolling. The birds had failed and because of that, they flew off in all directions. They soon disappeared, leaving nothing more than a memory.

"WJ221. If you are able, could you taxi to the eastern end of the airport, by the hangers? Over."

It was the closer end. "Roger that, Josè Marti Airport."

The Divine Ledger

The plane trundled to a stop and Jon stepped down from the cockpit. Having his feet back on the ground had never felt better. He'd had rough flights before, but this was ridiculous. After an hour with airport staff and customs, Jon grabbed his suitcase and passed through the front doors of the airport. With no commercial flights expected for half an hour, the line of cabs was non-existent and the ride they had sent him was surely gone.

"This is just great," Jon muttered. "How am I supposed to get to my hotel?"

A lone man stood quietly by the exit. He had a sign, although he wasn't holding it up any more. "That was quite the landing."

"It was." Jon looked at the sign. "Are you…"

"I'll be your ride to the hotel." He took Jon's bag and started walking toward a tan-coloured Lada. "I'm parked right over here. My boss has put you up at the National. I hope that's okay. It's the best in Havana."

"Thanks." His luck was changing. He waited until the man tossed the suitcase into the back seat. Then he held out his hand. "Name's Jon Martinez."

"I know." Victor grabbed it and gave it a solid shake. "You're on my list."

Chapter Twenty-nine

Violet didn't get out of the back seat of the cab when it stopped in front of the precinct gates. She took a second to stare at the face in the rear-view mirror. The one thing she knew she'd always lacked was people-skills. This was probably why she had no friends. Skills like these were wasted on victims and fellow cops. Otherwise, she never got out and socialised. It was time to start making a conscious effort.

"Is everything okay, Miss Violent? Should I wait for you?"

"I won't need you for a few hours." She opened the door but didn't get out. She needed to do this. "Hey, what do you want me to call you?"

"I like Sammy."

"Sammy?" She thought for a second. Call it a hunch. "Is that your name?"

He shook his head. "It is Sofia Benito Alvarez. It was my mother's choice. I think she was hoping for a girl."

"Then Sammy it is." She leaned toward the door, placed one foot on the ground and stopped, again. She needed to push herself. "Curious, Sammy. Why me?"

The Divine Ledger

"Business is slow. I will need money to buy a transmission clutch soon. You are sure money." He added, "All money is good money, but I sometimes go days and get no fares."

"How much for a new clutch?"

"I have a friend who will do it for four hundred pesos. He can get the parts on the black market."

"Why not get the money from the government. I mean, this is a Communist country, isn't it?"

"It doesn't work that way. I put in a request order nine months ago. I haven't heard back yet, and honestly, I don't think I will." He shrugged. "It often takes years."

"Well it's always good to find a system that works. Can I see you tomorrow then?"

"After what you charged your friend for the ride, you can see me every day."

She got out and watched him drive away. It didn't make her feel any better, but it was a start.

The precinct continued to be an anthill of activity. The Captain was busy on the phone, but one officer saw her and raced over with two sets of prints. She immediately sent a text to Bradley. A quick confirmation was returned. One belonged to a Bob Henley from Montreal, while the other was a Daniel Windham, also from Quebec, Canada.

The investigation had already started and Bob was assumed to be one of the victims. He was a missing person from that area. He'd left to watch a hockey game and never made it back.

The second victim, Daniel, was killed in his hotel room. Like Beverly, he had won a trip to Cuba. He was a student working on a psychology doctorate.

Bob had recently met a man called Victor. His wife had mentioned it in her statement. But this was Cuba and there were thousands of Victors.

Violet thought about sharing that she had a Victor in her sights. She kept quiet.

"These murders in Canada," Captain Careva asked. "Do you think it's the same guy?"

"I'd bet on it. We don't get a lot of head hunters."

"What happened up there?"

"We're not sure. Twelve murders in ten days and no motive. The victims were all decapitated and the heads were never found, until a couple days ago. Right after those twelve were killed, he stopped so the case went cold. He made no mistakes and left no indicators."

"Were the people ever linked?"

"If they were, we never found it. There was a doctor, two teachers, a banker, three administrative types, a journalist, two computer nerds, a lab tech and a police officer. We think the police officer might have been a case of wrong place, wrong time."

"Interesting."

"We tried using the letters in their name to see if they spelled anything. Maybe there was a message in that. There was nothing."

"Anything else."

"All our victims had lethal doses of Nembutal."

"They were euthanized?"

"I know. What a humane way to kill someone, eh. We also think they were chloroformed before that." She remembered the sweet smell from Victor's room and again remained silent. "This guy really didn't want them to suffer. It's not what we normally see in a killer. We had our theories and speculation. I thought it might have something to do with baking. A dozen murders and the first and last happened in the back alley of a bakery. Well, that and the guy was an obvious flake."

"Mr. Henley was a banker and Beverly Shipstone was a clerk for Her Majesty's Secret Service. Daniel was a student. I don't know if history will repeat itself. Maybe we should stake out the banks and bakeries."

Violet smiled. It was as close to a joke as the Captain would ever get. She thought of her people-skills, or lack thereof. These were good people, but they didn't have a chance. Should she give them the last name? They'd want to now how long she'd been sitting on it. She could say she wasn't sure.

But why wasn't she sharing? It was simple. She wanted this killer for herself. She wanted to be the one to stop him. It was selfish and she'd need to get over that or he'd kill again. This was called people-skills.

"I'm going to tell you something and I don't want you to get pissed off."

"I don't think I understand, Miss Stormm."

"Believe me, I have that effect on people." She forced a smile, hoping it might be contagious. "I have a name."

Her smile wasn't contagious.

Chapter Thirty

Greg and Juanita decided that a walk to the Malecón wouldn't take as long as it would to find a cab. Malecón, was the name given to the wide walkway that ran five miles along the city's northern shoreline. On clear days you could see the Florida Keys with binoculars. Cloudy days limited you to the odd freight ship or sailboat. No matter what the weather, it was always a pleasant walk and there was a good chance you'd run into Alzophine the Great.

Juanita took Greg's hand as they crossed the busy highway. She didn't let it go until they were on the other side. Greg tried to gently free himself a couple of times, like a child might from a doting mother. She held tight.

"Don't be like that." She snapped.

"Like what? I know how to cross a street." He finally managed to pull his hand away.

"That's not the real problem, is it?"

"What are you talking about?"

"Hold my hand then. We're not crossing the street anymore."

"I don't want to."

"Why?"

"It's just that..."

"Just what? You worried someone might see us? Maybe they'll think we're together and they'll talk? I'll bet they can't wait to get on the phone and call your wife. Do they even know your wife?" She let out a mocking giggle. "Are you afraid of her?"

"You're being ridiculous." But that was exactly what he was worried about. What if someone *did* see them? What if his wife found out? What more could she do to him? And then there was Violet. What was her role in this hodgepodge of feelings? Did she even have a role? Violet was damn cute and even though she was rough around the edges, she wouldn't have to be smuggled out of the country if a serious relationship was pursued. Did he even want a serious relationship, with either of them? His eyes danced around while these thoughts floated in the dead space between his ears.

Juanita saw the rusty gears in his head meshing as if they were about to seize up. "My God, Greg. You think too much, and you worry like an expectant father. Just enjoy the blue sky, the birds, and the fresh air."

"To hell with the birds." He was growing to hate birds. "Did I tell you I saw them again?"

"No, you didn't. Where?"

"Violet and I were driving past the cemetery and the birds started to swarm. That guy appeared again, you know the one, with the hat. When the birds dispersed, the man was standing there. I turned to Violet and asked if she saw him. You won't believe what she said."

Greg gave her a second to guess and when she didn't, he continued. "She said she hadn't seen him, but he was right there. You couldn't miss him and yet she did. Isn't that crazy?"

He waited through the silence for a response he'd soon regret.

Juanita dropped Greg's hand. "Who's Violet?"

"Uh, that's all you pulled from the story? Not that she didn't see him?"

"Whatever." Without warning, the warm Cuban air chilled. "We're here."

Greg looked over to see a pair of chairs with a good-looking woman sitting in one of them. He had expected the darker Cuban skin, straw-like grey hair and a customary wart on the end of an oversized nose. He'd expected someone no less than a hundred years old. And where was the crystal ball?

The woman was either an extremely well kept fifty or still looking damn good in her forties. Dark crimson hair was wrapped in a scarf and the only thing grey on this woman was her eyes. They reminded Greg of smoke from a campfire, unpredictable and fuelled by an unbridled sense of spirit.

Juanita quickly sat in the chair across from the woman.

"Juanita. Is this your friend, Greg Miller?"

"You might say that."

"Give me your hand, Juanita's friend," she commanded.

Greg leaned forward and did as he was told. Her hand was smooth and tender. When a spark jumped from her fingertip, he tried to jerk his hand away.

She held tight. "No, Mr. Miller. I'm not done."

"You zapped me."

"It's a connection and it's as much from you as it is me." She turned his hand over and spat on the palm. Again, he tried to pull away, but her grip was strong. "Relax. It makes a better bond, for your secrets to escape."

"I don't have secrets."

Her eyes pressed his. "Everyone has secrets, Mr. Miller, like these dreams you keep having."

"What do you know about them?"

"They are not dreams."

"I have them when I'm sleeping. I think I know dreams when I have them."

"Our minds are most vulnerable when we are asleep. A softer mind makes finding others on a subconscious plane easier."

"A what?" His eyes flared as he shot Juanita a dirty look. "Did she just say I have a soft mind?"

The woman ignored him. "When you see the boy, you are leaving your consciousness and actually visiting him on a subconscious or neutral plane. It's a reverie connection of sorts."

"Let me get this right. You say my brain is soft, and that it takes a flight to Cuba for the night?"

"Please, Mr. Miller, give your mind more credit. Those who don't believe, are prisoners to the lies they are told. Imagine there are two of you and only one body. American Greg lives his life in the States while Cuban Greg lives his own life here. Normally neither knows the other exists. The dreams you are having is American Greg having a peek into the life of Cuban Greg."

Greg looked over both shoulders. "But there's only one of me, unless you know something I don't. Have you seen this guy, because I'd like to meet him?"

"The mind can exist in many places."

"Are you saying there's two of me?"

She let go of his hand. "That we know of."

"There's a man with the birds," Greg said, changing the subject. "What's his deal?"

"The man with birds is your destiny."

"Is he dangerous?"

"To me, no. To that couple standing over there, no."

Greg looked over to see the old couple sharing a bench and looking out at the ocean.

She tapped Greg on the back of the hand. "To you, the man is very dangerous."

Chapter Thirty-one

Ocean waves crashed hard against the seawall as Juanita and Greg made their way back downtown. Juanita had wanted to talk to him about what the woman had said. She even started the conversation twice. It died both times. Greg just wanted to put as much distance as he could between them and that woman.

"Subconscious planes, destiny, what a load of crap. Do you believe her?" Greg asked.

"We'd be fools not to."

"I can't believe you bought that."

"Everybody in Havana knows her. Many have gone to see her. Usually it's because they've lost something important or they're struggling with a life choice. She always knows. The woman is brilliant."

"Do you think she can read minds too?"

"Of course she can, but I'm sure she doesn't hold it against you. She's a professional and wouldn't let it bother her that you can be a bit of an ass at times."

The Divine Ledger

"Really? I think I'm a nice guy." He rolled his eyes, making sure she saw. "I'm going to the University. Do you know if he's there today?"

She shook her head and looked away. "I haven't heard from him."

When they reached the next bus stop, he stopped. "Can you at least tell me which bus I should take?"

She put her index finger to her chin and pretended to give it some thought. "That depends."

"On what?"

"On whether or not you're going to tell me who this Violet is."

"Is that what this is all about? I thought you weren't interested in me."

"What can I say. I'm a little hurt that I could be replaced so quickly."

"It's nothing like that." It was an easy decision to tell her what she wanted to hear. It was a trick he'd learned from all those years with Anne. "Violet's just some detective working a case. She's older, not attractive, and hard to get along with."

Juanita also lied. "There. Now we're good."

"Good."

As promised, she put him on the right bus.

As the bus lumbered along he tried to shake all the women from his mind. Each one was an unneeded distraction. These women couldn't compete with finding his tombstone, or meeting the boy. That being said, the tombstone had been just a dream. He hadn't actually seen it, didn't know if it was really out there. Heck, why was that man with the big black hat there then? It wasn't coincidence.

He looked out the window of the bus to see if anybody was following. There was nobody. A large complex began to sprawl several city blocks and a sign came into view, Universidad de La Habana. This was his stop.

He stepped off the bus and started to count the one hundred steps as he climbed them.

She came out of nowhere. "Hi Greg."

The girl, a shy little local with long ringlets and black-rimmed glasses, bumped into him from behind and dropped a couple of books. She bent down to pick them up. Greg knelt to help her. "Good morning, Simonne."

Her eyes met his. It was an intense stare, like a child daring her friend to eat a bug. "Did you still want to meet Ricky?"

"I do."

"Are you going to tell me how you know him?"

"I, uh..." Could he tell her? What would he say, he's an astral plane acquaintance or a dream buddy? Maybe he should try a well-crafted lie. Except he'd never been any good at well-crafted lies.

She repeated herself. "I need to know how you know him."

"I've been dreaming of the kid ever since he was about three." He abruptly stopped himself. It was blurted, an act of desperation.

"Thank you, Greg," Simonne whispered. "He's in the Psychology Complex, room four eighty-seven."

"Hold it. What I just said didn't bother you?"

"Hardly."

"And this Psychology Complex, is it on the map?"

"No, it's not, but I can take you there."

"And it's psychology?"

"That's correct," she said as she stood up. She spoke loudly enough for anyone within earshot to hear. "The teacher's lounge is this way, Sir. I can take you there."

Greg followed her up the steps and through the courtyard. "He's on the lower floor of this facility." She pulled out a set of keys and unlocked a door at the back of the lecture building. It led to a staircase.

"Why do you have keys?"

"All the research basements are locked. You have to be involved in one of their programs. We're usually hand-picked"

"Why didn't they know him at the office?"

"He was never a student."

"What does he do here?"

Her face contorted for a second. "I think I should let him explain. Is he ever going to be surprised to see you?"

"Why do you say that?"

"Again, get that from Ricky. I don't know enough to explain any of it properly. He knows everything. The guy's a genius."

Ricky was talking to another kid when they entered the room. He had his back to them but was easy to spot. Greg had twenty years of looking at that head of hair. Ricky's conversation came to an abrupt stop. He didn't have to see Greg to know he was there.

He turned and came right over. "It's you!"

Greg held out his hand. "I'm Greg."

"Oh, I know who you are." Ricky took his hand and shook it for all he was worth. "My God, it's really you. You're real."

"I am."

Simonne's chubby cheeks dimpled as the grin stretched across her face. "I found him wandering the courtyard yesterday."

"And you brought him here." Ricky was still holding on to Greg's hand, his stare as thrilled as a small boy's eyes on Christmas morning. "I had another dream last night. You were visiting my Aunt."

"Juanita, she's your Aunt?" Greg asked.

"I call her that. I'm not sure what else to call her. All I know is that I feel safe around her. Some days she's like a big sister and others, she's more like a mother. We look out for each other."

"She's a good woman."

"She is." He took a step back to take Greg in. "My God, I can't believe you're really here. Do you want to go for a coffee or grab a bite of food?"

Greg looked down at Ricky's outstretched hand. It was still holding his almost a minute after the handshake. He used it to pull the boy in for a hug. And why not, he had known him for close to twenty years. "Sounds good. Damn, I'm glad I came."

Ricky smiled and wished he could say the same.

Chapter Thirty-two

Violet had been right about Captain Careva being upset at her holding back information, especially when it was the name and address of the killer. But a professional scolding of sorts was all he could give her. They needed her as much as she needed them. Violet was the only reason why each victim wasn't a Jane or John Doe. That being said, pushing her luck with the ones who gave her access to the bodies was poor judgement.

In her warped threads of thought, she could justify holding out on them. She was on the case first. They were professionals and never would have allowed her to sit in that chair with Victor's beer. That wasn't playing by the rules. The room would have been crawling with third world forensics. They would have stopped her from touching anything and thought her nuts for even wanting to. You just don't tamper with the evidence. But she was a little nuts. That was what gave her the edge.

She was glad to see that Greg and her cabbie friend weren't around when she left the precinct. It was time to concentrate. She didn't need to be thinking about clutches, a cemetery full of birds or the dream boy. They weren't the components of her case. All that really mattered was what motivated her killer, and which poor sap he was going to butcher next. So far, they'd all been tourists. So, who else had won contests where the prize was a trip to Cuba? She fired off a text to Bradley. He could run the airline tickets, see if there had been a block of them bought by the same person or company.

Violet had only taken a dozen steps past the precinct gate when the birds started to gather. For the second time today, they were in huge numbers and swarming like bees. She turned back to the guard. "Does this kind of thing happen often?"

"A handful, sure. Never this many."

As they got closer, the guard started to inch for cover. Violet inched towards a pair of parked cars. There was nowhere else for her to run. The swarm moved in quickly and instantly enveloped her and the two cars. They squawked and flapped like someone shaking angry budgies out of a wet umbrella. Birds bounced off the fenders and off windows, some landing on the ground. They sat stunned for a few seconds before shaking it off. Some were bleeding. All of them were out to get her.

Violet drew her gun. It was an instinct, much like handing a fake number to a guy in a nightclub. They fluttered over her head, slapping her with their wings. How many could she cap? Was she allowed to discharge a firearm in a Communist country?

She waved the barrel of the gun at them as she crouched lower. One bird struck the trunk and somersaulted toward her face. She turned her head, but it still hurt as it bounced off her temple and got tangled in her hair.

Running wasn't an option. She could barely see. At least they weren't pecking at her. Then, as her sanity reached its limits, the attack stopped. The black mass lifted, moved right and left, then disappeared down an alley. Violet stood up slowly, her hair in a mess from the effects of assaulting wings and feet.

Her gun was still drawn and loosely aimed at the alley as she tried to catch her breath. The hell with Cuban laws, if the birds returned, she'd kill as many as she could.

A few seconds passed, followed by a handful more. The guard returned to his post and tried to get Violet's attention. "Ma'am. Put the gun away, please. The birds are gone."

The birds were gone, except for a few that had broken their necks on the fenders and bumpers. They remained on the ground at her feet. One still dangled from her hair. Violet ignored it and poised herself for the mob of birds to return. Instead, a frail old woman made her way out of the alley. She walked with a limp and should have had a cane, if only to beat off the birds. A lone bird sat on the woman's shoulder. It looked a bit like a pirate's mini-parrot. Violet had to check to see if the old woman had a wooden leg. They were skinny and bent, but they were real.

"Ma'am?" It was the voice again.

Violet didn't hear him. Instead she focused on the shawl that was draped over the old woman's shoulders. Closer to white than pink, it might have been red in its day. That must have been back when dinosaurs traipsed through swamps, and the sun still revolved around the earth. The old lady carried a purse and a book under her arm, both made of black leather. They were slightly worn and looked like they'd been cut from the same side of beef.

"Please Ma'am." The cop put his hand on her shoulder. "You need to put the gun away."

"Yes. Of course." Violet let the guard gently hold her forearm and guide the gun back into her purse. "What just happened?"

"Birds, Ma'am." He pulled the dead bird from her hair and dropped it to the ground.

"Where'd they go?"

"I'm not sure."

"Damn, I hate those things." She tried to smooth her hair back into place. "I think it's time for a drink. It's gotta be five o'clock somewhere."

The guard was lost on the sarcasm. "It's barely noon."

"Did you blink and miss all this?"

The guard frowned at her comment and took a step back. The Captain was coming.

"Good, Detective Stormm. You're still here."

Violet turned around. "Yes, Captain Careva?"

"There's been another murder. It just got called in."

"Okay." Violet watched the old lady make her way down the street. Then she took another glance down the back alley where the birds had fled. The Captain started for the precinct and Violet slowly followed. Over her shoulder she could see the bird that had been trapped in her hair and the ones on the ground with broken necks. They were standing, stretching their wings and rolling their necks. Seconds later they were taking flight.

"Damn." Violet picked up the pace and bumped into the back of Captain Careva.

Chapter Thirty-three

Most cafeteria food was known for being fair at best. At the University of Havana, Greg found it a delightful treat. It made him wish that he'd found this place earlier. Other than the restaurant with the long line-up, this food looked and smelled amazing. Ricky watched as Greg filled his plate. He watched as if they'd done this before.

Greg looked back and gave him a fatherly shove. "Come Ricky, you have to eat something."

Ricky broke his trance and chose a sandwich. There was a quiet table in the corner and they made their way over to it.

"So what courses are you taking?"

"No courses. I'm studying the mind."

"Like brain mapping?"

Ricky took a seat. "Not really. I'm trying to figure out what the Russians are doing."

"The Russians?"

Ricky looked around. "I shouldn't say anymore."

"What are you talking about?"

"No. Not here." He put his sandwich down. "You shouldn't have come here."

"But I…"

"Don't get me wrong. It's great to see you."

"But you don't want me in Cuba?"

"I can't protect you here." His voice rose as the sentence came out.

Greg didn't argue. "I believe you. In my dreams I saw my own tombstone."

"For real? Then we need to talk." He grabbed Greg's arm and pulled him up from his chair. "Come with me."

Greg grabbed his sandwich as they fled. "Where are we going?"

"Somewhere safe, so we can talk." Ricky dragged Greg out of the cafeteria. They exited the building and headed for a four-door BMW sedan. Greg tried to keep up as he ate.

"This is *your* car?" Greg asked.

"Simonne's car. I have a spare set of keys."

Ricky did a quick shoulder check and sped out of the parking lot. The ride was short and neither of them spoke. Greg wanted to, but Ricky kept stopping him. There was only one place where Ricky felt safe telling his story. He had found the place as a child and remembered it whenever he wanted to purge the madness from his brain. A favourite stuffed teddy bear heard most of his theories and confessions. There'd be no judgement from the fake brown fur stuffed with fluff.

He parked the car in a courtyard a block away from Juanita's apartment. "Come quick, before they see us."

Ricky took Greg's hand and just like in the dream, dragged him down the street and through the doorway. It was *the* doorway. All his life he had wanted to talk to Greg and wanted to tell him his story. Instead, the bear had been the proxy.

In the main floor closet, large electrical wires hung down like jungle vines. Ricky chose a spot on the floor and sat. Greg never bothered to question how strange this all seemed and took the spot beside him.

The words couldn't come out quickly enough. "We have Russian scientists experimenting on stray cats. It's a mind discipline thing, communication without words. I hear they're getting close to making this happen."

"And you're trying to get a hold of their notes?"

"I work for them, in their labs. I've seen their notes, even talked to them. It's crazy stuff and way above me. The science isn't hard. It's how they're getting the results that make no sense. Our math doesn't figure into their work."

"Science without math? Is that even possible?"

"No." He leaned closer. "You've heard of Hemingway and his love of cats?"

"Sure, he had a house full of them."

"He also had a lot of Russian friends. They'd sit out at his place and drink their faces off. It's rumoured that one of the Russians saw something in the cats."

"The cats?"

"There were so many of them and they were somewhat feral. Mr. Hemingway wasn't feeding them because the grounds had mice and birds. He was only giving them water and shelter."

"What did this guy see in these cats?"

"They were starting to hunt in packs, and not like dogs or wolves. These were advanced packs. They'd hunt with a precision that couldn't be explained. It was like each one knew what the other was thinking. Without any communication, these cats would herd their prey to the others. The kills were then shared."

"Cats don't hunt like that."

"Domestic ones don't, but if the conditions are right, they do." He nervously tapped at the wires while Greg tried to absorb what he had said.

Greg had to wonder how many times the boy had sat there and tapped the wires while the bear looked on with an expression as blank as his likely was.

"Raptors were the only other creatures presumed to hunt by reading each other's minds and that's only speculation. You can't learn much from that."

"What about birds? Are they sharing a mind when they fly in swarms?"

"It's different with birds, fish too. In those, each bird only worries about the birds in their vicinity. It's a well played game of follow the leader and their reflexes are amazing. These cats are actually sending thoughts to each other."

"And the Russian want this for…"

"Their armies. Imagine the ultimate radio silence."

"Is that what's going on between you and me?"

"That's what I'm trying to figure out. I've caught wind of a drug that might induce this effect."

"And you think you might have been given this drug?"

"Me, you, Juanita. We're all linked. I just don't know how it's administered or whether both parties need to be taking it. I mean it could be in the food, water, maybe even airborne. I just don't know."

This was big. Greg felt a shiver in his spine. If the Russians, or anybody for that matter, developed that kind of technology, it would be a game-changer. "What's this drug called?"

"I have no idea. I call it the Hemingway Serum." He got up, grabbed two sodas from the fridge and returned to the closet. He opened them and handed one to Greg. "Nobody can know about this, so say nothing. I haven't even told Auntie Juanita."

"Why tell me then?"

"Last night I had another dream. You were being attacked and a gun was being fired. Have you seen anything odd?"

"Just the guy at the cemetery. I've seen my headstone there, in my dreams."

"Is it the guy with the birds? He freaks me out."

"It is. How long have you seen him?"

"My whole life. I used to imagine you walking me home, so the guy couldn't get me. He was always watching, and you kept me safe."

"I remember the dreams, but I never saw him." Greg thought of the drug. If it was real, then this kid must have been drugged as a child. It also meant that the kid had found him, so he likely wasn't the one being drugged. Hell, maybe he was and he found the kid. But the boy was the stronger force, which made sense because he had only dreamt of Cuba. So how did the boy know about him and what did this make them. The kid felt like family. "How'd you find out about all this?"

"I was dating a girl, still dating her. She's the daughter of one of the scientists here. You've met her."

"Simonne?"

"Yes. I found out about the serum through her. She was drunk and going on about one of her father's conversations that she overheard. It was too weird for her and she had to tell someone. I never mentioned it again and I doubt she remembers telling me."

"You think she forgot?"

"That, or she loves me enough to pretend."

"You and your aunt need to get out of Cuba."

"No, Greg. You need to get out of here. I think they've used me to lure you here. They want to see how we tick as a team. You being here is dangerous for both of us."

"But the tombstone?"

"Think about it. How can there be a tombstone with your name on it unless you die here. If you're not here…"

Greg finished his sentence. "Then I don't die here and there's no tombstone." It made sense.

"You're not safe and being here is dangerous for anyone you come into contact with. Can you understand that?"

"I'll think about it." Greg held one of the wires. "Why here?"

"The electricity seems to scramble the transmission of my thoughts. We can talk and think freely without him finding out."

"Him? You mean the man with all the birds?"

"No. Not him." Ricky got up and stepped out of the closet. "I've said too much."

Chapter Thirty-four

When Greg finally made his way back to the hotel, there was a lovely blonde in a black bikini lounging at the pool. A single golden silk tassel hung off her right hip, almost touching the ground. There was a cold beer in her hand and three empties beside her. They were neatly lined up like sentries, unlike the folders of past victims. Those were scattered on the ground as if pee-training a new puppy. He noticed the beer in her hand was almost empty, so he grabbed two more and headed over.

"Mind if I sit here?" He offered Violet one of the beers.

"Knock yourself out." She took it, downed the last of hers, and set the empty with the others. "And before you start anything, I've had a rough day."

Greg took a seat on the lounge chair beside her, feeling a little odd being fully dressed. "Tell me about it."

"Ladies first," she joked. "How was your day?"

He ignored the insult. "Well, I saw this deranged voodoo lady who went on about my brain being in two places. I also met that boy I was telling you about."

"The dream kid?"

"Yes. He was at the University. I found out some crazy shit."

"You just met a kid you've known for two decades, a kid that you've only seen in your dreams. No shit you're going to hear some weird crap."

"I suppose."

"What about the woman, Joanne is it?"

"Juanita. She's mad at me."

"I doubt that, more likely she's messing with you." She took a swallow. "You shouldn't have slept with her so fast."

"I didn't…"

Violet cut him a daring glance. "I'm a detective, remember? You have way too many tells. You might as well tattoo single and desperate across your forehead. Nobody wants to be a conquest, Greg."

"I think it had more to do with how weird we felt afterward. I mean, have you ever done it and regretted it right away?"

"Sex is passion. It's not something you should be analysing. And it's definitely not something to regret." She reached for her purse.

Greg stole a glance at her chest while she took a quick look at her phone. He noticed her fullness, the golden skin wet with sweat and the fabric stretched to the contours of her nipples. He wouldn't regret having anything to do with those. Beads of sweat pooled in the recesses of her collarbone. It was captivating. They'd be salty. Everything tastes better with a little salt. "So…"

She set the beer down. "Don't know how…to sew that is."

That was a joke. Was she being playful? Her eyes were a little glassy now, the beer taking over her senses. She was flirting and this time he'd play it cool. "You had a bad day?"

"Two more dead and I was attacked by your fuck'n birds. That's when I decided to call it a day. Let the clues come to me for a change."

"You saw the birds, downtown?" That put his eyes back in his head. "Did you see the guy this time?"

"No, I did not see the guy. I did however see a walking fossil of a woman. Bottom line, my death toll is rising and the perp isn't dropping any leads."

The Divine Ledger

"No guy with the birds? He wears a big hat and a coat."

"So you told me. Didn't see him."

"He wears leather gloves and boots."

"Still a no, Greg."

"That sucks."

"Ya know what sucks?" She waited for a second. "This guy could kill another ten times. Ten times and I know for a fact that there'll be no clues." She took a long swig, which took the bottle to half full, or half empty, depending on whether you were buying.

Greg let his eyes wander back to her flat waist. Was that a six pack? Wow. He couldn't stop himself as his eyes drifted over the curves of her hips, and down those long slender legs. She was a damn attractive woman. Was he wrong to want her so soon after being with Juanita? He was pretty sure they were finished with whatever they'd dabbled in. The woman was sweet, but the weirdness didn't need repeating. "You know, I could grab a few more beers and we could take this up to my place."

"Really, Greg?" Her eyes narrowed. "Did you know I spent the afternoon with a corpse? I was scraping fingernails, toenails, taking hair samples."

"Hair? I thought you said the body was headless?"

She raised an eyebrow.

"Oh." The mental image disgusted him.

When her phone chimed, she took a peek. It was Bradley. This was the message she had been waiting for. She started reading.

Greg persisted, "I was just thinking…"

She stopped reading and looked up. "Do you pride yourself in making the same mistakes over and over again? I mean, that fucking dead guy has a better chance at getting me in the sack." She shot him a half-drunk wink, "rigor mortis and all."

"I never said anything about…"

"Seriously. No wonder this Juanita woman is messing with you. You're like a teenager on his first band trip."

"I'm sorry."

"I wasn't asking for an apology, just trying to let you down easy."

"That was easy?"

She laughed. "You make it way too easy. And here I thought today was a total write-off." She tossed the phone in her purse. "Are we good?"

"Sure." He'd been caught, caged and clipped. "Was that more dead-guy news?"

"My buddy Bradley." The bottle went back to her lips. It was drained. "He found something in common with the Vancouver victims."

"That's good news, isn't it?"

"Good news, bad news. They were all adopted. That's a link, but it makes it tough. Bradley's been trying to pull up shit on their birth parents. He's not having much luck. Here's the fun part. Each one had a mother named Mary. That was the numerology name Bradley pulled from the snapshots of skull patterns in Sayulita."

"The killer sounds like he's messing with you?"

"Nah, I think it may be religious."

"And the last names?"

"He can't find any surnames or father's names."

"Isn't that a little strange?"

"Strange, but not that uncommon. Records get lost and orphans seldom look up their real parents. Everything they need comes with their adopted parents; birth certificates, social insurance numbers, passports."

"Still, that's one hell of a coincidence. I don't buy it."

"Thanks." Violet spun around and sat up. "I thought it was just me being overly suspicious. I think the killer knew the parents. This is either a revenge thing, or a cover-up. That would make these people nothing more than loose ends."

"That's a pretty wild assumption."

"No, you thinking we'd have sex is a wild assumption. What I've got is a theory. Wanna hear another one?"

"If you promise to drop the whole, me hitting on you."

"Already done."

"Ouch." Greg shook his head. God help the one that does win her heart. "Okay, what's your other theory?"

The Divine Ledger

"What if there's some secret society behind all this. People disappear, names vanish, and all because they have to protect their secret. It would explain the ritual killings."

Chapter Thirty-five

A fifth beer was a must, after the day Victor had just endured. But, as bad as it had been for him, it had been worse for the man he had killed earlier. A weight of remorse grew with every victim and the day wasn't over. The golden ale not only helped him cope, but allowed him to focus. The waitress brought the beer, opened it, and set it down.

"Last one. It's closing time."

Victor grabbed her wrist. "Wait. Where are you going?"

"Pardon?"

"You're leaving before I can give you a tip." He handed her five convertible pesos and immediately let go of her wrist. "You didn't grab one last time either. Where I come from, the girls don't leave until they've received their tip."

"This isn't that place." She smiled back at him. He meant no harm. "Most people here don't mind if I leave before getting a tip."

"The hell with those people."

"Look around." They both gazed across room. "Everyone's on vacation. It's not about me."

"But this is your livelihood. Tips are a big part of it."

"That's a noble thought, but we're a little short-staffed. I really need to keep moving."

The Divine Ledger

"I understand." He waved his hand. "Go, take care of the cheapskates and deadbeats."

"Don't worry. I won't forget you."

Victor watched her leave. That wasn't his concern. She was off to fill trays with drinks, deliver them and, on occasion, get a peso or two. It was one hell of a way to scratch a living. Meanwhile, fellow Cubans did less or nothing and still got their apartments and food stamps. It was a system that didn't reward hard work. Nothing in this world was fair any more.

"Hey," Victor shouted. He watched as the fat woman, too caught up in her moment to see him, stepped back into his table. His beer teetered and fell to the floor. The cold suds shot from the bottle as it spun to a stop.

The lady looked back and then down, shrugged and started for the door. Victor watched her leave before picking up the near-empty bottle. He wanted to throw it at her but stopped himself. Was it the clumsy cow he was mad at, or the path his life had taken?

It didn't take long for the waitress to show up with a rag. "Sorry about that. I'll get you another one."

"Isn't it closing time?"

"I'll let you take it with you."

Victor handed her the bottle. "That sounds more than fair."

She brought the beer and politely escorted him to the front door. "Have a good night."

"You too."

He tried to hand her a few pesos, but once again she was gone. Closing time meant there were tables to clear and, although it wasn't her job to lock up, it was to get the tables wiped and the chairs put up. Tomorrow the carpets would be vacuumed and the beer coolers would be restocked. For now, it was late and more about getting the customers out the door.

Soon the tables were bare, except for the turned over chairs. The bartender walked her to the front door and locked it behind her. Outside, Victor was standing on the edge of the curb, nursing the last of his beer.

"Hey big tipper, you still here?"

He shrugged. "I'm guessing cabs don't run this late."

"They do, but not around here. Are you far away?"

"No. I'm just a few blocks. Um, I'm just not sure which direction. I usually toss out an address and the cab driver does the rest."

"Is it safe to say it's not the distance, but the direction?"

"Yes."

"Do you have the address?"

Victor was clumsy as he pulled a card out of his pocket. He held it at arms length to read. "Some Hotel Issabella."

She took the card, read it and handed it back to him. "That's the Hotel Santa Isabel?"

He took the card and flipped it in his fingers before putting it away. "I just need you to point me in the right direction, maybe give me a heads-up on how many blocks. It all looks so different at night."

"I live just up the street from this place."

"Really? I'll give you ten convertibles to be my guide."

That was a week's worth of groceries. "You're being ridiculous."

"Not really. I'd pay that much for a cab. How is his time worth more than yours?"

Her eyes casually swept over him. She considered herself a good judge of character. "You can walk with me part way. I'll think about the money."

"Thank you." He held out a ten and then an arm for her to take. "Please take it. I thought I'd be sleeping on a park bench."

As if ashamed, she took the ten and slipped it into her pocket. "Come, before I change my mind."

She took his arm and let this perfect gentleman of a man escort her across the street and along the sidewalk. Most people had turned in for the night. The odd car drove by and on one corner a group of teenagers were smoking.

Victor thought about the twenty-eight acres of Yesler Terrace back in Seattle and the slums in the Bronx. These were areas where you wouldn't walk at two in the morning. Every town had an area like that, every town except Havana. These folks were safe anywhere in the city. Was it a lifestyle thing or because the laws were tough on crime?

"It's a beautiful city," Victor admitted.

She smiled. "It has its challenges. Tourists don't often stay long enough to see them."

"I've travelled the world. You can't hide from the challenges."

"What are your challenges, other than finding your way back to your hotel?"

"Work." It came out quicker than he expected. "I don't like what I do, but how many people do? We all have to do things we don't like."

"You can always change it."

"Just like that?"

"Yes." She gave his arm a friendly squeeze. "Just like that."

"I wish I could. Responsibility has a pretty tight stranglehold on me."

"Change isn't hard. The inability to see the need for it is the hardest part, and I think you've got that covered."

"I suppose you're right. If only it was that easy."

Her apartment came into view as they rounded the corner. She slipped her arm free. "This is my place."

"And I think my place is that way." He pointed down the street. "Am I right?"

"You are." She started for the doorway and stopped in the threshold. Then she turned back to him. "I've found that if you can't change what you do, then you really need to embrace it. Fighting it doesn't help."

"That is very good advice. Thank you." He reached inside his pocket and pulled the cloth from the plastic bag. She didn't see it as he stepped toward her. "You've been a big help."

Kevin Weisbeck

Chapter Thirty-six

Violet set her coffee down at Greg's table with a heavy clunk as she took a seat across from him. Most of the breakfast crowd had already passed through. The stragglers were bright-eyed and looking forward to a day of old buildings, history and shopping for souvenirs. They wore khaki shorts, bright skirts, tank tops and t-shirts with stupid sayings. And unlike Violet, they weren't hung over.

She was dressed in jeans and a favourite heavy cotton white blouse that had been stitched several times to mend bullet holes. "Mind if I sit with you?"

"What, no Danish? No insult?" Greg pulled a bottle of Visine out of his shirt pocket and slid it over to her. "Here, I thought you might need this."

The Visine was pushed back toward him. "Save it. I already got the *time to grow up* speech from Bradley an hour ago."

"You were awake an hour ago?"

"Thanks to him I was."

"Hey, about last night. I was being a bit of a dick and you were kinda being the other genitalia."

The Divine Ledger

Her eyes flared as she cocked her head and nodded. "Well put, Gregory."

"I'm sorry. You were drunk and I…"

"I wasn't drunk. I was on the road to drunk." She put the mug up to her mouth using both hands and savoured another sip before continuing. "I finished the trip in my room."

"I can see that."

"Haven't you ever wondered why I'm single, Greg? I mean, I'd consider myself cute, right?"

"I'll give you that," he cautiously answered.

"And I've shot three people. That's kinda cool. It's always a good icebreaker."

"You're definitely a double threat, being able to take care of yourself."

"I speak Russian, German, French and Mandarin." She rolled her eyes. "Never thought I'd need Spanish."

"Wow, I'm impressed."

"Thing is, there's a lot of damage with this package. It's like I was dropped and run over a few times by the delivery truck."

Greg had to think before responding. Was it a trap? "Come on. You can't be that bad."

"That's because you're not paying attention to what's inside." She casually reached across the table and took the Danish off his plate. "Look, there's nothing wrong with enjoying yourself while you can. You're a good guy and you'll be married again soon enough. I don't need a crystal ball to see that. It's what guys like you do. Just remember, when you do, the fun ends with the diamond ring. That thing has a hidden power that you guys don't see until it's too late."

"I know it sounds crazy, but I'm looking forward to being settled again."

"That's because you're extremely insecure and you don't know any better. If I wasn't so damaged, I might drag you through the sheets once or twice, give you a taste of the other side. I'm just fighting too many demons myself right now to help you out."

Greg returned a blank stare. His mind had become lost in those sheets.

Her phone chimed. "Okay if I check this?"

"Go ahead. Another killing?"

She read for a second. "What else. They've sent a squad car. It should be sitting out front."

"I hope your day goes better than yesterday."

"I just need him to screw up and leave me a lead before he's done. Hey if you need a cab, use Sammy. He needs a new clutch."

Greg gave her a thumbs up. There was a heart in that chest. "Will do."

Violet got up, tucked the phone away and let the squad car take her across town to the Ingesia Del Santo Cristo Del Buen Viaje. It was a church. Two towers rose three stories from the stone walls. A squad car was parked at the edge of the gathered crowd.

Violet took a look at the eighteenth-century building. Even to her, who wasn't that impressed by the Havana skyline, it was breathtaking. The forty-foot bell towers stood at the front corners. Stained glass hid behind the shrubs, all enclosed by the wrought iron gates.

"The body's in the church?"

"No." The officer exited the car and started to push his way through the courtyard. Violet followed.

"Our victim's down the alley."

Violet tried not to lose him. "Why is it so busy today?"

"Up until now the murders haven't been downtown. They were in quiet back alleys and lonely back streets. We can keep them out of the news and more importantly, away from the tourists."

Violet didn't need to ask when the murder had happened. Downtown was a busy place during the day. The only time Havana was quiet was when it was sleeping. "The killer's getting brave."

The officer grabbed her by the arm and started to drag her through the crowd as it thickened. "People here don't see a lot of murders. Havana has known only a little crime. No one steps out of line because the penalty is too high. We must protect our tourism. It cannot get out that it is dangerous to come here or we all lose."

"So…"

"These crowds have formed on their own. They've created this barrier to keep the tourists away. These locals are protecting their interests. You wouldn't be getting through here without me."

The crowd reluctantly broke, revealing a body propped against the wall. It was covered with a blanket. Violet walked over to the blanket and pulled it back. There was no purse, no identification and once again, there was little blood. The victim looked like a prop out of a movie scene.

She got down on her knees and leaned in close to put her nose up to the severed skin of the neck. "Smell that?"

The officer leaned forward, closed his eyes and took a sniff. He did smell something. "It's sweet."

"That's chloroform. Check to see if anybody has bought or stolen any. Try pharmacies, chemistry labs, and hospitals."

The officer took off. There was no doubt this was Victor's handiwork. Another officer took the corpse's hand and ran one of the fingers over an inkpad. Then he rolled the finger onto the pad of paper and handed it to Violet. "The Captain said you wouldn't mind."

She took it. "Of course."

Taking out her phone, she snapped an image for Bradley. The phone made a whooshing sound and the text was sent. Then she set the phone down and started scratching for clues. It was more out of habit than necessity. She knew who was doing the killing, and she knew what he looked like. Havana police knew what he looked like too. She'd had the sketch forwarded from Sayulita and given them the photo from Bradley. It hadn't helped.

This crime scene was a waste of time so she dialled Bradley.

"I'm not done yet, Stormm."

"I know, but I'm not going to find this guy unless I can get to know him better. What have you found out?"

"It's like the guy doesn't exist. I've tried school records, criminal records, traffic fines. He's not a part of any volunteer groups. He owes no money, doesn't have a mortgage. I've even tapped into tax records for a dozen countries including Canada, England and the United States. There's nothing."

"How is that possible? Everybody owes something?"

"I don't know. It's like he's lived his whole life in his mother's basement being home schooled and paying cash that he gets from an undocumented paper route. That kind of fits the bill though, for a serial killer, doesn't it? It's not like your average Joe has time to do this sort of shit."

"Okay. Keep searching. Try and see if there's anyone that matches his MO. Same person, different name? Any more on Mary?"

"Nothing. Maybe when he dumps these skulls it'll give me his father's name."

"That numerology shit?" Violet joked.

"It's not shit. It lined up with the victim's mothers. That's not a coincidence."

"True, but I don't want to wait years for that to happen."

"I'll text you that name in a second."

"Thanks, Brad."

Violet hung up and went back to the body. There was a thin flat square in her front pocket. "Could I get a hand here, please."

Two of the officers came over.

"Can we move her yet?" Violet asked.

The two looked at each other and shrugged. "They have their photos so I don't see why not. We'll have to move her to get her off the streets."

"Good. Flatten her out on her back. I want that square in her pocket."

She tried to slip the square out. Could it be a book of matches? This would put her somewhere, maybe a place she frequented. Maybe she met this guy at that place. Maybe he'd come back. This was hope. "You're slipping Victor."

The jeans were tight. It took a minute of wiggling to extract the matchbook. They hadn't been used, but that wasn't what caught Violet's eye. It was the fact that they'd come from the Copacabana Hotel.

As she read the hotel's name her phone chimed. She didn't need to look at the text to know who the victim was. For the first time, nausea settled in her stomach. She fought it and checked the text for confirmation. "Damn it."

Chapter Thirty-seven

Violet took the front stairs of the Copacabana one slow step at a time. She needed to be the one to tell Greg, but how? He'd slept with the woman. She kept reminding herself that it wasn't love between the two of them. Still, Greg was an emotional guy who would take it hard. He hadn't been hardened by death and probably never would be.

She spotted the one-eyed cat walking along the edge of the pool, so she cut through the restaurant for a slice of cheese. It was like he knew she was coming and waited by one of the lounge chairs.

"How about I give you this and you tell him?"

The cat purred as it nibbled the orange square smaller. It allowed Violet's thoughts to tumble, like water over rocks. Greg was a bit on the soft side as far as men went, but he could handle it. But unlike telling the Captain about Victor's name, she'd need to use tact. Developing that was a work in progress.

She looked up to the window of his room. The curtains were being jostled around. Was it the housekeeper, vacuuming them? In Cuba? It looked more like a body was being pressed against them in a scuffle. Violet drew the gun from her purse and started for the stairs.

She took the steps two at a time. When she saw the door ajar, she put her shoulder into it and slammed it against the wall. That stopped the intruder from strangling Greg, who was trying to wheel around and get free. The man slammed an elbow into Greg's throat, knocking him to the floor.

Violet raised the gun and locked it on her target. "Freeze!"

The man remained calm as he backed toward the patio. He put his left palm up and slowly passed in front of his face from right to left. Violet pulled the trigger. The shot missed left, as if he had willed it that way. The glass door shattered.

She squeezed the trigger again as the man crashed through the spider web of fractured glass. This time the gun's hammer jammed. She dropped it and charged across the room. Greg tried to get up and Violet shoved him back to the floor as she stepped over him.

From the balcony, she saw the man land on the ground twenty feet below. He rolled, got up and headed for the pool. Her purse was still sitting on the chair where she'd tossed it. The man grabbed it, turned back and took a second to study her. She took that time to study him. It was Victor.

She leaned over the railing and willed herself to jump. She couldn't. She'd only break her neck. "Fuck!"

Greg met her on the patio. "He jumped? That's thirty feet."

"More like twenty, but it's more than I'm willing to attempt."

"What are you doing here, not that I'm not happy to see you?"

"Damn it." She pulled her eyes from the chair where her purse once sat. Her hand slapped at her back pocket. At least she had her phone. That purse was her lifeline.

"What's wrong?"

"The guy grabbed my purse, wallet, ID, passport."

"Shit. He was rummaging around my room when I walked in." Greg ran to the safe. It was open. "He's got my passport too."

"Anything else?"

The Divine Ledger

"No. I think I caught him off guard when I arrived. The guy was probably looking for money, cameras and whatever else he might be able to sell."

Violet nodded, but she had to wonder, why was Victor in Greg's room? Did Greg know him? Either way, she had been begging for a clue and she just got it. Victor was starting to slip up. "We should call the police."

"I thought you said you were a cop."

"Not here."

Violet called the Captain and he quickly sent a car. She eavesdropped as Greg told his story to the officer. He didn't tell his story with the conviction of a man who had just been robbed. He confirmed what he'd told them and that became the statement for the record. When asked if they got a good look at the assailant, both Violet and Greg said no. He was Caucasian, darker hair and about six feet tall. In other words, he looked like half the tourists in Cuba

It took an hour to give the statements and for Greg to get a new room. Violet grabbed two beers and headed for a spot by the pool. "Come."

Greg didn't buy Violet's good cop act. "You're holding back. What aren't you telling me?"

"You spill first. Why were you being robbed?"

"I don't know. I'm in Cuba?"

"Okay, tell me when you're ready."

"There's nothing to tell." Greg leaned back and switched gears. "You had another murder this morning?"

"I did." She put her hand up to stop him from saying something stupid. "Let me finish. The killer was downtown Havana this time."

"That's brave."

Violet struggled to get comfortable in her chair. How should she break the news to him? Should she drop hints and let him guess, shed a few tears so he could be the gallant male or... "I'm sorry Greg, it was Juanita." She decided to go at it with the band-aid approach.

Greg almost dropped his beer. The colour drained from his face and his mouth dropped open. Nothing came out.

"I know it doesn't help, but I can promise you she didn't suffer."

"What, was she in a car accident or…"

The second band-aid was quickly yanked off. "It was the killer."

Greg made the common mistake of trying to picture the crime scene in his mind. He almost wretched, but instead downed more beer. "Why her?"

"Why any of them? There's no way these can be random killings. There's just nothing linking any of them yet. Did you know if Juanita's mother's name was Mary?"

"We didn't get that far."

"Hey, I am sorry."

Greg took a deep breath. He knew he had to man up. "I hadn't known her all that long. Damn, she was such a nice person. She took Ricky in when he had nowhere to go. God, how am I going to tell him?"

"I can do it, if you like."

"No. I need to be the one."

Violet waited for him to catch his bearings before continuing her questions. "Did she have any enemies? I know it sounds stupid, but this guy has to be picking these people for a reason."

Greg scratched at the stubble on his chin. "Who would kill a waitress?"

"A waitress?"

The one-eyed cat rubbed against her foot before jumping onto her lap. It startled her, but she let it curl around for two laps before tucking into a ball.

Greg also waited for the cat to settle. "I'm pretty sure she was."

"I went by her place before coming over here, as part of the investigation. The place was normal, in a crawling-with-police kind of way. I saw the picture on the fridge.' She unfolded it and handed it to him. "You didn't get this from me."

"Thanks."

"I also saw all the textbooks. They covered some pretty serious science shit."

"I saw them too. They belong to Ricky."

She cleared her throat. "You mean they belonged to Juanita."

"What? That's impossible. She serves drinks."

"Did you open any of them." She stroked the cat while she waited for his response. He remained quiet. "Well I did. All the hand-scribbled notes were in the same handwriting as the cookie recipe on the counter. Those were her recipes, right?"

"She baked me cookies."

"You slept with her and you must have talked to her. Who was she, Greg?"

"I honestly have no idea." He pulled himself out of his chair. "I need to call work. You don't mind, do you?" He started to walk away before she could reply.

"Where are you going?"

There was no looking back. He'd raise red flags if he did. "I can never get service by the pool. I'll be right back. I'll grab us a couple more beers."

Violet watched him leave and then slipped her phone out. She had full bars and pressed Bradley's number. He was in good spirits, likely a Jack Daniel's night.

"How's my favourite pain in the ass?"

"I'm good Brad. Hey, how's that skull coming? I'm kinda waiting for you to give me a positive ID so I can call the Sarge and get him in the loop."

"You should get him in the loop now."

"Hell no. If he knew I was in Cuba, he'd snap. Hell, if he knew I had lost my ID and badge he'd snap."

"What?"

"This Victor guy was at the hotel roughing up a guest. I had met the guest, nice guy. He knew the last victim. Long story short, the perp grabbed my purse."

"Think this guest is going to be the next one?"

"No, but he knew Juanita. The killer was probably curious as to how?" She paused, like she always did when she needed a favour. "Hey, could I get you to do a couple things for me."

"Shoot."

"Wire me a few hundred dollars and run a check on a Greg Miller. He's about forty and works in DC. I don't have a middle name. I doubt he's anything but boring. I just need to be sure."

"Miller, eh? You couldn't have picked a Smith or a Johnson."

She knew there'd be thousands to sort through. "I know. Sorry."

"I'll get right on it. Hey, are you okay?"

"Things are weird down here. Thanks for asking. It would sure help to get some answers on that skull, sooner the better."

"Have I ever let you down?"

"I doubt you ever could."

Violet continued to pet the cat after she hung up. The purring ball of fur was almost asleep in her lap. Then without warning it perked up, jumped down and joined two strays that were waiting at the far side of the pool.

She watched him leave. "Well isn't that odd."

Neither cat had made a sound.

Chapter Thirty-eight

Five passports landed on the coffee table in Victor's room as he headed for the fridge. A beer was in order. Four of the small blue books had come from the purse he'd taken. He had hoped for an ID, because this girl was a bit of a wild card. She had an agenda and she'd befriended Greg. It was a bonanza to find four different personas attached to the woman. He hadn't even looked at the wallet yet. After finding the passports, the wallet seemed insignificant.

He cringed as he sat. The two-story fall hadn't agreed with his hip and the muscles in his leg were a little tight. Maybe when he was twenty a fall like that would have been fun, exhilarating. It would have got the heart beating like the drums in Mozambique. He hadn't been twenty in some time though, nor did he want his heart beating that hard.

The top passport belonged to Greg Miller. He looked at it for a second before tossing it aside. That one was like opening a Christmas present when you knew you were getting socks. "Good luck leaving without this, Greg."

The other four passports were the gifts you wanted to shake. They were the ones that had you tearing at the corners. He opened the first one to find it belonged to a beautiful blonde named Victoria Sawyer. She was a Canadian and although the hair was darker and straight in the picture, this was definitely the woman with the gun. Victor flipped through the pages and found an ID. This woman was a Canadian Diplomat. It made a bit of sense that she'd be hanging out with Greg. He was a bit of a diplomat himself. The two things that made absolutely no sense were that she was toting a gun and she had multiple passports.

He opened the second one hoping for a clue. The photo was almost identical, but instead of straight hair it was shorter and curled in on her face like a young Bridget Bardot. "Veronica?"

Veronica Schultz was also a Canadian and according to the Press Pass, slipped into the last page, this woman was a journalist. Again, he could see her being here. Journalists could be found anywhere, but that didn't explain the gun.

The third passport also had an ID slipped between the pages. The face, the lips and the eyes were the same. This time the woman had long exotic hair. They had to be extensions. People just weren't born with hair that thick. Victor rubbed at his own thinning hair, a little jealous.

"What are you doing with a gun, Vivian Torrence?" Victor flipped through the passport before stacking it with the others. There was a pay stub from one of the Banking companies. She made good money.

That left one last passport. Hopefully this one would explain the reason why this woman had a gun, why she had several passports. Victor couldn't wait to find out. Was she an enforcer, a gun runner, or perhaps a…? A parking pass fell out onto the table as he lifted the passport. It read *Vancouver Police Department*.

Suddenly the importance of the wallet was back. He rummaged quickly. There was a card tucked under a clear plastic sleeve. It was her ID.

"Hello Violet Stormm. It looks like you're a Vancouver Homicide Detective. I did not see that coming."

The pictures on the passport and Police ID matched the woman with the gun. Her hair, sandy blonde and wavy, was just like the woman's in the hotel room. The pieces started to fall into place.

They had found out about Sayulita and had reopened the case. So why did a Vancouver Homicide Detective, a pillar of honesty and justice, have so many illegal aliases? And how did she find out about Cuba so quickly? It was a safe bet that she had friends working for her, friends to feed her information.

Victor also had friends who could find out things. He picked up his phone and started to tap at the numbers.

Chapter Thirty-nine

Violet waited damn near half an hour before Greg returned from his phone call with the office. He had done some thinking and made a few decisions while he was gone. The dreams had brought him here and although he didn't believe in hocus pocus, he also didn't believe in pushing fate. "I just called Ricky. I've asked him to help me get back to the States."

"You didn't mention…"

"Not over the phone."

"How's he going to get you out? You don't have a passport."

"I don't care. Juanita's dead and that guy in my room was the killer, wasn't he?"

"Good chance."

"Then I'm getting out of here."

Violet needed a minute to wrap her head around this cowardly approach. Bottom line, he was just a regular guy on vacation, piecing together some odd dreams. He wasn't used to getting roughed up. "Why were you gone so long?"

"I was checking out."

"You're kidding, right?"

"My bag is packed and it's sitting at your door. You able to put me up?"

She laughed. "Is that your idea of a pick-up line?"

"I know it's nuts, but I can't jeopardise Ricky's life. People need to think I'm gone and the sooner the better."

"Okay, I think you'd better start spilling."

Greg started to explain the voodoo reading, which she passed off as spiritual mumbo jumbo. Then he mentioned his talk with Ricky. It was like something out of a James Bond movie except, instead of Greg going all superhero and turning a fountain pen into a rocket-propelled missile, he decided to go back to his room and pack. It was what the pencil-pusher types did. She didn't blame him.

She thought about what the Ricky kid had told him. "You honestly think this Hemingway Serum exists?"

"How else can I explain the boy appearing in my dreams. He said that he and Juanita would be in trouble by my being here. Now she's dead."

Ricky's story had sent a numbing feeling through her head, especially when Greg mentioned the cats and how they could communicate using thought alone. That feral little shit had been asleep on her lap when the other two had called to him. There was no meow, no scratching on a door. They had shown up and he had sensed it.

"Okay, Greg. I won't rule out the serum. It's possible, remote, but possible. All I'm asking is that you don't do anything foolish. How are you even going to go? You have no passport and you don't have an embassy here. I think for now, you should stay put. If you're worried, I have an embassy. I'll take you there."

"Ricky says he's got a plan. I need to trust him."

"Just don't let this go from bad to terrible." She peered deeply into his eyes. "You're still not telling me something. Why?"

He gave a neurotic chuckle. "There's nothing to tell."

"Oh seriously, Greg? You just failed *lying through your teeth 101* big time."

"What are you talking about?"

"You laugh like Dr Strangelove, you leave to make calls." She showed him her phone. "I have full bars on mine. And what's up with that nervous lack of eye contact. Don't get me wrong, I know you're hurting, but you're also lying. I can help you."

"I swear I'm not lying."

"You're over-selling. That's another fail. Who was that guy in the room? How do you know him?"

Greg looked away as he tried to come up with an answer.

Violet made a buzzing sound. "Wrong answer, you shit. Now who the fuck is this guy?"

"Okay." He took a deep breath and exhaled very slowly. "I know the guy, but I've only seen his picture. We've never met. There isn't much I can say other than that."

"You know damn well I want this bastard more than anything. Had my gun not jammed, I'd have emptied a clip into him. Who is he?"

"That phone call I left to make, it was for you. I'm hoping you'll get an email at some point over the next day or so. It should give you everything you need to catch, or kill, this guy."

"How about you verbally give me this stuff, right now."

"I don't have that information on me."

"Damn it, Greg."

He cleared his throat. "I want you to catch this guy, so I'll come clean on what I can."

"Do I need paper to write it all down?"

"I deserved that. First of all, I didn't know this guy was the killer until I saw him. Secondly, I'm not leaving because I'm afraid. I don't want Ricky getting hurt. Thirdly, I'm involved with National Security and I need to get back to my boss. I'm not sure what they'll do when I tell them my wild story about mind serums and dream children, but I can't sit on this."

"Aren't they able to come get you?"

"They can't chance it. And this Victor guy, he's dangerous, and by dangerous, I mean professionally trained, so watch yourself."

"I could get Bradley to do a little digging on that serum."

"I'd rather you didn't. It'll raise red flags at his end. I don't want this getting out. I have my responsibilities. You must understand, being a detective and all."

The Divine Ledger

Violet broke into a full laugh. She struggled to control it and people were starting to look over from the other side of the pool. "I'm sorry. You have no idea how badly I suck at responsibility. You should talk to Bradley. He thinks I'm the most irresponsible person alive and I can't argue the fact. I mean, the guy's in a fucking wheelchair because of me."

Greg sensed the emotions being held back. He had a hanky but left it in his pocket. She'd strangle him with it. "I think it's your turn to spill."

"You know what, why not?" She'd always wanted to get it off her chest and since she didn't have any close friends, this guy would have to do. Besides, he'd likely get himself killed before the week was over and her story would be safe. "We had responded to an average call, chasing a bank robber. You see Bradley was my partner."

"I get that."

"Hell, he was a lot more than a partner at that point, but nobody knew. We kept our living together a secret. Anyway, this perp wasn't going to stop until he'd killed somebody and we didn't have back up. I should have backed off. It's protocol. I didn't. It was reckless."

"You said the guy robbed a bank."

"He only got eighteen hundred dollars. His gun was a toy. It wasn't like this guy was Al Capone. I fucked up by making it bigger than it was."

"You couldn't have known what he was."

"I was all ego at the time, unwilling to let him get away. We could have got him next time." She wiped away a tear with her thumb and studied the wetness before wiping it on her pants. "If you ever tell anybody any of this I will shoot you."

"Understood." And he believed her.

"We chased him up an overpass. The idiot lost it and slammed into the barrier. We were too close, got collected in the crash and Bradley hasn't walked since."

"You blame yourself?"

"Hey, I was the one driving." She took a swig of her beer. "There's more."

"Like what?"

"I ended up with Bradley's car, a black '68 dart with a custom fit 440 Magnum. Now I give him fifteen hundred a month. He doesn't know it comes from me."

"A settlement?"

"In a way. I let him think it's a secondary disability."

"That's nice of you, but it's anything but fair. You have to tell him. He deserves honesty."

"No. He deserves legs that work."

"Sounds like he needs a friend, and friends don't lie to each other."

"He pushes me away. Doesn't want me stuck with a cripple." She downed the last of her beer. "He's a bigger pain in the ass than you are."

"Sounds like a decent guy. As for tonight, can I stay? I'll take the couch and I'll be gone first thing."

"I've got a driver, remember? I'll give you a ride when we get up. How do you think he's going to get you out of here?"

"I'll take anything but a catapult."

Chapter Forty

The Havana Market was usually a bustling place first thing in the morning and today was no different. The coffee flowed, sugar-coated doughnuts were devoured by the dozen, and tour buses lined the front of the market like the sections of a large metal caterpillar. Each bus had a purpose. Tourists, eager for adventure, would be whisked off to white, sandy beaches, to the splendours of the jungle, to go hiking or to the tobacco plantations at the far end of the island.

Victor sat quietly at a table nursing a strong black coffee. He had started his day by looking over Violet's passports again. Out of the four, he found Violet the Vancouver Homicide Detective to be closest to reality. It felt sincere, more so than the other three. Still, there was no way to be sure she was any of these people. Lord knows he had run through a few different names himself and he wasn't any of them. Soon he'd receive a phone call and he'd know more. She had pulled a gun on him, thought she could stop him. Nobody could stop him.

He reached into his pocket and took out the picture he had pulled from a file. Chelsea McKlente was a junior legal assistant for a huge law firm in Winnipeg. They represented an international clientele including a lot of Oil CEO's from Calgary and politicians north and south of the Canadian border. The girl was in her mid-twenties with unnatural scarlet red hair. Victor couldn't understand why women would dye their hair such phoney colours. At least it wasn't Kermit green.

He took a second look at the picture before slipping it back into his pocket. What if she'd changed colours again over the last couple days? Younger women were hard enough to spot without losing the obvious features. Some days the hair was up, the next time it was down. They wore shorts, dresses, blue eye shadow or no eye shadow. Regardless of the look, he'd find her because she was on the list.

Chelsea, much like the others, had won a trip to Cuba. She had slipped her name into a raffle box at a home show, hadn't she? Anything was possible. She and her friend had meant to enter their names in every box at that home show. Who could remember what boxes she'd put her name in, or what the prizes were? She could have won a trip to the moon from a furnace duct wholesaler for all she knew.

What she had won was a dream trip. She'd always wanted to see Cuba. As a bonus, it had included last night's complimentary dinner at the infamous Hotel Nacional de Cuba and a tobacco plantation excursion that included a tour through a cigar factory. Victor, or Sven as he'd be known today, had also bought a spot on the bus and it was boarding time.

Victor finished the coffee, left a single convertible peso on the table beside the stained mug and got up to leave. Outside the bus was loading. He wasted no time finding a seat. This was the bus heading up the island to the town of Pinar del Rio. It was a cheesy tourist town, but a wonderful place to see the tobacco grown and rolled into Cuba's finest.

Working his way through the bus, his eyes began to scan the faces. Most were too old or the wrong gender. At the back of the bus he turned and thought of leaving. The girl wasn't on board yet. Should he go looking for her? The last thing Victor needed was for the girl to miss the bus because she'd decided to buy a set of souvenir salad forks for her grandmother, or a stupid key-chain for a lacklustre boyfriend.

He dropped his bag and looked out the window. What was she thinking? He did another quick check of the bus. She was not there. He sat back. She'd show. It was a free trip.

The driver checked his watch and started his head count. He wanted to get going. They were already five minutes behind. "Please Sir. Ticket?"

Victor said nothing and handed the man his ticket.

Slowly the man walked back and did a recount. There were twelve. Victor could have told him that. The driver took his clipboard and scribbled a number on it. Then the engine of the bus fired up.

Would she have slept in? That was the other problem with young people. They were irresponsible. The elderly ones, who had a much harder time getting around, had no problem making the bus. They had paid for this trip and they were going. It was as predictable as the bladder twinges that would start a mile down the road.

The doors swung shut, the brakes hissed as they released, and the murmuring stopped. It was time to start the adventure. Victor's eyes remained glued to the sidewalk.

They started to pull away from the curb when Victor yelled. "Stop!"

The bus ground to a halt. Victor waved at the girl to hurry as she raced up the sidewalk. She waved back. The doors swung open and an out of breath young woman handed the driver a ticket. He changed the number on the clipboard to lucky thirteen.

Again, the engine revved and the bus left the curb. The girl slowly swayed back and forth as she made her way to the back of the bus. Her hands grabbed the back of each seat as her eyes remained fixed on Victor. "Thank you, Mister. That was close."

"I'm glad I saw you." She wasn't as cute as her photo. Her hair was still wet from the shower and there wasn't a hint of make-up.

"Name's Chelsea."

"I'm Sven, but everyone calls me Sticks." He'd chosen a hipper persona for this girl.

"I'm guessing you're a drummer?"

"I am, studio stuff more than live. I've played with Peter Gabriel, Floyd, Supertramp and Katy Perry." He hoped he'd given her enough variety to hit one that she knew and worshipped. He guessed it would be Pink Floyd.

"Oh my God. You know Katy Perry?"

And why was that a surprise? Today's youth had no bonds to the classics. He'd seen Peter Gabriel and Pink Floyd and they were amazing. He'd never seen a Katie Perry concert, never wanted too, but he wasn't an adolescent girl. Neither was Chelsea. He shouldn't judge. "Yes, great gal. You know she writes her own stuff?"

"Yes, I know. Wow. I'm not going to let you out of my sight."

This girl was a *drop the hook in the water and pull* kind of gal. She'd bite on anything. "I also toured with Garth Brooks."

"No way. That's nice. Have you ever seen Katie's house?"

He pulled two Cohiba cigars out of his front shirt pocket and lit one up. He handed it to her and slid a window down. "Seen her house? Hell, I helped her rearrange her kitchen. Poor girl has no organisational skills."

She took a puff and kicked her feet up. "That is so cool."

Yes, dealing with youth had its struggles, but it also had its rewards. Victor lit his cigar and leaned back into his seat. "You know she watches my cat when I'm gone?"

Chapter Forty-one

Violet made a point of giving Sammy a proper hello before she and Greg got in the back seat of his cab. Once again, he slipped and called her pretty woman. He had seen Julia Roberts all decked out in a red evening gown and knew that Violet could look as good as Julia, given the chance.

She remained quiet until the cab pulled away from the curb. "Are you sure about leaving?"

"I think it's best for everyone. I just want to talk to that gypsy woman at the Malecon before I go."

"You think Hocus Pocus lady knows something?"

"She knows more than she's saying."

"So, when she doesn't talk, are you prepared to get rough with her?"

"What?"

"Look, you need answers and she has them. Don't wimp out on me, Greg."

He rolled his eyes. "What do you propose, we rough her up?"

"Give me a break. I haven't beaten anybody up in days." She looked at the rear-view mirror to give Sammy a reassuring wink.

"Don't worry Sammy. I'm a nice girl. I don't beat people up until I have to. It's a last resort thing."

The warm ocean air filled the car, tossing hair and easing Violet's frame of mind as they turned onto the six lanes of 5ta Avenida. She was hopeful that this woman would divulge how she thought Greg was involved. The woman would come across as an idiot and he would change his mind about leaving. Then she could work on him. He knew something.

Violet checked her phone for a text from Bradley. There was nothing. Greg kept an eye on the seawall for the gypsy lady.

Sammy saw her first. "There she is. Right up there." He sped past the woman. It had been too late to pull over. The car slowed as Sammy moved over to the inside lane.

"She's back there Sammy," Violet announced. "We need to pull over."

Sammy said nothing. Instead his eyes danced from the windshield to the rear-view mirror. Then, as Violet was about to repeat what she'd said, he cranked the wheel into oncoming traffic. They shot in front of another cab, dodged a heavy truck and then he eased his way to the curb lane. Violet, now sprawled across Greg's lap, clawed her way back to her own side and straightened her shirt.

Sammy shrugged. "It would have been too dangerous for you to cross the street on foot."

"Uh, thanks." Violet appreciated the act of kindness, even though she was almost thrown out the side window.

Sammy stopped by the gypsy's table and they got out.

"Can you stay, Sammy? We might need to give the dough-head a ride. He plans on doing something stupid and he needs our help."

"I am happy to stay then."

The woman recognised Greg immediately. "You have returned. Sit down."

He took a seat. "I need to know more about this paranormal plane you say I'm living in."

The woman eyed Violet up and down. "Where is Juanita?"

Violet offered first. "She's…"

The Divine Ledger

The woman recoiled. "She's dead, isn't she? How did this happen."

Violet wanted to mention that a good psychic would already know, but refrained. "It was murder. Do you know anybody that might want her dead?"

She reached out to Violet. "Give me your hand."

Violet ignored her.

The lady grabbed her hand. "This is important. You are involved."

Her eyes closed as she took in Violet's energy. She knew better that to try and spit in this girl's palm. Violet felt the energy. It wasn't that different than that chair at Victor's hotel room. It opened a connection.

"I see a killer." Her eyes deepened. "He has a girl with him. She will be his—"

Violet finished her sentence. "Fifth. I know. Where are they?"

"They're not here in Havana and she's not dead yet. She's sleeping right now. She will be dead soon. The drugs will take her."

"Shit." Violet pulled her hand away. "We've got to get going. Where?"

"You can't get to her in time." The woman pursed her lips. "Why do you say fifth?"

"Right. He killed twelve the first time so seventeen, maybe eighteen." She thought of the thirteenth mystery skull. "We could be talking nineteen?"

"I see thirty-six people in total."

"Victor's killed thirty-six?" Violet gasped.

"Please." The woman took her hand again. This time it was to comfort her. They had a connection, a trust, doing what they do…reading energy…seeing what others couldn't. "My Dear, His name is no more Victor than it is John, Andrew, Sven or Sticks. This man has many names. He has many faces. And I know you will find it hard to believe, but this man is not your enemy."

"Over thirty people are dead. How is he not the enemy?'

"I cannot see that. He is hiding behind something dark. Some of those names, the earlier ones, were bad, but he is good now."

"That's ridiculous. Is Greg safe?"

"He is not, and should leave Cuba immediately."

Greg pulled her hand from Violet's and clutched it in his. "My tombstone, can I change that by leaving?"

"Fate for most is stationary, like the stars. Your fate, however, can change. Do not ask me how, because it makes no sense. I see a blonde woman standing over you. She will be the one to change it."

"Who, me?" Violet asked.

"No." Her eyes closed and then reopened. She looked up to Violet. "I see you standing before the killer. You have your gun on him. You don't shoot him."

"That happened. My gun jammed. I've fixed the problem."

"This is your future. Your gun is working, but you don't shoot him."

"That's crazy. This whole damn thing is crazy." She grabbed Greg's hand and dragged him off toward the cab. "Let's get the hell out of here."

They remained quiet in the car. Eventually, Greg broke the silence. "If you get the chance to shoot him you'll take it, right?"

Violet couldn't believe he'd even ask. "Oh, shit yeah."

Except there was something about that crazy lady's energy, something that was hard to deny.

Chapter Forty-two

The cab entered the Havana Tunnel, leaving the city and heading east. Violet fumed while Greg stared off at the ocean. He'd had the audacity to ask her if she'd shoot him, given the chance. What a dick thing to ask. Why wouldn't she cap this guy? Why was there any doubt? He had killed not only the nineteen that she knew about. It was possibly double that amount. Even if she had a chance to take him alive, she might just empty a clip into him for shits and giggles. No one would miss such a man and you couldn't always trust the courts. One silly loophole, or bag full of cash, and this monster could end up a free man. Why take that chance?

Sammy wheeled through a subdivision of low-cost houses, each one identical to the other. It looked like one of those scaled down scenes from a model train set. Perhaps the builder got a deal on one particular model and over-used it. Every street was the same scene, house after house.

The beach came into view and the cab rolled into a sandy parking stall. Ricky was waiting down by the water with an old wooden fishing boat. He met them halfway. "It's the best I could do. I know it's small, but the weather is nice and the boat doesn't leak."

Violet and Greg looked it over. It was a fourteen-foot rowboat with an old motor that hung off the stern like a child's backpack slung over one shoulder. It had an extra oar and a few supplies that included a badly torn tarp, a small tank of extra fuel, several bottles of water and a sandwich.

"It seems sturdy," Greg said.

Ricky shrugged. "It's a hundred miles to the Florida Keys, which is quite a distance. You only need to get close. The American Coast Guard will pick you up. They constantly patrol the coastline for illegals. You'll be okay once they check your story."

Violet's face had lost all expression. "You know you're a dead man if you go, right? There's no way you'll make it."

"I don't have a choice." He looked over to Ricky. "Do I?"

"This is better than staying."

"Well I don't like it." Violet crossed her arms. "I mean, if you stay I'll keep an eye out for you."

"You can't catch him and keep me safe."

"I could use you for bait."

"Well I don't like that idea." He turned to Ricky. "Before I go, you and I need to talk. Walk with me."

They started down the beach. Violet stayed with Sammy and they watched as Greg did the talking. After a couple minutes, Ricky broke into tears. Greg wrapped his arms around him in an awkward embrace.

Violet gave them a few minutes before joining them. "I'm really sorry."

Ricky nodded. "He needs to go or he'll be next."

"I agree." Greg pushed the boat into the water with Sammy's help. "Wish me luck."

"Hey, call me when you make it across." Violet waded out to her waist. She grabbed his left hand and wrote her number in his palm. "Or call me if you're just thinking about me. You're right-handed I hope."

Greg grimaced. "Ouch. I'm going to miss that wit of yours."

Violet pointed to one of the freighters. "Just watch out for the big ones. I think they have the right of way."

"I'll take that on advisement. Just remember you don't get any brownie points for bringing bullets home."

She shot him a wink. "No worries there."

Her phone rang. She gave Greg an awkward boat-hug before heading back to the shore. It was Bradley and he had news. "What have you got Brad?"

"I finally got the beads and shit off the skull and the results are in. You'll never guess who that skull belongs to."

"You know, you're probably right. So how about you tell me."

"You don't want to guess?"

"Okay fine, Jimmy Hoffa, Fred Flintstone, or how about that guy that sells mattresses on forty-ninth street."

"It can't be Morty Mattress. He's still alive. I saw him on TV just yesterday."

"Damn it, Bradley!"

"Sorry. Are you sitting?" He waited for an answer that didn't come. It quickly became awkward, so he blurted it out. "It was Vincent Wainsworth."

There was a log on the beach and Violet took a seat. "You're kidding me, right? Isn't Wainsworth the killer's name?"

"Very good." He continued, "Vincent Wainsworth lived in Seattle and I've pulled a set of prints. He was working in England three years ago. I think he's a teacher, but I wouldn't bet money on it."

"Why do you say that?"

"I've sent you a recent picture of the man. You tell me."

Violet checked her phone and allowed the picture to load. "Hold it. That's Victor. What does that mean? Does he have a brother, like a twin? Could that be possible?"

"What it means is that he killed this guy and stole his identity, looks and all. He's a serious player, Violet."

"Serious indeed. I think the guy's actually good for thirty-six murders."

"Shit."

There was silence as she looked up to see Greg trying to get the motor started. What a Dufuss. This guy wouldn't make it a hundred yards. "What did you find on Greg Miller?"

"He's government, but I can't get much more than that. I can tell you he's recently divorced and that his wife took him to the cleaners. Isn't love a wonderful thing?"

"Keep digging. A gypsy told me there might be another murder today. She said the woman was sleeping but would be dead very soon."

"Did you say gypsy? Sounds like you're getting pretty desperate."

"Fuck you too, Brad. She's the one who told me he's killed thirty-six. She had answers for me. You should try it some time. Do some digging and keep me posted. Maybe they've got a few headless bodies in England."

"I'll check that. Hey, this Victor guy, he's pretty elusive."

"You couldn't find much on Greg either. I think you're losing your touch."

"Greg's government. If you ask me, Victor or Vincent is the same, only higher up. Watch your back and try to get me a print. I want to see if they match Vincent's."

"I'll see what I can do." Violet watched as Greg finally got the motor running. He was putting distance between them. With a little luck he could be hitting Florida by nightfall. "Hey Brad, why do you think Victor's government?"

"You'd need some serious resources to steal an identity like this. That, and I've had a black SUV parked out front of my place since yesterday."

Chapter Forty-three

The thought of Greg bobbing on the ocean was all Violet could think about as the cab pulled into the turnaround at the Copacabana. It was the stupidest thing she'd ever seen anybody do, but he was a grown man, not that he ever acted like one.

She got out of the cab, handed Sammy ten pesos without arguing and dragged herself up the steps. She'd stopped by the precinct, on the way, and told the Captain about Victor being a Vincent. There may have been more aliases and tying him to any one name was a mistake. The face however, was the same. She had made full disclosure, for what it was worth. This was progress in her learning to be a team-player. It wasn't great progress. She hadn't told them that Victor was a match for a thirteenth skull.

She grabbed a beer and a hotdog and set out for the pool. Her one-eyed furry friend was sitting on the pool wall with his back to her. As a test she tried to send him a signal. Hot dog kitty, kitty. Turn around, kitty, kitty. The cat continued to stare off at the ocean. When another cat strolled through her legs and stopped in front of her. The one-eyed cat immediately turned around. The two took off toward the bar.

Violet stood there with the hotdog in hand. "What the hell?"

She broke it into pieces and left them behind one of the planters. They'd find it later. With no leads and more confusion, she started up to her room. On the way she thought about Brad's report of the black SUV outside his place. Victor, or Vincent, had to be American and if that SUV was because of him, then he was government. The SUV could also have been connected to Greg. So, what was his angle?

The air was fresh, so she planned to change into her bikini, go poolside and go over the files one more time. She could work on her tan at the same time. At least she would get something accomplished. From down there she could also keep an eye on Greg's room. Would Victor return?

She thought of the Sarge as she started up the stairs. Maybe if she could knock back enough beer, she'd phone the man and let him know where she was. There had been a few texts exchanged with him, but they'd been kept random. They had made her sound like she was still in Mexico, yet none of them were actual lies. It was all in the wording and he wasn't asking the right questions.

Violet opened the door to her room and stopped. She drew her gun and aimed before he could say anything. What arrogance. This bastard had not only made her look bad, but he had been the one responsible for Greg taking off. He'd also be the one responsible for Greg's death if anything went wrong.

Victor returned a half-cocked smile. "Hey."

He had done his homework on her, and although she was becoming a royal pain in the ass, he had already decided to spare her. Killing her would only happen if she got in the way and hopefully she wouldn't take it that far. His friends had done some digging. This woman was about doing the right thing, at any cost. That put them on the same team. "It's Violet, right?"

Her finger tensed as it rested heavily on the trigger. All she wanted was an excuse. Would he give her one? Did she honestly need one? Thirty-six dead. This guy deserved to die and this was Cuba. They wouldn't care as long as the killings stopped. That being said, his eyes were throwing her off. She hadn't noticed it the last time she had seen him, but they didn't look like the eyes of a madman. They were placid. And then there was the gypsy lady, telling her that he wasn't the enemy. How?

"Can you lower the gun? I'm not running."

"Give me a reason you piece of shit," she barked. "You can run."

"And have you shoot me? You're not that kind of cop?" He slowly raised his hands. "You're so much better than that, Miss Stormm."

With his hands in the air he slowly turned a complete three-sixty. He was wearing jeans and a t-shirt. It was easy to see there was no gun and no apparent knives.

"I came unarmed."

"Too bad for you."

"You're a good cop, colourful among other things, but you stand for justice. I just want the same."

"By killing people?"

"People?" He calmly shook his head. "It's not like that."

"What is it like?" This wasn't a question as much as a smart-ass remark.

"You wouldn't believe me if I told you, so I won't begin to explain. I will give you a heads up. You should be looking for a book. Find the book and you'll understand why I'm doing what I'm doing."

"A book?"

"You're different. I saw that right away, so I trust you'll know the book when you see it."

"Is that why you're in my room?"

"I wanted to see what you knew about Greg. His boss is responsible for all this crap. I think Greg knows about this book and we could use his help in finding it."

Violet studied him as she took a step closer. He was an average build, full hair that was greying and he had a tattoo on his arm. It was a cross with birds, lots of birds. What was with birds in this damn country? "What's the ink?"

"I'm a part of something. Call me a righteous man."

"Righteous? I outta shoot you for saying that."

"Look, you know there's more to this than just a few random killings. I'm no nut-job serial killer, getting my willy wet by lopping off heads. To be honest, I can't stand cleaning those damn things."

"Then why?"

"Because it's the only way it works. We can't take any chances that the Russians might get to them. They'll torture them. The things they'd do, hell, it would make me look like a boyscout." He put his hands down. She'd have shot him by now if she was going to. "You need to find the book. And when you do, bring it to me. I need to make it disappear. I promise you, I'll disappear with it."

"Again, with the book? What's in this book?"

He started inching toward her, innocent steps. "I think you have to see it for yourself. I managed to get it after the last set of killings and tried to destroy it. Fire didn't work and throwing it in the ocean with a rock obviously didn't work either."

Her gun was becoming heavy and complacency had dropped her aim. A lot of it was the tale he was telling her, lulling her. "Does this book have a title? How do I find it?"

"I'm hoping Greg knows. Make him help you. It's important. Oh, and I'm sorry."

"For wha—"

He lunged, knocking her over, and grabbed the gun. Her guard had dropped. The gun was tossed on the bed, and the clip was slid toward the bathroom while he pinned her to the floor.

"This book is all about energy, Miss Stormm. I've talked to a few people about you. You're no more a cop than you are a diplomat or a journalist. You're resourceful and I can work with that. Our types need that in our line of work. If anybody can do this, you can."

With that he got up and started for the door.

"Oh no you don't, not again." She scrambled to her feet.

Chapter Forty-four

As a teenager, Greg had spent a lot of time on boats fishing with his adopted father. He had hated the water then and he hated it now. It was nice to have a motor and although it took a bit to get the damn thing started, it ran like a charm once it had warmed up.

As the Cuban beach shrank, the once tiny stick people dissolved into the treeline. The beach, fifty yards from water to trees, had narrowed to a barely visible beige strip. But the once-small waves had grown into face-slapping swells and the freight ships had become mountains.

At one point he thought he saw his blonde in the white dress. She was standing at the water's edge watching him. She watched him for a good five minutes before disappearing with all the others. Except she literally disappeared in the blink of an eye. The others had shrunk into the shoreline. He shook the thought. There was no point in hitting all eight cylinders of crazy this early in the trip. He had the better part of the day ahead of him for that.

Above, a few cottony clouds dotted the blue sky. One looked like a rabbit, or maybe it was a long-eared cat or a snowman with horns. It was a welcome distraction from his arm, which was starting to cramp from the vibration of the motor. He'd read a story once in one of those empowerment magazines. A woman had swum this stretch of water. It was years ago. She wasn't escaping the poverty of a heavily sanctioned country. She did it because she could. If she could swim it, surely he could crank the damn handle without complaining.

Reaching down into the boat he picked up one of the bottles of water. It was no longer cold, but still tasted good. He didn't stop until it was half gone. There were four one-litre bottles of water. He hoped it would be enough.

The air tasted different this far out. It wasn't sandy or fishy anymore. Nor did it smell like the coconut lotions that always accompanied a beach of tourists. It was salty and fresh and it carried a breeze that was picking up. Suddenly a horrifying thought came to him. The water was deep. How deep? It had to be a mile, or more. He'd never taken swimming lessons.

Giving the handle of the motor a sharp crank, he accelerated and straightened himself out. He looked at the number on his left hand and turned his thoughts to Violet. Would she get this madman? He hoped that by the time he got to the other side, there'd be a newspaper with the headline *Canadian Detective Ends Dangerous Serial Killer's Reign of Terror*. Then he shifted his thoughts to the woman poolside in her bikini. That would be the image that sold papers.

The motor hummed as he guided the boat away from Havana. He was becoming one with the boat, a machine. He'd need that if he wanted to keep the damn thing heading toward the Keys. Soon Havana would be out of sight. When that happened, would the Keys come *into* sight, or would he be travelling blind? And how far was Africa, if he veered off course? There wouldn't be enough gas, or bottles of water for that trip.

The sun was hot now, blistering. When it finally took a break, Greg wiped his brow and looked up. A dark cloud was edging in from the north. It was a nice break from the searing heat. Muggy would be easier to deal with.

"Where the hell did you come from, Mr. Cloud?" He cranked the handle again, making sure he kept the pace. "Don't matter. Feeling groovy."

There were gloves in the boat and although he didn't like the idea, he took a minute to put them on. The last thing he needed was a blister. He changed hands for the next hour and decided to finish the first bottle of water. The first swallow was warm. Squinting through the vibration of the motor, he thought he might have seen land. It was distant, but it looked like land. Behind him Cuba was still a lot closer. He started up again, feeling a little less concerned.

Head down, he motored on. He did this without thinking. It had to be instinctive. There was a rag in the bottom of the boat. He wet it and threw it on the back of his neck. Every little bit helped.

He spent an hour like this, in a trance, bowing and bobbing, his grip locked on the handle. Another hour would have passed had it not been for the blast of a ship's horn.

"Shit."

The boat was far enough away, but he was in its path. His heart began to race as he twisted the handle for all he was worth. A second blast came from the other direction. They were passing, honking at each other. They didn't even see him.

The motor sputtered twice. "What? No, no."

It sputtered a third time and quit.

"What the…" Greg screwed the gas cap off and looked inside. The tank was bone dry. "No, not now."

He scrambled to grab the extra fuel and dumped most of it into the tank. Some also landed all over the motor and in the boat as he rolled with the waves. Greg threw the empty can to the front of the boat. Then he grabbed the chord and pulled.

Nothing.

The two ships blasted their horns again as if engaging in a friendly conversation. It was much louder this time.

He pulled the chord four more times before the motor sputtered to life. The handle was cranked, and the boat lunged forward. Greg needed to make his way past the first ship without getting hit. The two ships would be passing at a safe distance, so he wasn't too concerned with the path of the other one.

Overhead, the clouds were rolling in thicker. The skies were darkening. Was that a raindrop? Greg looked back towards Cuba. It would have been one hell of a swim. How'd that woman do it?

The ship was growing fast. They hadn't seen him. Who'd be looking for a rowboat this far out? With the boat-sized white caps, and the rain squall, he was pretty much invisible. The ship's hull was a lot closer now. It looked more like a cliff.

"No!" Greg could see his tombstone as he watched the ship close in on him. So, this was how it happened. He suddenly knew where his body would wash up. It was Cuban soil. You can't cheat death when it's meant to be.

Overhead, the drizzle had become a deluge. A swell, not related to the ship, grabbed the small boat and lifted it a good fifteen feet. Greg grabbed for the side of the boat as he fell from his seat. His jaw struck the oar as he toppled over the side.

Below the ocean's surface his world lost gravity. Was he upside-down, right side up, left-side right? Which way should he swim? Greg decided to let his buoyancy bring him to the surface, at first. After forty-five seconds he hadn't found his next breath. He was still tumbling in the currents. Greg thrashed around and fought to find his way. The sky was dark when he finally surfaced.

He'd just filled his lungs with a fresh breath when the currents pulled him back under.

Chapter Forty-five

Violet chased Victor down the corridor and out past the pool. When he went straight, she ducked into the dinning room. With supper in full swing, this quickly turned into a bad idea. She knocked one plate out of a woman's hand with her elbow, sending the lady and the plate flying. Her hip knocked a table of glasses over when she cut a corner too sharply. Neither slowed her down.

The back door swung open, almost pulling the hinges off the frame. Victor raced past her and she hooked a finger in his collar. It wasn't enough. She was two strides behind him as they crossed the street, heading down a back alley. This was his territory now; back alleys, quiet parks, and places without witnesses.

"Stop, you bastard."

He raised his tattooed arm as a disclaimer. "That's righteous bastard."

"I won't give up."

And he believed her. For that reason, he started to slow down. His days of outrunning someone this young had passed years ago. Besides, he wasn't afraid of a Vancouver cop. What was she, a hundred and twenty pounds? "Okay, okay, you win."

She went for the takedown. He countered it, throwing her hard into a row of trashcans. "I said 'you win', Stormm. We don't have to do this."

Violet sprang to her feet and charged. She drove her shoulder into his gut. It wasn't soft, nor was this guy of average build. The man was solid. Still, she managed to slam him hard against the wooden fence. The air left his lungs as she swung an elbow toward his throat. In return, he grabbed a handful of hair and peeled her off.

She spun free and put her foot on a collision course with his manhood. A knee came up, blocking her. He didn't see her fist as it slammed hard against his mouth. Four clenched knuckles split his lower lip right down the centre.

"Damn it, Stormm. I don't want to hurt you."

"I can tell." She recoiled and connected again with his jaw. "And thanks for that."

That shot rattled teeth. He grabbed her by the shirt as she threw a glancing shot off his cheek. He spun around and held her tight against his chest. She kicked wildly as he wrapped her up in a one-armed bear hug. Then he lifted her off her feet and drove her into a garbage bin. A cold steel blade was quickly pressed against her throat. "Enough already."

She tried to squirm free. "Big mistake."

"I don't wanna hurt you." He squeezed harder. "You're not on my list, Stormm."

"Screw your list." As she said that, a bird passed in front of them. It landed on the edge of the bin a few feet away from them.

"That list is saving humanity."

"The book, the list." She continued to struggle. "Can't you see how stupid all this sounds?"

Violet was a lot stronger than he'd have guessed. He pressed more of his weight against her. "Damn straight, I do. I'm living it and have a hard time believing it myself at times."

"You collect skulls. You ditch skulls. I don't get it. And who was the thirteenth skull?" She gulped to get a breath. "Who was Vincent?"

"I collected those skulls to save the souls. They're wasted otherwise. I have to keep them, so they don't come back."

The Divine Ledger

"Now I know you're crazy." She thrust her knees to the left, twisting just enough to get her right arm free. An open hand found his cheek. The stinging blow caused his eyes to water. It weakened his grip as she spun to face him. Both hands were now gripping his forearm, keeping the scalpel at a safe distance from her throat. A drop of blood trickled down her neck from the nick.

Victor thought he'd squeezed the fight out of her. He was wrong. Using his weight, he dropped her to the ground and quickly pinned her on her back. It worked, but it had seemed too easy. "I assure you, none of this is crazy."

Violet brought a knee up and nestled it gently in his groin. "Tell me about Vincent and why you look like him."

He felt the knee, did a quick shift of his shoulder into her chest, and jammed his left hand down on her leg. "I look like him because I *am* him."

She felt the gravel digging into her shoulders, into her back. Through the dust she could see birds landing on the ground beside them. "I'm not kidding. I had the skull checked. Who is Vincent and why'd you kill him?"

"I'm Vincent." He struggled to hold her knee back.

"You're here. How is that possible?"

"I wish I could tell you. You've got my blood all over your knuckles. Do a DNA test on it."

Her arm came up and shoved the barrel of a gun against his throat. "Maybe I will."

He softened his grip. "Second gun? I should have known."

"Wanna know the calibre?" She looked over to see more birds gathering on the bin and a row of them on the fence.

"Doesn't matter." He looked down to see her pant leg pulled up. The knee to the groin wasn't the threat. It was the gun she wanted. "Do me a favour. Find the book and give it to me. I'll show you what it does and then we'll destroy it, if we can. If not, I'll hide it where no one will ever find it. I'll spend the rest of my life guarding the fucking thing. All hell breaks loose if I can't. The Russians don't understand the power. Nobody could. They just see opportunity."

"You're American?"

"I'm whatever I need to be, just like you." He lifted himself off her and extended his hand. She took the hand and let him pull her up. That was when he saw the knife. It was an eight-inch blade and the handle was genius.

"That's your gun?" He had to chuckle.

She stepped back and flipped the chromed knife around as she slipped it back into the holster on her calf. The handle of the knife was the barrel of a forty-seven magnum. It was the first gun that she'd been shot with. It would never fire again. It would however fool Victor and others into submission. "A girl's gotta have an edge."

"Edge. That's a good one, shiny too." He licked at the corner of his mouth. She had bloodied him remarkably well. "Where'd you train?"

More birds landed on the fence, bringing the numbers to well over a hundred. "I have a friend and you?"

"Rattlesnake Ranch." He'd also noticed the birds and her reaction to them.

"The Rattlesnake Ranch?" She'd heard rumours about the place. There was a place just outside of San Antonio, deep in the Grey Forest. It was a Special Op training camp. "And what are you?"

"Don't worry about me. You're a smart woman with a solid support group. Find the book."

"You don't know me. Where are you getting your intel?"

"I have a boss, just like you. And I know you better than you think. I know you have some pretty deep secrets."

"What do you mean, the passports?"

"That's such a small part of you." He left it at that as he dusted himself off.

Violet left the dust on her. Instead, she concentrated on his eyes, but saw no signs. Oh, the man was good, unquestionably trained. What did he know about her and how could he have found out? "Who's your boss, the birdman."

He made a hand gesture to the birds, like everything was okay. They took flight and were gone in seconds. "The man has no name, just one hell of a lot of sparrows." There was an aching in his jaw as he hinged it open and shut. "And yours?"

She looked over to the fence where the birds had been. Had they come to protect him? "Sergeant Crowley, Vancouver detachment of the Vancouver Police Depart—"

"Sticking with the Vancouver Homicide Detective story, are we?"

"For now."

Chapter Forty-six

A full minute passed before Greg could take his next breath. The current had finally released its grip when the stern of the ship had passed. There was no further undertow or weird sensation of being dragged under. It wasn't something he'd ever wondered about until now. The hull gave the illusion that he could reach out and touch it. He was too tired to try.

Greg treaded water as he looked for the shore. He'd have accepted it in any direction, but with the swells and waves, all he could see was the turmoil of ocean. Then he looked for the rowboat. Where was the damn rowboat?

He spun around as he treaded. The swells and waves might as well have been mountains. Heavy rain continued to pelt him. Drops felt like hail as they hit his face. It was all so cold. How could the rain or this ocean be so cold in such a tropical world? Even the sound of the rain had dropped a blanket over him. It was deafening, as if a million marbles were dropping on a metal roof.

Such large waves were sinister by nature. They rolled and crashed into each other in a sloshing chaos. There was no direction, no order. One wave slapped Greg sideways, filling his mouth and

The Divine Ledger

sinuses. There was a cough of water, a sputter, and a swell of panic. He needed a second to recover. He wouldn't get that. Other waves promptly followed.

Staying above the surface had become impossible. Shoes and dress pants weren't helping matters. Anyone that had ever fallen into a pool with clothes on would understand. His shirt had become a parka. For that reason, it had to go. The pants also had to go. He pulled the belt out, unclasped the top, and unzipped the fly as he was pulled under. Was it hope or stupidity, that he grabbed his wallet and stuffed it in the front of his form-fitted boxers? The phone was in the other pocket and he pulled it out, thought for a second, and let it drift down to the depths.

Stripping down was a good idea and Greg knew he'd swim better without the bulk. What he didn't think about was how hard it would be to pull his legs out in a choppy ocean. Bending his body in half, the waves tossed him around and pulled him under again and again. One leg came halfway out, the other didn't. The pant leg was now inside out. It was as if he'd been wrapped up in a bed sheet. Why hadn't he kicked his shoes off first?

He continued to work at the pants, getting them over the knees and pulling one leg over the shoe. He'd been under a while now and had to give up and grab a breath. Instead, he gulped a mouthful of water. The salt burned his lungs and he coughed hard. Above him, the hull of his fishing boat appeared. He quickly swam for it.

It wasn't the entire hull, just four feet of it, but it floated and that was all Greg cared about. Hugging it for all he was worth, he cleared the rest of the water out of his lungs, stopping occasionally to take in more.

Greg's arms were throbbing. He wanted to hold on. It just seemed like so much effort. This was an ocean, powerful, unrelenting and much bigger than he was. Still, he needed to fight.

After a half an hour of coughing up water, Greg tried to remember what he was fighting for. Was it that damn dream about his headstone, to prove it wrong? Was it for his ex-wife or the recently deceased Juanita? He had gone to Cuba, and because of that, she'd been killed. Ricky would be next. Cuba was a lot better off without him.

And what about Detective Stormm? He had promised her an email, knowing it wouldn't be sent. It was a classified document and no favour was that big. He pictured her stretched out on a lounge chair. If his life was about to pass before him, he'd want it to start with that moment. Contours and stretched fabric was what he wanted to be thinking about when he went, not the stinging in his sinuses.

Another wave washed over him, filling his lungs, crushing the last of his strength. Everyone was put on this planet for a reason and Greg had hoped for something life-changing. Sometimes the purpose wasn't for anything more than to enrich somebody else's life. Was he put here for Anne, for Ricky or was his death the most important part of his being?

Close to an hour had passed since the swamping of his boat. He had found four feet of the boat and clung to it debating whether or not it was worth letting go. The muscles in his arms burned and the waves showed no signs of calming. Greg had been lucky to find that section of the boat. He was about to find more of it, another eight feet of it.

A flash of white caught his eye as it approached from the right. It struck him hard, driving him under the water. Again, the darkness of the ocean tried to consume him.

This time, he'd let it.

Chapter Forty-seven

Victor walked through the door, threw his keys on the table, and went to the mirror to check the damage. Damn it, he was trying to help her. Then again, if he were in her shoes, he'd have done the same. The real story was something straight out of a movie.

His lip wasn't as split as the bleeding made it look, but you could tell he'd been hit. She had caught him with a few quick ones. If he had to look for a silver lining, it was that she wasn't the kind of girl to wear a lot of jewellery. A few flashy rings might have torn chunks out of him. Thing is, he should have seen it coming. He'd been warned. She was all fight and he admired that. Instead of admiring it, he should have responded to it.

The lip could be passed off as a cold sore. The cheek was red, but would look okay in an hour. He grabbed the facecloth and wiped away the blood and dirt. The cloth would get pitched out later.

And when was the last time he'd been hit like that? There was that bodyguard in Prague and that gunrunner's henchman in Morocco. One was three hundred and fifty pounds and the other had friends pinning his arms, not a fair fight. This girl was a featherweight, but she held her own. He smiled as he rinsed the cloth and set it down. It would be a shame to kill her.

His suitcase stood beside the bed. He popped the locks and flipped it open. First, he grabbed a case and went back into the bathroom. In it was a variety of moustaches, make-up and glue. He chose the Tom Selleck.

It looked good on him. He gave his upper lip a wiggle and it held fine. He undid his pants, shed them and put them on the bed. A pair of old Levi's would be a part of his new look. They were faded, the back pocket worn to the shape of a wallet. The hems at the end of the legs were boot-frayed.

Then he pulled out a plaid shirt. There were no buttons. The shirt had snaps, making it a fighting shirt. He'd been told that by a girl he met in the bar. Fight shirt she had called it and for good reason. He looked a little lost, so she gave him a demo, pulling the shirt apart exposing his chest. The sex was rough, a fight he didn't mind losing.

There'd be no fighting now, not with names still on the list.

The cowboy boots had been resoled more than once. Finally, he grabbed an old straw hat that had been folded up like an old napkin. Then he selected a dark blue Canadian passport and slipped it into his back pocket.

He turned to the mirror and attempted his best John Wayne. "Well, we should get them wagons in a circle, pilgrim. And be quick about it. Them Indians ain't gonna shoot themselves." It was good, but not about to land him a gig in Hollywood.

In the lobby he picked up a pack of cigarettes and lit one. He missed the filthy habit. Police had filled the lobby of his hotel. He walked past them tipping his hat to the one by the door. "What's all the hub-bub 'bout?"

"We're looking for an Englishman and heard he might be hanging around here." He flashed a picture. "Have you seen this man?"

Victor gave it a fleeting stare. "He doesn't look like he could wrassle a gopher on his best day."

"Have you seen him?"

"Nah." He reminded himself he was a Canadian cowboy. "Sorry."

He turned from the officer and moseyed to the front desk where he booked himself into the hotel as Rick Herrington, a chuck wagon outrider from Brooks, Alberta. The man handed him a key and he went back up the elevator. The new room had a better view of the ocean and a king-sized bed.

Later he took the elevator down again and made his way through the lobby. This time he left the hotel and walked straight over to a cab that sat out front. He joined the driver, who was leaning against the driver's door and offered him a cigarette.

"Hey partner. Do you know a driver, hangs out at the Copa? He's been doing a lot of driving for a blonde girl." It was a long shot, but he wanted to keep an eye on this girl.

"*Si*, Sammy. Why do you want to know?" There was an instant suspicion, and understandably so.

"Blonde's a damn fine filly, if ya know what I mean."

"*Si*, I've heard about her. She pays well."

"That gal and I went out dancing last night. We had an incredible time. I told her I was going to buy her lunch today, but I was a little drunk. I forgot where we were supposed to meet. I'm hoping this Sammy guy knows where to find her." He held out ten pesos.

The driver pulled out his phone and dialled. There was a brief conversation that ended it with *gracias*. That was a good sign.

"I know where he dropped her off. It was fifteen minutes ago."

"Can you take me there?"

"I need thirty pesos; ten for Sammy, ten for me, and then ten for the ride." His smile widened.

"Ouch." Victor pulled a few more bills out of his pocket. "I hope this gal's worth it."

Chapter Forty-eight

Karolina Encinoe sat quietly on a wooden park bench and watched as the children brought the playground to life with the innocence of their youth. She was twenty-eight again. Her hair, no longer grey, was a deep chestnut brown and tied up nicely with a red satin ribbon. Legs, once mapped with varicose veins, were firm again. She had them crossed as they protruded from the knee length tweed skirt. It was the perfect skirt to go with her favourite white blouse and red shawl. Bought in the States, before Cuba had become an enemy, this outfit was the only elegant thing she owned. It would be the outfit she'd wear when she died.

She looked up to see Robert on the hill.

He was a dashing young man as he sat with his new girlfriend, their relationship only weeks old. Robert had kissed her twice, both times pleasantly awkward. But twenty-eight was an age to take chances, so he'd continue to woo her. He just needed to grow into his skin.

Nita was the bookworm, too busy reading to find love. She had three books spread out on the blanket as she went through them looking for logic and reason. It was hard for Karolina to understand a brain so devoted to finding answers. On her stomach, and propped up on her elbows, Nita allowed the words on the page to flow through her and over her like the air that filled her lungs or the breeze that teased her hair. She was eleven.

Nita waved when she noticed Karolina. Her smile was so noble, and Karolina waved back. She was such a sweet thing.

Bee was an older sister, one who had just turned fourteen. She hung from the monkey bars by her knees. There was a book in her hands as well, but it had no answers as to how or why. Her book carried her away to a place where men were gentle and placed coats over puddles. Women dressed in fancy evening gowns and frequented lavish balls every night. She read of these places while hanging upside down, because in the real world everything was the opposite. Men were arrogant and didn't think women could keep up. She'd prove them wrong someday.

Karolina shook her head. The poor dear should have been born two decades later. That world had changed and no longer belonged to these men. Now women and minorities called the shots. Bee had also noticed Karolina and quickly waved.

These were just two of the many kids that crowded the monkey bars, swung on the swings and chased one another through the trees and down the trails of the park. Robert was the oldest, not really a child anymore, while Richard was the youngest. He was three days old. There would be more in time. Each one would have a life, complete with dreams and aspirations.

Richard had been sleeping in his baby carriage as the others played. Then, as if shaken awake, he started to cry. Was he hungry, wet? Karolina got to her feet and took two steps before stopping. There were rules. She wasn't allowed to tend to these children. She was only allowed to watch them.

But Richard was crying and she was the only adult around. She had to tend to him. What if he was choking or being suffocated by a blanket. How could she stand by?

Karolina decided to ignore the senseless rules and started for the baby.

A dark cloud formed in the distance. She caught it out of the corner of her eye and quickened her pace. The darkness soon engulfed half the sky. Karolina was running hard now, the ribbon falling from her hair to the ground. Baby Richard's cries were drowning in the thunder.

"I'm coming, Richard." Her voice broke as she fought back the tears.

She had been told, watch but never intercede. How could the man expect her to ignore these cries? Karolina looked up to see that the sky had blackened, choking out any remnant of the sun. Around her the kids continued to play as if nothing was happening. They hadn't noticed the darkness, hadn't seen the birds.

The cloud of birds had beaten her to the playground. They had beaten her to baby Richard. She fought through them to get to the baby carriage. It was empty. The roar of birds quickly turned to laughter as they dispersed.

She dropped to her knees with Richard's blanket in her hands. The birds had ended Richard's cries by taking him. Karolina looked up as the birds began to circle the park. The darkness began to lift. Soon the sun returned and the birds were gone. The children were also gone.

She was alone.

Karolina Encinoe woke up from the dream in her rocking chair, tears streaming down her cheeks as she looked around the room.

She was alone.

Chapter Forty-nine

There was something about a police station that gave Violet a sense of belonging, and it didn't have to be her station to make her feel that way. It was the excitement, the camaraderie and, of course, the gamesmanship that was required to catch the bad guys. As expected, another headless body had been found. She was a young girl from one of those day tours.

Violet snapped a picture of the fingerprint, sent the text to Bradley, and in minutes confirmed a name for the Captain. The fingerprint, and the ID in her purse, both matched that of a Chelsea McKlente, twenty-four, born in Toronto, Canada. The gypsy had been correct in her prediction. She'd keep that to herself.

The Captain turned to Violet. "You look like shit." He thought it needed to be pointed out.

"What can I say, Cuba's a happening place." She filled a paper cup with the thick goo they passed off as coffee and started for the door. Victor had told her there was a book. He'd also told her it held the answers. That damn thing had been the only thing on her mind since talking to him. What did the book have to do with all these murders and what was it about him that she trusted? She did trust him. She also kept that from the Captain.

Violet left the station, deciding to head toward the Malecon. Perhaps a walk would help her find the answers. Who was she kidding? She needed to see the Ocean, see how Greg was doing. The wind had picked up and the storm clouds had started to roll in. He was a fool to try such a ridiculous trip.

She climbed up on the seawall and slouched as she stared off toward the Florida Keys. Dark clouds had enveloped half the sky and they looked angry. Violet checked her phone to see if there'd been a text from him. Her heart sank. Surely he'd had the sense to turn back?

A sparrow landed on the cement wall, three feet from her. "You're a brave little shit. I'm not one of your boss's friends, so go away."

He cocked his head and hopped closer.

Violet tried to shoo him away with her hand. He didn't move. Instead he continued to stare, as if expecting a handout.

"Well you're in the right country."

Any love she might have had for birds had withered, especially after being attacked over by the precinct a while ago. What a mess that had been; hundreds of birds, chattering, swarming. Then, all at once, they'd disappeared. That was when the old lady had appeared. It had been madness.

Violet was allowing the image of the old lady to surface when a shiver startled her. The old lady had been carrying a book. It was leathery and probably older than she was. A crazy energy had accompanied the old woman, or so she thought. Whatever it was, it was off the charts. She had just assumed the energy had came from the bird attack or even that freaky old woman. Was it possible that it was coming from the book?

She got to her feet and raced back towards the precinct. That alley was right across from the precinct entrance. The first drops of rain were starting to fall as she got closer. They started small, but by the time she got to the alley they were as big as grapes. The storm had arrived.

The Divine Ledger

The dead-end lane was deserted, yet she could feel the eyes. They were watching her. She looked around expecting to see birds lining the rooftops, ready to attack. She saw three. They were sitting on a doorframe guarding the opening. Violet swallowed hard and started for it.

The door was left ajar and neither it nor the birds did anything to stop her. Did this mean she was welcome? It wasn't the feeling she was getting.

Inside the apartment it was dark and it reeked. The stench was unfamiliar at first, musky, dirty. Soon the odour was unmistakable. She stepped into the living room. There, the light flooded in through the broken windowpanes, illuminating the source of the smell. It was bird shit and lots of it. It clung to the furniture, hung from the light fixtures and blanketed the floor like a runny carpet of curdled milk. Violet put a hand up to her nose.

In the middle of the room, an old lady sat in a rocking chair staring off as if in a trance. It was the lady from the street. She had a blanket draped across her lap, covering her tweed skirt. Birds sat on the blanket, on the shawl that covered her shoulders. They perched on shelves and on tabletops. There were hundreds of them.

The old woman clutched a book tightly to her chest.

"Excuse me?" Violet didn't mean for her words to come out so nasal. It was the smell of the birds. The last thing she wanted was for any more of the foul air to enter her lungs.

The old lady turned her head. She'd been crying. "He never told me."

Violet reluctantly took a step closer. "I'm sorry, what didn't he tell you?"

The old woman's eyes were weary. How could she have known any of this was coming? "He never warned me about the birds. What have I done?"

Violet couldn't take her eyes off the book. Victor was right. It captivated. There was a primal desire to touch it, to hold it, to have it. "Can I see that book?"

The old lady's eyes dropped down to it and then to Violet. "You really shouldn't."

"Just a quick look." Violet inched forward. "I'll give it back."

The old lady clutched the book tighter. "I can't."

Violet stopped. "What is that book?"

"Once the dreams of a young girl." Another tear started down her cheek. "Now it's just the nightmares of an old lady."

"That's very cryptic." It wasn't what Violet had asked for. Didn't anybody give straight answers any more? Violet pulled her gun out and took aim. "Look, I don't want to hurt you, but the book is a part of a murder investigation. You're going to hand it over. Alive or dead, it's your choice."

Violet had played enough poker to know when a bluff would pay off. She'd taken hundreds from the gang back in the Vancouver Police Department. This was an old lady and her chips had an expiry date. She wouldn't want to lose them.

"I can't."

Then again, there had been the odd night when Violet had left the poker table wondering how she was going to eat. She lowered her gun. "Look, I need you to give me that—"

A deafening blast cut through her plea for the book. Violet froze as she waited for that hot surge that often accompanied the bullet as it ripped into her flesh. Instead, it was the old lady's head thrown forward with such a force that it recoiled as if on a spring. Her blood sprayed the papered walls and ivory carpet of bird faeces like paint bursting from an exploding balloon.

Violet spun around to see a cowboy holding a Glock G27. The smoke was still hanging in front of him as he pushed the barrel of her gun aside. "It's me. Grab the book and let's get the fuck out of here."

They were Victor's cold, grey eyes. "Why'd you kill her?"

"Because you couldn't." He stared for a second, grateful that she couldn't pulled the trigger. "We don't have time right now to discuss this. Get the book and let's go."

"Why? What's…"

Birds started to pour into the room by the hundreds. They came from the bedroom, the bathroom and the kitchen. The room darkened as more birds joined those that were already there.

The Divine Ledger

Violet lunged through the flapping of wings and grabbed the book. Turning and slipping on the floor, she followed Victor out of the apartment into what had become a deluge. The flapping storm of feathers followed them. The birds shrieked, squawked and fluttered as they flew after them down the alley and out into the street.

A cab was idling at the curb while the driver stretched his legs under an awning. Through the rain he could see the man and woman as they jumped into the front seats of his Lada. He yelled, but they didn't stop. The engine was revving before he could get to his feet. The car's tires spun on the wet pavement, there was a brief lurch and his cab was gone.

The alley and the precinct shrank in the rear-view mirror as Violet and Victor made their getaway. Two cars quickly appeared from side streets and gave chase. Instinctively, Violet pulled out her gun.

"Forget it." Victor told her. "They're cops."

Chapter Fifty

Victor drove the car through the streets like he had stolen it, which was fair, because he had. Violet hung on. She had wanted to tour Cuba, but not like this. Street signs were ignored and red lights were blown. Behind them, the two cars were gaining. Was it fair that Violet couldn't use her gun, yet they could? Their first shot shattered the back window. Another found the trunk.

"Can't you go any faster?"

Victor didn't respond. His eyes scanned for traffic and pedestrians. They might be able to ditch the police in the traffic, but the flock of sparrows wouldn't be as easy. They were obsessed with the book and killing the old lady didn't help.

Violet looked over at Victor. The boots, the moustache, it suited him, but wasn't he a bloody Englishman? The gypsy had said he went by many names. "So, what's with the Halloween get-up, Jesse James?"

"I'd prefer you call me Rick if anybody asks."

"You mean if we go out on the town, dancing, maybe a movie or drinks? What are you, a cop?"

"I'm surprised you haven't asked your boyfriend yet." He cut a corner, bouncing the car off the curb. "Do I act like a cop?"

"I've known worse." She pointed her gun at him. "How about *you* tell me how you know Greg?"

"I don't work that way." He ignored the gun. The car drifted around the corner. "Maybe it's better if you think I'm a killer. I mean there's nothing magical about what I do."

"Sounds like you don't enjoy your work."

He briefly took his eyes off the road and made contact with hers. "Would you?"

"No, but I'm…" She couldn't find a word for sane that didn't come across as condescending, or make him sound nuts. "Why then?"

"It has to be done. I'm the one that pulls the trigger when others can't, like back there."

"I see that."

"I have a friend. He did some digging. I'll bet you already know what he found on you." He slammed the brakes and cranked the wheel hard to the left. The tires shuddered as he stomped on the gas pedal. "You have some pretty unique friends. Maybe you should start explaining yourself."

He waited for an answer. His researchers didn't run across people like her all that often. "Well?"

"Sorry." Violet opened the car door and rolled out. She took the brunt of the impact on her shoulder, flipped across the curb, then tumbled and somersaulted down a grassy slope. At the bottom she shook the wet grass from her hair and watched as the brake lights flickered. Then Victor and the two police cars raced down the street and out of sight. "Victor, my good man, you ask too many questions."

The rain continued to fall in sheets. The police hadn't seen her exit the car. They were having a hard-enough time keeping Victor in their sights. But the birds had seen her escape and they only cared about the book. Violet got up to run. In seconds she was overcome and abruptly knocked to the ground by the feathery swarm. Fighting through the mass of wings and claws, she spotted a large tree.

In the roots of the tree was an opening in the muddy soil. She took the book and stuffed it as deep into the hole as she could. Then she stumbled and crawled away from it. The birds remained, swarming around the tree. Damn, how she hated birds.

From the wet grass she watched the birds through the rain. There was a bench nearby and she eventually dropped her battered, mud-soaked body onto it. Birds covered the tree like angry bees, scaring off anybody that walked by. It took half an hour for them to calm down, much like they had been at the old lady's house. Soon they all found perches in trees and along power lines. The chirping and chattering, once a deafening roar, had become an ominous silence. The sinister wet birds, rain dripping off their beaks, had found peace. They sat quietly, staring at Violet.

Rain dripped down Violet's cheeks and off her nose as she studied the tree. The answer lay in that tree, in those birds and in that book, but it was no closer now than it had been that morning. In the distance the sirens wailed. First there were two, but that soon became many. Victor had his hands full. With any luck they'd catch him, realise who he really was and throw a rope around his neck. He had admitted to being a killer, because somebody had to do it. That was good enough for her.

Violet's only concern was that she had been seen with him. By now they'd have found the old lady, with her head blown open like she'd been cleaning her ear with a Q-tip made of dynamite. They'd link her to the old lady's murder and think she was the shooter. She also had a Glock that fired 40mm and the Captain knew it.

That meant her hotel room was no longer safe. They'd have a team watching it. Could she explain her way out of this? Anything was possible, but she'd also lied to them earlier. Strike three was her pulling a gun on that nerd in Mexico. As usual she had dug the hole and fallen into it.

"Damn it." For a second, she thought about phoning Bradley. Calling him was always her fall-back option when she was in it deep, and she had stepped in it good this time. The wailing of sirens, once distant and chasing Victor, were also closing in on her from all angles.

The birds, startled, had started to stir. About half of them took flight. Violet watched as they did a couple of loops, closed in tightly on one another and headed off. That still left hundreds to guard the book, but that wasn't the problem right now. The sirens were.

They must have seen her jump from the car.

Chapter Fifty-one

Elizabeth watched Greg's near-naked body as he lay motionless on the beach. He was handsome man, but unbelievably careless. The men where she came from were conservative and practical. She looked down at him and smiled. Soon he would wake up, which was only thanks to her intervention. Because of that he would owe her a favour. That was how it worked here.

Being naked herself for the better part of an hour, she had enjoyed the sun's warmth as it baked her skin. It was intense here in Cuba, but everything was different if compared to back home. For one thing, there was the concept of tanning. The idea of using the sun to toast your skin seemed ridiculous until she had tried it. Her new friend, Jenny Davies, had introduced her to it in the back yard of their home. It was relaxing and actually improved her mood. How was that even possible? There was no science behind it. The tanning soon became a late afternoon ritual. There was nothing better than setting a couple hours aside at the end of a hard day for a good toasting and an ice-cold tea.

She looked down at her naked frame and smiled at how her once white skin had started to bronze. Back home Nicole, her closest friend, had a hard time believing she was doing this. Why change what you were given? But Elizabeth loved how her curves seemed enhanced by the shadows of the tinted skin.

She looked out over the ocean and sighed. How long had it been since she her and Nicole had talked? Other than a recent communication warning about Greg's situation, it had been weeks.

A little voice in the back of her head started to chastise her. It was Jenny. If she were here she'd be telling her to put her dress back on, that nudity was frowned upon. But her dress had got wet and needed to dry. There was no reason to feel shame. The human body was an instrument of beauty, not embarrassment. That being said, there were laws about public nudity and she didn't need any trouble.

With the storm clouds distancing themselves, people started returning to the beach. Elizabeth walked over to the tree where her white dress was hanging. She slipped it on and smoothed it over her body. Greg was also starting to stir. He'd been peaceful, lying on his back. Who could blame him? She'd be tired too, had she spent that much time under water. At least he was alive.

When she'd first arrived at Jenny's, she was lost. Their two cultures were very different, but she had been chosen for a reason. Elizabeth's ability to charm, convince, and if required, manipulate people was exactly what was needed. There was also the fact that she could speak seven languages and was a science major. Being called a science major was putting it mildly. Now in her late twenties, she was one of the brightest scientists of her time. It came with a lifetime of dedication.

A half-winded grunt told her that Greg was coming to. She walked over to him and crouched down. "Are you okay?"

"What? Where am I?"

"Don't try and get up. Give your body a chance to catch up."

Greg blinked and rolled his eyes as he tried to focus on the woman. He knew her, didn't he? He tried to remember, but only brief flashes of recollection came to him. "What have you done to me."

It was time to weave her story. She didn't dare tell him the truth. He wasn't ready for that. "I was walking along the beach and I saw you in the water. I had to stop."

"What do you mean, you saw me?"

"You were just floating out in the currents, in your underwear. You had your pants around one ankle. I couldn't just let you drown."

He looked down. True to her word, he was in his underwear. An embarrassingly large bulge was pressing against the fabric of his shorts like a tent pole. "Awe, shit."

Reaching in, he pulled out his wallet. It was all coming back to him. He had left Cuba in a fishing boat. A freight ship had almost struck the craft. No, it *had* hit him. After that, the events blurred from bad to worse. He'd been ready for death, had almost welcomed it. Now it looked like he had cheated it.

"I'm sorry, my appearance. I…"

"I hung your pants on the branches to dry. I'll go get them."

Thank God, at least he had pants. He sat up and pulled his legs into his chest. The ocean was out there and it had tried to kill him. It had him in its grasp and there had been no escape. Then, for whatever reason, it had decided to cast him free.

He looked out at the ships and the blue sky. Then he looked down the beach for a clue. Had he made it to the Keys? There was a handful of people, but were they Americans or tourists?

"Hey, uh…"

She handed him his pants. "It's Elizabeth."

"Elizabeth, that's nice." He started to slip on a leg. "Am I in Florida or Cuba?"

She knew what he wanted to hear. He wanted to hear that he was in the good old US of A, but she hadn't brought him to that side. She'd brought him back. There was unfinished business. "You're in Cuba."

"Damn it."

"You wanted to go to the States?"

He stuffed the other leg in the pants. "I sure as hell don't want to be here anymore."

"What happened?"

He hiked his pants up. "I was on a boat, trying to get to Florida. The weather turned and I capsized."

"Isn't Cuba a better option than the bottom of an ocean?"

The Divine Ledger

"When you put it that way." Greg zipped his trousers. "I'm sorry. You don't understand. And I haven't introduced myself." He held out a hand. "I'm Greg."

She took it. "I'm still Elizabeth."

The hair, the cheekbones, she was beautiful. Her dress hugged her curves like a second skin and then there was that smile. It was infectious. But the quality that truly captured Greg, actually trapped him like a fly in honey, was her eyes. They were blue with mystical hints of grey and purple. They fascinated him, diminishing the rest of the world along with all the shit that came with it. They were magical and cast a feeling of enchantment on him that he didn't dare fight.

He knew her, sort of. She was the woman that he had seen at the cemetery and then again in the alley by the mall.

"Do I know you?"

"Seriously, Greg." She playfully batted her eyelashes. "Do lines like that ever work?"

Kevin Weisbeck

Chapter Fifty-two

The car door slammed shut as his blonde passenger leaped for her freedom. In the rear-view mirror her body rolled and tumbled. He tapped the brakes, but quickly decided against stopping. She was better off without him. This way she could put some distance between the cops and the book. Now his job was to drag these law-abiding do-gooders to the other end of town. He'd find her later.

He made a hard left down a back street and slowed to make sure he hadn't lost them. When the flashing lights came into view he hit the gas and let the desperation of losing them surge. He needed them to believe that he was the one worth chasing. Had they seen her jump?

The next corner was cut a little closer than he'd wanted. He clipped a magazine kiosk and sent people running for doorways. The owner fell in the melee and scrambled on his hands and knees through the mess of falling papers and magazines.

That stunt had gained a few feet of separation, but it had also loosened something in the steering. On his next left-hand turn he had to crank the wheel twice what he should have. And driving

The Divine Ledger

straight was no better. The car swayed to left and right as it brushed parked cars.

One of the cars that got nudged was a '56 Chevy. It was red and white and as beautiful as any muscle-car in a show room. All it needed was a set of Micky Thompson tires on Cragar mags and it would have been perfect. It was somebody's baby and a damn shame that he'd grazed it.

Victor watched the damaged car disappear in the rear-view mirror. He also watched two Ladas become four as they rounded the corner with sirens blaring. He knew he couldn't outrun them and pulling over wasn't an option. He debated going straight or around another corner. The choice was made for him.

The passenger-side front wheel folded under the car. The Lada bucked right and slammed hard against a retaining wall, knocking out a good section of the bricks. The car rolled through the barrier and over a twelve-foot ledge. The passenger door swung open and Victor flew through the opening as it flipped.

Landing upside down on the grass, the roof of the car crumpled to the door handles. Victor landed on the grass several feet away. The not-so-lush grass caught him with a thud as he rolled ten feet into a park bench where a mother and son sat.

Back on the street the police cruisers ground to a halt, lining the escarpment like Cherokee warriors in an old western. By the time Victor caught his bearings, ten police officers had lined up at the hole he'd put in the wall. Guns were drawn and aimed. Commands were shouted, and bystanders were running in every direction. Victor used that moment of confusion to go over his injuries.

His right leg was bleeding, but not sore enough to be considered serious. He'd ripped it open on the shifter. Both shoulders had been rough-tumbled on the roll, but again, nothing serious. The blur in his eyes was clearing and his ears rang, but they had done that for years thanks to the shooting range.

No, the biggest problem was his shooting hand. It had gone numb. He realised that when he reached behind his back for his gun. Should he run? He wouldn't get ten feet without being shot dead.

The police continued to yell at him as he tried to stand. He knew they wouldn't shoot him for that. They would however, lose their patience quickly if he didn't clasp his hands behind his head and drop back down to the ground.

Victor thought about grabbing the boy, who had sat frozen to the bench. His mother had bolted and now stood twenty feet off to the side. She was trying to coax her son over. With the feeling in his hand slowly coming back, he could grab the kid and use him as a shield. He imagined grabbing his knife from its holster and putting it to the boy's neck. None of the police would take the shot. He also imagined losing his grip on the kid. He'd be peppered with lead.

Then he saw his escape. On a rooftop, two buildings over, he saw the man in black. He was standing there, wearing that big black hat. His menacing birds were behind him in the distance and closing fast.

Victor started to inch away from the bench, hoping to work his way toward the shrubs. The shouting continued, but not at Victor. They had also seen the birds coming. There was a stairway that led down to where Victor was and several officers were running for it. The birds swooped down and met them halfway. They also curled around the police still standing by the broken wall. One officer panicked and squeezed off a shot. It cut through the mass of birds and caught Victor in the arm.

Victor didn't wait to see what happened next. He slipped through the bushes and down the narrow space between a couple of buildings. From there he disappeared into the crowd.

Now to find that crazy bird with that book.

Chapter Fifty-three

Violet had always played in trees. A treehouse was the only thing her father had ever built for her. He had a huge heart, but was never much of a handyman. The rickety ladder was more dangerous than climbing branches, so it had been quickly discarded. Besides, it was *her* tree house and she didn't like sharing. Soon she was climbing the tree like a cat.

And why stop and sit in a structure that creaked and moaned when there were branches ten or fifteen feet above. That was where the fun was. Last night, as the rains poured down and the police scoured the park, Violet brought those childhood skills back into play.

While the police spent hours searching the pathways and bushes, Violet found peace in the crotch of a sturdy branch, fifty feet above the ground. She fell asleep wondering if she'd wake up with a broken neck from a fall, or with a hundred guns pointed at her. She'd been known to snore. There had been neither.

The sore back, the stiff neck and the soggy clothing made her wonder whether a broken neck might not have been a better ending. With the police gone, she climbed down and took a seat on the park bench. The tree, with the book concealed in its roots, still had birds on every limb. Their numbers had returned while she slept. Even the muddy ground had feathery little sentries standing guard.

"Shit, you guys really need to turn it down a notch."

She was about to look for a coffee shop when her phone rang. She wiped the mud from the screen to find the answer button.

"Violet?"

"Greg? Is that you?" She changed hands and cradled the phone closer to her ear. "Where are you? Did you make it?"

"Long story there. I'll have to fill you in. Where the hell are you? I went to check your room, but there are cops everywhere. What have you done?"

"Where do I start?" And why was it, whenever she got to know a guy, they suddenly became *that* guy, the one that asked what *she* had done? Nobody ever regarded her as an innocent victim. Then she remembered the hole in the woman's head. "Let's say I'm no longer working with the precinct on this one."

"Whereabouts are you?"

She looked around and spotted a sign. "The El Parque de La Normal. Normal Park?"

"What's down there?"

"Come on over and I'll show you."

"Okay. We're at the Malecon. I think you're really close."

"We?"

"It's part of my long story."

"Make it quick." Violet ended the call. And what was up with the *we*? Let's hope this wasn't another one on Victor's wish list.

Across the street from the park, a coffee/gift shop/bookstore sat nestled between a couple of apartments. Rolling her hair up, she grabbed an *I love Cuba* hat and stuffed her hair up into it. She also bought a three-dollar pair of sunglasses and a cup of steaming black coffee. It tasted like breakfast. Walking back into the sun, she started rubbing the dry mud off her face. Last night's drenching had left her damp on the outside and cold on the inside.

"You look like shit." Greg quipped as he took her hand and dragged her out of the welcome sun into a shady alley. "You know, even with the hat and glasses, you stand out like the kid who peed herself."

"I'll bet you know all about that." Violet turned to face Greg's new friend. "I see you found a stray."

Elizabeth smiled as she stepped forward and rubbed a chunk of dirt from Violet's eyebrow. "Like I'm the stray."

"Really?" Violet took a threatening step toward her. Her make-up had been washed away, leaving her looking more like an Alice Cooper wannabe. It had been a rough night.

Elizabeth stood her ground. Greg's stray wore a formfitting dress and looked like a million dollars.

Greg stepped between them to end the stand-off. "Elizabeth found me on the beach. That storm last night capsized me. I'm lucky to be alive."

"Elizabeth, eh." Violet leaned toward him. "And do you trust this woman with your life?"

"Uh, yes, considering she just saved it. Are you okay? You seem a little…"

"I'm not the problem here." Violet held her arms up before dramatically dropping them to her side. "We've got shit to do and just because this woman saved your life, it doesn't make her a part of the team. I don't trust her."

"Relax." Greg insisted, "She's fine and we don't have time for this."

"Whatever." The man was like a kid with a new toy, so she started on her story. "Victor says there's a book. He also says it can explain why he's on this killing spree."

"You saw Victor again?" Greg grabbed her by the arm. "Did you get him?"

"This is my story and I don't like starting in the middle."

He let go. "By all means, continue."

"There's a book. He told me it has the answers to why he's doing what he's doing. Then I remembered seeing this old lady with a book. I went to check it out."

"Was it the book?"

"It was."

Violet went on to tell him about the book, cowboy Victor the sharp shooter, the old lady's exploding head and all the bird shit. It wasn't what Greg had wanted to hear. He'd wanted to hear that Victor was dead and he wanted answers to the serum issue. Violet had delivered neither.

"You should have killed him."

"We need answers. Now it's your turn." Violet remembered what Victor had said about Greg. There was one thing that had resonated, no, had wormed its way into her brain. "Victor said you know him, and so does your boss."

Chapter Fifty-four

Greg put his hand up to stop Violet from asking, because his knowing Victor wasn't a topic he wanted to talk about. Everything he had heard about Victor had been based on what others had told him. None of it was first hand information. Bottom line, Victor was a complicated threat. He also knew that if he said anything, the questions wouldn't stop there. She'd want to know where he got his information. She'd want to know how he had acquired his contacts. He couldn't tell her any of that. "Why didn't you just pull the trigger?"

This time it was Violet's turn to ignore his question. Not shooting Victor was something she felt in her gut. "We need him alive. This guy knows an awful lot about this book. He also knows something about the serum. I think we need to talk about why you just risked your life to get away from him."

"I can't tell you."

"That's fucking rich, yet I'm supposed to shoot him?" She took a step toward him. It was meant to intimidate and it worked. "He said he's not a cop, but he fights, thinks, and acts like he's a professional. This is not some random guy who watches TV in his parent's basement. He's got skill-sets."

Elizabeth was curious. "Skill-sets?"

Violet rolled her eyes. "He removes heads with surgical perfection, he's an expert shooter, he's trained in martial arts and the man can drive. There's more. I just haven't spent a lot of time with him … and why am I explaining this to you?"

Elizabeth shrugged. "I'm thinking you have a theory?"

"He's CIA."

They both turned their attention to Greg. Neither had to wait for Greg to answer. They saw it in his eyes. She was right.

Violet crossed her arms across her chest in disgust. While some of her anger was aimed at Greg, most of the blame fell on her own shoulders. She had toyed with the idea and ignored it, ignored it despite the fact that all the signs pointed to him being a CIA agent. Her gut was hung up on the killing. "What's his role, Greg?"

Greg turned away and tried to swallow, but it was like sand had replaced the saliva in his throat. "Okay. The American government trained him, and yes, he was CIA. I was briefed on him, but I never met him, officially. Unofficially, he came to me once. He was looking for help. It was some project that he didn't agree with. He wanted out."

"But there is no out with the CIA." Violet added, a comment meant more for Elizabeth.

"Never say never, but it often depends on the sensitivity of the mission. I had friends working on that project. They wouldn't tell me anything, couldn't, but they also disagreed with what was happening. Nevertheless, Victor was on his own."

"And when he couldn't get out…"

"He went rogue." Greg paused. "I heard he killed two people and kidnapped another."

Violet's gut hadn't been totally right, but it wasn't wrong either. He was CIA, but not anymore. "What happened to the one he kidnapped?"

"Nobody knows, and if they do, they're not talking. There was a lockdown on the information. I saw a redacted file. Someone had gone nuts with the felt pen."

Violet shook the bag to find the last of the puzzle pieces. "Okay, so this guy was CIA, he killed twelve people in Vancouver and he's killing again in Cuba. Oddly enough, he strongly believes that he can justify the killings and claims that the answers are in the book. My question is what does Victor want from you? Do you think he's still sore because you didn't help him?"

"Not his style. The woman at the Malacon said his name wasn't Victor. I believe there's some truth to that. I met him as Victor, but he didn't respond to that name very well. You know what I mean?"

"Kinda. So why didn't you cough this up earlier, like at the gypsy's table?"

"Same reason you didn't tell the police everything. Sharing limits your options and it negates the ability to colour outside the lines. I'm sure you know what I mean?"

Elizabeth cut in. "I don't."

Violet explained, "It's all about the grey areas. If I act stupid and people buy it, they won't link me."

"Sounds like you've got that mastered." Elizabeth couldn't resist.

"Screw you." Violet turned to Greg. "Why is she here?"

He put his hands on her shoulders. "Can't you get along with anybody."

"That depends on who the 'anybody' is." She squirmed free. "What happened to Victor?"

"Victor ended up on the Laundry list."

Again, Elizabeth found herself at a loss.

Violet rolled her eyes and surprised Greg with her knowledge. "It's a list of, let's call them traitors or spies, who've been earmarked for elimination, like tidying up the loose ends. There's often an internal bounty put on them. Some agents use the challenge to advance their careers. Was Victor turned? It's not like CIA agents get cold feet."

"Everyone thought that the Russians were involved but, honestly, there was no way of knowing."

"And here we are in Cuba, a former Russian stronghold, talking about conspiracies and mind-control serums." It made sense, except for one thing. "I'm not sure it's him. I found a thirteenth skull. It was tossed into the jungle back in Sayulita." Then she showed him the text from Bradley confirming that the thirteenth skull had been Victor's.

"And what do you think?" he asked.

"He's committed to being Victor and he admits that Bradley's DNA results are correct. It's like he left it with me as some kind of riddle. Call it an incentive. The book has the answers and he needs me to find it so I can have those answers."

Greg asked the obvious question. "Do you have any idea where this book is?"

Violet pointed to the tree. "The damn birds have it."

Chapter Fifty-five

Hundreds of sparrows sat, fluttered, and twittered on and around the tree. At one point, Violet had started counting them, but gave up. A calculated estimate was fifteen hundred to two thousand birds. That was a shit-ton of nasty claws and sharp little beaks.

The bench was a safe fifty feet from the tree and it was fifty feet from the book. It was in the DMZ. Greg spoke first. "How'd you get it in there?"

"Desperation. They were attacking me." Violet pulled her hair aside to reveal a number of peck wounds. "It was a lot easier to get rid of it."

Greg nodded. "I see."

A cat appeared from behind a shrub. Spotting a couple of the birds on the ground, it edged closer but stopped when the other birds came into view. Hair rose on its back and its tail bushed up like a squirrel's. In seconds the feline was bounding across the grass in full retreat. Lunch would have to come in the form of a mouse, bug or an open trashcan.

Elizabeth stared as the cat left. "Where I come from, they eat birds."

Violet got to her feet. "They do that here too, but these aren't your everyday birds." She edged toward the tree and the fluttering began. She turned to Greg. "After you."

"What?"

"Seriously? You're the guy here. Man up and take one for the team."

"Not a chance."

This wasn't the first time someone had tried to bully him into doing something stupid. He remembered a high-end nightclub a few blocks down his university. He'd frequented the club as a first-year student. One night a friend tried to get him to kiss one of two girls at the end of the bar. Normally, boys no longer living at home didn't need much coaxing. The girls, however, were somehow different. Although they were adorable, something didn't seem right. It turned out they were dudes in heels. Greg had been right to fight off the peer pressure and he was right now.

"Here's a thought then, your new friend can do it?"

He looked over to Elizabeth.

She stepped back, surprised that he might even consider asking. "I'm not doing it."

Greg waved his hand like it had never crossed his mind, but it had, and they had both seen it. "I think we need more cats."

Violet looked around. It was Cuba, land of the strays. "How many do you think we'll need?"

Greg remembered stepping on the birds and having them come back to life. "Too many."

"If cats won't do it, then how?" Again, Violet was hinting for him to step up. There was still time for him to show some gumption. The threat was from birds, after all, and not from a crocodile or a grizzly bear.

"Fine. I'll do it."

Violet smiled. The bullies had won.

He pretended to push up the sleeves of his white *Welcome to Cuba* T-shirt and headed toward the tree. The birds started up. Over his shoulder he could see that Violet and Elizabeth were retreating towards the bench. The two Benedict Arnolds were wide-eyed. He took two more steps and about eight birds took flight.

"Go ahead, Greg. They're just birds," Violet coached. "Just birds."

Elizabeth added, "The sooner you get it done, the less pecks and scratches you'll have."

"There're not *just* birds." He muttered. "And how many birds does it take to peck an eye out of its socket?"

Violet had to yell over the chirping. "What was that?"

Greg ignored her. He was close enough now to ruffle every feather. Like synchronised swimmers diving into a pool, one by one the birds took flight. Within seconds some two hundred birds had knocked Greg to his knees. He swatted the sentries from the hole, but that was as far as he could get.

His hair was pulled and his skin was bitten and perforated. He swiftly retracted his hand from the hole to swat at a bird that was hanging from his left earlobe like an earring. As he did that, another pecked at his lip and another at the tender flesh on his chin. "Damn it! Ouch! God no!"

Birds fluttered as he shook his head and flayed his arms. He dove for the hole and once more had to stop to knock birds from his face. Two of them had a hold of his eyebrow.

Violet cupped her hands to her mouth. "Grab the book, Greg."

"I'm fucking trying."

When a beak locked onto the sensitive skin between his nostrils, the full-on retreat began.

"No Greg. Go back," Violet cried. "Get the book. You were so close."

Greg stumbled his way back to the girls. The birds retreated and returned to their roosts. He started wiping the blood from his face. "You get the damn book."

"Whoa," Violet laughed. "Relax, eh."

Elizabeth also chuckled. "Come on. They're so small and you're so big and strong. I know you can—"

"Save it. I'm not going back. That's one crazy flock." He walked over to the bench and sat down.

Elizabeth joined him. "At least you tried."

"Look." Violet pointed across the park. The cat from earlier was sitting with two other cats. After this last display from Greg, they had seen enough. Two more cats had been watching from a safe distance on the other side. "I wonder what's going on in their heads?"

"They don't know the half of it. You see, when I was…" Greg was about to tell them how he'd seen the crushed birds come back to life when he stopped himself. It had given him an idea. "I think I know what it's going to take."

He got up and headed for the street. Violet and Elizabeth got up to follow.

"No. You two stay here. It won't work otherwise."

"What's the plan?" Violet asked.

"Meet me at that good restaurant in an hour." Greg gave her a stay-put wave as he sprinted for the bus. "And bring the book."

Chapter Fifty-six

Greg left with a plan. Violet wondered if he was picking up guns, grenades, or a flame-thrower? She smirked at the thought. Could they get away with burning down a tree full of birds in Havana? Think of all those charred wings, and her with no hot sauce. Then, as if flicking on a switch, she realised she had Elizabeth all to herself.

"Elizabeth? I like it. It suits you. So tell me, out of all the choices, why the hell did you chose Greg?"

"It's good to see you again." Elizabeth added, "Violent, is it?"

"There's no n. Why is that so damn hard? Violet Stormm. It's my detective name."

"Can you see how people could make the mistake?" She laughed. "It sounds a lot like Violent Storm, and that might suit you a little better. I say put the n back in it."

"Funny, but it was never there." Violet sat down beside her. "I've missed you guys."

"How's it going down here?" Elizabeth asked.

"You know, lots of contacts, lots of learning. I'm sure you've see my reports."

"Nicole gets the reports. I'm busy in DC. I almost didn't recognise you ... the hair, the jeans, and what's with all the attitude?"

"I'm living the life of a bad-ass detective."

"You always wanted something bigger than what you left back home."

"I did." Violet pushed the reunion aside. "So why this Greg guy? Who is he?"

"It's more like, who is he connected to."

"Is he our liaison?"

"He is."

"That must mean we're getting closer. I'm guessing you found a family?"

"I did. I'm staying with the Davis family, Jenny and her parents Tom and Claire. They're good people. I'm in position."

"I like the tan."

"Don't you just love toasting." Elizabeth stretched her arms out. "Remarkable, isn't it."

Violet stretched her arm out beside Elizabeth's to compare. She wasn't as tanned as Elizabeth was. "Don't you work?"

"I help the family do charity work in the mornings. I do toasting in the afternoon."

"Seriously? It's called tanning and charity work is boring. You should try being a cop? I could pull some strings."

"The idea is to blend in, learn what you can and not get shot. We're getting tired of you being patched up."

"Bullshit. You learn by doing, not by handing out sandwiches."

"You haven't changed." Elizabeth shook her head and then gasped. "Oh, I get it. It's Greg. You're trying to impress him, aren't you?"

"Hell, no. Trust me, I'm not after him. He's just bait to find Victor."

"Not any more. I need him alive." Elizabeth looked over to the tree. "What's with that book? Is it a part of some case you're on?"

"It's so much more than that. You remember that crazy dialect that Nicole was trying to decipher?"

"She's still obsessed with it. Why?"

"This book had something on it that looked very similar."

Elizabeth inched closer. "Are you sure?"

"Not a hundred percent sure, but it's pretty close."

"That's remarkable. Don't put any of that in your reports. Nicole doesn't need the distraction unless it's true."

"Okay, but for the life of me, I can't imagine how her research could be linked to my murder case." She shrugged. "Tell me what you can about Nicole's work."

"She talks about it when I see her, but I seldom listen. It's not a part of my mission. Maybe I can do some digging."

"Please do. I need some of this to make sense." Violet put a hand on her shoulder. "It really is good to see you again. Sometimes it feels like I'm all alone out here."

"Is that why you got the tattoo."

"I know, stupid, right?"

"Not at all. The slang, the tattoo and the attitude makes you one of them. I know the others are proud of you. So why this case?"

"It came to me and I knew right away that it was where I was meant to be. I have no idea why, but I feel this."

"Then go with it." She put a hand on Violet's hand. "I heard about Bradley. I'm so sorry. I wish I could have been there for you."

"Hey, it is what it is."

"You can knock it off with the tough gal act. It's me, remember?"

"Why do things like that happen to me? I find these guys, I fall for them and they're assholes, or in Bradley's case, crippled."

"Don't give up on Bradley. It won't be long. Soon we'll be going forward with the next stage. We won't forget about him."

"It's hard to watch him struggle in that fucking chair."

"Fucking? You sound like you found a new favourite word."

"Let me give you some advice, my friend. You have to let their culture come to you. Cursing is a big part of it in my line of work and so is attitude. Let your hair down and embrace them.

You'll find it easier to understand them. They're all about emotion and expression."

"For me it's all about image. I'll be on the world stage soon and I can't be seen swearing, and acting all..."

Violet finished the sentence for her, "like a gun-wielding crazy?"

"Yes. Help me understand. As a Vancouver Homicide detective, are you Russian, American or Cuban? Like I said, I haven't read many of the reports."

"Canadian."

"But they're so gentle, so..." Elizabeth laughed when she figured it out. "Pretty nice cover."

"So why don't you get that book for me? I know it wouldn't be that hard for you."

Elizabeth looked around. "Too many witnesses. I'm a liaison, not a magician. Give Greg a chance."

"And what about Greg?" Violet asked. "He's your type, isn't he?"

"Oh, that's just what I need. No, I'm not getting involved." She gave a deep sigh. "But he is cute, isn't he?"

"In a goofy kind of way. So how does Greg fit into your plan?"

"He's my way in."

"But he doesn't even know you."

"Yes, but he owes me for saving his life. That's going to come with a hefty price tag."

"Really? Sounds devious, especially for you."

"Greg Miller doesn't know it yet, but he's a critical part of our mission." She added, "but first I have to win his trust."

"Well, you saved his life, you're a good-looking woman and he's recently divorced. He's hitting on anything that moves. Getting into position shouldn't be that hard, if you know what I mean."

"That isn't the plan." She gave Violet a horrified scowl. "You're evil. What's this place doing to you?"

"I'm just saying." Violet cocked a brow and shrugged. "We need results anyway we can get them, right?"

Chapter Fifty-seven

A double-decker bus left the curb with a belch of diesel smoke that was as dark as the swarm of birds. It was the bus that Greg had needed and missed. He slapped at the side of the bus as he awkwardly ran through the cloud. A young girl quietly watched from her window as Greg chased the bus through the green light and the two blocks to the next stop. He got on, giving the bus driver five pesos and a very dirty look. Then he grabbed the first available seat beside the girl.

"You could have said something to the bus driver."

"You're bleeding, mister."

Greg saw her pointing at his forehead. "Yes, thank you."

He wiped it, smiled, and moved to a different seat.

Sure, his forehead was bleeding, but it was the ear that stung like it was on fire. Rubbing it between his index finger and thumb helped.

When the bus reached the cemetery, Greg got off and ran across the street. Beyond the gates, one hundred and forty acres of headstones waited. Every time he'd visited this place the sparrows had come. The birds brought the man, with a spectacle that freaked him out. He hoped it would be the same again.

The air was hot, yesterday's rain not even a memory now. Dust lifted with every step Greg took. Where were they? After a couple of minutes Greg gave in to the obsession and started searching for his tombstone. His name had to be somewhere in this place. The names rolled past him like pickets on a fence. Twice he had found a Gregory, but he wasn't a Gregory. He also wasn't a Jimenez or Fuentes.

He looked up. The sky was still clear. "Shit. Where are you guys?"

Rosa, Maria, Vincent, Robert, Marie…there were a lot of Marie's and Maria's. There were also many Anthony's and Hernando's. Some of the graves had wilted flowers, while others hadn't seen flowers in years. Then he saw a tombstone that reminded him of the girls. There was an Eliza Strom. She had been born in 1924 and had died in 2002. There was something written below her name. The spelling wasn't even close on either name, but it got him crouching down to wipe at the dust. *Buenas Noches Mi Amigo* - Good Night My Friend. A shadow spread across the tombstone as he read it.

Greg looked up to see the feathery cloud forming.

Elizabeth and Violet sat staring across the park at the tree. There were so many birds. Elizabeth broke the silence. "So why is Greg divorced?"

Violet shrugged. "Not sure. He's a stand-up guy. No doubt he's got a few quirks, but who doesn't."

"This coming from you."

"Be nice or I'll—" She ducked as a bird rocketed past her.

What started with one bird soon became hundreds. They dropped from the branches and swooped into flight. Within seconds the majority of the birds were in formation. Violet pushed Elizabeth aside. "Look out."

The birds came at them in a steady stream and in seconds they were gone.

"Quick, Violet. Grab the book."

She fought off a handful of stray birds that had stayed behind, grabbed the book from the hole and ran. The birds would return and she had no intention on being anywhere close when they did. Elizabeth followed. They cut through yards, parking lots and buildings, staying away from the parks and trees. After a few blocks, the restaurant where she and Greg had met came into view and they dove into it. Being a few hours between mealtimes, there was no line up.

Elizabeth grabbed the book as soon as Violet sat down. "What is this thing?"

There was definite energy to it. She opened it, hoping to learn what all the fuss was about. Violet watched from across the table. Her heart sank as she saw the first few pages. They were blank.

Greg showed up an hour later. "What did you find?"

Elizabeth slid the book over, along with a napkin for the blood on his lip. Greg picked the book up and opened it. They both watched his smile fade as his eyes scanned page after page. "Are you serious?"

Violet took her phone from her pocket. She sent a text to Bradley informing him that the book was a red herring. Furthermore, it was a death sentence for Victor.

Greg continued to scan page after page until he reached the end. They were all blank. Elizabeth excused herself and Greg's eyes followed her as she went to the washrooms. Violet noticed his eyes studying her walk. It was a smouldering saunter that she herself had never learned. For a reaction like that, she might have to.

"Don't worry. I'm so gonna cap that son-of-a-bitch next time I see him."

That brought Greg back. "There's the Violet I know and love."

Violet sneered as she thumbed through the menu. "Are we ordering?"

"We might as well."

The waiter came and Greg ordered for Elizabeth. Violet made the meal choice unanimous. They'd all have the chicken. Eating any kind of bird after the day they'd just had would have done. The food came shortly after Elizabeth returned and they all ate without speaking. There was nothing to say.

Kevin Weisbeck

When they got up to leave, Violet half expected to see the policianiolas waiting for them outside. She was now a wanted felon. Greg was expecting the birds to be lined up across the street on the Capitol Building. Every sill and rooftop would be lined with beady eyes and sharp beaks. They'd be waiting for them. Elizabeth merely hoped that someone else would carry the book.

But there were no birds, no police, and Elizabeth found the book to be heavier than she thought. Violet had, however, noticed something that she didn't expect. She was in full sprint across street before the other two realised she was on the run. Her gun was drawn.

Chapter Fifty-eight

Greg wasn't sure why Violet was running until he caught a glimpse of Victor across the street. The woman dodged cars while tires squealed, and horns honked. What was she thinking, going after this guy in broad daylight? Would she shoot him if she got him cornered? He didn't give it a second thought as he stepped off the curb and took off after them.

Elizabeth, a little more in control of her emotions, saw how everything was coming apart. Violet was drawing unwanted attention and Greg was heading into traffic without looking. Violet had also raced into traffic, but she was used to doing that kind of thing. It wasn't just luck running with her as she scooted past a bus, then two cars and a motorcycle. She had done this kind of thing many times before.

Greg wasn't nearly as catlike or as quick. Three steps into the first lane of traffic, the blaring of a bus's horn froze him in his tracks. The bus showed no signs of stopping.

In the next second, Elizabeth was wrapped around him in a bear hug, the breeze from the passing bus licking at their hair. They were back at the curb. Greg struggled to get his words out. "What just happened?"

Elizabeth released her grip on him and reached down to pick up the book that she'd dropped. "I saved your life. I guess that's two favours you owe me."

"Sure, anything, but that's not what I meant." He looked around to see that they were on the same curb that they'd been standing on earlier. The bus hadn't stopped. They were staring at the back wheel when it finally ground to a halt. "What did you just do?"

"I shoved you out of the way."

"No, you didn't. That bus was about to flatten me and there was no way you could have shoved me that hard. Besides, how could you have shoved me backwards?"

"Look, I saved you. I'm sorry. Is that what you want, an apology?"

"No. Don't get me wrong. You saved my life and I'm grateful, but it makes no sense."

"You're alive and I'm calling in my first favour." She held up a single finger. "Favour one, accept the fact that you're okay."

He looked back at the bus.

Elizabeth started to scan through the crowd. "I think we lost them."

Greg couldn't take his eyes off her. This tiny creature, one hundred and twenty pounds of blonde hair and silken skin, had just moved him a good ten feet. To top it off, she stood there like it was no big deal. He couldn't stop trembling. It was insanity.

"I said, Violet's gone. We have to get going."

"I agree." Greg nodded. "We should head back to the hotel. I need to regroup, call Ricky, and fill him in."

As they walked, people backed away to give them as much space as they needed. Everyone had seen what she'd done.

Chapter Fifty-nine

Down the back alley, through a hole in the fence and into the back street with the grace of a gazelle, Violet managed to keep Victor in her sights. She'd also been led down alleys, between parked cars and past an old man in a rocking chair. She hadn't been paying attention. Unlike many of the back alleys, this one was a dead end.

"Freeze, asshole."

Victor obliged her. He knew her gun was now trained on him. With his hands in the air, he wiped the smile off his face and slowly turned around. As he did, Violet let the vision of the dead woman's face wash over her. Pulling the trigger for that old woman should be easy—Victor was a killer. But nothing was easy anymore. Hell, if anything, she was an accomplice. She was there when he pulled the trigger. She'd had her own gun trained on the old lady.

In her defence, the place had consumed her. It had been surreal with all those birds, the shit and that stench. The crazed bird-loving woman had a black rippled book. Violet wanted it, badly. Victor had said it held answers, yet it held nothing. The old woman had died for nothing. The anger returned and she started to squeeze.

"You know there's more to this, Miss Stormm."

She kept a firm pressure on the trigger. He wasn't lying. That old lady had been crying. She had said that the book had become a nightmare. Violet hadn't understood. Now she was even more confused. It was blank, worthless. Had Victor's bullet been a welcome escape for her? Was that why he had lied about the book?

She aimed carefully and fired off a shot. "You lied to me?"

Victor kept his hands up as the bullet grazed his right arm. He didn't flinch as the bullet creased his flesh. "Lied?"

"The next one's gonna hurt a whole lot more if you don't start coming clean with me. The book was nothing more than empty pages."

"What? You mean to tell me it was blank?"

"That's what I said." She slowly put pressure on the trigger again. This would feel good. Closure usually did.

He laughed as he ran his eyes up and down her body. "I never would have guessed you to be a...."

"What the fuck is so funny? Tell me why I shouldn't just shoot."

"Why?" His smile widened. "Because you and I both know you need answers more than you need to cap me. Why am I killing? Why these people? What's the book about? I need to ask, did you open the book or did Greg?"

"Greg did. Elizabeth had it too."

"You never held it while it was open?"

Violet tried to remember. She hadn't opened it. "Why would that matter?"

"It's everything. What do you know about this woman, this tag-along?" He took a step toward her. "She seems a little too convenient."

"Greg ran across her."

"Trust me on this." He walked up to her and put his hand over hers, lowering the gun. "This girl is anything but random. You know that."

Violet did know that. "What's up with the book? Why was it blank?"

"You need to be the one holding the book in order to see its power. Open it and read it. I doubt that it'll be blank when *you* read it."

"The damn thing was blank. I saw it."

"It was blank for Greg and that girl. What did the old lady tell you?"

"She said the book had become her nightmare."

"You can't really believe it's blank then, can you? You've had your gun on me more than once and I'm still standing. There's a reason for that, even if you don't want to believe it."

It was true. She could have finished him and been on the next flight home. He had killed over thirty people. She'd seen him murder the old lady. Mercy-killing or not, it was cold-blooded. "Why can't I kill you?"

"Because you're better at your job than you'd like to admit." He hinted a smile. "You're smart enough to trust your instincts and to see the bigger picture."

"Having a hard time at the moment."

"Go look at that book again, hold it, and feel its energy. Then you'll have what you need. I'll be around."

"And if it's blank?"

"It won't be, and don't forget to lean on Greg. You're a detective, damn it. Get him to tell you who I am. He doesn't know the whole story, but he knows enough. But first, read that book. Then I'll tell you everything. Hell, I'll even tell you all about that thirteenth skull. But then I'll need a favour from you."

"A favour?"

"It'll be one you can't say no to."

She watched his eyes. They were steady, honest. "I don't want you killing anyone."

"I don't want to kill anymore either. I liked Bob and Beverly. I also liked that little rodeo girl, but this isn't my call."

In his eyes, she could see his commitment. There would be no stopping him, except for the bullet she couldn't seem to fire. "Give me some time. I'm guessing you have a number in your head. How many?"

"I have a list. Like I said, nothing is random." He took a quick glance at his arm. The blood was trickling down to his elbow. "It's sixteen this time. That doesn't include the old lady."

"Are they linked?"

"You still want to solve this and stop the killing, don't you?"

"I do."

"Get that thought out of your head." He clapped the dust off his hands, off his jeans. "I'm not at liberty to tell you anything more. Grab that book, Miss Stormm. Open it and I guarantee you'll have your answers. Not saying there won't be a different set of questions though."

She had him in her sights. It could all end now. "How can I trust you?"

He stopped, reached into his back pocket and pulled out the passports. They were hers and Greg's. "Your purse is in a grocery bag, in the bushes over by the trash bin where we first met."

"And the killing?"

"Make you a deal." He started to walk away. "I'm gonna grab a couple cigars. Then I'll come find you. You've got two hours."

Chapter Sixty

Back at the hotel, Violet could sense a trap. The police were nowhere in sight, but their cars were. Although they were all unmarked Ladas, many of them had the light blue licence plate associated with police only. Sammy reluctantly parked across the street. He didn't say anything. Instead he went to the trunk of the car and retrieved the wheelchair, stolen from the pharmacy down the street.

Violet changed and put her hair up into a large straw hat. Sammy pretended to help her into the chair before wheeling her into the lobby. Then she handed him a hundred pesos, watched him leave and wheeled her way to the stairwell. Where was everyone, hiding in her room?

In hindsight the wheelchair was a bad idea. She'd never make it up the stairs without giving herself away. Besides, what front desk would ever put a handicapped guest on a second floor? Her friends had either been scared off or arrested. "Shit."

"Language, Miss Stormm." Hands grabbed the rear handles of the wheelchair and pulled her away from the stairs. It was a woman's voice. "Right this way."

Instinct told Violet to get up and run. A firm hand shoved her back down.

"Stay put." It was Elizabeth's voice. "We have a different room. Say hello to Allan and Donna Reid."

"Good move."

Near the end of the corridor, Greg held a door open. "What the hell happened to you?"

"I saw Victor." Violet peeled off the hat and sailed it onto the bed. "Where's that book?"

"Don't tell me he got away, *again*?"

"All I had to do was squeeze the trigger." She closed her eyes. "I couldn't."

"Why the hell not?" Greg fumed.

"He wanted me to read this damn book first. He was adamant."

Ricky was in the corner, thumbing through the book. "I've got it right here." He got up and handed it to her. "Nothing in it though."

"Victor insists it's special."

"He's lied to you," Greg scolded. "You know that book is a joke. You saw it in the damn restaurant."

Violet had intended on giving Greg his passport. Instead she left it in her purse, which she tucked under the bed. "The guy let me catch him, Greg. He wanted to know what I saw. I doubt he would have done that if that thing was a dud."

Violet took the book from Ricky and placed it in her lap. She closed her eyes and placed her hands on it, palms down. Energy surged through her fingertips. It was emotional; fear, love, hope and hurt. They were all there. She pulled her hands back. "What the fu…"

"What?" Greg asked.

"Didn't any of you feel anything when you touched it?"

Greg picked the book up from her lap. He shrugged and dropped it back down. "It's a book, nothing more."

Violet looked at both Ricky and Elizabeth. They shrugged. There'd been nothing.

The Divine Ledger

She placed her hands over it again and let the energy surge through her. The leather undulated under her fingers. She could feel the cover crawling, shifting, as if it had come to life. Something was surfacing. She slowly pulled her hands away. It had changed. Once a single shade of black, it was now a smokier ripple of ebony and inky greys.

In the middle of the book, letters and numbers rose from the leather, *WS14J694124S-25*. To Greg and Ricky they were random letters and numbers. To Violet, they represented something far more important. She said nothing but saw the shock in Elizabeth's eyes. This was impossible. How could this book have known?

"Where'd that come from?" Greg moved closer. "What is it?"

The lie came automatically. "That was an identification number I was given as a child. It's a Canadian thing." She knew that none of them, other than Elizabeth, had any way of knowing what it really meant.

"That number belongs to you?" Greg asked. "How does this thing know that?"

"You act like I should know," she snapped. "It's a fucking book; paper, leather and cardboard. How the hell could it know?"

"Then how…" Greg reached down and ran his fingers over Violet's ID. Little curls of smoke rose from the leather. He drew his hand back. The tips of his fingers had been scorched. "Ouch. Son-of-a-bitch."

Seeing that, Violet ran her fingers over the letters. Nothing happened to her. They felt velvety. Then she took a corner and opened it. The book was now filled with words. She started reading … out loud at first, but her words tapered off as she continued.

Nicole Stevenson - born June 24, 2005 - Blue eyes, blonde hair, 4' 6" tall, 89 lbs.

Currently attending John Robson Elementary School, excelling in math, English and social studies. Will become a school teacher, grades two to four, and marry at the age of twenty-two. There will be three granddaughters: Marlis, Dorothy and Nikky. She will live to ninety-one years of age and have seven great-grandchildren.

Jennifer Stevenson - born June 27, 2005 - Blue eyes, blonde hair, 4' 6 1/2" tall, 86 lbs.
Currently attending John Robson Elementary School and excelling in soccer, ice hockey and girl's rugby. She will become a police officer with the New York Drug Enforcement Agency and marry at the age of thirty. Her husband will be a fellow officer. They will adopt a child, Patrick, from Germany.

Violet had to stop reading. There were more, but the lump in her throat was beginning to choke her. "This is impossible."
"Who are these people." Elizabeth asked.
She wanted to stop reading but couldn't. The next name she read to herself while her fingers traced the words on the page. She could feel the connection as the tears began.

Michael Stevenson – born July 03, 2005 - Blue eyes, blonde hair, 4' 8" tall, 88 lbs.
Currently attending John Robson Elementary School and excelling in science, math, ice hockey and painting. He will become a writer and publish forty-two novels. Most will be a mystery series based on his mother's career as a homicide detective. He will marry only once and father four boys: Bobby, Derrick, Steven, and Johnny.

Greg moved Violet's hand off the page. "Violet, talk to us. You act like you know him."
"I know all of them." Another tear started to trickle down her cheek as she flipped through the pages full of names. "These are my children."

Chapter Sixty-one

Violet took a short break to compose herself, then she reopened the book. There had been a gap of three months before the names carried on. She wanted to know, had to know. Her eyes danced in their sockets as she scrambled to get the book open to where she'd left off.

"No." Greg grabbed the book away from her. "You need to talk to us Violet. Who are these kids, and when did you have them?"

"I didn't."

Elizabeth moved between them. "Any ideas?"

"I dated a Danny Stevenson years ago. He was a handsome boy, an orderly at the hospital. I was twenty and had just moved to Canada." Her mind began to drift. "I met him at a football game. He helped me after I slipped on some ice. If I remember correctly, it was the last time I wore a dress. My legs were kicking at the sky as I landed hard on my back. My tailbone was bruised, and I was bedridden for a week. Danny took care of me. He brought me food, taught me to play cribbage and even bought me a teddy bear."

Greg crouched down in front of the wheelchair. "You had kids with him?"

"There were no children, ever." She tried to shake the confusion. "We started dating. It was like we'd found something magical. We got drunk and had fun in the back seat of his '68 Impala. It was a hot car with a conveniently large back seat. He told me he loved me. It was wonderful, but we were careful."

Tears threatened to come in waves, but she fought them off. "He told me he loved me. It was the first time I had heard those words."

"What about your parents?"

"I'm sure they loved me, but love was never talked about. I'm not sure if it was because their parents never said it to them or it was just a she-already-knows kinda thing. It didn't matter. The first person to say it to me was my Danny. After he said that, I was his ... mind, body and soul."

Elizabeth asked, "Yet you didn't conceive with him?"

"No, and I didn't want to. I made sure he used a condom. One day he went off with a pair of his friends. It was a weekend of hiking in the Okanagan. I wasn't going to see him for a couple of days. He wanted to go and asked me if it was okay. Who was I to say no? They were off on their big-boy adventure."

Again, she stopped to compose herself.

"I got a call the day after they left. It was Stan. They'd been cliff-diving at Kalamalka Lake. Danny had jumped in doing a somersault. He'd come close to the rocks and never surfaced. The scuba divers searched for hours while his friends stood on the shore with the police."

"Violet, I'm so sorry."

Violet turned to see Elizabeth. She'd never shared that story with anybody. It wasn't important, as far as the mission went. She turned back to Greg. "Give me the book."

"I don't think that's a good idea."

"I need to see something."

"I'm not sure you should," Elizabeth added.

"Look. I didn't date for six months. Eventually a guy named Tom Werthington found his way into my heart. It became a physical relationship that lasted six months."

Elizabeth asked. "What happened with him?"

"He made the mistake of telling me he was married. Thought it might be time to come clean when I found his wedding band. It had fallen out of his pocket when he got dressed. With the sex over, he had to get home. It was a big day at his house, a kid's birthday or something."

Violet snapped her fingers and Greg handed her the book. She had slept with this asshole fourteen times. In the book there were fifteen names, eight boys and seven girls. Two of the girls were twins. "They were called Jaclyn and Jade."

"Shit." She started thumbing through the other pages.

"What is it Violet?"

"I was attacked once. It was dark. I'd been jumped from behind and struck on the head. That was all I could remember. When I came around, I was right where I'd fallen, my pants around my ankles. I showered for an hour when I got home and I prayed for weeks that the nightmare wouldn't continue. I got lucky."

Elizabeth placed a hand on her shoulder. "Did you ever find out who did it?"

"No." She stopped flipping through the pages and her heart sank as she read the name, Morgan Fitzpatrick, born April 9, 2008. "There was a Darren Fitzpatrick in my training class, tall kid, shy, looked like trouble."

It was the only way the bastard could have had her. Her nostrils flared as she contemplated how to torture him, and torture him she would.

Greg was still trying to catch up. "What the hell does all of this mean?"

Violet held his gaze with an I-told-you-so look. "It means Victor wasn't lying."

Chapter Sixty-two

Ricky sat quietly on the bed, deep in thought. The gears in his mind kept returning to the same question—how was the ledger linked to the serum? Several theories were bouncing around in his head. Did the book hint at time travel or was it subliminal suggestion? There was no time to waste. He got up and started for the door.

Greg caught this out of the corner of his eye. "Where are you going?"

"My serum. I need to check something. This book is an eye-opener. I don't know how it knows these things or why it didn't work for me, but I need to go over a few calculations."

Violet asked, "Like what?"

"Does the serum induce a delusional effect or is this real? It makes me wonder whether we should be grouping delusions or categorising them. We all saw the book change, yet none of us believe in magic." He stopped at the door. "Oh, I should get a blood sample, Violet, if that's okay? The book works with you. Maybe you're a..." The gears were turning, searching for the right words. They weren't coming.

The Divine Ledger

"It's okay. None of this makes sense to me either. I'll give you my phone number as well." Violet lifted her pant leg and removed her knife from the sheath strapped to her leg. She pierced the skin on a finger. "Call us if you learn anything."

"I will." He caught a few drops of blood in a drinking glass and handed Violet a wad of toilet paper before hurrying off to the university.

"Do you think he's safe on his own?" Elizabeth asked.

Greg shrugged. "I hope so. He's resourceful and this is his home. Besides, we need to find out why this book only works with Violet?"

They both looked at her as she swabbed the blood with the toilet paper. It caused her to wheel the chair backward a foot. "Hey, I'm not the bad guy here."

"Nobody said you were," Elizabeth assured her.

Violet continued to dab at her finger. "Good, because none of this is my fault."

"Try to remember everything Victor said to you. I mean, he told you that the book would provide the answers." His eyes returned to the book. "What are they?"

"All we've got are names, possibilities. I never actually had any of these kids."

Greg continued to press her. His people would have to know everything. "The old lady said they were nightmares. Do they feel like nightmares?"

"Not at all. It's more like an overwhelming good, or a novelty, like seeing a good card trick. I mean how can this book know this." And then there were the numbers and letters on the cover. Trick or no trick, only she and Elizabeth could have known where they came from.

Elizabeth sighed. "I don't know. We all saw it change when you let your energy run through it."

Violet checked her cut. It had almost stopped bleeding. "What do you think Ricky knows? He was in quite a hurry, don't you think?"

Greg looked at the door. "He was."

Violet turned more pages as she remembered her third love, the third beetle on her tattoo. Franco was Italian and a summer fling. He was never supposed to be anything more than a fling, but she had let it go on far too long. When he went back to Italy, like he had promised he would, she was ready to go with him. Whether it was lust, love or stupidity, she thought he'd take her with him. He had no intentions on furthering that relationship. Franco had twenty-one children listed in the book, mostly dark-haired boys.

No one could ever accuse Violet of being promiscuous. There was only one other beetle in her book of what-might-have-been, bringing her total of intimate encounters to four men ... and a rapist.

The fourth name was Bradley and they had been together a couple of years. In that time there had been eighty-two entries. Bradley had always kept a jar on his headboard. Each time they'd made love, a jellybean went in that jar. When she asked about it, he mentioned that if you put a jellybean in a jar every time you had sex before marriage, and took one out ever time after marriage, you'd never empty the jar. He saw it as bullshit. She saw it differently. The man had intentions to marry her someday.

Now all that remained of their relationship was a jar full of stale candy, eighty-two pieces to be exact.

Elizabeth gave Violet a consoling wink as she closed the book and took it to the far side of the room. Greg watched and continued to rack his brain for an answer that wasn't ready to surface. The book was odd, perhaps magical, and yet it had done nothing for him, for Ricky or for Elizabeth.

But Elizabeth had seen the emblem that Violet had mentioned earlier. It had sat in the bottom corner of the cover like a little wallflower at an elementary school sock hop. It wasn't embossed and didn't disappear or come to life. Only an insignificant inch tall and worn to almost non-existence, she had seen it the first time she saw the book. She'd also seen one that was almost identical. She gave it a closer look. It almost looked like a rounded Arabic script, but it wasn't. If Nicole was right, it was a much older dialect than Arabic.

The Divine Ledger

With everyone in deep thought, Elizabeth got up and made her way to the bathroom with the book. She needed to know more. There had been twelve deaths in Vancouver and several more in Cuba.

Had all of this been their fault?

Kevin Weisbeck

Chapter Sixty-three

Greg got up and walked over to the bathroom. Three cups of coffee had finally caught up with him. He knocked softly on the door. "Hey, Elizabeth, are you going to be long?"

He knocked again, this time a little louder.

Violet shook her thoughts. "I don't think she's in there? I thought she left a few minutes ago, went for a walk."

"I didn't see her go anywhere." He turned the knob and slowly swung the door open.

The room was empty. He looked for an open window. There was no window. There was no trap door or gaping hole in the wall. "I guess she slipped past me. I really wish she'd say something when she goes. We need to stick together."

"Seriously?" Violet snapped. "Where is she going to go? Maybe she'll bring back beers."

"Are you kidding? She'd bring sodas before beers. I just don't want her getting caught by Victor."

"Victor doesn't want her."

"Because, what, suddenly you know him so well." Greg scanned the bathroom again looking for escape routes, like a loose vent cover. Then he looked behind the door and in the cabinet under the sink. She was gone.

"Quit being a mother hen, Greg. She'll be back. I mean you found her on the beach and she's still here, right? I doubt she's going anywhere."

"Again, she found me. When the boat capsized I was washed ashore. She saved my life."

"I'm just saying, it was all very convenient." She was going to add more but didn't want to ruin anything for Elizabeth. It was his mindless doting that pissed her off. "You really need to grow a pair."

"You should talk. You could have shot Victor three times and didn't."

"You don't like him, and I get that. He's a killer, but I can't afford to kill him. Not until I know more."

"That makes no sense. How can you trust anything he says?"

"I have to trust somebody." It was mentioned as a shot. "You've been playing games. You know this Victor guy except you're not allowed to say anything. I've already figured out he's CIA. I've also figured out that he's on the Laundry List. You have to be a pretty bad guy to make the Laundry List. This guy kills people at will, but he only roughs you up and takes your passport. What aren't you telling me? Oh, and what ever happened to that email you promised me?"

"I keep telling you, I don't know much."

"Then phone your boss. Ask him, because Victor says your boss knows all about him. It sounds like your boss screwed him, maybe a double-cross? Am I getting warm?"

"I have no idea."

"At least tell me who your boss is, Greg? Are you CIA?" She regretted the question immediately. He wasn't CIA and giving him that kind of credit was simply embarrassing.

"I work for Uncle Sam. That's all you need to know."

"So does the guy that delivers your mail. Don't you see how dysfunctional this all is? Look, I came here looking for a killer, but this is bigger than that. And this killer, he's the only one trying to help me understand."

"All I can say is you're making a mistake keeping him alive."

"You want to hear a shocker? I think I trust him more than I trust you." She flopped back in her wheelchair, glad that she had kept his passport. "Just tell me who you work for already. You know I'll find out eventually. This way you can save face."

"Look, if it was relevant, I'd be happy to tell you. It's not. This guy took my passport and he took your purse. I notice you got your purse back. Where's my passport? If this guy was trustworthy, he'd have given our passports back. He doesn't want us to get out of here. Ask yourself why."

"He can keep my shit. I'm not leaving until I find out what's going on here. Aren't you curious?"

"I'm more curious about that serum. Twenty years of dreams are linked to that drug. It's dangerous. I just hope Ricky can find a lead."

"And let's hope he's not pig-headed and shares."

"Whatever."

"Good one, Greg." Violet's phone put an end to the conversation. "I need to get this. It's probably Bradley."

She hoped it was Bradley, hoped he had found out a few things about Greg, like how he was linked to Victor and why he was so afraid of telling her who his boss was. Victor had dirt on him and on his boss. Greg's involvement in all this was no coincidence. She looked down at the number as she brought the phone up to her ear.

It wasn't Bradley.

Chapter Sixty-four

Victor pulled out a cigar and put a match to it. The end of it came alive and he offered it to Violet as she wheeled toward him. She took it as she got out of her wheelchair and ran her hand along the hood of the '57 Bel Air. Victor offered her the passenger door with a wave of his hand before tossing the wheelchair in the trunk. Then he climbed in the driver's side.

The bucket seats held her like a lover as she leaned back. "This is a pretty nice trade-in."

"Just a loaner. The last one had issues with the steering. How'd you get away from Gregory?"

She enjoyed that first drag as he lit a second cigar for himself. "I told him I was going to the cemetery, to see you."

He pulled away from the curb. "I bet he was happy to hear that."

"He really wants me to get off my ass and shoot you, along with a few thousand birds."

"But you know I'm not the problem here and they're not just birds, they're sparrows."

"Do I, and who cares what kind of bird they are?"

"The fact that they're sparrows is pretty important. Did you give the dumb shit his passport back?"

"No."

"I'm glad. What's with the chair?"

"Thanks to you, I'm an outlaw."

"We all fall from grace eventually."

"Where are we going?"

"Just up the coast and back. I like to keep moving. How'd you make out with the book? Not going to find that one on Oprah's must-read list, are you?"

A shiver climbed her spine and nestled hard at the base of her skull, raising goose bumps. "It definitely grabbed my attention. What is it?"

"Did you like reading about all the children you would have had?"

"You could have warned me about that."

"I could have. Would you have believed me, or would you have shot me on the spot? I was betting on a bullet."

"Good call." She motioned for him to pull over. "So how does it work?"

"That, I have no idea. What it does, I know only too well." He took a lungful of smoke and blew it skyward. "You can't imagine how good it feels to finally talk to somebody about this."

"Pull in over there for a sec." She exited the car and entered what looked like someone's garden shed. She returned with a couple of cold beers. She cracked both cans and handed one to Victor. A good cigar was wasted without an accompanying cold beer. "I found the place a day ago."

He took the beer. "Good on you."

"Don't you get to talk to the man with the birds?"

"We talked once. I mean, he talked and I listened. He told me who he was, his origin, and what he needed from me. After the initial shock, I agreed to his terms and we've never spoken since. There was no need. And can you call them sparrows, for me?"

"Okay, sparrows. Have you ever talked to your family about any of this?"

The Divine Ledger

"I don't have family. My parents are both gone and I have no friends, which makes my job easier. I couldn't do this without a clean break from everyone. It's better for them, better for me. Killing like this changes a person. It takes the *person* out of you and replaces it with..." He tried to find a word. "A machine."

"But you don't kill like a machine. You took Beverly out for pizza, didn't you?"

"I did. And Bob watched a hockey game with me. It was nice to get to know them ... harder, but nice."

"But then you..."

"I kill them. It's calculated and cold. It bothers me, but that's my problem, not yours. What's important is that I stop them before the others find them. You see, to me they're still human."

"I'm confused. When you say others, are you talking about the Russians?"

"Surprisingly, we have no idea. They're an untraceable bunch. My best guess is Russian, but I think they're being played." He signalled and made a right turn. "That book. You saw the names?"

"I did. The others didn't when they held it. Why was that?"

"That's because it shows you the kids you would have had. How many men or virgins have you seen get pregnant? Which surprises me about that blonde. She's damn cute."

"What do you mean?"

"The book only works for people who have had sex." He laughed at the thought Elizabeth being a virgin. "The book lists each sexual encounter and generates an actual result, had you conceived. The names you saw were the children you would have had. It's a ledger of sorts, a divine ledger. Now here's where it gets tricky. Imagine you could bring certain names to life. Their existence conjured up from a spell or an incantation."

"I'd say the marbles had left your marble bag."

"That's what I'd have thought too, until I saw it for myself."

"You saw this happen?"

"Years ago, a group of scientists from Kiev stumbled across the book by chance and saw what you saw. They saw an opportunity, if they could figure it out. They were making good progress. Thing is, American Intelligence caught wind of it. The CIA used one of their own, who had already infiltrated the Russian organisation, to get a hold of that book."

"You? Is that how you were involved?"

"As CIA agent Ivan Dbrocknicov, I was doing a lot of work with the scientists in Kiev. We specialised in mind control and implants that could set off trigger responses remotely. Then the book came into play. It was found in Eastern Canada."

"Canada's involved?"

"They never knew about it. Russian teams scour the Arctic Circle all the time. They're small parties, recons, looking for resources, secrets and keeping an eye on NORAD bases. They're in Alaska too."

Violet wasn't surprised to hear that Russia roamed undetected in Canada and Alaska, or that Victor was a spy in Kiev, but she was shocked about one thing. "You were a brain surgeon?"

He looked at the mitts holding the steering wheel. They weren't the hands you'd expect to see doing such a delicate job. "I specialised in placing the manipulants in the various regions of the brain and spinal cord. The CIA wanted me to keep an eye on their progress."

"Does that mean you were working on the book?"

"Not exactly. We'd heard about it and decided to wait until they figured out what it could do. No point in wasting our own resources. When the Russians figured it out, the book disappeared."

"What did the CIA do with it?"

"The bastards kidnapped my mother. They took her while I was off in the field. She was staying with me at the time and I was only gone for a couple of days. My mother and I were very close after my father died. The CIA lied to her, told her I'd been killed while on duty. She was taken to one of their secure sites, for her own safety."

"A lie? Why her?"

"Bart Gunn, one of my Directors had it in for me. I made him look bad, back when we were both agents. He was the one who told her that she could bring me back. They had a book, but she had to act fast, couldn't hesitate. It must have been hard for her to believe. That would have changed when she started going through all the names. You know how that feels. She was desperate. The verse cinched it. All she had to do was look at my name while she recited it"

"I never saw any verse."

"Not everyone can make it appear at first. They're too wrapped up in the names and the language is such a strange one. My mother couldn't make any sense out of the verse until she touched it. A couple of co-workers were there. They said it began to glow and when she touched it, she started to chant. It was like speaking in tongues. Her eyes rolled back in her head and it scared the hell out of them. Then she snapped out of it and nothing more was said. The CIA considered it a failure at the time."

"Nothing came of it?"

"That night she had a dream. Her son was living in Sacramento, except it was more a bewitched twin. She claimed the dream was very real, very vivid. A CIA team did a quick pick-up. The guy was taken to my mother, but she saw the difference right away. That night they overheard her talking about going public."

"And they killed her?"

"They made it look like a suicide. She'd become a loose end."

"I'm sorry."

Victor finished his cigar and flicked it to the sidewalk. "I found out from a friend on the inside, so I made a play for the book. I clipped the two guards and broke Vincent out. He was the same age and looked just like me, but he didn't belong."

Two killed and one kidnapped, just like the gypsy lady had said. "God, that had to be hard. Did you..."

"Kill him? Not right away. It took a while for it all to sink in. Eventually I had no choice. They wanted to dissect us both, figure out how the similarities worked. I took his life to prevent him from being hunted and tortured. He was too frail for what they'd do to him. Besides, he freaked me out. The whole damn thing freaked me out."

"So, this book can..." Her words died as it started to sink in.

"Those kids that you saw in the book, they're not real. They're what might have been and nothing more. The people conjured up and walking among us, they also don't belong. They aren't the same as us, and they're targets."

"Targets?"

"The CIA figured out how to bring these names to life, but at the cost of twelve lives, plus Vincent's. I got rid of the book, but somebody found it and recruited that old lady. You remember that Birdshit Hotel? It used to be a brothel of sorts. She was a Cuban prostitute."

"Oh, lots of options there."

"Thousands, and all different fathers. Can you imagine the variety?"

"I'm guessing she could also see the verse. Did she pick the names?"

"She had help and, like my mother, I'm sure she had dreams about finding them. The dreams not only told her where to find the conjured up children, but also gave her limited control over their thoughts."

"I bet that's where the serum comes in?"

"The stronger connection would ring the control. That's why I had to shoot her. Thanks for leading me to her. I had faith in you."

"What's up with the birdman?"

"I know this is gonna sound crazy, but he's in charge of the souls. He wants his sparrows back. Back in Mexico I released the souls of the first twelve, and that of my brother. He's given me a list of sixteen more."

Violet remembered that day in the jungle. The cat had helped her find the skull and the bird had flown from its eye socket. "Then these sixteen are conjured people?"

"Yep, and in case you haven't figured it out, each sparrow in his flock is the soul of one of those children in the book. He decides which souls to release and who will be born into this world. Souls that were brought to life unnaturally are the taken ones. He wants those ones back."

"You're not a killer as much as a bird collector, I mean sparrow?"

The Divine Ledger

He turned the car around and headed back for the hotel. "It sounds a little nicer when you say it like that, deranged but nicer."

"I think it's deranged no matter how you say it." She turned inward, leaning her back against the passenger door. "So those first twelve, was there a reason for them to be in Vancouver?"

"It was a military test. They were supposed to shut down a power grid in North Vancouver. They chose that city because it was in Canada, an easier target to walk away from if things turned sour. The experiment was a huge disaster. It only succeeded in getting them all in one area, which suited me. It took a few days, but I got each and every one of them."

"Why keep the heads?"

"It was a Haitian Vodun woman's idea. She told me to keep the skulls. They couldn't be brought back that way. Not that any of that would be possible as long as I had the book."

"How'd you get rid of it?"

"I attached a big-ass rock to it and dumped it in the middle of the Atlantic Ocean. I wasn't popular with the CIA, KGB or Interpol for doing that, but there was no way I was letting them have another crack at it."

"That's why you're on the Laundry List."

"They'll have to find me first." He shrugged as he parked in front of her hotel. It had been a nice drive along the ocean, and insightful. "Regardless, I get an envelope and catch wind of a book in Cuba. The damn thing must have washed up on shore. I get here and a man with a shitload of birds greets me. I can't win."

"Well, I have it now and I see why you didn't tell me until I saw the book in action." She stuffed the butt of her cigar into the empty beer can. "So how do I turn my back while you continue to kill?"

"Turning your back is the easy part. You have bigger problems than you realise." He finished his beer and handed her the can. "If you want something to do, try to find out more about that blonde. She's not what, or who, you think."

"Why? Do you think she's trouble?"

"Let's just say I've never been a fan of coincidence."

Chapter Sixty-five

The book was on the table when Violet wheeled her way back into the hotel room. Elizabeth had returned and found a spot on the bed. Ricky was still gone.

Greg met her at the door. "How'd it go? Did you see the man with the birds?"

"They're sparrows." Violet let her eyes linger on Elizabeth. She wanted to pull her aside, find out what she'd learned about the book, but knew better. That disappearing trick with the book meant that Nicole, a colleague, had also seen the book. If anybody could make sense out of this, it was her. No doubt she had been all over it and had her notions. What were they?

Greg did a shoulder check. "Turns out she was down the hallway the whole time."

Violet took a deep breath before starting. "There's no easy way to explain this so I'm gonna just say it. The book brings people to life, people that don't belong."

Greg laughed, watching her eyes for the punch line. There wasn't one. "You're serious."

Violet explained the book, the conjuring, and the mission that Victor was on. She told him about the souls and the crazed

The Divine Ledger

birdman at the cemetery that controlled the sparrows. It was the ranting you'd expect from a mental patient in the dark halls of some hilltop asylum. She went on to explain that Victor was the thirteenth skull, one of the abominations. Violet made a point of using the word abomination.

Greg sat quietly for a second. A part of him still wanted to laugh. It was all so ridiculous. "If that's the case, then I have to take this guy's side. These aren't people. So where do I fall into this? He tried to kill me? I'm as real as they come."

"What do you expect! You were trying to stop him, and you wanted me to shoot him. I think he'll cut you some slack once he knows you're on the same team."

"What, you're team Victor now?" Greg asked.

"I don't know. I mean, I think I am. It's just, what if he is a killer and it's all bullshit? I'm already an accomplice to the old lady's murder. Do I really need to take this any further?"

"You saw what the book did. You can't deny it. And I cannot deny that crazy birdman."

"You mean Victor's boss. His sparrows watch us because he's afraid we're going to conjure from the book. The sparrows defend the book. They don't want to lose any more souls. Victor said he'd talk to him."

"His boss, book guarding birds..." He started to pace the room. "This is utterly ridiculous."

"I agree and now it's your turn. Everybody else has come to the party. Who's your boss? Tell me before this Victor guy does. He knows. He's just giving you first chance to come clean."

"I..."

"Look I know this serum thing is scary, national security and all, but I can't help you, or trust you, if you're going to keep me at a distance."

"I work for..." Greg took a deep breath and revealed his boss as he exhaled. "The President."

"Now we're getting somewhere. President of what?"

"The United States of America."

"What!" She slammed her hand down on the table. "*That* fucking President."

"The one and only."

"Shit. No wonder Victor hates you. I'd want you dead too. Your boss is doing everything in his power to kill him and get that book back. He's as corrupt as the damn Russians."

"He's not like that."

"Oh, you're gonna tell me all these organisations have our best interests at heart. I bet that's what Ricky is. He's some top-secret agent and he's playing us."

"If that was the case, why wouldn't he just take the book and shoot us?"

"Because he needs us for something. The book is useless to them without the serum. That's what it is. He's close to finishing the serum. He's already got the connection with you. Victor said the twelve in Vancouver were trying to take out a power grid. They failed because their communication skills weren't quite there. That's what he's doing. He's trying to strengthen the connection. Think about it. Imagine the army you could create. Conjure a small group of ordinary people, soldiers, and inject them with a drug that gets them hunting like Raptors or those damn feral cats." She thought of the one-eyed cat by the pool. "They're getting close."

Greg thought about the closet with all the connection-blocking wires. "I think the kid's okay."

Elizabeth nodded. "I agreed. So why these sixteen people."

"I think we need to go and find out." Violet secured the hat to her head and slid her sunglasses on. "Grab the book, Greg."

Chapter Sixty-six

Both Violet and Greg were both hiding behind hats and glasses as they stepped off the double-decker bus. Wanted posters for the two of them had started to pop up like hotdog stands at a circus and, like those hotdogs, they were of poor quality. Thankfully, no reward had been posted yet. These locals worked better with incentives.

Outside the precinct, police officers shuffled around with purpose. This new presence of officers was something she hadn't seen in the past few days. But there had been several murders, including that of a female scientist named Juanita, which put additional pressure on the Captain to find the killer.

Staying within the crowds, Violet and Greg kept a safe distance as they skirted a number of shops and ducked down the back alley to the old lady's apartment. They'd expected a guard and they weren't disappointed. He was in the doorway and armed with an old AK-47.

"Okay, Greg. Do you think you can take him out?"

"What?"

"Well I can't get near him. Even with the hat and glasses, he'll recognise me from the posters."

"But, I've never knocked anybody out."

"You work for the President. You've never received any fight training? What if somebody jumped out of the crowd with a gun?"

"We've got other people to take care of that. They're part of the crowd, dressed like regular folk. We've also got our men in black."

Violet looked around and then past him. "What do you do there?"

He chuckled. "I talk, advise."

"You mean you never got into a schoolyard brawl when you were eight? Tell me you bloodied some little boy's nose for stealing your lunch money."

"I always talked my way out of getting my own nose bloodied."

"Okay. New plan." She grabbed him and planted her lips on his as she shoved him into the view of the guard. Slammed into the wall, she had him smothered.

Lost, as usual, Greg played along. He grabbed at ribs and got daringly close to her breasts. With their lips locked, she grabbed at his shirt, pulling it out of his pants.

The guard quickly rushed over. "*Excusa. Excusa, usted no puede hacer eso aqui.*"

Greg's lips moved to her neck, up her ear. "I think he wants us to stop."

Violet giggled as she reared her head back. "Oh ya. Take me right here. Oh ya baby, that feels good."

"*Escusa!*" He started to push them apart. "You no do that here. Stop now."

With that Violet started to peel her t-shirt off, exposing the lower part of her lacy red bra. "Oh, hell ya."

The officer grabbed her shirt before she could lift it over her head. "Senorita. This is not allowed. Control yourself."

Violet spun and drove a fist into his gut doubling him over. Then she wrapped an arm around his neck and squeezed her biceps muscle into his carotid artery until the man dropped to the ground.

"Hey Greg, ever move furniture as a kid. Maybe your parents bought a new TV or something?"

"Very funny." Greg grabbed the man by the feet and helped drag him into the apartment.

Violet started for the living room. "What's that pickle doing in your pocket?"

Greg ignored the comment as he tried to step in spots not covered in bird feces. "Why are we here?"

She held up the book as she entered the living room. "I need to know who's on this list. Victor said he's got sixteen this time. He wouldn't share names."

"Why do you want to stop him?"

"Shit Greg, I'm still a cop. I can't stand by and allow this."

"I'm not saying that I condone murder, but these aren't people. They're abnormalities. They need to be stopped."

"Still, there's a reason why these sixteen were picked. I want to know why. And even though they weren't born like you or me, they're human and they have no idea what's happening here. Someone brought them here. Maybe they're going to be injected, inspected and eventually dissected. I imagine if there's something there, or if they figure out that serum, they'll mass-produce these people and use them for taking out power grids, blowing up buildings…"

"Or assassinating Presidents," Greg added. "Where'd this book come from?"

"Ask your boss." Violet gasped when she saw the empty chair. The body had been taken. The corpse would be in a morgue, lying on ice. She looked around and saw nothing but dust, bird crap and the blood spattered on the wall. "That's it."

Grabbing a cloth, she blotted one of the blood splatters. It reddened the white piece of cotton and Violet smiled. Then she set the book down and touched the blood to the cover. A name appeared on the cover - Karolina. With the cloth still in hand, Violet opened it and started turning pages. She needed sixteen names and there were so many to choose from.

A sparrow flew in through a broken pane in the window. He landed on the open page of the book. It started to rub its beak on one of the names. It was Bob Henley. "That's right. He's one of them."

Violet turned the pages as the bird watched. On the seventh page it rubbed its beak on another name - Juanita Perez. "Very good."

Greg quickly wrote the names in his notebook as she turned the pages. When sixteen names had been revealed, the bird flew off. Violet grabbed the pad. "Like you know what to do with these names?"

"Victor has this list?"

"He does."

"*Hola. Gustavo, dónde estás? Gustavo?*" The frantic voice came from the front door and it didn't sound friendly.

Violet stuffed the bloody cloth in her pocket, scooped up the book and shoved Greg toward the stairs leading up to the bedrooms.

"Run."

Chapter Sixty-seven

Violet almost carried Greg up the old wooden stairs as they fled the living room. A second-floor hallway led to three rooms. The closest was a bedroom that smelled of dust, an old woman and, of course, the birds. Breathing into her sleeve, Violet let go of Greg's hand and headed straight for the window. Years of paint held it shut as she tried to force it up. Two of the panes were missing. She tugged on it there for a better grip. In the background, Officer Gustavo's unconscious body had caused a frenzied plea over the radio. With the precinct a half a block away, they had no time to escape.

"Quick, grab a blanket and get under the bed."

Greg did as he was told, correctly assuming that the blanket was meant to be placed over the crap-coated floor. Violet put her phone to vibrate before picking up a chair and hurling it through the window. Then she joined him under the bed with the book. "You might find this next part hard, but keep quiet."

"Me?"

She pulled her gun and waited. "Shh."

Two officers entered the room and raced over to the window. A voice boomed into the radio. *"Que están escapando. Escapando!"*

Within seconds, a squad of officers ran through the apartment, exiting through the window. Their boots stomped, lifting dried bird shit and dust out of the carpet.

Violet's whisper was barely audible. "Damn, that smells awful."

"I want my notebook back."

"Why? You wanna help Victor and prove yourself a man? Trust me, that ship has sailed."

"Victor's not a man because he kills."

"I agree," Violet answered.

"He's a man because he's doing what others can't."

"You can't even knock out a guard. I say you let him do the dirty work. These names are more important to us than the actual people. If we can find a link between these names, then maybe we can figure out their plan."

"And if there's no link?" Greg asked.

"Then either we're not looking hard enough, or they aren't as advanced as we thought."

"How do you think Elizabeth is involved in all this?"

"Where'd that come from? I thought you liked her?"

"I do," Greg admitted. "But what if she's a spy?"

"Shhh." She elbowed him. "What do you mean?"

"Look, she's anything but random so let's look at this. This adorable gal comes out of nowhere and says everything I want to hear. I think she's a plant. I mean, let's face it, I'm close to the President. Hey, you said you speak Russian?"

"I do. You want me to see if she does?"

"I don't think it can hurt. Why else would she save me?"

"Give her a chance. I don't think you, or the President, are the targets here."

"I have to believe the worst. Hell, for all we know, she's one of those abominations and she's on Victor's list. Was there an Elizabeth on the list?"

"Spygirl 101, Greg. She'd never use her real name. Victor has a file on each of these people. He knows their real names, ages, heights, hair colour, likes, dislikes, and he has photos. It makes

The Divine Ledger

everything foolproof. We just have names. But Elizabeth isn't a threat."

"You know that for a fact?"

"I have a pretty good read on people."

"You can spot a fake?" He asked.

"Uh, ya."

"Like when I kissed you down on the street?"

"Try and keep up. I kissed you." Violet smiled. "Oh, and that wasn't real."

"Right." He replied.

"Why, did you and your pickle feel something?"

"Like you didn't?" That kiss had screamed passion. He knew Violet had felt it too. He leaned over to steal another kiss, to prove to her that the emotions were real.

"What the fuck." Violet pulled away and shoved a hand in his face. She pushed him back. "Police, guns, jail…remember? Pay attention."

"I, uh." He looked away. "How long are we going to be stuck under this damn bed?"

"You're not claustrophobic, are you?"

He ignored her. Women were evil. Elizabeth was playing him and so was Violet. He crawled out from under the bed and brushed himself off. "I'm done with this. These cops are out there looking for you and Victor, not me. This place is empty. That means I can leave. I don't have my mug-shot on the wall. You have a great fucking day."

Violet crawled out after him. "Look, get back here."

Greg took one step toward her and embraced her. The kiss he planted on her lips held every ounce of passion he could muster. The initial fight quickly became a shared moment. When he pulled away he laughed. "And I didn't feel a thing."

"You're a child."

With that he slipped quietly down the stairs and out of the apartment. Two officers in the back alley, not having noticed where he'd come from, didn't give him a second look.

Violet peered through the window. There were still too many cops out there for her liking, so she sat on the bed and opened the book. Her ID reappeared on the cover and she looked over the children that she and Brad might have had. Twice she stopped to think about Greg's kiss. Twice she smiled and shook the thought. The man was a tool. She and Greg were oil and water.

Then the craziest thought came to her. Did this nice guy have it in him to kill, to do something corrupt or stupid? Why not? She was a sweet kid once and look at her now.

Violet reached into her pocket to go over the names. "Aw, shit."

She had failed distraction 101 and, like Greg, the notebook was gone.

Chapter Sixty-eight

The old woman's apartment remained quiet for a good ten minutes after Greg had ran off with the list. The police were obviously spreading the search from a single block to a quadrant of the downtown area. It was time to take a chance. Violet got up from the bed and stretched her sore muscles. The week had taken a toll. By now the police had searched the alleyways, knocked on doors and exhausted most of their leads. They were scrambling up and down the city streets at this point, chasing tails and widening the search area as desperation set in. For them, Violet had escaped.

Getting up to the rooftop would be her best choice. A fire escape clung to the side of the building like a bookcase being climbed by a gun-toting toddler. From the far edge of the rooftop, she stared at the eight-foot gap to the next building. She jumped. A ten-foot jump put her safely across. A four-foot drop with a seven-foot gap took her to the next rooftop. Down below, the crowds went about their daily business.

Her heart raced as she made her way north. The next rooftop was one floor down and fourteen feet away, divided by a narrow alley. She gave it a quick assessment. This one would be a challenge. If she missed, an upper floor balcony might catch her. Would the balcony hold? If she made that rooftop, a fire escape led down to a busy market. She could disappear into the crowds. All she had to do was make the jump.

Violet backed ten steps away from the edge and readied herself. Fourteen feet wasn't that far to jump, was it? Hell, it was a ten-foot drop. This would be easy. As she took that first step, the door opened behind her.

"*Parar alli!*"

She heard him with her second step. He sounded official. She took a third step, much quicker than the first two. When she took the fourth and fifth, there was no looking back. The voice yelled again, demanding she stop. Six, seven and eight were a sprint. If she obliged her curiosity and stole a peek over her shoulder she'd, no doubt, see a police officer and he'd have…nine, ten, jump…a gun.

The first shot hit her in the back of the shoulder as she travelled through the air. She tumbled into a face-plant as she landed on the rooftop and quickly scrambled to her feet. A second shot ricocheted off the galvanised iron by her feet. A third hit the railing by the fire escape as she started down it. Violet made her way down the steps, three at a time. She landed on the sidewalk with both feet and lost herself in the crowd. She thought she was safe when a familiar voice startled her.

"Pretty Woman. I no see you lately."

"Sammy! Where's your cab?"

He pointed across the street. "You need a…"

Violet was across the street and reaching for the door-handle before he could finish the sentence. He quickly ran for the driver's door.

"Hurry, Sammy." She jumped into the front seat. "Go, go, go."

Sammy pulled away and made an immediate left to get on the main street. "You want to go to the precinct?"

"Hotel, Sammy. No, wait." The hotel wouldn't work. Greg wasn't going there. She quickly opened the book to see her children. "Shit."

The bloody cloth was still in her pocket so she pulled it out. The old lady's name quickly surfaced. The list of names formed, and she remembered the order the bird had given them. If Victor was as OCD as she thought he was, the next victim would be a Chad Alvin Remmy. Violet dialled Bradley.

"Huge favour, Brad. A Chad Alvin Remmy, can you find him? He'd have come to Cuba, so check airport arrivals. I need to know where he's staying."

"Always the same with you. Brad I need…"

"Look, I owe you. I get it. I need to stop a murder and I've just been shot so I'm kinda pressed here."

"You've been shot? Are you okay?"

"I sure hope you're typing. And yes, I'll live."

"Just a sec, I'm getting something."

Violet reached back to see how bad the bleeding was. Her fingertips glistened with the fresh blood. She could feel the warmth from the slug, burning. But she knew better than to do anything about it. That was how it felt when it was up against bone.

"You hurt Pretty Woman?"

"I am Sammy and I'm sorry, but I'm bleeding in your car."

"Sammy take you to hospital."

"No!" She held up a bloody finger while Bradley read her off the address. "Sammy, I need you to take me somewhere. I need the corner of Calle 48 and Avenida 7 c."

"I go there, then hospital."

"Sure." She put the phone back to her ear. "Thanks, Brad."

"Take care of yourself, eh?"

"I will, and I'll call you later. Ciao." She hung up and slipped the phone into a pocket. "Good days, bad days, huh Sammy?"

"Si." Sammy couldn't look away from the pain in her eyes. "I wait for you there. You do what you need, then I take you to a doctor."

"Sounds good, Sammy."

She'd expected a hotel, but this place was a bed and breakfast. She broke through the front door to see Greg. He was standing in shock. There was a body at his feet. The head had been removed. "You didn't…"

He retched but didn't vomit. "I, uh, no. It was like this when I got here. I heard a noise from the other room. I think Victor just left."

"Not a pretty sight, is it?"

Greg backed away from it. "How could he just… I mean it's just so…"

"He has to. If you couldn't do this, why take the notebook?"

There was a hesitation before he spoke. "I was worried that you could."

"Seriously? How fucked up do you think I am?"

A third voice interrupted them. "To be honest, you are a little scary."

Greg and Violet turned around to see Victor. He was carrying what looked like a bowling bag.

He walked straight up to Violet and spun her around so that he could see her back. "What the hell happened to you?"

"It's just a flesh wound." She pulled away from him. "I was jumping rooftops and got clipped. It's nothing."

Victor pinned her against the wall. It required a closer look. "You know the slug's still in you. You want me to get it out?"

She closed her eyes and relaxed her shoulders. "Only because it'll save me a trip to the hospital."

"And having to answer all those embarrassing questions from the nurses," Victor added. He started to tear a larger hole in her shirt.

"Hey, this is my lucky shirt so be nice to it."

"Gotcha. Would you prefer to take it off?"

She looked back at the two of them. "No."

"Just asking." He opened the bag and pulled out a scalpel. "It's clean enough. Greg, find her something to bite down on. A wooden spoon or a rolled-up towel."

Greg didn't hesitate.

Victor wiped the scalpel with an alcohol swab and stuck his pinky finger in the wound. "Bout an inch in. Seems to be lodged against the shoulder blade."

The Divine Ledger

Violet cringed as he tried to free it.

"You doing okay?"

"Just get it over with. I'm not good with the attention."

He delicately pried the bullet from the bone. Violet held out her hand. Victor dropped the slug into her palm. "You collect them?"

"Maybe." She slipped it into her pocket.

Greg could only stare at her. "How many of those do you have?"

"Three. This one makes four."

Victor grabbed a needle and some surgical thread and closed the wound with seven stitches. Then he gave the wound a final wipe with alcohol. "Sorry I don't have a dressing on me. I haven't needed one, up until now. Tell me Stormm, how is this shirt lucky?"

"I'm still here, aren't I?"

Greg wanted to shake his hand, thank him for fixing her up. He didn't. Victor was still a wildcard. A tuft of hair poked out from his bag. It was from the body that lay only feet away. Yes, a handshake was out of the question.

"Why me?" Greg asked.

"What?"

"You tried to kill me. Should I be worried?"

"No."

"How come?"

Victor finished packing up his bag and started for the door. "Maybe I'll explain it some day, if we live through all this. Right now it's time to get out of here."

"Where are we going?" Greg asked.

Victor looked back from the doorway. "We?"

Kevin Weisbeck

Chapter Sixty-nine

Violet gave Greg a polite shove as Sammy drove them to the cemetery. She knew what he was thinking, knew those thoughts. She'd had the same ones in the beginning, before taking up drinking. Headless bodies were undeniably out there. "Hey, you really shouldn't do that to yourself. It'll drive you to drink."

Greg remained quiet. It was a lot to process; seeing the dead body and the compassionate side of Victor. A day ago he had wanted him dead. The thought was still bouncing around in the back of his head after seeing the body. Only an animal would act like that. He thought about the bar at the hotel and could almost taste the beer in his mouth. "A drink sounds like a good idea. We'll have to be careful though. We don't have the wheelchair."

"There won't be any police. They've already ransacked my room. What else is there? They think I'm downtown, not stupid enough to return. To be safe, we should go in the back. Just go ahead of me and make sure it's safe." She leaned forward and tapped Sammy on the shoulder. "Don't drop us off in the turn around. Drop us off by the garbage bins. Then stay for thirty minutes. Greg will give you a few extra pesos."

Sammy nodded and in minutes he was backing the car into a stall. "I stay here."

The walkways were clear as they made their way back to the room. Greg pulled the door card out of his pocket and reached for the lock.

Violet grabbed his arm.

Strange voices were leaching their way through the door. Violet and Greg listened. They were too muffled.

"What are they saying?" Greg asked.

"Shh." Violet put a finger to her lips. "I'm trying to hear. I count three, with accents." She put her ear back on the door.

"Want me to go find a glass?"

Her eyebrows dipped. It was a sure sign not to bother. His shutting up would suffice. She closed her eyes. "I think it's Russian." She leaned in closer just as the door opened, spilling her into the room.

Two guns were immediately trained on them, one for him and one for her. A runt of a man standing by the glass doors to the balcony held a PSM pistol. A tall stick of a man held a Makarov. The third man was a meatball. He sat at the table, too lazy to draw his weapon and too slothful to get up. They were all wearing the same black suits.

Stickman spoke first. "Nice of you to show up. You have something that doesn't belong to you. We want it." He walked over, reached behind Violet to take her gun and lifted her to her feet. With his free hand he reached for the book. Her right hand shot out, striking him in the throat. As he fell backwards, she drove her shoulder into his gut. Her knee was about to pin his throat to the floor when a shot grazed her leg.

"Hand over the book, Miss Stormm."

She winced as she looked up. "Not going to happen."

Ricky was sitting on the bed. "You best hand it over to them."

"Talk to me Ricky." Violet swayed as she stood. "Why'd you bring your friends here?"

Greg recognised them as the ones that were parked in front of Juanita's apartment. They were the ones at the University. "You don't know these men, do you Ricky?"

"Their boss is funding the lab at the University. The serum is no good without the book. You best hand it over."

"The serum is ready?" Greg asked.

"Juanita finished the serum years ago, when I was young. It needed more strength."

"Enough talk." The man pointed the gun back at Violet. "Give me the book before I blow your head clean off your shoulders."

"Did you say *off*?" Violet shook her head as she laughed. "That gun couldn't…"

Heads turned when the bathroom door swung open.

Elizabeth took her place between Violet and Greg. "I just talked to my people. We're going to be taking the book."

Violet gave her a double take. "Nice of you to finally show up."

Greg took a step toward her. "How the hell do you keep doing that?"

"Not now, Greg." She turned to the man pointing the gun at Violet. "My people are willing to pay for this book. I'm guessing gold is a viable currency for you?"

"This book is not for sale. Who are you and where did you come from?"

"We don't want trouble." She took the book from Violet.

Rubbing his throat, the other man got to his feet. "I say we shoot them all. The police cannot touch us here."

"Too bad you couldn't handle a little girl," his partner chuffed. The gun remained on Violet. "So, Blondie. Hand over the book or I'll blow your friend's head off."

Elizabeth inched away from Violet, toward Greg. "I can't do that."

"Seriously." Violet snapped. There was an instant regret in handing her the book.

He swung the gun to Greg. "And what if I shoot this one?" He saw the unmistakable concern in her eyes. It was all he needed.

The Divine Ledger

"Ah, so I should shoot this one first. I mean I'll shoot all of you if I don't get the book, but him first."

His chuckle was cut short as Victor put his shoulder through the door and came in shooting. The man roughed up by Violet took the first bullet, a head-shot that dropped him. Elizabeth lunged for Greg. She wrapped her arms around him, the book pressed between them. They both vanished. Even Victor had to blink twice.

The man in charge returned fire. A bullet ripped through the door-jamb, driving splinters of wood into Victor's face. Before he could fire a second shot, Violet drove her head into the man's chest, sending them both crashing through the glass door to the balcony.

The third man, the spectator seated at the table, reached into his jacket. A bullet to the temple rocked him in his chair. He dropped like a slow falling tree. Victor stepped over him as he made his way to the patio. Violet was pinned against the railing, struggling to get the gun free. The man was freakishly strong and about to win the battle when his face exploded. The force of the shot pushed her back on her ass. The blast covered her in blood.

"What the fuck, Victor." She wiped at the side of her face, her neck, and the white shirt. "That's just fucked up."

"I'll let you thank me later." He grabbed the man's wallet and extended a hand to help her up. "We gotta go."

"Sammy's still downstairs." She scrambled to her feet and grabbed a facecloth as they started toward the door. "You're an asshole."

Victor squeezed off another shot. She turned back to see Ricky's head jerk left.

"Why'd you kill him?"

"He was on the list." Victor knelt and started going through pockets. "Grab that one's ID. We need to find out who these thugs are."

"You mean were." Violet hobbled over and rifled through pockets. "Got it."

"You okay to walk?" Victor asked.

"Please." Violet shoved him toward the door. "You getting soft on me?"

"Wouldn't think of it. Grab a pillowcase and we can wrap it up in the cab."

The stench of burnt gunpowder lingered in the room as they left. Violet struggled two steps behind as they went down the stairs and was four steps behind by the time they got to the cab. It felt good to sit down. She pulled out her phone and shot a text to Bradley. These three names belonged to the dead men, the men that were willing to kill for the book. Hopefully, Brad could find something on them.

"Cemetery, Sammy." She slipped the phone into her pocket and turned to Victor. "Hey, why'd you come here?"

"The Boss told me to. First time we'd talked in quite a while."

"What did he want?"

"Sparrows are the life-giving birds. These birds carry the souls and only he has the power to hand them out. He doesn't much care for it when you take them."

"Why are you telling me something I already know?"

"Because the man shared a very interesting fact about your blonde friend."

"Why? Did she take the wrong bird?"

"No," Victor replied. "More like she doesn't have a bird. Not one that he knows of."

"I didn't think that was possible."

"It isn't. Tell me, Violet, or whoever you are, where did your friend take Greg?"

Chapter Seventy

Tourists and locals walked sidewalks, crossed streets and shopped in small stores while Sammy wheeled his cab toward the cemetery. For them there was no Divine Ledger, no man lopping the heads off tourists or women vanishing. For them it was just another day. It was a day like yesterday and would be a day like tomorrow. None of them had televisions, nor did they care about anything that didn't directly affect them.

Violet leaned against Victor as he calmly tore the pillowcase into long ribbons. It kept her from falling over. He admired her pain threshold. "You're a regular magnet for gunfire."

"Good thing I was wearing my white shirt."

"It's not that lucky."

"I was being sarcastic." She stuffed a blood-splattered sleeve in his face. "How am I supposed get this stain out?"

Victor shrugged. "You think she took him to the cemetery?"

"Where else?"

He held the strips out for her and then pulled them back. "What are you guys, some secret society?"

"Nothing like that." She took them and started to wrap her leg. It was her turn to clam up as they headed to the only place that made sense. If they weren't there, then she'd have no idea where to look. There was a sigh of relief when her phone rang. She answered hoping it was Greg. It wasn't

"Got your text. Glad to hear you're still alive."

"Got another hole in me, but I'm hanging in there. What did you find?"

"How the hell did you find those three?"

"Hey Brad. You give the answers and I ask the questions, remember?"

"You've stumbled across three North Koreans. They're members of the Comradeship of Truth. They're hunters, interlopers."

"Like foreign diplomats?"

"No. More like ET's, freaks, ghosts, people with super powers, you know, like Santa Claus."

"They're certifiable?"

"Certifiable, maybe. Dangerous, definitely. These guys have killed hundreds for their cause. Word has it they were formed years ago when they caught wind of the Chinese being visited by aliens. They've hunted scientists in China, Russia, the States and England. They've been looking for some space book. It's a critical part of their mission."

"And what mission is that?"

"Why, to prove that ET exists of course."

"Are you for real, Bradley? North Koreans?"

"They're heavily funded and whoever hired them wants them to keep a close eye on China. And hey, if they're after you then you best lay low. They aren't afraid to do whatever it takes."

"I'll take that under advisement. Thanks."

"I need you to quit getting shot, Stormm."

Violet hung up and grabbed at her leg. "Brad says they're North Korean spies looking for ET."

"The spaceman freaks?" Victor shifted closer and helped her loosen her dressing. It oozed blood for a minute and then he tightened it back up, properly.

"You've heard of them?"

"Bits and pieces, Aliens, China, and technologies that are beyond anything on this planet. I never thought it was real."

Her phone rang again. It had to be Greg. "Where the hell are you?"

"Vancouver, where do you think?"

She looked down at the number on display. It was Bradley again. "I was hoping to hear from Greg. We've had a bit of a strange day here."

"Strange? Don't tell me, let me guess."

"We don't have time and you'll never..."

He cut her off. "A blonde woman just disappeared with some guy in a hotel room. I'm guessing he's this Greg guy that you lost. Am I right?"

Violet sat stunned as the bumps from the road gently jostled her around in her seat. "How the hell..."

"Nothing mystical. I just saw you on CNN. You're also becoming an Internet sensation. There was a live-feed camera hooked up in that room. What the hell is going on down there? I thought you were trying to find a serial killer."

"I was. I mean I am."

"You found that space book, didn't you? When were you going to tell me about it? I mean don't get me wrong, I laughed when the blonde picked that guy over you. You have a real knack for making friends, don't you?"

"It's a long story, twelve-beer minimum."

"Fair enough. Just so you know, the video's gone viral and it's hitting all the big news channels."

"Damn it. What else did they say?"

"Oh, they had lots to say. And now somebody's leaking a non-redacted government file about a book that creates people. That's an even bigger story."

"There's also a drug called Hemingway. Crazy shit," Violet added, "What do you know about it?"

"I haven't heard much, definitely nothing concrete."

"Say, Bradley, how clear was the footage and how did they get CNN to pick it up so quickly?"

"It was a CNN camera from what I've gathered. They were doing a piece on the Comradeship of Truth. They asked CNN for the camera set up. Sounds like that blonde was set up."

She tried to clear her voice. "So, everybody's seen it?"

"Be easier to count the ones who haven't. Sarge has called me twice asking if I know where you are. He seems to be under the impression you're still in Mexico. Talk about being pissed."

"Shit."

"Oh, it gets better." Bradley took a minute to send Violet a picture. "They think they've spotted blondie's spacecraft. Damn thing's invisible, but detectable."

The picture he sent was an image with a blue and black background. "What the heck is this, Brad?"

"To you, just a blob of colour. To NASA it's a spacecraft that's a half-mile wide and close to two miles long. They figure it's big enough to have seventeen levels. The damn thing is frigg'n massive."

"No, no, no…"

"Oh ya, ya, ya. I think NASA would have preferred to keep this story Area 51 quiet, but that's not going to happen now. The ship had been partially hidden behind Mars. Who knows how long they've been here or what they want."

Victor, who had been on his phone, reached for the door handle. The cemetery was coming up. "We need to go."

"Gotta run, Brad. Keep me posted."

"Hell girl, you keep me posted, and get home safe. I'll even spring for the beer on this one."

Violet ended the call and turned to Victor. "You leaked that file about Vincent?"

"I was bored while you were wrapping your leg. I had to."

"What all do you know?" Violet asked.

"I don't know much of anything, obviously. I mean Violet Stormm, really?"

"What are you talking about?"

"You've hidden your identity well. I thought you and this blonde were some mercenary group. You know, sell anything for cash, including crazy books. You let everyone think you're going after a killer when all you ever wanted was the book, but you're no mercenary. You're one of those damn aliens."

"A what?"

The cab stopped. Victor and Violet got out arguing like a couple that had been married ten years longer than they should have been. They continued as they started for the cemetery. As expected, Elizabeth and Greg were waiting.

"You're crazier than I thought." Violet snapped.

"It's okay to tell me," he pleaded. "I'm good with secrets."

"There's no fucking secret to keep, asshole."

"You're a little defensive, maybe too defensive, don't you think?"

"I'm not a stupid alien."

"If you say so, but I'm CIA. I was trained to read people." Victor grabbed her by the shoulders as they crossed the street. He remembered what his boss had said, that Elizabeth didn't have a bird that he knew about. He wasn't sure about Violet. Elizabeth had done the alien thing by disappearing and now her ship was front-page news. It only made sense that Violet could do the same. She would never admit it. She couldn't and he got that. She was a lot more professional than she looked. He'd have to force the truth out of her.

As a car passed by, he shoved her in front of it. He knew she'd disappear, and then he could say his I told you so. Except Violet didn't disappear. Instead, the car ground to a screeching halt. Violet slid up the hood, landed hard against the windshield and tumbled over the roof.

Victor's jaw hit the ground about the same time Violet did.

"Shit." Victor ran to her as the car sped off.

Greg stood dazed. "Did he just…"

"Shove her in front of that car?" Elizabeth answered. "I think so."

Chapter Seventy-one

Greg made a fist while he ran into the street. It made no sense. What was Victor thinking? "You bastard."

Elizabeth followed, not as concerned. "It'll take more than a car to stop her. I feel sorry for Victor. She's not going to be happy."

Victor grabbed at her knees, feeling her legs for breaks. "Damn it. I thought you were…"

"I fucking told you I wasn't one of them. Now get me to the sidewalk, before someone calls the cops."

He pulled her in and started to pick her up.

"Get your grubby paws off my ass. I can walk."

"You're a piece of work, Stormm." He grabbed her good arm and slung it around his neck to help her to her feet. "You've probably got a broken leg."

"Serial killer, CIA, and now you're a bloody doctor." She put some weight on her leg and it held. "Just get me to the cemetery. I hate having all these eyes watching us." She waved her hand at the crowd and smiled. "I'm okay. Hubby here has a strange sense of humour, that's all."

The Divine Ledger

The smile worked. Realising she'd be okay, the crowd started to disperse. She continued to smile for the tag-along types and even put decent weight on her leg.

Greg reached them first and drove his fist into Victor's face. Victor spun Violet between them to stop a second blow.

Violet elbowed him in the chest and broke free. "Damn you two. We don't need the attention. Now stop it."

Victor let her go and put his hands up. "She's right. We need to move it into the cemetery. I'll let you man up there."

Hopping twice, she put her arm around Greg and pulled him away from Victor. "See, I knew you had it in ya. I'm impressed. The President's coffee boy has a good right hook."

"I do more than grab coffee for him."

"Sure you do." The words bled with sarcasm. "Have you heard, we've managed to make all the headlines."

Elizabeth's eyes widened as she hurried to get closer. "What do you mean, headlines?"

"CNN. They're one of the biggest news agencies in the world. They caught you doing that thing with Greg, you know, poof. It was caught on camera. Everybody's seen it."

Victor followed a step behind. "Are you going to tell us who you are, Elizabeth?"

"I can't get into details." She added, "It's not my call and you of all people know how orders work. If I had my way, I'd tell you. Except for tossing Violet in front of a car, you're good people, but it's not time yet."

Victor lit a cigar and wished he'd picked up a beer to go with it. "How about I tell you then. Tell me if I'm close."

He moved a little closer to Elizabeth. "You're not from here and, considering what you can do, you're not one of us. I heard a rumour, quite a while back, that there might have been an alien encounter with China. Normally alien encounters aren't taken all that seriously, but this was China. They're known for their level-headed behaviour. The States, in fact most other countries, would have made up some smoke-and-mirrors story. The accusations would have been laughed off. China, however, neither admitted nor denied the encounter. It's bad karma to lie, best to say nothing, which is what they did. How am I doing so far?"

"I can't…"

"I'll continue then. China knows about you, although what they know is anybody's guess. Russia and the States found out and pulled out all their spy technology. I think Russia even went as far as recruiting the North Korean space cadet club, the Comradeship of Truth. Thing is, I really doubt anybody missed a ship that size. We've seen too much to think we're the only ones out there. The hardest part would be keeping the scientists quiet. A ship that size would create quite a buzz. So where did she take you, Greg?"

Greg shook his head. "I uh…"

"Good answer," Victor continued. "The President would be proud. China has done a good job of keeping this under wraps, so what's in it for them? Did you promise them the world? Since you haven't blown us up yet, I'll imagine you're peaceful."

Elizabeth nodded. His theory was on point and she had to work at holding back any signs that he was right. Saving Greg had been a serious screw-up, but what choice did she have? The assassin would have shot him and she couldn't afford that. Greg had no way of knowing it, but he was about to be her liaison to the most powerful man on Earth, the President. "I suppose I should be going. I need to get back and see what kind of damage we're dealing with."

Violet's eyes were spinning in their sockets from the pain. "Why aren't you denying any of this?"

"She can't, Violet. She's a liaison." Victor interrupted. "She can't tell the truth, nor can she lie. And hey, I'm sorry about the push. I'd have sworn you were one of them."

Greg laughed. "You thought she was an alien? Is that why you pushed her, to see if she'd disappear?"

"Not every theory's a good one," Victor admitted.

Elizabeth looked down at the rag tied around her leg and moved in for a hug. "And I'm sorry for getting you involved in all this. We can fix that."

It was tempting. "Nah, I'm good."

"But you need to be…"

"Asshole-face is my doctor."

"Are you sure? It'll take weeks to heal and it'll be painful. We can…"

"No, I'm good." Violet smiled. "Not my last rodeo. Getting shot and run over is what I do."

Victor leaned in and whispered, "That's first, first rodeo."

"Whatever. I'll heal my way."

"If that's what you want." Elizabeth said. "Then I guess I should go."

"And how do I fit into this plan?" Greg asked.

"I'll be in touch when you get back to Washington." She forced a smile before vanishing.

Victor held out his hands, palms up. "I guess it's safe to say, there's no need for me to continue killing."

Greg hadn't thought about the book since the apartment. "How many did you…"

"All but one."

Violet looked down at his hands. They were still being held out toward her. "Why are you doing that?"

"You're in a lot of shit with your boss. Taking me in might appease the powers that be. Besides, with the book safe, I could use the rest."

She looked at his wrists and imagined her handcuff on them. She had wanted this for some time. And he was right. The Sarge would be all over her ass if she didn't bring back a killer. A collar wouldn't save her from a good dressing down, but it would net her a citation and perhaps a raise. It was hard to argue with results like that.

"Forget it. I'll face the music."

Greg looked down at Violet's leg, over to Victor and then to the sky. "Am I the only one freaked out by all of this? There's a space ship up there. We're not alone."

"We've always known that," Victor chuffed. "I say we go grab a forty-pounder of cheap rum and we let the dust settle. I think life on this planet is about to get very interesting."

Violet looked up to the sky and shook her head. "Interesting indeed."

Chapter Seventy-two

Elizabeth appeared on the stainless-steel platform, coated with a non-slip teal skin. It was the safe zone of the Mother Ship's Transportation quarters. Nicole was waiting just to the left of the platform, thumbing through the pages of the ledger. She didn't look up when Elizabeth's body reatomised, but she'd heard the faint popping sound. "This book is amazing. The markings are identical to the others."

Elizabeth stepped off the platform. "Others?"

That pulled Nicole's eyes off the page. "We've found several items at the other cache. I was gone for three months on the Edify Expedition back on Alzie. You don't remember?"

"I, uh, do so."

"No you don't, but that's okay. My team found a broken capsule back home. It was torn apart and the debris was scattered everywhere." She continued, "there were a few artifacts, older than anything we'd ever found. They had markings just like the one on this book."

"I thought the Edify was a science course." She caught herself sounding angry. "I mean, I don't remember you ever telling me about them."

"I never carried on about it because I didn't want my findings to interfere with your training. That, and I've been subject to a T-7 protocol."

"When has that ever stopped you?"

"It's protocol, Elizabeth. It always stops me. It stops everybody. What's happening to you?"

This was where Elizabeth knew to back off. Earth had changed her. Her new friend Jenny had changed her. T-7 protocol was nothing to mess with. She knew that. But on Earth the rules bent, bowed and even broke on occasion. "Sorry. You're right."

"I know."

"This book helps?"

Nicole nodded. "Finding similar relics here on Earth is momentous."

"I guess you owe me?" Elizabeth hinted.

"Did you think I brought you along on this mission to keep me company?"

"Who brought who, kiddo?"

"Kiddo?" Nicole shook her finger. "Careful. You're starting to sound like one of them."

Elizabeth shrugged. "Uh, thank you? And what does an Earthling sound like?"

"Undisciplined, unprofessional, impractical. Need I go on? They have slang, or as we call it, an early chaotic breakdown of the vocabulary structure. They add words to the list all the time. Uh, eh, and thank you are not structurally relevant. Neither are redundant questions. They are add-ons, and annoying. Are we supposed to acknowledge them, ignore them? They're awkward."

Elizabeth stood quietly like a small child being chastised for her immature behaviour. Jenny, a friend she'd made during reconnaissance, was full of these early chaotic breakdowns and some of them were funny. They had rubbed off on her over the last few weeks. At least she wasn't using words like cool, far out, or groovy … yet. The silence, although always fine with Nicole, bothered Elizabeth. It had become habit to talk, share and express. "Can I ask you something?"

"Since when do you need permission for that?"

"You don't seem upset about the current course of events. Why is that?"

"You may have compromised the mission by saving your liaison, but my research is unaffected. And this book is a wonderful acquisition, Elizabeth. Do you have any idea what this means?"

"Would you hate me if I said no?"

Nicole could only stare. "I swear you're becoming one of them. You might as well be wearing a Hello Kitty ball cap. I'm actually ecstatic that they found out about us, and I'm even happier that it had nothing to do with any of my endeavours. Now we can start the next leg of our mission and I can get down to Earth and search for more relics. If you ask me, our playing policy has taken too long. I don't see how we can build trust with spy satellites and time wasting recon missions."

It was Elizabeth's turn to shake her head. She also rolled her eyes, something she'd learned from Jenny. "You make it sound like we're going down there to have tea, that they'll welcome us with open arms."

"They have no reason not to. All the changes we'll be expecting from them make perfect sense. They should be asking themselves why they never thought of these things first."

"Perfect sense, except these are Earthlings. They have no idea what or who we are. They've never experienced life other than that of their planet, and what we're going to be asking of them is huge."

"They've seen aliens before, and we'll go over everything before we enact the changes. We have formulas and a proven module with our own planet. It's not like we won't keep them informed."

"You forget, they've never been to Alzie." Elizabeth watched as Nicole held the Ledger like a newly born baby. Too bad she couldn't muster the same respect for the Earthlings. Even though her dark brown eyes were as warm, if not warmer than most, inside that head of hers was the brain of a computer. Most of the crew on this ship were just like her. It was why they were here. Science wasn't about compassion, emotion or apologies. It was about practicality, progress and the acceptance of proven theories.

The Divine Ledger

Back on Alzie, it was standard logic that spurred results, but this wasn't Alzie. On Earth there was little gravity placed on logic. Elizabeth had found that these people lived and led with their hearts. Their actions were based on either fear or greed and their leaders led with agendas based on personal gain, not the improvement of their civilisation. The people of Earth wouldn't easily accept their Alzien logic. They'd fight change and fight it with everything they had.

Elizabeth sighed. "We really need to adjust our objective."

"Everything will be fine." Nicole patted her friend on the shoulder. "We're giving them our best and all we ask in return is that they give us a chance."

"I don't know. I've studied these people. I've spent a month living with them. They're pretty comfortable with their ways."

"Change is coming. They'll have to embrace it." Nicole started to walk away but turned and held up the ledger. "Good job on this. You can't even begin to imagine how important it is."

Elizabeth shrugged. "Whatever." She vanished, reappearing in her bedroom back at the Davis house in Washington DC. Even though it had only been a couple of days, she missed this family. Here she could be herself, her new self. And here she could start the damage control. Greg would be flying back in the next day or two and she needed his connection to the President.

Ready or not, their mission had started.

Kevin Weisbeck

Chapter Seventy-three

For two hours, Violet, Victor, and Greg sat in the cemetery staring up at the sky. They passed around a bottle of Rum and not a word was spoken. Victor's killing spree had ended, Violet's leg was, at the very least, fractured, and the aliens had arrived. Everybody on Earth had always known that there could be life out there in space but, much like dying, most wouldn't believe it until that day came.

    Greg thoughts stirred around the stunning young blonde with a persona wrapped around whatever was inside that body. And what was in that body? As good as she looked, that wasn't her. Was the real Elizabeth a flesh-eating lizard, a vapour of energy, or was she some hideous creature like the one in Alien, with a mouth jutting out from an already grotesque mouth? With Area 51 off-limits to the public, if it even existed, television was all they had. Greg wanted to ask Violet what she thought, but he also didn't want to get her started.

    Violet took a swig. The rum was as good a painkiller as anything she'd ever taken. The last time she was shot, they had given her Codeine. The time before that it had been Demerol. Both put a fog in her head that hung around like soft butter on a dishrag. The fog from booze was a welcome one, a familiar one.

Victor couldn't shake the thought that his intel was correct about China. Too bad his instincts on Violet weren't as good. At least he didn't kill her. He decided to break the silence. "Be quite a bonanza for them if they want us for food." Then he added, "brings a whole new meaning to eating Chinese, French or Italian."

At that point Violet rolled her eyes. She politely gave him a drunken smirk and looked over for Greg's reaction. There wasn't one. "And what's your problem, Smiley? Hand sore from punching old Vic, here."

"I don't think any of this is funny."

"No, but it's kinda funny. I mean, I know you're stressed and all, but at least one of the aliens is cute, don't you think?"

"Not the alien part. Victor tried to kill me. I'm…it's just that…"

"For real?" Victor asked. "Do you want me to apologise? Here goes, I'm sorry." Victor's apology was a sincere one, even if it didn't come out that way. "I tried to kill her too and she's over it."

"Fuck you," she slurred as she went for another swig.

"No hard feelings." Victor held his hand out for Greg to shake.

Greg looked at it briefly. He'd been taught to forgive, to turn the other cheek. "No. There's more to it and I can't just pretend it's okay."

"Nope, fair enough." Victor dropped his hand. "What will it take to make it up to you? Do you want me to take you out and get you drunk, laid? Or would it be better if I gave you a free shot?" He stuck his chin out.

Greg studied his jaw line, even made a fist. His knuckles were still tender.

"Go ahead. Give me a good poke. I promise it's a free shot." He put his hands behind his back and held his chin out further.

Greg didn't move.

"Getting a little uncomfortable here." Victor waited another ten seconds before straightening up. "Fine. What then?"

"Just tell me the truth."

"Aw, come on. Pick something else. I once met a hooker from Marrakech that could…" Violet's I-dare-you stare killed the sales pitch. "I could line you up with the woman. You'd be smiling for weeks."

"Say no." Violet waved the bottle. "I doubt you want to catch anything."

"I'm just saying, there's only one apology-wish granted so he should pick something memorable."

"You could tell me why," Greg insisted. "That's all I want."

Victor stood there, silent.

Violet gave him a playful kick in the leg. She was feeling playful after drinking the lion's share of the rum. It was purely medicinal. "Don't be such a douche. Just tell him. I wanna know too, and you owe me."

"You're drunk."

"Feel'n no pain, baby. Now tell us."

"Fine, but don't say I didn't warn you." He turned and started to walk away. "And you stay put Stormm. You can barely stand."

"Screw that. I'm curious."

Victor walked along the graves. Small dry puffs of dust lifted from his boots with each step. Greg became a human crutch for Violet as she tried to keep up. "I've already checked this section."

Victor kept walking. "I'm sure you did." He continued, his steps as deliberate as a hammer's blow. "Ever wonder why Ricky came to you, so many years ago?"

"Always." Greg struggled as Violet teetered against him. "Where is he anyway?"

"Not now." He glanced over to Violet, who was rolling her eyes again. "You said he was injected with the serum as a small child."

"Of course." Greg stammered. "Juanita must have finished it when he was a little boy. That was when he started to appear in my dreams."

"They were using him to get to you. It was all an experiment to see if the connection could be made."

The Divine Ledger

"And it did. So why didn't they bring me here earlier? Why after all those years?"

"Because you were just a test subject and never supposed to come here, and it wasn't as many years as you might think. I'd also bet that Ricky wasn't working on the serum. He was using them, working on a thought-blocking counter serum."

"Like the closet?" He stopped to look over at Violet. "Ricky had a closet that could block the signals."

"Nothing surprises me." Violet coughed as she waved the bottle. It was becoming hard to breathe in the heat. "Anything surprise you, Vic?"

"Your right hook was a bit of a surprise. So was the disappearing blonde at first." He turned back to her. "Surprises are like shit in that way, unavoidable when the storm hits."

"Storm, ha, good one. Hey, was that a dig?" Violet tried to stop in protest, but Greg dragged her along.

"Not at all, Miss Stormm." Victor stopped. "You're still curious as to why I tried to kill you?"

Greg nodded as he shifted Violet closer for a better grip. "Yes."

"I'm surprised you haven't figured it out. Ah shit, you do work for the government, so I shouldn't be surprised." Victor looked down. Greg and Violet's eyes followed.

The tombstone at Greg's feet looked just like the one in his dream, if you could call something that wakes you in a cold sweat a dream. It read *Gregory Michael Miller, September 24, 1962 – Died September 24, 1962*. It also read *Rest in Peace*.

Violet looked over to see Greg's reaction. It was confusion. "I don't get it."

Violet already had a hand on his shoulder and gave it a pat. "You're a smart man. Do the math. Shit, I'm corked and I get it."

"But that's impossible. I remember my childhood."

"They all thought they did. Tell me about your sixth birthday."

Greg tried to recollect it but couldn't. "Well I can't remember everything."

"Then tell me about the day you learned how to ride a bike. I remember bleeding for an hour after I skinned my elbow."

Greg couldn't. "There's no way I was zapped out of a book. Besides, I exist. I have a wife and she cheats on me. I just moved to an apartment, but I lived in this big-ass house."

"I know, and you remember the last twenty years, birthdays, anniversaries and the day you realised she was cheating on you. Do you remember a week before you met her, or what you were doing the day you graduated high school? Isn't it odd that some memories are so strong, while other are non-existent?"

It was extremely odd.

Victor took a seat on Jorge Alverez's headstone. It was a stand-up stone right beside Greg's. "You were never carried to term. You died before you were born. That being said, you did get a bird, while your heart was beating. My boss just took it back when it stopped. The old lady brought you back, but she stole a sparrow to do it. It made you a bit of a wild card with these people. Not just a shot in the dark like the rest of them, but an actual fetus with an original sparrow."

"So, I had a heartbeat, brain waves and the conjured ones didn't?"

"That's right. You were more than just a name in a book and normally a child not carried to term isn't worthy of a funeral. You must have meant something to her." He paused. "It was all in your file."

"I'm one of them?"

"Yes, and the day you were conjured, the world changed to accommodate your existence. Your wife's life transformed, because suddenly you were a part of it. She was never supposed to marry you. She was meant for someone else. The man she should have married had to change, never meeting her. And on and on it goes. And what if one of her kids was meant to be President? Bob, Beverly, all of them, they put ripples in the truth."

"Was I conjured as a child? I mean I remember a fair bit of my childhood."

The Divine Ledger

"It was probably done about twenty years ago, when you started having the dreams. It seems like a lifetime because the book loosely created the twenty years prior."

"You changed the world, Greg." Violet said as she took a seat beside Victor.

Victor added, "And you're changing it every day. Every person you meet has changed. Some more than others."

"Me, barely at all." Violet rambled. "I mean I just met you."

"You more than most," Victor corrected. "You're here because of these people. You were shot twice this week, because of these people."

Greg thought of Anne. It was like Juanita had told him, that they simply didn't do it for each other. He'd always thought it was her, maybe both. The truth was that he never should have been with her. He had ruined her life.

"Does Greg still get to be, Greg?" Violet gasped.

"Of course. I talked to the birdman, as you call him, and he's okay to let this end here. Greg was given a sparrow once. This is *second chance* Greg." He turned to Violet. "And you owe me big time for that."

"You threw me in front of a car and broke my frigg'n leg. I think we're square."

Greg interrupted what would have been an entertaining spat. "Were Ricky and Juanita family?" He thought back to the awkward sex.

Victor shrugged as he thought of the old lady with her head blown off. They were all her could-have-been children. Greg didn't need to hear that though. "Hard to say. The only connection you two had was that book."

"What happens to me now?" Greg asked.

"You live, because I don't feel like pissing off your blonde alien friend. She wants you alive and who knows what they'd do to me if I changed that."

Violet dropped the bottle and picked it up. "Well I'm gonna finish this thing and get on a plane. I'm about to be fired and I'd hate to miss it." She held the bottle out to Victor for one last slug. "What are you going to do?"

"I'll do what every ex-CIA agent does, I'll disappear." With that he shook Greg's hand before crouching down and planting a long lingering kiss on Violet's lips. "I'm sure we'll meet again, someday."

Violet, a little dazed by the kiss, tipped the bottle back and let the last of the rum sanitise her mouth. "Don't count on it, Vic." She got up and started for one of the gates. Her stagger wasn't from the fractured leg as much as it was from the rum. "Come on, Greg. I'm sure I can smuggle you through Customs."

"And how are you going to do that?"

She pulled the passports out of her pocket and fanned them out on Carlito Suarez's tombstone. "I'll take Veronica Shultz, the ditzy reporter from Kelowna British Columbia. You can be Victoria the diplomat, Vivian the investor, or Greg the guy with the smok'n hot reporter chick on his arm. Oh, and she has a limp. She buggered her leg surfing." She gave him a colourful wink. "Means ya gotta go through Vancouver to get home."

"I guess it could be worse."

She thought about the little girl and the ride back from Sayulita. "It beats the hell outta bag of beads and a bottle of glue."

Chapter Seventy-four

Nicole watched as Elizabeth rendered herself back to Earth. With a slight distortion of molecules, she was gone. Nicole had promised Elizabeth that she'd take the book to the leaders, but how could she? It was proof that she was right, that she had been right all along. Her lie to Elizabeth was a necessary one because she knew their leaders would screw this up. They'd see the book as mystical, something science couldn't explain. Fearing the unknown, they'd bury the truth under some scientific rationalisation, or worse, they might confiscate the book and make it disappear.

Hiding the book amongst an armful of data tablets, she slipped into her quarters. No one needed the distraction now that the mission was moving forward. Better they pressed their eyes to the news feeds that were streaming in from Earth. The footage of Elizabeth and the Earthling named Greg disappearing was being replayed over and over. Each time it was accompanied by a reporter's opinion on what had taken place in Cuba. The accounts were surprisingly accurate. For the Alzien leaders and the Leaders on Earth, this was chaos. For Nicole it couldn't have been a better outcome.

Had what happened been that big a deal? Elizabeth had revealed her people in a desperate attempt to save her American liaison. Sure, it was a careless move, but as far as Nicole was concerned, the big reveal was long overdue. What were they waiting for? Earth needed help and they were in the position to give it. Why else had they come? Sure, it was a political nightmare, and it could have damaging consequences on Earth, but this was a practical move.

The book tingled in her hands as her name became embossed on the cover. Inside would be the names of five children, three boys and two girls. Nicole didn't care to read them. That wasn't what mattered. This book was so much more than a list of might-have-been offspring. It tied in nicely with her research on the origin of humanity.

She placed the book on her lap as her mind swam with the possibilities. Why was this book on Earth, a planet so far from Alzie? Alzie had sent spy satellites to orbit earth, to land on the moon, to capture radio and television signals. The data had been studied, but it hadn't been enough to explain how human life had started here.

During her schooling, a few years prior to leaving Alzie, she had made a discovery. She had found a small cache of relics that were as old as the planet itself. It had sparked a theory. Had these items, in some strange way, created life? And if so, where had they come from? Sure, it was pure speculation, but wasn't that what science was all about—proving the crazier theories? This was what she tried to sell to her leaders, her once-upon-a-time mentors. They had considered her findings and did everything but laugh at her. At that point she agreed to drop it, except she couldn't.

All these controversial meetings were kept from Elizabeth. Even though she had gone to the same school and they'd become best friends, their lives had taken completely different directions. Elizabeth was groomed to be the liaison between Alzie and Earth, should that ever be required. She had been bred and educated, almost foreordained, for the role. While this was happening, Nicole was doing whatever it took to secure her chance at going to the only other planet that held human life, Earth.

The Divine Ledger

On Alzie, the artifacts, the papers, pottery, and petrified wood had been accompanied by a unique language that was almost impossible to decipher. *Almost* meant that a vague understanding of it soon took form, albeit with no alphabet and no structure. It wasn't a language to be read but more one to be experienced, like an enchantment. It was a language unique to Alzie until the appearance of the book.

Working alone, she had originally passed it off as an archaic and perhaps an extinct culture. She came up with a theory that life had taken root on Alzie millions of years ago and that it had died. Miraculously, it had returned to give them a second chance. That theory soon dissolved because these weren't primitive hieroglyphics. They were futuristic, futuristic and yet older than the Alzien civilisation. None of it made sense.

Nicole had loosely translated one of the symbols into the word 'Eve', but was that a name or a moment in time? She remembered seeing the name in the Earthling's bible. It had a serious significance. Eve, and Adam, had been the biblical creators of humanity. That was more than a coincidence.

Another anomaly that had always puzzled her was how Earthlings had learned to speak Alzien? The planets were five light years apart. Had Alziens migrated to Earth after the Great War? Had the Earthlings come to populate Alzie? She pushed both thoughts aside. Earth had a hard-enough time getting to the moon. The idea of a migration from either planet, thousands of years ago, was absurd.

But this was how science worked, with so many questions and so few answers. She picked up the aged leather book and placed it in the drawer beside the dated relics that she'd brought from home. The journal didn't fit. She had to shuffle a few items. As Nicole made room, one of the Alzien pieces of petrified wood fell out of the cloth that it was wrapped in. It landed on top of the book they'd found on Earth. The cover slowly changed.

She leaned closer to get a better look. How was that possible? A name she'd never seen before embossed itself across the leather. It wasn't an Earthling or Alzien name. She picked up the wood and ran a finger along it. Nicole had been wrong.

She'd assumed this was petrified wood, much older than any bones they'd ever found. Who'd have guessed it belonged to a person, a woman. This was proof that a book like this could not only bring life to Earth and Alzie, but somewhere far older than either planet.

Nicole could feel it. The name, now embossed onto the cover of the book, was the name of someone from a third planet. Was that where these books had come from? If so, Eve had to be a place, perhaps a planet where humanity had begun.

"Eve," she muttered to herself as she stared through the window of her quarters at the stars and planets. "Now I need to find you."

The Divine Ledger

Enlightenment

Book two of the **Eve of Humanity** Series

Chapter one

Washington, DC

Jenny raced down the stairs of her parent's two-story home on a mission. Normally this decent was a float, or a carefree glide, but today was different. There was no time for gliding. "Morning Elizabeth. Are you ready for our big day?" As an afterthought she looked over to her mother and father. "Oh, hi guys."

"Hello?" Father Davis stood slightly dazed at the sight of his overly chipper daughter. He'd never seen her that awake, this early.

"Ya, ya, Dad." She turned back to Elizabeth. "Are you ready?"

"I'm very ready." She'd been looking forward to touring the university and thumbing through a few of the textbooks. For the last two weeks she'd been helping Jenny with one of her projects. They should be able to wrap it up today.

"Shall we then?" Jenny grabbed Elizabeth's hand and gave it a tug. This day wasn't about finishing a project or touring her school. No, today was about showing off her new friend. "We'll see you both at supper."

The two girls left the house and piled into Jenny's car. The drive took half an hour and with the windows open, the music cranked, Jenny pulled into a parking spot that was reserved for visitors only. Elizabeth pointed to the sign.

"What?" Jenny waved the sign off with a wrist twirl. "Like you're not a visitor."

The University sprawled for several city blocks, but for Jenny it was no harder to maneuvering than the mess in her bedroom. "We should get you a visitors pass and then hit the Library. Did you enjoy hanging with Dad yesterday?"

"Yes. We had a candy thing. The fixation on sugar here is a little insane."

"Are you serious? Wait, don't tell me…"

"I feel I have to. Your dad bought me some pink cotton and a chocolate stick." She ran her tongue over her teeth. "It caused my teeth to ache."

"Where have you been living where they don't have *candy*?" Jenny grabbed her arm. "Never mind. Tell me you liked it."

"It was definitely flavourful. What other kinds of odd foods do you have?"

"We'll stop by The Sweet Tooth on our way home. They've got everything from chocolate, to fudge, to toffee. You'll love it there." Jenny remembered her first time in the store. Her stomach ached for a week. If it had sugar in it, they sold it and it was a definite must for the new girl.

Elizabeth forced a smile through a scrunched face. "I couldn't finish the pink cotton though. I would have been ill."

"That's okay. You shouldn't eat too much of that stuff at a time. It's more of a treat thing. Wanna do chicken wings for lunch?"

Elizabeth just stared. Wasn't that the worst part of the bird?

Jenny signed Elizabeth in and dragged her off to the labs. They weren't that different from the labs Elizabeth grew up in. Jenny noticed her professor in the back corner of the room.

"Hi Teach, This is my friend that I told you about."

"Hello, I'm Professor Lawton. It's a pleasure to finally meet you, Elizabeth." For the last two days he'd endured numerous stories about her. "Do you plan on going to school here?"

"The pleasure is mine, and no. I've reached my education quota."

He cocked a brow. "Okay… Did you study here, in the US?"

Elizabeth was tired of not being able to answer questions like these. She decided to make up an answer, call it a lie. Maybe it was Jenny's youthful energy taking charge of her. Perhaps it was the fact that her colleague, Nicole, had told her to loosen up. Regardless, it was time for a little fun. "Actually, all over Europe, China, and Russia."

She had his attention. He had also studied overseas and knew little English was used in the universities there. It had made learning nearly impossible. She was either gifted or making it up. A little test was in order. "*Kennst du die sechs verschiedenen* Quarks?"

"I understand German." Her smile broadened. "*Kaum ein* Test. *Sie sind unter oben unten, bezaubert, merkwürdig, Spitzen- und. Die aus Gebühren sind Elektronen, muons und taus.*

"Really, well *Так вы думаете недавних выдвижений в исследовании днаа?"*

"*Бедный человек іий считало его вс то просвещая.* And yes, I speak Russian." She had him on the ropes. "*Inoltre parlo Italiano et Français assez bon.*"

Jenny was staring now. "What's going on here?"

"Your professor is testing my integrity," Elizabeth replied. "I can speak eleven different languages, including Mandarin, Cantonese..."

"Okay, okay. You win." Professor Schewe knew when to admit defeat. "Well I'll be. You've been a busy student. Dare I ask what areas you practiced in?"

"I studied them all. Biochemistry, Quantum, Astrophysics. It's been time consuming, but it was necessary."

"That's amazing..." Again, he found her a little eccentric. "What are your views on String Theory?"

"I'm not sure I understand. That's a term I'm not familiar with."

He started to explain. "It's a theory that protons can be broken down beyond quarks into billions of small strands of electricity..."

"Oh, you mean energy bonding. Billions of little strands of electricity, proving Einstein's $E=MC^2$. These strands are held together by contrasted frequency enticements and can be stretched, with increases in speed, causing the..."

He cut her off. "What are you talking about? I've never read anywhere that frequencies hold them together, or that they can be stretched."

Not yet she thought. "It's just a theory of mine. Maybe someday I'll formulate a paper."

"You should. That makes a little sense, perhaps." He wasn't quite sure. String theory was a deep science and better left to the experts. Apparently, she was one of them. "So, what's your secret to learning?

Sorry but it's almost impossible to believe anybody could learn that much, that quickly. You're awfully young to be such a scholar."

Elizabeth confessed, "eidetic memory."

Again, Jenny was left in the dark. "Pardon?"

The Professor knew what it meant. "Photographic memory. I knew a guy that had that in Undergraduate school. He was the life of the party. We'd give him a novel and within the hour he had it read. All night we would ask him questions like, what's the 43rd word on the 289th page? I lost a lot of money on those nights. He was never wrong. What brings you here?"

She looked at Jenny and in a poorly learned slang replied, "I'm just hanging with my Jenny."

That got a grin out of Jenny. They'd be talking tonight. Elizabeth had been holding out on her. There was more to this girl than she had let on, and she owed it to her to spill. Besides, she needed a few more lessons in talking the slang. *Hanging with my Jenny?*

They carried on with the tour, hitting the library. Jenny signed out an armful of books for Elizabeth, mainly books on new advances in Biology and Economics. They finished the project and checked out the cafeteria. It was worth a slice of apple pie.

"Well this was a blast, but we should head if we want to hit the Sweet Tooth. But tonight we're going to talk about what happened with the whole eleven-language thing. You know there's no avoiding me. You want a Pepsi?"

"A what?"

"Give me a break! You can't be serious." Jenny couldn't put the money in the machine quick enough. She grabbed a can and opened it for her. "Sip it though."

Elizabeth took a sip from the can. "It's hissing." She looked in the opening of the can. As with everything, it was sweet and very tasty, but there was something else. "What's in it?"

Jenny was watching intently. "You mean the CO^2?"

"Why? It makes no sense."

"It's fun. We have wine like that too. All pop has fizz. It won't hurt you."

The Divine Ledger

Elizabeth tried to curb the curiosity. This was a strange land indeed. "First candy and now Pepsi. I won't have teeth by the end of the week."

"Don't be a baby. You haven't even tried fudge," Jenny beamed.

More than she thought possible, the day had been quite an education. "Your Mom said you have a tattoo? She tried to explain what it was, but it made no sense."

"Oh my God! I got in so much shit over that. I think Dad was more upset about where it was, instead of what it was."

"In shit?" Still confused and trying not to picture Jenny neck deep in human waste, Elizabeth asked again. "What is it?"

"Oh, I'm sorry. It was a little cat paw."

"A what? I still don't get it."

"I had a little cat paw put on my left breast."

Elizabeth was instantly appalled. "That's just wrong."

Jenny returned her dirty look. "No. It's cute. What's your damage?"

Fully flustered Elizabeth looked at her blouse. "Your mother said it was permanent. Is it still there?"

"That's what permanent means." Jenny looked around to make sure they were alone. She unbuttoned a couple of buttons and pulled her blouse open exposing her bra. Her hand quickly grabbed the lacey garment and tugged it off to the side exposing the tiny grey and black cat paw.

Elizabeth moved closer as she stared at the image. Instinctively she licked her thumb and tried to rub it off. Jenny backed away and started to button up her shirt. "What are you doing?"

"I'm sorry. I wasn't thinking. It's just that I've never seen anything like that before. How is it on you?"

"Really. You've never seen a tattoo before?"

"Never."

"They put ink in a needle and poke it in you like a thousand times."

"That sounds painful. So it doesn't rub off?"

"Nope. That was why Mom was so mad. Dad was upset because some guy saw my breast. If Dad only knew, the guy was handling my girl for like half an hour."

"Girl?" That had to be a nickname. There seemed to be a lot of that. "Sounds like it was rebellious. It sure is cute, not that I plan on getting one myself."

"Yeah, well the bra covers it up so it's not on display for the world. It was kind of an independence thing for me."

"So, are you considered a *brat*?"

Jenny's eyebrows dipped. "I guess in a way."

"I'm sorry about the touching." For that split second she had forgot that these people had so many modesty issues.

"That's okay. I'm kind of shy that way, so it just spooked me a bit."

Elizabeth stared at her shirt. "A tattoo. That's a peculiar ritual. It is a ritual thing, right?" How else could you explain such a primitive act for such an advanced culture.

"No and peculiar is you gawking at my chest so knock it off. Now let's go check out the candy store."

Elizabeth often found herself staring at Jenny and how she acted so childish at times, most times. And then there was the slang. It was such an important part of her culture and definitely worth learning. Elizabeth knew she'd have been beaten if she ever carried on like that or came home with a tattoo. Their cultures were worlds apart.

The candy store ended up making them late for supper and Father Davis laughed harder than he dared to remember when he saw Elizabeth walking in the house with the brown bag full of sweets. *Déjà vu* he thought. Jenny had done the same thing when she was fourteen.

After the supper dishes were cleared Elizabeth poured the paper bag of treats onto the table. There was no way she was going to finish it by herself.

That evening, Elizabeth helped Jenny with a final read on her school paper. Jenny was even more confused by the conversation that followed. They had talked like Elizabeth had promised, but she had been spun in circles. In the end, all she was sure of was that

The Divine Ledger

Elizabeth was indeed gifted and planned to use her ability to somehow better mankind.

Elizabeth was starting to nod off when the small coin-like token on her nightstand started flashing. It was her people, likely Nicole. She quickly changed into her tight white dress and disappeared.

She reappeared on the transfer platform of the mothership. "I was almost asleep, Nicole. What did you want?"

Nicole walked over and the grin that was spread across her face was as malicious as Elizabeth had ever seen. It had been a look that she had seen before.

"What now?"

Nicole pushed a clear tablet toward her. On it, a holographic image was playing. "Did you know your liaison is trying to make his way across the Gulf of Mexico in an old fishing boat?"

"He's what?"

Kevin Weisbeck

Calm before the Stormm

Book one in the Violet Stormm Detective Series

Chapter one

Vancouver – Post Cuba Debacle

The sign was a simple cardboard square, held by a man who would rather be anywhere but at the airport. Two Vancouver City cops stood on either side of him like clumsy bookends. The sign he held, scribbled in black felt pen, read Storm, with one m. The misspelling had been intentional.

Violet limped toward them.

Sargent Crowley handed the sign to the officer to his left, Simmons, as he stepped forward. He didn't speak. His eyes, however, put Violet on the defensive.

"Hi, Sarge. Thanks for picking me up at the airport." Although she knew his actions weren't any personal favour or professional courtesy. He was corralling her so that she couldn't run. "Am I…"

He held his hand out. "Gun and badge."

"Seriously?" Not that she was all that surprised. She was an accomplice to an old woman's death, she'd withheld evidence from the Cuban police, and she'd destroyed Canadian relations with the Cuban and American governments, albeit with a little help from her friends. She was lucky to get out of Cuba before Captain Cerava connected the dots.

"What were you thinking?" The Sarge asked.

"I was thinking I wanted to stop the killings." She rummaged through her purse and slowly handed him the two most important pieces of her life. "This is bullshit. You know that."

"I don't know anything any more. Hell, I thought you were in Mexico. Imagine my surprise when the Mayor's office calls me, telling me

The Divine Ledger

to check the news. I do and there's my agent, in Cuba with some alien. All of a sudden, my precinct is under investigation by the feds."

"Sorry, but about that…"

"No. I don't even want to hear your crap. You were a good cop and you showed a lot of promise. This is a shame." He turned to walk away. "These two will be escorting you to the hospital because your injuries take precedence over the investigation. After you're been patched up, I want you in my office."

"Not a problem," she replied. "Just a couple gunshot wounds and a possible broken leg from when the car hit me, injuries incurred in the line of duty I might add." She'd hoped for some sympathy. There was none as he made his way down the corridor and out of sight.

"What an ungrateful shit."

The officer holding the sign took her by the elbow. "This way."

She tugged her arm away. "I got this."

As Violet pulled free from his grasp she bumped into a small boy. His hair was long and blonde, swept off to one side. His eyes were blue and his nose was dusted with freckles. He looked seven, maybe eight years old.

"Sorry kiddo. Didn't see you."

His eyes immediately found hers. The connection was intense. "Are you that lady in the video?"

"I am." She shot him a smile. "Did you want an autogra—"

"Sorry kid," Officer Granger interrupted. "It's imperative that we get Miss Stormm to a hospital."

The boy, uncertain and intimidated, stepped aside as the two officers escorted her down the hall and out to the squad car. Like a criminal, she was thrown in the back. The only thing missing was the handcuffs. Was what she had done so terrible? She had stopped the killings, albeit only one short of Victor's full list of sixteen. Greg, an American diplomat, was safe because of her, although he would be scarred for life. She didn't deserve this. That kid didn't deserve this.

"All he wanted was an autograph."

"You aren't supposed to talk to anybody. That includes kids that think you're some kind of freak hero."

"Besides," Officer Simmons added, "we don't need that kid getting shot."

"Oh, you're funny." She leaned back and stared out the side window.

Familiar buildings passed as the squad car rolled through Richmond. They passed over the Oak Street Bridge and headed into Metro

Vancouver. Most of the buildings she noticed were restaurants. Her stomach growled. "Hey! Can we stop for wings?"

"No."

"How about poutine?"

"No."

"Fine." Violet sat back until the hospital came into view.

Officer Granger pulled into the turnaround and stopped. Both he and Officer Simmons exited the car and started for the sliding emergency doors. As the doors opened the two men looked back. Violet was staring like a puppy waiting for the come-here command, except she couldn't. The door was locked.

Simmons returned to let her out. "And we're going to need a written statement."

Violet pushed past him. "Sure. I'll get right on that." She hobbled through the doors and up to the far-too-chipper young woman at the front desk. "I think I have a reservation."

Her brows arched. "Uh, I don't think we do reservations. Do you want to see a doctor?"

Violet looked at the blood stains on the sleeve of her shirt, at the bandage on her leg, tied over her jeans, and then back to the woman. "Do you sell poutine or ice-cream here?"

"Uh, no."

"Then I'll take a doctor."

Officer Simmons leaned over the counter. "Actually, Doctor Anderson should be waiting for her. We called this in."

"Oh. This is *that* girl." She took a closer look. "You look much prettier in real life than in that video. I've seen it a dozen times."

"Thanks." She turned back to officer Simmons. "Can I give this one an autograph?"

"No."

"The nurse got up and grabbed the clipboard that had been set aside. "Right this way. I gotta ask, did that guy and that woman really disappear?"

"Totally gone, splitsville. I never sh—"

Officer Simmons cleared his throat.

Violet ignored him. "She took him up to their space ship."

"Knock it off already." This time he stepped between them. "We said no talking."

"Sorry." She shrugged to the girl. "I guess I'm not supposed to talk about the killings or the book, either."

"There's a book? What kind of book?"

"Well…"

"Okay, enough already," Officer Simons hissed. "I'll sneak you in some wings if you'll just shut up."

"And a couple of beers?"

"What the hell. Who needs a pension."

The young woman led them to an empty bed. "What's this about a book?"

"I was just kidding about the book."

"Really?"

"No, but I want beer and wings."

Doctor Anderson didn't look like a doctor as he entered the room and pulled the privacy-curtain around the bed. The man looked more like an undercover DEA agent from the seventies … and was that a handlebar moustache? The face fur, the tinted sunglasses and the earring didn't suit the MO of a doctor. "What are we dealing with?"

Violet took a seat on the bed as she worked the pillowcase bandage off her leg. "Two gunshot wounds, shoulder and leg." She tore her jeans leg open down to the knee. It exposed the most recent gunshot wound, a lot of dried blood and even more bruising. "And then there's this."

He squatted down to get a closer look at her leg. "And this is…hit by a car?"

"Very good."

"Okay, we'll start with the shoulder, so off with the shirt."

"We'll have to ditch the flatfeet before that happens."

The doctor looked back at them. "Out."

"I'm not sure we shou—"

"Unless she's a prisoner, get out!"

Violet threw them a widening smile.

"We'll be right outside."

Dr Anderson waited for them to leave while Violet slowly slipped her shirt off. He gave it a quick inspection. "Nice work. Was this done by a Navy Seal?"

"Ex CIA."

"No such thing, but I think you know that."

"He did a good job?"

"Better than I would have done. In the field they use a different stitch technique. It holds the stitches better, but you'll have a scar." He looked down to her leg. "May I?"

"Knock yourself out."

The bullet had sliced through three inches of her flesh. The wound was deep enough for staples, but the doctor grabbed for a needle. "I can freeze this if you like."

"Don't bother."

"That's what I thought."

The needle dipped in and out of her skin. After nineteen tight stitches, the doctor put the needle down and pulled the gloves off. "You look tired. I bet you can't wait to get home."

"Home is a shitty little trailer out in Surrey. Trust me, I can wait."

"Then how about I get you up to x-ray for that leg. While they snap a few pictures, I'll get you admitted. Clean bed, supper, breakfast and if I can pull it off, cable TV."

"I say sign me up. Why are you doing this for me?"

"You come in shot up, you've been stitched up by an agent and you just let me stitch your leg without freezing. You remind me of me, twenty years ago."

"Are you talking Vietnam or Korea?"

"Those conflicts are a lot older than I am. Nah, I'm talking the Santa Marta hills of Columbia."

"Why Doctor, it sounds like you have a bit of a past?"

He fetched a wheelchair from the corner. "Everyone has a past."

She sat down and let him wheel her out of the room. There was a boy standing in the hallway. It was the same boy from the airport. He politely stood aside as the doctor pushed her toward the x-ray lab. His eyes immediately locked on Violet's as she got closer.

Her mouth opened as if she had something to say.

She couldn't find the words.

Then the boy stepped in front of them, causing the doctor to stop.

The doctor leaned down. "Hi, sport. Can I help you?"

"Is my Mom going to be okay?"

The 7th Crow
A Victor Wainsworth Mission

Victor's morning started with a strong cup of coffee, watered down with a couple ounces of scotch. He set the two empty mini-bar bottles down on the café table and then calmly took a drink. Across the room, a fair-skinned redhead was walking toward him. Her eyes were fixed on his as she took a seat across from him.

"You look like shit, Victor."

"I always look like shit, Cara."

"I meant worse than usual." She pointed to the right side of his face.

Victor reached up and touched his cheek. The Violet Stormm's right hook was a slow healer. "It was a little thing in Cuba. I have to ask, how'd you find me? I mean I thought I was doing a pretty good job at hiding."

"Come on. I'm CIA, remember?"

"You're an administrative accountant. Who's helping you?"

She reached for a lock of her hair and started to twirl it. Her coy smile disappeared. "We uh…"

"Are you watching me?"

"There's a group of us that still consider you a friendly."

Victor chuckled and took another gulp at his coffee. "Are you trying to tell me I have a babysitting club?"

"We never believed in what they did to you and we simply run interference." She reached for her purse. "Do you remember Charlie?"

"Charlie Hodgens?" He nodded. "Old Charlie went to Lima with me once. He dared me to drink this goat milk paralyzer. Thing was made with home-made hootch and gave me the worst hangover. Charlie tried to drink three of the damn things. He kept chucking them up. Tried to tell me he was lactose intolerant."

"Sounds like Charlie." A folded newspaper clipping was retrieved from her purse. "What was in Lima?"

"There was a Columbian hiding out there. We had to go find him. He'd taken twenty kilos of cocaine from us, and by us, I mean your boss."

"You're boss too."

"I don't think Uncle Sam likes me anymore. So, how's Charlie doing?"

Cara unfolded the paper and slid it over to Victor. It was an obituary. "We had the service three days ago."

Victor skimmed over the article. "Says a car accident."

"They staged it, more for his wife and kids."

"Was he even in the country?"

"You know how this works, Victor. I give you, like, no information so that I don't incriminate myself and you do all the work."

"Did *we* kill him?"

"I honestly don't know who got to him. We got an anonymous call and found him in the trunk of a stolen white caddy. He'd been beaten to death. Damn funeral was a closed casket affair."

"That bad, huh?"

"Charlie was beaten in such a way to induce maximum pain. They started with ribs and kneecaps. It was like they took pleasure in what they were doing."

"Bastards." Victor shook his head and downed another mouthful of coffee. "I doubt it was CIA. They'd have capped him or run him off a road. Again, I gotta ask, who do you think did this?"

"Here's where I give you that morsel of information. Ever heard of an organisation called the Nest of Crows?"

"Money laundering folk out of Vegas. We've used them to clean our drug money if I remember right. I mean, that was back in the seventies when we had to fund our own black-ops. I can't believe it was these guys. They were just a bunch of nerdy money crunchers that made a shit-ton of money off of us. They're not killers."

"They aren't the same group anymore. All that money put them in with the big players."

"The evolution of a criminal."

"It gobbled them up like a stoner eating Doritos. Charlie was supposed to infiltrate them and get an update. We just wanted to know what they were up to, find out their worth, and see if the six players were the same ones from before."

"You guys knew what a seventh crow would signify, didn't you?"

"That's just a myth."

"No myth, Cara. In real life, the seventh crow constitutes a murder. These guys obviously live by that motto."

"But these guys were our allies once."

"You don't infiltrate allies. They knew Charlie, or knew of him. The lack of trust must have spooked them. They've heard of me, I'm sure. What makes you think I'll have better luck?"

The Divine Ledger

"If they've heard of you, then they know you're on our Laundry list. They'd likely trust you if they knew we wanted you dead more than they did." The newspaper clipping was folded up and put back in her purse. She replaced it with an envelope.

He opened it to see a folded piece of paper and a first-class airline ticket to Vegas. "And this is?"

"Another crumb." With a quick glance over her shoulder, she gathered her stuff and moved in closer. "This was the last guy Charlie talked to, before…"

"Friend or foe?"

"Don't know," Cara said as she shrugged, got up and walked away without looking back.

Victor watched her sultry swagger as she left. Then he panned the room for any eyes that might also be watching her. There were none. He looked down and unfolded the piece of paper. The name was that of John 'Dynamo' Peterson. It was a name he knew, a name that everybody knew. The guy was a congressman and as honest as they came. His reason for entering politics was to bring down the establishment and his constituents loved him because of it, the always-admired crusading underdog. The man had positioned himself for taking a run at the Democratic candidacy for President.

"What the hell were you up to Charlie?"

Victor got up, drank the last of his coffee, and left the plane ticket on the table as he walked away. He liked Cara, would even dance with her under the stars if given the chance, but he was alive because he didn't trust anyone. He'd rent a car under an alias and drive down there.

Heading for the door, he fumbled the paper in his hand and dropped it to the floor. As he reached down to pick it up, he pinched a glimpse out the main window of the café. Across the street, a man in a car was staring at him through the lens of a camera.

The man looked a lot like Charlie.

Kevin Weisbeck

Other Books by Kevin Weisbeck

Madeline's Secret

Madeline suffers from amnesia when she wakes from the car accident that killed her sister. Her parents, husband, and small child are all strangers. As she accepts these people into her new life, she uncovers a secret, one so dangerous that it could ruin her if it ever got out.

The Darkness Within

A victim of his own bad choices, Johnny Pettinger is stranded following a plane crash in a remote mountain wilderness. His injuries are serious, but they're not the only factors preventing him from getting home. In order to do that, Johnny needs to shine a light on the very reason for his being there, the **Darkness Within**.

Calm Before the Stormm (coming soon)

Book one of the Violet Stormm Detective Series

Back from a case that could end her career as a homicide detective, Violet Stormm meets a boy who wants to change her life. He claims to be her son. The child has a persuasive story, but she's never been pregnant. Still, every child deserves a mother, so Violet vows to find his. That would soon become a decision filled with regret.

Enlightenment (coming soon)

The Eve of Humanity – Book Two

With the exposure of her people, Elizabeth has no choice but to start their mission. Will Earth welcome the changes that will be expected of them? The rewards for both planets are worth it, but it would mean all countries of Earth doing what they're asked. The alternative could be costly.

The 7th Crow (coming soon)

A Victor Wainsworth Thriller

Rogue CIA agent Victor Wainsworth needs to infiltrate a secret organization called the Nest of Crows. They're responsible for the murder of Charlie, a good friend of his. That being said, Victor knows that this group lives by the motto that seven crows make a murder.

Kevin Weisbeck

About the Author

Kevin Weisbeck is a Canadian author, born in Kelowna, British Columbia and currently living in Okotoks, Alberta. He's had several short stories published in magazines and newspapers and currently has one in the Canada-wide McGraw-Hill's iLit Academic Program.

He can usually be found on the couch with his laptop and his Ragdoll cat, Franklin, on his shoulder. It's not an ideal set-up, but Franklin doesn't mind. Otherwise Kevin enjoys hiking, kayaking, camping, photography and golf (when the weeds and water don't get in the way).

Made in the USA
Columbia, SC
01 September 2018